The Warlock Senator

By

Sam Ferguson

This is a work of fiction. All of the characters, organizations, and events portrayed in this book are either products of the author's imagination or are used fictitiously.

THE WARLOCK SENATOR
Copyright © 2014 by Sam Ferguson

ISBN: 1943183015
ISBN-13: 978-1943183012

Front cover art by Bob Kehl

For my friends Anthony and Andrew

Other Books by Sam Ferguson

The Sorceress of Aspenwood Series

The Dragon's Champion Series

The Wealth of Kings

The Netherworld Gate Series

The Dragons of Kendualdern series

The Fur Trader by Sam Ferguson

Other Books by Dragon Scale Publishing

The Protector of Esparia by Lisa M. Wilson

Kingdom of Denall Series by Eric Buffington:

The Troven
Secrets at the Keep
The Changing

Tales of the NoWhere and NeverWhen by Jason Hauser

Wisp the Wayfinder
Puck the Pathwinder
Nobb the Nightbinder

The Lost City of Alfarin by Keaton James

Gryl the Enchanter by Tamlin Moore

Also available exclusively on the Dragon Scale website:

Tharzule's Tome of Wishes by Malinda Smiley

Orcs and Elves by Bethan Owen

Table of Contents

CHAPTER ONE

Lord Lokton pulled his sword free from the body on the ground before him. He stood, turning about to survey the scene. His heart frantically throbbed in his chest. His lungs gulped air, heaving his chest up and down with each breath. The shouts and cries of battle began to die down. House Cedreau's army had turned on its heels and was fleeing from the field. Lord Lokton looked down to the man at his feet. His eyes were still open, the anger and heat of battle still painted on his still, unmoving face.

"My Lord, the battlefield is ours. We have routed them. Shall we give chase?" a lieutenant called out from behind.

Lord Lokton bent down to the man at his feet and closed the corpse's eyes. "No," Lord Lokton said with a shake of his head. "Do not give chase."

"My Lord?" The lieutenant moved up beside him. "If we do not run them down, they may have a chance to regroup."

"I said no!" Lord Lokton bellowed. "Let them go. There has been enough blood for one day." Lord Lokton stood and returned his sword to its sheath. He pointed off to the trees at the edge of the battlefield. "I want to know where that arrow came from. Send three men into the woods and find the man who slew Lord Cedreau."

The lieutenant nodded. "It will be done."

Another armored guard came running up to Lord Lokton. "Sir, are you hurt?"

Lord Lokton recognized the guard as one of the corporals. He examined himself for the first time since the battle started. Blood was dripping out from under his left gauntlet and his armor was bent in at his right hip. "It is nothing, I will live."

"With respect, I should take a look," the guard said.

Lord Lokton looked up to see the lieutenant still standing

1

near. "I thought I told you to go and find the assassin," he growled. The lieutenant nodded and hurried away, shouting for a few of the others to join him. Lord Lokton then turned back to the corporal. "Very well, but let's be quick about it."

The corporal reached out and unhitched Lord Lokton's armor to inspect the wounds underneath. "You were struck in the shoulder, but it is not serious," he said. The corporal unceremoniously threw the armor down on the ground.

"We were in parlay," Lord Lokton said as he looked down to his bloody shoulder. "Who would have gone after Lord Cedreau during parlay?"

"I don't know, my lord," the corporal said as he pulled a field kit from a satchel on his belt. "Please hold still while I clean the wound." The corporal gripped Lokton's left arm and scrubbed his shoulder. Lokton grimaced, but didn't pull away.

"Have you seen Sir Duvalll?" Lord Lokton asked.

The corporal shook his head. "No, my lord. I have not."

"Do you know how many casualties we have suffered?"

Again the corporal shook his head. "We should have the count later today, my lord. Please hold still so I can finish." The man pulled a thread through the gash in Lokton's shoulder, pulling the skin a bit as he closed the wound.

When it was finished, Lord Lokton was quick to find a horse and make his way back to his home. As he galloped through the battlefield he was hailed by those among his retinue who still lived. He stopped when he saw his blacksmith, Demetrius standing over a trio of dead men and nursing a cut in his thigh.

"Are you all right, Demetrius?" Lord Lokton asked.

"I am all right," he responded. "Have you seen Sir Duvalll?"

Lord Lokton shook his head. "No, I was going to ask if you had seen him."

Demetrius' face turned sour. "There is a part of me that would call your attention to the bad omens, and Tukai's prophecy."

Lord Lokton shook his head. "I don't believe in those," he said. "Though I understand that you do."

Demetrius nodded knowingly and pointed to one of the dead men in front of him. "I don't anymore. Do you recognize this man?"

Lord Lokton dismounted and looked closer. "One of ours,"

Lokton said flatly. "I was not close to him though. Do you know him?"

Demetrius shook his head. "I only know that he was one of the guards who watched Mr. Stilwell." Demetrius looked away and spat on the ground. "Do you know what he told me before he died?"

Lord Lokton folded his arms. "What?"

"He said that the night Timon Cedreau was killed he was the guard watching Mr. Stilwell."

"That's right, his name was Ben, I believe," Lord Lokton cut in. "I spoke with him briefly the morning after Timon was murdered to make sure that Mr. Stilwell was still in his cell."

Demetrius nodded glumly. "Before Ben died, he told me that Mr. Stilwell had not been in his cell that night."

Lord Lokton stood rigid and clenched his jaw. Cold, hard eyes turned on the dead man. "What do you mean?"

Demetrius stood up and placed a hand on his master's good shoulder. "He said that Sir Duvalll paid him ten gold pieces to allow Stilwell out for the night."

"What was he thinking?" Lokton fumed. "He should have told me."

Demetrius shrugged. "I guess at the time he thought it was the right thing to do. He said that Sir Duvalll had told him you would not hold Lord Cedreau accountable for the magistrate's murder. Since Ben knew the magistrate was Mr. Stilwell's cousin, it didn't take much more convincing than the ten gold Duvalll gave him."

"Did he have any proof beyond his word?" Lord Lokton asked. Demetrius shook his head. Lord Lokton kicked a clump of dirt through the air and slammed a fist into an open palm. "Sir Duvalll went into the parlay with me," Lokton said, "so it couldn't have been him in the woods."

"Yet, neither of us know where he is now," Demetrius put in. "So perhaps he knows who was in the woods."

Lord Lokton nodded. "Take a few men and scour the woods. I have already sent a few others there. Bring me back the arrow that killed Lord Cedreau. I would be interested to see if it bore Mr. Stilwell's markings."

"Isn't Mr. Stilwell back in his cell?" Demetrius asked.

"If Duvalll could get him out once, maybe he was able to do it again." Lord Lokton clambered atop his horse. "I will see if the treacherous leach is still there, and if he is, I will get a confession out of him so we can end this blood feud."

Without another word he spurred his horse on, tearing clods of dirt and grass out of the ground behind tempestuous hooves. His anger burned hot in his blood. Could the guard have been telling the truth? Why would Sir Duvalll betray him like this? He couldn't comprehend it. He had known Sir Duvalll for many years, and he had always been a true friend.

The horse panted and jerked beneath him as it plodded up the last hill to Lokton Manor. The wild grasses of the field gave way to manicured hedges surrounding a well-kept lawn of emerald blades tucked inside an inner border of tulips and roses. Lord Lokton trampled through them and leapt off of his horse just a yard away from the steps leading up to the front door of his manor. He landed hard, bending down to steady himself with his good arm as he fought to maintain his balance.

"My lord, are you all right?" one of the guards shouted.

Lord Lokton looked up and rose to his feet. "I am fine. Where is Braun?"

"He is inside, my lord," the guard replied.

"Have him meet me in the dungeon," Lord Lokton instructed as he bounded up the steps.

"Lord Lokton, please wait a moment," the guard pleaded. "Your son was here."

Lord Lokton turned on his heels. "Erik was here?"

The guard nodded. "Erik and a dwarf were ambushed in the forest."

"What? Is Erik all right? Is he here?" Lord Lokton all but forgot about Mr. Stilwell at the news of his son. He hadn't seen him since the night the manor had been attacked by a throng of Blacktongue assassins.

The guard patted the air with his hands. "Braun is in the southern guest room with the dwarf. He can tell you everything about it."

Lokton barely let the guard finish before he ripped through the front door and sprinted through the halls to the southern guest room. His heavy boots clanked against the marble floor, chipping

4

hunks of stone as he ran.

He found the door to the southern guest room closed. He reached down and turned the knob. The door opened easily and he spied Braun standing next to the bed wherein a dwarf slept. He stopped and looked at the dwarf. A long, thick beard trailed down from the dwarf's strong chin and flowed over the blue blanket. He was shorter than a human, but thickly muscled and obviously as hard as the stone the dwarves lived in.

"My lord, you are hurt," Braun called out as Lord Lokton walked through the doorway.

"I was told that this dwarf and my son were ambushed," Lord Lokton said, ignoring Braun's stare at the red bandage on his left shoulder.

Braun nodded. "It's a long story, but Erik is safe." Braun moved away from the bed. "Apparently they were coming to our aid and were ambushed in the forest by Janik, who was a warlock in disguise."

"Master Orres' brother was a warlock?" Lord Lokton asked. He folded his arms and furrowed his brow. "And he tried to take Erik?"

Braun nodded. "Erik told me that this dwarf saved him from Janik. The two were able to defeat the warlock together, but the dwarf was exhausted and required rest so Erik brought him here."

"See to it that he has everything he needs then," Lord Lokton said. "Does he have a name?"

"Erik said that the dwarf goes by Al," Braun replied.

Lord Lokton bit his lower lip and narrowed his brow. "Strange name for a dwarf."

Braun shrugged. "Erik said it was short for something, but he didn't say what. He said it was too hard to pronounce and would take too long to write out for me."

"Al it is then," Lord Lokton replied. "Were there any attacks here at the manor while I was afield?"

"No, my lord, except for your son, there were no others here." Lord Lokton nodded and rubbed his left arm with his right hand. "Is it bad, my lord?" Braun pointed to the bandage on Lord Lokton's left shoulder.

"No, it's a flesh wound, that's all."

Braun nodded and folded his arms. It was obvious that he

wanted more details. Lord Lokton thought Braun was much like an overprotective dog, always underfoot and barking at every creature within fifty feet of its master. Braun had fumed when Lord Lokton had told him to stay at the manor. The big man's face had flushed and he had begged to be allowed on the field with him. Not wanting to leave his residence defenseless however, Lord Lokton had placed Braun at the manor with a small detachment of men, just in case.

"Lord Cedreau is dead," Lord Lokton said with a sigh.

Braun arched an eyebrow. "How?"

"I'm not sure. One minute we were in parlay and the next an arrow went straight through his neck. It was an impossible shot. The arrow just slid between the bottom of the helmet and the steel collars of the hauberk." Lord Lokton shook his head and his eyes went distant. "Sir Duvalll and I galloped away then. Cedreau's whole army cried out that we had betrayed Lord Cedreau, but we didn't. I didn't have any man in the woods."

"Sounds like someone else took the opportunity to settle an old score," Braun said.

"I need to speak with Mr. Stilwell. Apparently he might have been released the night Timon was murdered."

Braun looked to the floor and held up his hand. "Shortly after you took the army this morning, one of the guards came to me and reported that Mr. Stilwell had escaped. I'm not sure how he did it. The guard on duty in the dungeon was also missing. I sent out a pair of men to track him, but I kept the rest here as you had ordered me to do."

"Good heavens, Braun, why didn't you send a runner to me?" Lord Lokton wailed.

"It wouldn't have done any good. You and I both know that if Stilwell doesn't want to be found, he could stand on your toes and you wouldn't see the man. Besides, I didn't want you to have yet another thing to worry about. I thought it best to tell you after you had returned from the field."

"If it was Mr. Stilwell that slew Lord Cedreau, it will be extremely difficult for me to end the blood feud between our families."

"I am sorry, my lord," Braun offered with a low bow of his head.

6

"I suppose you did right, Braun," Lord Lokton said at last. "I also have men in the forest, so hopefully between all of them, someone will find him and we can get to the bottom of this. We are also looking for Sir Duvall."

"Sir Duvall, what for?" Braun asked.

"The guard who was on duty the night Timon was killed said that Sir Duvall paid him ten gold to let Mr. Stilwell out for the night." He walked over to the bed and looked down at the gray-haired dwarf, ignoring Braun's dumbfounded stare. "Either way it matters little now. If he and Mr. Stilwell are working together, I doubt we will find them."

"I presume that we won the battle?" Braun asked, changing the subject.

"It's interesting, isn't it?" Lord Lokton asked, ignoring Braun. "The dwarf is quite a tough looking fellow, yet he sleeps as silently as a newborn. I would have thought that dwarves snored."

"Sir, what of the battle?"

"Yes, Braun, we won." Lord Lokton closed his eyes and laid his right hand to the hilt of his sword. "We routed Lord Cedreau's army and sent them home. But they will be back. With Timon and Lord Cedreau dead, you can bet that Eldrik will not wait for long before he brings an army back here to finish this business of blood."

"Then we should prepare," Braun put in.

"Excuse me," a guard called from the doorway. Braun shot the man an angry glare. The guard bowed his head reverently, but entered the room anyway. "Forgive me for disturbing you, but I thought you should know that Senator Bracken has arrived."

"What?" Lord Lokton asked. He shook his head and patted the dwarf's foot. "I presume he wants an audience?" The guard nodded his head.

"Well, don't stand there like a mute statue, boy. When is the senator going to want the audience?" Braun asked.

"Right now," Senator Bracken said sternly as he appeared in the doorway behind the guard. The room seemed to grow colder as he pushed past the startled guard and stepped through the doorway, as though he brought the chill of winter with him. No, it was the chill of death. Senator Bracken clasped his hands in front of his white flowing robes, thereby prominently displaying the purple stripes encircling the rim of the sleeves. A golden medallion, the symbol of his office, hung from his neck, sliding side to side with each step. His dark, oiled hair gleamed in the light, accentuating his cold umber eyes. His chin seemed to form a point under the thin lips that sneered at Lord Lokton. Something was terribly wrong.

"House Lokton welcomes you, honorable Senator Bracken. May I offer you some wine or perhaps some fruit?" Lord Lokton offered.

"Lord Lokton, perhaps we may dispense with the pleasantries," Senator Bracken replied coolly. "I am here on a matter of most serious business."

"The senate sent you to investigate the murder of the magistrate?" Braun asked.

Senator Bracken turned a fierce eye to Braun. The brown orbs looked up and down the captain of the guard disdainfully before the senator spoke. "I am here to speak with Lord Lokton, not the hired help."

Braun bristled, but kept his mouth silent. Lord Lokton stepped forward and took the lead. "What may I assist you with?"

"For starters, you can explain to me why you have started a war on the king's land? Do you not know that the kingdom is in dire straits as it is without your petty squabbles over land and wealth?"

"I did not start-" Lord Lokton began to reply but he was cut off.

"Do not play games with me!" Bracken yelled. He clapped his hands and two large, heavily armed sentries came through the doorway. They pushed the other guard into the room, toward the bed. Lokton's guard reflexively pulled his sword half way out of its scabbard and Braun went for the axe at his belt. "I see your help has no problems committing treason," Senator Bracken growled.

"Braun, stay your hand," Lord Lokton said, though he made sure his own sword was loose in its scabbard. "What is the meaning of this, Senator Bracken?"

"By order of the senate, you are under arrest for high treason, Lord Lokton. Your two guards here might be able to help you escape, but I promise there are more than enough men on their way to subdue your entire household, if that is what you would prefer."

"I am no traitor," Lord Lokton replied.

"Oh no?" Senator Bracken sneered. "I have more than enough evidence to convict you. It's simple really. You knew that the knife you found and sent me wasn't enough evidence to prove Lord Cedreau's involvement in the magistrate's murder, so you tried to enact your own brand of justice."

"That's a lie!" Lord Lokton growled.

"Is it?" The two sentries pulled massive swords free from harnesses on their backs and flanked the senator. "The knife was taken from Eldrik Cedreau by Master Orres at Kuldiga Academy. The boy could not have used it to kill the magistrate. But, because you were quick to judge, you sent your men to slip into Cedreau Manor and kill Timon, Lord Cedreau's youngest boy."

"I did no such thing!" Lord Lokton shouted.

"Do you expect me to believe you?" Senator Bracken growled. "You stand before me with an injury obviously received today during your massacre of House Cedreau's men. Lord Cedreau is dead, and many of his knights lie in the dirt as well. How can you justify this?"

"They attacked me," Lord Lokton replied through clenched teeth.

"Because you murdered Timon," Senator Bracken replied. He steeled his gaze. "You slew Lord Cedreau ignobly during parlay. Your depravity knows no bounds."

"I'll not hear another word of this," Braun said as he stepped forward. "Command me, and their heads will roll."

"Is that the wise thing to do?" Senator Bracken asked. "If you attack a senator, here and now, you will only prove your guilt. I will be forced to seize your manor. Your son and wife will be shunned from society and your house will be razed to the ground."

"Braun, hold your hand, and your tongue," Lord Lokton commanded. Then he turned to the other guard. "Put your weapon away, boy." The guard did as he was told. Braun slowly set his axe on the bed next to him, but his eyes threw daggers at the senator. "Senator Bracken," Lord Lokton began as coolly as possible. "I have not sent anyone to murder any member of House Cedreau. I am afraid that you are mistaken in this."

"You may tell that to the senate. They will assemble one week after we return to Drakai Glazei."

"You have no proof of these accusations," Lord Lokton said. "You cannot arrest me."

"Proof?" Senator Bracken quipped. "I have a pair of letters from two men in your service, announcing that you have falsely imprisoned one of your own men after the death of the magistrate. I also have the witness of all of today's survivors that say Lord Cedreau was slain during parlay. I have Lord Cedreau's own letter claiming that his youngest son was slain by your men. I have an arrow that bears the signature of your fletcher, Master Himmal, and I have a report from Kuldiga Academy that supports Eldrik Cedreau's claim that his knife had been taken from him. Apparently Master Orres took the knife from the boy only a few weeks ago. So, as you can see, there is more than enough to bring you in before the senate."

"None of these prove anything," Lord Lokton said.

"Perhaps not decisively," Senator Bracken said. "But, they will be of importance to the senate, I assure you. I should also warn you, that if I happen to find Sir Duvall or Mr. Stilwell dead, then your fate will be sealed for certain."

"How do you know Sir Duvall and Mr. Stilwell?" Braun asked skeptically.

"Be silent," Bracken hissed. "You have no authority to question me."

Lord Lokton fumbled for something to say. He thought of explaining Ben's testimony against Sir Duvall and Mr. Stilwell, but he knew that without proof he would not be able to convince Senator Bracken of his own innocence. He had to stall. "Sir Duvall rode with me into battle," Lord Lokton said. "He is alive as far as I know, though I have not seen him as of yet. But he has not been named among our dead."

"Interesting," Senator Bracken said as he stroked his pointy chin. "Then take me to Mr. Stilwell. I know that you have him in your dungeon as we speak. Two of your guards wrote and told me as much. If you are innocent and have no part in this madness, let him tell me."

Lord Lokton sighed heavily. "I cannot," he said.

"Why?" Senator Bracken raised an eyebrow.

"Mr. Stilwell escaped from his cell shortly before the battle began."

"Things are not looking very promising for you," Senator Bracken said. He glanced to the two gigantic men with him and nodded. "Take him, by any means necessary."

The two men moved forward and Lord Lokton removed his sword belt. "I'll be fine, Braun," he said as the guards bound his wrists behind his back.

Senator Bracken smiled wide and then he produced a sealed parchment from the folds of his robes and tossed it on the ground before Braun. "I heard that Master Lepkin was here recently. This is an official summons for him to appear for the tribunal that will determine Lord Lokton's fate. Can you get the message to Lepkin?"

Braun nodded. "I know where to find him, but it may take some time to reach him."

"Well don't delay, I am sure you know what happens if Lepkin fails to answer an official summons from the senate."

Braun bent down and scooped up the parchment. "By your command, honorable senator" he said.

Bracken sneered at Braun's remark. "Sarcasm is a weapon of choice among cowards and ankle-biters," Bracken chided. "The tribunal date has been set, and we will convene with or without the Keeper of Secrets."

*****

Al groaned and rolled to his side. Again something grabbed his foot and shook it violently. Slowly he opened his eyes. A large man stood over him.

"Wake up, good dwarf, I need your help," the man said.

Suddenly Al remembered why he had been sleeping. "Where is Erik?" Al asked.

"Erik is back at Valtuu Temple," the man replied.

"Who are you?" Al asked. The dwarf pushed himself up to sit on the edge of the bed.

"My name is Braun, I am the sergeant-at-arms for House Lokton. Erik told me that you saved his life and charged me with watching over you while you rested."

"What of the battle?" Al looked around. "Am I to assume that

11

we won? Where is Lord Lokton?"

"That is why I woke you," Braun replied. "Lord Lokton has been arrested by Senator Bracken on charges of treason and murder."

"We should summon Master Lepkin at once," Al said, but he stopped short when Braun raised a hand. Al could tell by Braun's expression that there was more to the story. "Go on," Al said.

"I have here an official summons from the senate. They are requesting Lepkin's presence at the tribunal. So, understanding the consequences should Lepkin fail to answer the summons, we sent messenger birds to Lepkin. We were answered by the Prelate of Valtuu Temple. There was a great battle there as well. A wizard led an army of Blacktongues riding upon a night shade. The Prelate said the attackers were defeated, but both Lepkin and Erik were injured and are currently unconscious."

"Are the healers with them then?" Al asked.

Braun nodded.

"Well, it seems I picked a very poor time to sleep," Al groused. "I miss all the action and even Lepkin can't handle himself well enough without me." Al chuckled to himself, but noticed Braun's disapproving gaze. "Just trying to diffuse the tension…" Al straightened his beard and slid down from the bed.

Braun bristled. "My master is on his way to face the senate tribunal in Drakai Glazei, Lady Lokton is in a fretful state of mourning, and I am too far away from Erik to provide any meaningful service. You will forgive me if I fail to laugh at your joke."

Al nodded. "Of course, Braun, of course." The dwarf stretched his back. "Then what is the plan?"

"I have left another in charge of protecting House Lokton while I go to free my master from Senator Bracken."

"You aim to attack a senator on the open road?" Al inquired.

"I see little choice in the matter. Do you have another option?"

Al nodded. "I will go and fetch Lepkin. There is much at stake should he fail to attend." Al stretched his arms and made fists, bending and extending his sausage like fingers a few times. "Besides, I am well versed in senate protocol. There is a good chance that if I get Lepkin to the tribunal, we can still save Lord

Lokton."

Braun folded his muscled arms and frowned. "Then go as quickly as you can. I will follow the caravan, but I will stay my hand. Just know that if Lepkin's injuries prevent him from attending the tribunal, or if my master is sentenced to death, I will lop off every head in the senate that stands between me and Lord Lokton."

"Then I must hurry," Al responded. "Wait as long as you can, Braun. I'll do my best to get Lepkin to the tribunal."

Braun nodded and extended a hand. Al offered his in kind and the two shook hands. "Take care, good dwarf. Cedreau's spies have been spotted on Lokton land. They are not pleased with their master's death, and they will strike like a pack of jackals at your heels if you let them."

Al nodded. "I can handle myself," he said with a wink. "I will prepare immediately and try to set out before the sun begins to set this day."

"Very well," Braun replied. "I leave immediately for Drakai Glazei. May the Gods smile upon you."

*****

"I am sorry, but you cannot go inside with him," Marlin said as he closed the door to Master Lepkin's chamber. "It's nothing personal, but the dark side of your aura could taint the healing process. We mustn't take any chances."

"Of course," Lady Dimwater replied softly. Her sky blue eyes bored through the wooden door barring her from her love.

The longing in Lady Dimwater's soul was more than obvious. Marlin could tell by the energy swirling through her aura how deeply rooted her feelings were. He patted her shoulder and gently turned her away from the door. "He is making quite a recovery. I don't think it will take nearly half as long as I originally predicted."

"How long will it take?" Lady Dimwater asked, glancing back over her shoulder at the door as the two walked down the long hallway.

"I would wager perhaps six or seven days, no more than that."

"What of Erik?" She watched as the slight smile on Marlin's face vanished. "How long will Erik need to recover?" Lady

13

Dimwater pressed.

"I'm not sure," Marlin said gravely. "His aura is not very strong right now. That makes it more difficult for me to know."

Lady Dimwater stopped and grabbed Marlin's shoulders, turning him to face her. She looked into his glazed eyes earnestly, trying to search them as she would a normal person's, but she couldn't decipher the cloudy orbs. "Will he live?"

"I am almost certain that he will live."

"Then tell me, Marlin, what is wrong?"

"It is very difficult to put to words."

"Try," she demanded.

"From what I can tell, the boy's brain is slipping away. It isn't as active as it used to be. I don't know what it means; I only know that his brain is, for lack of a better word, asleep."

"He's unconscious, of course his brain is asleep," she said quickly.

"No, you don't understand. Master Lepkin is unconscious, but his brain is still active. His aura is strong, strengthening all the time, and his brain is very active. The brain does not completely shut down when a person sleeps. Think about it. Surely you've seen a person who is sleeping but is having an active dream."

Lady Dimwater nodded. "So, Erik's brain is completely dormant?"

"Not completely, but close to it. I don't know what the effects will be when he wakes up. I have brought in the very best healers the temple has. They are working on him day and night. They come in six shifts, four hours for each shift. There isn't a single moment when he is not being attended to. I, myself, go to his room at least once a day. I can tell you that we are doing everything we can to bring him back as quickly as possible."

"If he is lost…" Lady Dimwater let her words trail off as her eyelids fell shut. "There is not another who can replace him. As it is we are hard pressed for the time required to train him for his role in the events to come. If you can't save him, then all of us will suffer the consequences of that failure."

"I know," Marlin assured her. "I know." Marlin again started walking through the hall and Lady Dimwater fell in step with him. The two walked silently along the corridor to a small dining room outside the kitchen. They could smell the stew left over from dinner that had come and gone over an hour ago.

They sat for a few minutes on a bench along the side of the room and Marlin leaned back against the wall. Lady Dimwater couldn't see aura's, that was a type of magic she didn't have or understand, but the dark purple bags under Marlin's eyes and his heavy, slow breathing proved how exhausted he truly was. She guessed that Marlin probably had slept fewer hours than she over the last two nights, and she hadn't slept more than an hour or two since the nightwing had come with the wizard Erthor on its back.

Her only comfort came in watching the priests tirelessly minister to Erik and Lepkin. The sight of them coming and going, aiding them in their time of need, gave her hope. She leaned forward and let her head sink to her waiting, upturned palms. Her hair slipped over, covering her face, and her tears.

Her tired eyes stung from the many tears she had allowed herself to shed over the last few days. Her throat was sore from sobbing and supplicating the gods to wake her Lepkin up. Despite everything else happening around her, her mind replayed Lepkin's promise to finally find a way for the two of them to wed. Her heart ached now, hoping that she had not been given this promise just to have something else take him away from her.

Her tears stopped falling. Not for lack of sadness, but because her body was unable to create any more. Her eyelids grew heavy as stones and she gave in to her fatigue. She breathed in deeply and began to dream in spite of her uncomfortable position.

Something tapped her shoulder. She shrugged it away with a slight grunt. She didn't bother to look up. Sleep was not eager to release her from its grasp. The tapping came again. She came up from her hands, ready to slap the beetle or spider that she was certain to find. Instead, she saw a man offering her a bowl of stew. She thought to dismiss him, but her grumbling stomach reminded her that she could use the nourishment.

"Eat child," Marlin coaxed. Lady Dimwater gave him a sidelong glance and saw that he also had a bowl. She nodded and took the bowl in front of her, whispering her thanks. Given the time since her last meal, the food should have tasted divine, but it was little more than warm sawdust. The chunks of meat and potatoes almost dissolved in her mouth. She didn't really think about chewing. Bits of carrots and onion had long ago lost their crispness and flavor. What did it matter? She shrugged. It all ends up in the same place anyway, crisp and tasty or not.

She finished the bowl and set it down beside her. She recalled something that Marlin had said right after the battle with Erthor. "You mentioned that you might know where to look for the Book of Light?"

"I did," he replied through his last mouthful of stew. He unceremoniously wiped his mouth and then set his bowl down. "We will need it if we are to stand up to what is coming. I too know a bit of the Wyrms of Khaltoun. They will be back sooner or later for Nagar's Secret."

"How do you know of them?" Lady Dimwater asked. "I learned of them when I vanquished a shadowfiend that had been working with them. How is it that a group of priests and monks holed up in a remote, isolated temple would know anything about the necromancers?"

"I read the books of prophecy child, I know many things." Marlin folded his hands in his lap and smiled slightly. "They are named in a few places."

"They are named? But, I thought that prophecies just alluded to events and people. I didn't think they ever named specific people and events."

"Normally that is the case, but sometimes specific details are given. It is quite rare though."

"So, where do we look for the book of Allun'rha?" Lady Dimwater asked.

"The Illumination," Marlin corrected. "I will have to go back and check a few things. The references I have found to it over the years are obscure at best. I want to clarify a couple of passages before I give you the answer." Marlin stood up with a groan and put a hand to his forehead. "I hate it when I stand up too fast," he said with a smile.

Lady Dimwater nodded. "I suppose we could both use the sleep," she said. "I will see you in the morning?"

"First thing," Marlin promised.

*****

Al grabbed his pack and plopped it on the bed. He flipped the flap back and spread the opening with his stubby fingers. He set a loaf of bread inside, careful not to squish it under his cooking utensils and hammer.

He heard footsteps approach and turned to see a woman in a green gown standing before him in the doorway. Recognizing the signet she wore on her left hand he dropped his pack abruptly and straitened his tunic.

"Lady Lokton," he greeted with a bow of his head.

"Why do you travel with a hammer?" she asked.

Al regarded her for a moment, noting her red, watery eyes and her longing gaze. "It's a part of me, I suppose," he answered. He pulled the hammer and turned it over in his hand. The finish was worn off the smooth handle from heavy use. The head was engraved with a shamrock design on one side and a shield on the other. "I made this when I finished Hamalsiran."

Lady Lokton scrunched her brow into a knot above her nose and cocked her head to the side. "What is Hamalsiran?"

Al smiled, "It's a preparatory university. The curriculum takes thirty years to complete."

"Thirty years?" she asked incredulously.

Al nodded, laughing a little at the anticipated reaction, "In Hamalsiran, we dwarves study the physical sciences for ten years, then metaphysical sciences for another ten years. Afterward, we study religion, philosophy, history, and language for the last decade."

Raisa walked into the room and gently reached out for Al's hammer. "Then, you move into a profession?" she asked.

Al allowed her to take his hammer. Her hands dipped under its weight, but she didn't drop it. "Actually Hamalsiran only prepares us for one of the Academies." Al took the hammer back and gripped it as if to strike an imaginary workbench. "I was destined to go into King's College. That is where nobles are instructed."

"But you didn't," Raisa asked.

"I always felt more comfortable with metal and stone than with people." Al shrugged. "I made this hammer to show my father what I wanted. We fought for weeks." Al slipped the hammer into his bag. "Finally my brother took my place in King's College and I was allowed to pursue smithing. I spent the next several decades

17

perfecting my craft. My father never accepted my choice to give up the throne. He kept hoping I would come around to the idea of ruling. It never felt right to me though. I hadn't asked to be king. I wanted to pursue my own life. When my father passed on I left Roegudok Hall. My brother assumed the throne and the hammer has been with me ever since."

Raisa nodded and folded her hands together. "So, if your father wished for you to be king..." her words trailed off.

Al guessed what she was getting at and nodded. "I am the eldest, the throne is mine if I choose to challenge my brother for it."

"Have you considered it?"

Al wrinkled his nose. "Why would I want to do that?" He looked into her eyes and immediately understood what she was digging for. "I never went to King's College," Al huffed. He started to close up his pack.

"Is that a requirement?" she pushed.

Al shook his head sharply. "I can't lead my people. They no longer want to follow the old ways, and I..." his words caught in his throat.

"If the time comes that you choose to be king," Raisa began as she laid a hand on his shoulder. "I believe they would follow you. It may tip the balance in our favor."

Al gruffed, but said nothing. He tied the flap over his pack, and looked up to her with a warm smile. "First, I need to get Master Lepkin to Drakai Glazei. Then, I believe the best way for me to help is to stick with your son. There will be difficult days ahead."

Raisa's shoulders slumped and she turned her face away from him.

"We'll get Lord Lokton back," Al promised. "Lepkin is a living legend, and with me at his side, no one can stop us, especially not a bunch of wrinkly, old, high-browed senators." He offered a smile but Lady Lokton's tears fell over her cheeks anyway.

"I can't get Tukai's words out of my mind," she whispered.

Al closed his eyes and sighed. "I haven't known Erik as long as you have, but Tukai is wrong. Erik has nothing but love for you both. Tukai's prophecy is a lie, nothing more."

Raisa raised a handkerchief to her face and wiped her eyes

clean. "We have prepared a horse for you," she said after a moment. "Please remember you are always welcome here, good dwarf," she said.

"I will protect your family to my utmost ability," Al replied. "I may not be a king, but I will always come to House Lokton's aid."

The two embraced and then Al hefted his pack over his shoulder and left.

CHAPTER TWO

"You wanted to see me, Master Orres?"

Orres set his cold, pewter mug down on the long table and looked up to see Master Wendal. The narrow faced, thin man stood stoic, showing little emotion. The man brushed aside his black locks from his brow and folded his hands together behind his back.

"I did," Orres said with a slight smile. "How long have we known each other, Master Wendal?"

Master Wendal scrunched his brow. "Perhaps twenty years."

Orres nodded. He pulled a short parchment from his lap and laid it on the table next to his mug. His pointer finger twirled the paper around so that the writing faced Master Wendal and then he pushed it toward him. "I should have noticed something," Orres said.

Master Wendal took the paper and began to read aloud. "Master Orres, it is with the deepest regret that House Lokton informs you of your brother's passing. During open hostilities with House Cedreau—"

Orres cut in. "During open hostilities with House Cedreau, Janik turned on Erik Lokton and revealed himself to be working with the warlock Tukai and his order. Erik survived Janik's attack with the help of Aldehenkaru'hktanah Sit'marihu. Enclosed is the amulet Janik wore around his neck when he attacked Erik." Orres finished repeating the note's message and clunked a golden amulet on the table.

"Janik worked with Tukai?" Wendal asked skeptically. "That doesn't make any sense. Perhaps House Lokton is lying, or mistaken."

Orres shook his head. "After I received the letter with the amulet inside, I went to his private chamber. I found a letter instructing my brother to travel to a tavern to meet and discuss how to 'deal with the boy' and proceed with House Lokton." Orres raised his mug and drained the contents. "I knew him a lot longer than twenty years, yet he deceived me."

Wendal shrugged. "The letter may have been planted," he suggested.

Orres nodded. "That is true, but my gut tells me that is not so."

"With respect, one should be careful not to let their emotion cloud their judgment."

Orres slid the mug away from him and rose from the table. "Come with me," Orres said. He motioned for Wendal to turn to the northern corridor. Orres scooped up the amulet, took back the letter from House Lokton, and then proceeded ahead of Master Wendal. He walked with a determined gait, forcing the tall Master Wendal to quicken his pace in order not to fall behind. They walked to a far corner of the academy that was well removed from the other offices and classrooms. They passed a few old storage rooms and then Orres stopped and pulled an old, tarnished brass key from his pocket and slid it into the lock. The tumblers clicked and the door popped open.

Inside the room stood a few barrels with labels on them. Some contained flour, others whole wheat grain, and others had labels that had been scratched out and appeared to be empty. A couple old brooms stood in the far corner, collecting cobwebs and old flies. Otherwise the room was unremarkable in every respect.

"Why have you brought me here?" Wendal asked.

"Because I feel you are someone I can trust, and I *hope* that my intuition will not let me down." Orres stepped up to the first barrel labeled flour and opened the lid. He placed his massive hand in the flour and pushed the white powder aside to revel an iron ring. He pulled the ring and a series of clicks and metallic *pops* echoed in the small room. A portion of the rear wall detached and swung away, revealing a passageway that led to another chamber. Orres replaced the flour and the lid before walking through the doorway.

Master Wendal looked behind him to the corridor before following Orres into the secret passageway. The air was warm and damp, but there was plenty of light coming from a series of oil lamps hanging from the ceiling. "I never knew this place existed," Wendal said.

"From time to time, some of us at the academy have been called upon to execute orders from the king," Orres said. "In order to aid us in our duties, those of us with special commissions meet here to organize information, discuss orders, and strategize."

"What kind of information?" Wendal asked.

Orres stopped walking and opened a heavy, iron door after sliding a long, hexagonal key into the lock. Orres reached up and took the nearest oil lamp from its hook on the ceiling and walked through the doorway. A moment later the room beyond was illuminated in warm, golden light. Wendal slowly walked in.

Several chests lined the left wall of the chamber. Each had bands of iron and three hefty locks holding them closed. Along the back wall stood a series of black bookshelves enclosed with iron mesh doors. A long wooden weapons rack stood along the right wall, and beside it stood a great mahogany wardrobe. Orres moved to stand at the head of an eight person table.

"Have a seat," Orres instructed. He went to the back wall and unlocked one of the bookshelves. He pulled a long parchment out and returned to the table. He eyed Wendal curiously. "It's all right, have a seat," he insisted.

Wendal moved to take a seat near Orres and watched the headmaster unroll the long parchment to reveal a map of the Middle Kingdom. "What is this?" Wendal asked. "Every noble family is listed on the map with their houses and lands clearly outlined."

Orres nodded. "Surely you are aware that there are factions conspiring to assume power when the king passes."

Wendal nodded. "I have heard the rumors."

Orres smiled and nodded his head. "Kuldiga Academy was founded during a time of great need. A group of shadowfiends had conspired to assume control of a region in the kingdom."

Wendal nodded. "And it was Master Heimdal with his mighty sword, Stormfang, who crushed the shadowfiends and established Kuldiga Academy over the ruins of their fortress. I know the legend."

"It is no legend," Orres countered sharply. "It is all fact." He gestured to the room around them. "Look at the stone in this room. It does not match the rest of the academy. This room was the shadowfiends' planning room. In this room, Master Heimdal discovered texts that revealed secret plans and plots, as well as detailed maps and records that listed the kingdom's resources, and details about various noble families and their true loyalties."

Master Wendal frowned.

Orres held up a finger. "After discovering this chamber, Master Heimdal worked with the king to create a special team of officers who would protect the information, and use it to foil enemies of the king."

"How did the information help them do that?"

"Not only did it indicate other potential people who threatened the kingdom's security, but the system of records itself showed Heimdal how such information could be recorded and preserved in an effort to stay one step ahead of further developments that could harm the kingdom." Orres tipped his chair back and kicked a leg out to the side. "Since then the task of monitoring, collecting, and acting on the information has passed from one headmaster to the next. As has the task of identifying other individuals who have the right skills and integrity to join the select group."

"Was Janik a part of this group?"

Orres nodded. "Ever since the battle that crippled him, he had been assigned to the group. He was a great asset, and helped us prevent several disasters."

"Lady Dimwater is also a member, isn't she?" Wendal guessed. "That is why she went to Kuressar."

Orres nodded grimly. "She first went to Spiekery, to deal with a shadowfiend that was forcing human sacrifice on the small town. Afterward she went to Kuressar to deal with Lord Hischurn. We had some information indicating that he was working with the warlocks of the Order of the All Seeing Eye as well as gathering resources for battle."

"She told us that the orders came from the Royal Court to arrest a suspected shadowfiend," Wendal commented.

"And she told you the truth," Orres said. "We gathered the information, but only the king or Judge McTeabe of the Royal Court can authorize the actions we take. That way the king maintains control over us."

"So, why have you brought me here?" Wendal asked.

Orres sniggered and pointed back to the map. "Several families have been making moves over the last several years to consolidate their power. While there are many that remain loyal to the king, there are others who are not only positioning themselves to take power, but they grow tired of waiting for the old king to die. I have some reason to believe that a few of the other Masters here at the Academy are aligning themselves with some of these impatient, power-hungry families."

"You can't be serious," Wendal scoffed. "Who here would do such a thing? We have all sworn our allegiance to the crown."

"But the king has not yet named an heir," Orres pointed out.

"That doesn't matter," Wendal argued. "In the event the king dies without a legitimate heir or appointed replacement, the senate and the Keeper of Secrets are to rule jointly."

Orres nodded. "I know the law, my friend. However, I also know that many of the senators grow hungry themselves. Many do not relish the thought of sharing power with Master Lepkin, and several noble families have grown very close to some of these senators."

"What you speak of is treason," Wendal said sharply.

"That is exactly why this special council was formed under Master Heimdal's leadership those many years ago." Orres stabbed the table with his index finger and locked eyes with Wendal. "Heimdal's mighty sword, Stormfang, rests in a glass cabinet not more than fifty paces from the armory next to my office. It is there not only as a reminder of the great battle Heimdal won, but the oath that I took as Headmaster. The battle continues today." Orres rose to his feet. "What I want to know from you, Master Wendal, is will you stand beside me and help me run these traitors down?"

*****

Lady Dimwater couldn't sleep. She tossed back and forth on her bed. She threw the blankets off and then pulled them back over herself. Nothing worked. Her body ached for rest, but her mind was far too active to allow her to sleep. Finally she left her bed and draped a dark robe around her shoulders. She slid her feet into soft leather slippers and quietly exited her room.

She walked down the hallway to a set of stairs. A couple of days previous, Marlin had taken her to a large archive of books and records in the basement level of the temple. Now was as good a time as any to go back and do some additional research. She saw only a few guards as she descended down the spiraling, smooth marble steps. She returned their nods and greetings, but did not slow her pace.

Once she reached the bottom she found the door to the archives already ajar. She slipped inside to discover Marlin sitting at a table near the entrance, a slew of books and papers strewn all around him.

"I thought you went to bed," Lady Dimwater said.

"I could not sleep," Marlin replied. "I suspect you have the same problem?" Lady Dimwater nodded and Marlin gestured to a chair across from him at the table.

"Have you found anything yet?" Lady Dimwater asked.

"I have found something, actually, though I don't know what to make of it." Marlin directed her attention to a dusty, green tome. "This is a book of prophecies, written by an ancient mystic. I believe I have stumbled upon something to do with Erik."

"What language is this?" Lady Dimwater asked.

"It is Taish, High Taish to be exact," Marlin replied.

"I can read High Taish," Lady Dimwater countered. "This doesn't look like anything I have ever seen before."

"True," Marlin said with a nod. "This as a very ancient dialect; several thousand years old I believe. I would wager that you would be hard pressed to find any among the elves who can read this."

"What does it say?"

Marlin leaned over the page and pointed to each word as he translated the passage for Lady Dimwater. "On the wings of death the champion will ride, laying waste to the seats of white. His anger ushers in the dark tide, and washes the world in the color of night."

"And that is about Erik?" Lady Dimwater asked skeptically.

"I believe so," Marlin nodded. "Several pages preceding this one speak of the Champion of Truth, and this passage references the champion in it. It seems to be about Erik, though I must admit it doesn't make much sense to me."

"How could Erik wash the world in the color of night? I thought his destiny was to save us." Marlin sighed heavily. Instead of responding, he sucked in the corner of his bottom lip and chewed on it a bit. "Marlin, I can see that something weighs on your mind," Lady Dimwater said. "What is it? What have you found?"

"There is another passage in this book here." Marlin reached to his left and pulled a blue book close to him, opening it to a bookmark he had left in it. "This is written by a different person; the language is the same but the strokes are made differently. Judging from the texture of the pages, it is from the same era as the other passage."

"What does it say?"

"Believe not your eyes, for a champion in false skin shall rise."

Dimwater watched Marlin carefully. "So, you think that Erik could be the false champion the prophecy spoke of?" She shook her head and crossed her arms. "There must be more than this." she said. "Surely we cannot abandon Erik just because of this one piece of paper."

"It is not one piece of paper, Lady Dimwater. There is a third prophecy that I believe deals with these two. It is written by a third person, but again it is from the same era."

"What does it say?" She watched Marlin reach for a book with a red cover. His fingers deftly found the bookmark and opened the yellowed pages to the desired passage.

"One touched of the dragon's might, but not born of it, shall save the world from darkest night, and rule from the Stone Pulpit." Marlin gently pushed the book away. "Each of these passages in each book is describing the same event, though they focus on different aspects of it. One is a warning that there is a false champion, the second warns what the false champion will do, and the third tells us who can stop the false champion."

"Lepkin," Dimwater whispered. "It is said that those who are dragon-born are touched by dragons and given a gift. They are called dragon-born, but they are not exactly born of dragons."

"That is the same conclusion I came to as well." Marlin pushed back from the table and wiped a weary hand over his brow. "You and I both know who steps in to rule the kingdom if the king fails to appoint an heir before his death."

"The Keeper of Secrets rules in partnership with the senate," Dimwater answered.

"Correct," Marlin said.

Dimwater shook her head and tapped a pointed fingernail on the table. "Are you telling me that Erik might be a false champion, and has the power to destroy us all?" Voicing the question aloud left a bitter taste in her mouth. "You are telling me that Erik, the same young man that risked his own life for an adoptive father, and saved Lepkin from the power of Nagar's Secret, could turn?"

Marlin sighed. "Up until now, I would never have believed Erik could so much as hold an evil thought in his heart, let alone act upon such a treacherous desire. But now..." He stood, displaying a grim expression on his face. "You know of the prophecy given by the warlock about Erik?"

Lady Dimwater nodded. "Of course, it has bothered Erik terribly. He has been racking his brain trying to figure out how his father could turn evil and need to be killed, or if there is possibly another son that the prophecy speaks of. It is hard for him to even imagine a situation where he might slay his own father."

"I wonder if anyone thought about the possibility that Erik might slay his own father because Erik is the one who turns to the dark side." His finger tapped the prophecy describing the false champion.

"The books of prophecy are difficult to decipher," Lady Dimwater stated.

"That they are," Marlin agreed with a nod. "I still have much research to do to uncover the truth behind these words, but until then perhaps we should endeavor harder to wake Master Lepkin before we pull the boy from his coma."

"If Erik turns..." Lady Dimwater closed her eyes and sucked on her lower lip. "May the gods be merciful."

*****

Al pulled up the reins and slowed his horse. He swung his right leg over to his left and slid off the horse. He untied his pack from behind the saddle and pulled out his small pot. He could hear the babbling brook just beyond the ferns, and his throat was in dire need of wetting.

He walked to the water and took a few quick gulps of the cool, crystalline water. Then he filled his pot halfway. He set the pot down on a flat rock and walked along the brook gathering mushrooms. When he had enough he cleaned the dirt off and rinsed them in the water before dumping them into the pot. Next he pulled a pair of fishing lines from his pack and went to work tying hooks every eight inches. Then he foraged for grubs, grasshoppers, and worms to bait the hooks on one of the lines.

After the fishing lines were ready, he attached one end of the baited line to an exposed tree root and threw the line into the water. After watching it unravel in the current and begin to sink, he dunked the other line into the stream, pulled it out and tied a rock to each end. He set the second line on a flat stone nearby and quickly went to work gathering wood and built a fire. He nestled the pot of mushrooms and water in the flames and erected a spit off to the side for later use.

Al rummaged through his bag and found a clove of garlic. He wrapped it in a small cloth and then mashed it between a pair of rocks. He took the mushed garlic and sprinkled the moist pieces into the mushroom soup.

Next, he put up a crude tent. He laid his blanket over a low hanging branch and pinned the sides in place with a couple of metal tacks.

The squirrels overhead stopped chattering. Al paused for a moment and listened. Hearing nothing, he tossed his pack into the tent and set his axe against a nearby tree trunk.

*****

"Don't muck this up, Blacktongue," Deglain said. He glanced over to the man next to him. The Blacktongue's shaved head was streaked with black, angular tattoos that accentuated the hard lines drawn in his face by his prominent cheekbones and pointed chin. The assassin's irises were as black as the ink in his skin. His slender, sinewy arms reached over his head to draw a curved, black sword. The Blacktongue slipped away without a word, barely disturbing the nearby bushes as he moved.

"Blacktongues," Deglain grumbled under his breath. He turned his attention back to the dwarf making camp. Deglain slowly raised his bow and arched his arm over his shoulder to retrieve a pair of arrows. Deglain slid a foot forward to position himself. He froze when he saw the dwarf pause. Deglain held his breath until the dwarf set his axe down and crawled into the tent.

Deglain readied his arrow and looked to his left. He scanned the bushes, searching for the Blacktongue. As his eyes studied the shadows, trees, and bushes, a chill ran up Deglain's spine. The assassin had vanished entirely from his sight.

He waited for two more minutes and then took aim with the first arrow. A slight lump bulged out from the side of the tent. Deglain lined up his shot and let it fly. The arrow exploded from the bushes, scattering a pair of finches and sinking deep into its target. Deglain heard a pained groan from the tent and smiled. As he fired his second arrow it only narrowly outpaced the Blacktongue assassin who emerged from the trees like a ghost from the shadows.

The assassin sprinted in and delivered a devastating chop. The tent was rent asunder by the swift slices and strikes. Bread, leather, and wood were strewn about, but Deglain saw no blood.

The Blacktongue ceased his savage attack and reach down, picking up a saddle bag and turning to hold it up for Deglain to see. Two arrows protruded from its side.

Deglain stepped through the bushes. "Where is he?" he shouted.

The assassin shrugged and prodded the tent with his sword. The blade sunk deep and easily below ground level.

"I told you not to muck this up!"

"I did not fire the first arrow," the man hissed. He flicked his sword to the side and removed the tent from its place. "There is a hole here in the ground," he said.

Deglain stopped next to the fire and kicked the dirt. Brown clumps of soil and grit sprayed over the campsite. "Find him you useless…" he stopped mid-sentence and pointed. A dwarf came running up from the stream.

"Here I am!" the dwarf shouted. A hammer flew from his hand and thunked into the Blacktongue's chest. The skinny assassin flew backward through the air, limbs flailing about until he crumpled to the ground.

Deglain reached for another arrow. The dwarf was spinning something over his head. Deglain set his arrow to the bow, but the dwarf was faster.

A wet cord wrapped around him clumsily, grappling onto him with blinding speed. Deglain stumbled back as a pair of stones slammed into his spine. Deglain moved his arms to shrug the cord off, but stopped abruptly as hooks clawed into his skin. Deglain recoiled and jerked against the pain before slamming to the dirt. He writhed around grunting and snorting.

"Stop fighting it," the dwarf said

"You are marked for death," Deglain growled. "I will not be the last."

The dwarf nodded and disappeared back down behind the hillock. He returned a moment later with a line of freshly cleaned fish. Deglain craned his neck around to look at his companion.

"No," the dwarf said. "The Blacktongue won't be getting up again." The dwarf stood next to a spit and began shoving it through the fishes' gills. "We need to talk," the dwarf said.

"I ain't got nothing to say," Deglain hissed.

"We can start with names," the dwarf said. "My name is Al, but you already know that I suppose."

Deglain clamped his jaw and turned his eyes away from Al.

Al chuckled. "You know, I hear bears roam these parts. Do you think the smell of fresh fish might attract them?" Al took a small fish and threw it in Deglain's face, smirking as the cold, slimy fish slid across Deglain's forehead and fell to the dirt. "That would certainly not bode well for you if a bear did show up and found you lying here in the dirt."

"You wouldn't leave me here," Deglain responded.

Al shrugged, pulled another fish and tossed it at Deglain. "Let's call it an experiment then." He reached down and pulled the pot from the fire.

"What's in the pot, some special spice to entice another predator?" Deglain snarled.

Al set the pot on a rock and walked toward the tattered tent, where his saddlebag was. He retrieved a metal cup. "No, my friend," he answered absently as he blew some dust out of the cup. Al returned to the pot, removed the lid and breathed in the aroma. "This is garlic mushroom soup. It's for me." Al dipped his cup into the pot and gingerly sipped the steaming contents.

"So then, what now?" Deglain asked.

Al shrugged and took another sip. He smacked his lips and

smiled to himself, wiping a bit of dribble from his beard. "Well, either you answer my questions and I let you go, or I have dinner and a show." Al paused for effect. "I don't imagine it will be too long before a hungry bear catches the scent of our fish though." Al smiled and raised the metal cup back to his lips, slurping loudly.

CHAPTER THREE

"Have you found anything else?" Lady Dimwater asked.

Marlin shook his head. "Not anything specifically relating to the false champion."

Lady Dimwater watched as Marlin studiously devoured page after page of ancient writings. She marveled at the speed with which he read. Then a curious thought came to her. "Marlin," she started. "How can you read these books if you have given up your natural sight?"

Marlin smiled. "The mystics who wrote these tomes used a portion of their magic. While I can no longer see the ink with which they wrote, I can see the magical essence in each stroke on the page. This enables me not only to see the words, symbols, and characters used, but also the mood and intent of the mystic at the time he or she wrote it."

Lady Dimwater nodded. "That is intriguing," she said.

"Let me show you something," Marlin offered. He grabbed a brown tome and set it before Lady Dimwater. He opened it and pointed to the third paragraph. As Lady Dimwater slowly stumbled through the archaic passage, Marlin grabbed another book and pointed to a paragraph in it. "These two passages describe the same event," Marlin said. Then he leaned back and waited patiently for Lady Dimwater to finish reading.

"I don't understand," Dimwater said when she finished. "These two passages contradict each other. I didn't realize the mystics could err in their prophecies."

"They made no mistakes," Marlin said cryptically.

Lady Dimwater pursed her lips and studied the two passages for a moment. A smile tugged at the left corner of her mouth and her eyes brightened suddenly. "I understand," she said as the answer dawned on her. "The mystics used false prophecies as a defense mechanism, in case the tomes fell into the wrong hands. The mystics knew all along which is the correct passage, but only the intended reader – you with your true sight – could decipher the mystery. Am I right?"

Marlin nodded with a pleased smile. "Well done," he said. "My gift of true sight allows me to discern between them. If a mystic were to write falsely, it left a visible mark on the text. Conversely, if a mystic wrote truly, it left a different discernable mark for me to see. Therefore, I can glance at opposing prophecies and know which is false, and which is true. As you can imagine, this cuts a lot of time out of the process for me, but would take the intruder years, if not decades, to go through all the versions of each prophecy. Then, to try and make sense of the many variations would likely drive him mad. The mystics were quite clever."

"That they were," Dimwater agreed. "Are there ever any prophecies from which you can't discern between false and true?"

Marlin sighed. "Prophecy is a difficult and dangerous tool to use. From what I understand, a mystic would have a vision, write it down, and then meditate upon its meaning. Once the meaning was clear, the mystic would write down a passage in a magical tome of prophecy. Most of the time a mystic knowingly records his or her vision accurately in one book and falsely in one or more other books, and I can always discern between the two. These books are then combined with that of other mystics into large, prophetic tomes, mixing false and real visions at random so that no one book can contain all of the answers. However, there are occasionally some passages that I cannot understand."

Lady Dimwater scrunched her brow. "What do you mean?"

"It is a rarity, but sometimes the mystics would have visions which they could not understand themselves, regardless of how long they meditated. These visions are recorded in a special collection of tomes. They are extremely dangerous to use, for none of our order can decipher their truth any more than the mystics could."

"Can anyone else decipher them?"

Marlin nodded slowly. "There are some references to an immortal mystic who resides in a faraway land. This mystic is said to be able to decipher the forbidden prophecies, but as of yet no one has been able to locate this mystic." Marlin sighed and closed the two tomes and pushed them away. "One of our order, a priest by the name of Tatev, knows more about this. He loves to study the more obscure texts. Perhaps we can talk with him if we need to find this immortal mystic."

Dimwater nodded and looked back to the closed tomes. "You didn't say which passage was the correct one," she noted.

"They are both false," Marlin said with a smile and a quick wink.

Dimwater laughed and shook her head. She opened her mouth to ask another question when the door to the chamber burst open.

"Prelate, forgive the intrusion, but Master Lepkin is waking," the priest said.

"Excellent!" Dimwater exclaimed as she flew off of her seat and made for the door.

"Hold on," Marlin said grimly.

Dimwater reluctantly turned and saw that Marlin was concentrating heavily. "What is it?" she asked.

Marlin kept his attention focused on the priest in the doorway.

Dimwater turned back to the priest. "Well, out with it!"

"I don't know," the priest said. "Lepkin's aura is different. I can't explain it better than that."

Without another word the three of them went straightaway to Lepkin's chamber. Though the walk seemed to Dimwater to take hours, it was only a matter of minutes before they arrived. Marlin stopped in front of the door and turned to Dimwater.

"I am sorry, but I must ask you to wait out here, just until I know what is going on." Dimwater frowned, but nodded her understanding. Then she watched Marlin and the priest enter and close the door behind them.

*****

"Has he spoken?" Marlin asked as he walked up to Lepkin's bedside.

"No, Prelate," one of the other healers replied. "But he has moved and started groaning a bit."

Marlin scanned Lepkin's aura. The intensity of the colors he found was astounding. White, yellow, red, blue, and green hues pulsed throughout Lepkin's body. A cord of purple coiled around the outside of the aura while an egg-shaped orb of white grew in his chest and cast golden rays throughout Lepkin's body.

"This is perplexing," Marlin said to no one in particular.

"When we saw the change in his aura, we slowed our healing."

"No," Marlin said with a shake of his head. "Let's finish waking him." He looked to the others and waved them over. "Join with me," Marlin directed them as he placed his right hand on Lepkin's forehead and his left upon Lepkin's chest, just over his heart. Two more priests came up and did as Marlin had, placing their hands directly over Marlin's hands. Green energy started to flow from the three, starting in their chests and coursing down their arms to their hands and finally mixing with Lepkin's aura. Once the connection was made, another priest came up and placed his hands on Marlin's shoulders, augmenting Marlin's efforts by sending his own energy through Marlin. Two additional priests augmented the other two healers.

No one spoke. The only sound in the room was the warm, vibrant hum of the healers' energy as it flowed into Lepkin. Their energy spread through Lepkin's aura, strengthening limbs and waking muscles. After twenty minutes had passed, Lepkin opened his eyes.

"It is done," Marlin announced wearily. The healers all broke the connection with Lepkin and stepped back, giving Marlin room to speak. Marlin studied Lepkin's aura. It was even brighter now than before, as though Lepkin was a prism before the sun.

"Can you move?" Marlin asked.

Lepkin nodded and rolled to his side before pushing up to a seated position.

"How do you feel Master Lepkin?" Marlin asked.

Confusion rippled through Lepkin's aura.

Marlin placed a reassuring hand on Lepkin's shoulder. "You may feel a bit strange for a few minutes as your body adjusts. You went through quite an ordeal during that battle. I'm sorry to press you so soon, but we need to talk, Lepkin. I have discovered some things…" Marlin let his words hang unfinished. He saw the confusion growing in Lepkin's aura. "Master Lepkin, what is wrong?" Marlin asked.

Lepkin looked up with a frowning face. "Why do you keep

calling me Lepkin?"

*****

Lord Lokton wiggled his fingers behind his back. His wrists had long ago ceased aching and he had resigned himself to the ensuing numbness. He tried to twist his torso to loosen the iron's grip on him, but instead it only seemed to pull his shoulders farther behind him. The wagon lurched into a rut, slamming his head into the wooden wall. He shook it off and looked up to the barred window above him.

A toothy grin met his gaze from behind a bush of black hair under his guard's short, wide nose. "Havin' fun, my lord?" the guard mocked.

Lord Lokton grinned up at him. "I always have fun looking at freak shows," he shot back. "Which circus did the senator pull you from?"

The smile disappeared. "I would keep my insolent mouth shut, if I were you," the guard warned. "The senator will stop to eat in the next village, and when he does you will be under my supervision."

Lord Lokton winked. "A dinner date sounds lovely," he said.

The guard growled and moved away from the window. Lord Lokton let his tough façade fall away as he looked up to the starry sky. His eyes watered and a tear slid down his left cheek. Another bump in the road jerked him to the other side. The iron chain snapped him back to place. He leaned his head against the side of the wagon and stared at the brightest star he could see.

"Just let me see my boy one more time," he whispered to the heavens. "That's all I ask." A dark cloud blew in from the side, obscuring his view through the window and hiding the stars from him. He dropped his head and looked to the floor of the wagon.

Some time later the wagon rolled to a stop. Lord Lokton heard shouts and hollers mixed in with heavy footsteps. The guard popped back to the window with a wide, evil sneer.

"We have arrived," he said.

"Step back from the window," someone said. The guard obeyed immediately, disappearing from the window once more. "Open the door," the voice said.

A series of locks clicked and popped as they disengaged and the wagon's rear door was opened. Lord Lokton looked out and saw Senator Bracken standing there. He grinned and stepped up and into the wagon, closing the door behind him.

"I trust you have enjoyed the journey thus far?" Senator Bracken smirked.

"Oh it has been delightful," Lord Lokton replied. "You'll have to allow me to return the favor sometime."

Senator Bracken closed the gap between them in an instant and slammed his fist into Lord Lokton's left cheek, opening a gash along his cheekbone. Lord Lokton's head rang from the force of the blow.

"That statement summarizes exactly why you are in this predicament," Bracken said. Lord Lokton glared up at the senator, but remained silent. "What? No pithy insult or sarcastic remark? Lord Lokton, I am dumbstruck."

"Let me loose, and you will surely be struck," Lord Lokton growled.

Bracken backhanded Lord Lokton with such fury that Lord Lokton's neck popped.

"Let's not play games," Bracken said. "I am here with a proposition." Bracken moved to sit on a stool nearby. "I have more than enough evidence to convict you. You do know that, yes?"

Lord Lokton shook his head. "You have no evidence against me. I am no traitor."

Bracken nodded. "I know."

Lord Lokton raised a curious brow. "You know?"

The senator sneered. "I know you are innocent," he clarified.

"Then what in the name of Hammenfein am I doing in here?" Lord Lokton demanded.

"Tsk tsk," Bracken said with a wag of his finger. "One should not evoke the name of realms which they neither control nor understand."

"What do you want from me?" Lord Lokton asked.

"Ah," Bracken said with a smile. "That is the first smart thing to leave your mouth all day." Bracken rose to his feet and the stool disappeared. Bracken paused, waiting to see if Lokton had noticed. He had.

"I am not impressed by parlor tricks," Lord Lokton said. "Tell me what you want."

"I want your fealty," Bracken said openly. "Poor King Mathias grows old, and he has no apparent heir. Align your house with me, and assure me of your loyalty."

"I will do no such thing," Lord Lokton said. "That is not how the law works." Lord Lokton turned angry eyes up at the senator. "You set me up didn't you?"

Bracken smiled and nodded. "I may have orchestrated a few things," he admitted.

"You did all of this just to put me in a position of need so I would jump at your offer," Lord Lokton surmised. "It will not work. My honor is not for sale."

Bracken knelt down in front of Lord Lokton and leaned in close enough for his hot, putrid breath to assault Lord Lokton's nostrils. "Without my help, you will die a traitor's death," Bracken warned. "I have many allies inside the senate who follow me. They will give the verdict I tell them to give. Even if I had no evidence, you would swing on the gallows."

"You are mad," Lord Lokton said.

Bracken reached up and seized Lord Lokton's shoulder with otherworldly power and dug into his skin with his nails. "I am neither mad, nor a fool. A new tide is coming in. Along with it, all families who swear fealty to me will rise. Those who defy me shall be obliterated as though a tempest swept over them. You have a choice, here and now. Join with me and I make all of this disappear. If you continue to rebuke me, I will destroy you, and your family. Your lands will burn and your wife will die a scorned widow. Your adopted son will be hunted down and gutted like an animal in the forest."

Lord Lokton jerked his shoulder free and spat in Bracken's face. "May Khefir take you and drag you to Hammenfein."

Bracken laughed as he slowly wiped the spittle from his face. "It doesn't have to be this way. I can just as easily pin the blame on the real culprits and allow you to walk away. Your family will be taken under my wing and protected once the new era begins."

"You will not succeed," Lord Lokton swore. "Lepkin and my son will stop you."

"No, they won't," Bracken hissed. "Should Lepkin, or anyone

else, come against me, I will have them branded traitors just like you. Every proud head that refuses to bow to me shall be lopped off." Bracken stood and backed away. "This is your final chance, Lokton. Tell me where you stand. Are you willing to forfeit your life and the lives of your family and friends just so your petty 'honor' remains intact by stubbornly serving a ghost of a king?"

"House Lokton serves the king," Lord Lokton said.

"What if I told you that Sir Duvall and Mr. Stilwell were the true murderers?" Bracken asked. "Duvall placed the dagger in the magistrate's back and helped Stilwell escape from your prison."

"How could you know this?" Lord Lokton spat.

"Because I am the one who hired them," Bracken smiled. "Ironic how the 'honor' you hold so dear means so little to those you have surrounded yourself with." Bracken turned and went for the door. "No matter, your death will allow me to pull House Cedreau under my wing." He glanced back over his shoulder. "It might interest you to know that I have Mr. Stilwell's and Sir Duvall's bodies with me. I will present them as evidence of *your* treachery."

"You hired them, and then you killed them?" Lokton asked.

"Delicious, isn't it?" Bracken cackled.

"You are a monster," Lord Lokton said.

Bracken nodded and exited the wagon. "He's all yours," he said to someone standing out of view. "Just leave enough of him so I can hold the tribunal," Bracken instructed.

The bearded guard stepped into the wagon. "I'll try to keep him alive," he promised.

Bracken sneered one final time at Lord Lokton and then slammed the wagon shut.

CHAPTER FOUR

"What do you mean?" Dimwater demanded.

Marlin shushed her and put a finger to her lips. "Please, keep your voice down, he is only in the next room, and he is just as confused as we are about the whole thing."

"How did this happen?" Lady Dimwater asked as she tossed a book to the table.

"I wish I knew, Marlin replied. "I only know that it is so. I examined him thoroughly."

"So Lepkin is now inside of Erik's body and Erik is inside Lepkin's. That is what you are saying?"

"It would appear so," Marlin said.

Dimwater placed a hand to her forehead and sighed. "How did this happen?" she repeated.

"I'm not sure," Marlin replied. He kept his nose buried in the black, leather bound tome, pouring over its contents. "But, I have a theory."

Lady Dimwater tapped her finger on the table. "You going to share it with me?" she nagged.

Marlin nodded. He pulled back from the thick tome and wiped a hand over his face with a sigh. "The magic Erik uses is unique." Marlin leaned back and pointed to a book on a shelf. "Can you send that book to me?"

Lady Dimwater waved her hand and the book flew from the shelf to hover in front of Marlin's face. "Shall I open it for you as well?"

Marlin gave a wry laugh and pushed the book to the table. "How did you do that?" he asked. He could see the confusion and anger swirling in her. He held a finger in the air. "I mean, do you understand the mechanics of your magical power?"

"My power grabbed the book and brought it to you," she

replied impatiently.

"Exactly," Marlin said with a nod. "Your power acted upon the object, like an invisible hand."

"Marlin, Lepkin lies in a coma, trapped inside Erik's body while Erik has woken to find himself in Lepkin's body. Can you get to the point?"

Marlin blushed and nodded. "Of course, I apologize. I assumed a scholar such as yourself would want the detailed theory."

"Not in this case."

"Erik's power doesn't work like yours. While your magic acts upon objects, his acts within objects."

"What's the difference?"

"For one, it makes him more powerful, potentially. But mechanically speaking, your magic forces an object to act in the desired manner. Erik's power connects to the object and elicits a change from within so that the object itself chooses to obey and align itself with him."

Dimwater frowned. "Marlin, nothing you said makes sense. I have researched magic for most of my life, but I have no idea what you are talking about."

"Have you heard of inherent intelligence?"

Dimwater nodded. "The theory that everything has capacity for thought and choice. But that is not one of the magical laws."

"When I trained Erik, one of the tests required him to eliminate magical shades. I made copies of myself, and he had to find the false images and dispel them." Marlin rose from his seat and walked to his left. His body then split as several Marlins filled the chamber.

One of them spoke. "I know which one is real because I created them."

Another continued, "However, each Marlin has an identical aura, so I can't look and see the difference."

A third stepped forward. "Can you spot the real me?"

Dimwater waved her hand and the false Marlin next to her faded away as mist before the dawning sun.

"How did you do that?" another Marlin asked.

Dimwater arched her brow impatiently. "I dispelled him." She waved her hand again and all of the Marlins in the room disappeared. She gasped and her mouth dropped open. "Marlin?"

Marlin laughed and reappeared in his chair by the table. "I never left my seat," he said slyly.

"Well played," Lady Dimwater offered. "But what does this have to do with Erik?"

"You see," Marlin started. "You counteracted my illusions by acting upon them and overpowering them. Erik, on the other hand, would have used his power to reach into everything around him. He would have tapped into the inherent intelligence and each illusion would have dispelled itself in an effort to please him."

"But he still wouldn't have found you," Dimwater asserted.

Marlin shook his head. "His power has an area effect. It would have found me and counteracted my invisibility spell as well, even against my will. Once his training is complete, he would be able to counteract all magic around him and even bend living beings to his will."

Dimwater sat silently for a long while contemplating. Marlin waited, allowing her to work it out for herself. "So," she began, "how did they switch physical bodies?"

"A part of Erik's energy is used in his magic. When he focused all of his power on Lepkin, I believe his spirit went inside Lepkin in order to counteract the power of Nagar's Secret."

"So, Nagar's Secret acts upon inherent intelligence too then?" Dimwater mused.

Marlin nodded. "I believe it does. That is how it can bend the will of all beings to align with it."

"Even the will of dragons," Dimwater added.

"Everything has intelligence," Marlin said. "A chair is made of particles of intelligence. Our magic can rip them asunder by force, destroying the chair…"

"But Erik's power can reach inside and make the chair choose to dissolve itself."

"Precisely," Marlin said. He sighed and slapped a hand to the table. "I can't be sure, but my theory is that Erik's spirit entered Lepkin's body and attacked the dark magic from Nagar's Secret, thus displacing Master Lepkin's spirit."

"Are you saying that Lepkin is dead?" Dimwater asked.

Marlin shook his head. "No. Erik was focused on saving Lepkin, not killing him. Somehow I think he separated Lepkin's spirit from the evil magic. Lepkin's spirit then was compelled to comply with Erik's desire, so I think it realized the only way to align itself with Erik was to escape Lepkin's physical form and allow Erik to dispel the blight. Then, because Lepkin's spirit wanted to comply with Erik's desire for Lepkin to survive, it saw an empty body nearby and occupied it."

Dimwater sat and rubbed her shoulders. Her face then brightened and she smiled. "Well then, it is simple. Erik can change them back." Her smile vanished when she saw Marlin's shoulders slump. "What is it?"

"It isn't simple at all," Marlin countered.

"You just said that Erik caused them to switch in the first place."

"I said that was my *theory*. I don't know if I am correct." Marlin shrugged and went over to her, placing a hand on her shoulder. "Even if I am correct, Erik won't be able to switch them back."

"But if he switched them in the first place, then why wouldn't he be able to reverse it?"

"I once stayed with a family while I journeyed to Valtuu Temple for my initiation. I went out with the father and his son, who was about Erik's age at the time, to cut down a tree. It had rained the day before and the ground was still slick in spots. When the tree fell, the man slipped on one of these slick spots and was pinned. I was too far away to help him. The man's son lifted the entire tree and threw it off of his father. The tree was easily three feet in diameter at its base. There was no way the boy could have done that. Yet, somehow, he tapped into an ability within himself he didn't even know he had." Marlin patted Dimwater's shoulder and backed away as he knelt down to look into her eyes. "After we realized the father wasn't seriously injured, I asked the boy to lift the tree again. He couldn't even raise it from the ground an inch. He tried several times, but it wouldn't budge. It took all three of us to lift the tree just a few inches."

"So Erik has the potential, but lacks mastery," Dimwater noted. A tear slid down her left cheek.

"Precisely," Marlin replied. "A moment of extreme need coupled with Erik's love for Lepkin summoned the best from within, but he likely won't be able to come close to that kind of power again for many years."

*****

The hot sun reached through Leanor Cedreau's black, heavy dress and warmed her skin. Its heat mocked the cold, barren hole torn in her soul. Her wet, stinging eyes locked onto the stark, marble casket only three paces in front of her. Her gaze fixated on the narrow slit between the lid and the stone box, as if staring would awaken the body inside and he would emerge from death's unforgiving clutches to hold her once again.

Strong fingers pried their way between her clasped hands and squeezed.

"The arrow was meant for me," a voice said.

Leanor slowly pulled her eyes away from her husband's casket to see Eldrik, her eldest son. His eyes were red and moist, but no tears stained his cheeks. Crying was not becoming of Cedreau men, she knew, but his unrelenting grip allowed her to feel the grief under his stoic mask.

"I should have been there," Eldrik said. He turned to face her and opened his mouth, but nothing came out. His jaw quivered and his shoulders slacked.

"There is nothing you could have done," Leanor whispered. She held his hand with her left hand while disentangling her right to gently caress his face. As her fingers pushed back a lock of his blonde hair, Eldrik set his jaw and turned to face the casket. A tear fell down Leanor's face and she pulled her hand back.

A hand fell on her left shoulder and squeezed gently. She looked up to see Mikel. His beard hung low, covering his neck, but it was neatly kept and freshly oiled. It hovered only a few inches above a golden amulet of a rainbow settled neatly over his black, hooded robes. His left hand held a black, leather bound book.

Leanor looked up to Mikel's wrinkled, leathery face and did her best to return the priest's kind smile.

"I am ready to begin," he said simply.

Leanor gave a nod and turned back to her husband's coffin.

Mikel walked beyond her, robes grazing the grass as he stepped behind the marble box. He took the large book in both hands and opened it atop the coffin.

Leanor's throat seized as if an egg had suddenly materialized inside. Her stomach flipped and lurched, her forehead burned, and her vision narrowed as darkness wrapped around her.

Eldrik squeezed her hand, pulling her back from the brink.

Mikel looked up at her for a brief moment before scanning the others that had gathered behind her.

"Today," he began solemnly. "I have come to bury the body of one of the great men of our day." Mikel's right hand pressed flat against the coffin and he held a page down against the wind with his left hand. "As a priest of Icadion, the All-Father, I wear the rainbow amulet. It is a reminder of the bridge between our world and heaven. It serves as a symbol of the connection between Terramyr, the land where we sojourn during our mortal lives, and Volganor, the heaven city."

Mikel looked down to the coffin for a moment before continuing. "Once the last rites have been performed, Lord Cedreau's soul will be granted passage to the hall of his fathers." Mikel paused and looked to Leanor, then to Eldrik. "When the next rain comes, Nagé will come for his soul, and guide him back over the rainbow where his soul may find rest."

Leanor looked to her feet. She could hear Mikel performing the final rites, but she couldn't understand the words. The Old Tongue was as foreign to her as if Mikel were speaking Taish, but she could understand the idea. Mikel was reading from the Valkernium, announcing to the gods that Lord Cedreau's soul was ready to return home, and suitable for Volganor.

While it was customary to perform the ritual, she wondered whether Nagé would judge her husband worthy, or allow Khefir to take his soul to Hammenfein to face the wrath of hellfire. Leanor loved her husband dearly, but she knew his character as well as her own. Tears fell freely and she looked to Eldrik. As she watched her eldest sit through the ceremony, she knew there would be no rainbow crossing for her husband. She also knew that she, herself, would most likely follow her husband when her time came. Their sins were too great to escape judgment.

A gong rang out from behind, ripping her from her thoughts. The ceremony was complete. Mikel closed the book and stepped back. He motioned to a few men who came forward and took hold of thick cords under the casket. They lifted the stone cocoon and suspended it in the air while two more men removed sturdy planks from covering the grave below.

Leanor let her tears fall, but she managed to maintain a semblance of composure. She owed him as much as the lady of the house. She gripped her son's hand and sat rigid, fighting against the urge to sob, to scream, to let her anguish out and escape the torment inside. She felt Eldrik remove his hand in order to wrap his arm around her shoulders. She closed her eyes, absorbing her son's strength and pushing the sorrow deeper inside.

She opened her eyes, wanting a final glance at her husband's resting place. The casket descended below and the priests stepped aside to grab the shovels. As they moved away, Leanor saw another marble coffin. This one was thinner and shorter. The sight of Timon's coffin pulled her from her seat. She ran forward, screaming and shaking her fist at Mikel.

Darkness closed in around her as she cursed the bewildered priest. The ground beneath her lurched upward and she sprawled into the dirt in a fit of sobbing shrieks. Dirt and stone meshed with her tears on her cheeks as hands tugged and pulled her back. She dug her fingers into the grass, clawing her way toward Timon's coffin. Then, all went black and her strength was gone.

CHAPTER FIVE

Master Orres opened the secret passage and walked through to see Wendal sitting at the table, pouring over a series of scrolls. "Master Wendal, I wasn't expecting to see you for another hour," Orres said.

Master Wendal turned. "Forgive me, Master Orres, I overheard something during the lunch recess today and came here to see if I could make sense of it."

"Surely you know Lady Arkyn?" Master Orres asked.

Wendal leaned back to peer around Orres' girth and saw Lady Arkyn step into view. Her long, blonde hair rested over the front of her left shoulder in a single, neat braid. Her green eyes looked back to him warmly as she smiled and waved.

"Yes, of course," Master Wendal said. "The crusher of many fourth-year apprentices' dreams." He smiled and waved back to her.

"I also have other skills," she teased as she moved over to the table and looked down at the items Master Wendal was studying.

Master Orres laughed and closed the door behind him. "She is also joining us," he said. "We could use a ranger, I believe."

Wendal nodded and looked back to the map in front of him. "Shall I bring you up to speed?"

Orres sat two chairs away and slid the map closer to him. "Please do," he said. Lady Arkyn went to the chair on Wendal's left, turned it around and sat leaning her chin upon the back of the chair with her hands crossed on the table in front of her.

Wendal glanced to the two of them before proceeding. "Your brother was killed in a battle between House Lokton and House Cedreau, somewhere here," he said as he pointed to a spot on the map between the two manors. "I thought it might be noteworthy that Senator Bracken arrived at Lokton Manor not long after the battle to arrest Lord Lokton."

Orres shrugged. "Doesn't seem out of the ordinary," he said. "I would expect arrests to be made after such events."

"But what is weird is the timeframe," Wendal pointed out. "In order for Senator Bracken to have arrested Lokton so early, he would have to have been in the area already."

"Master Orres said that the magistrate was murdered a few days prior to the battle. Perhaps the senator was on his way to investigate that murder and then stumbled into the battle," Lady Arkyn put in.

Wendal smiled and put a finger in the air. "That's what I thought at first, but while I was eating my lunch, I heard Master Greenwood and Lady Hanzor speaking. Master Greenwood was discussing a recent trip he had taken to Drakai Glazei to purchase some alchemical supplies for his class. As you know, he is close friends with some of the senators, including Bracken. He said he had tried to call upon Senator Bracken during his visit, but that Bracken was traveling on business and was not expected back in the capital city for at least a week."

"Where was he?" Orres asked.

"Greenwood said that Bracken had been tasked to travel to Roegudok Hall, and afterward he had scheduled some other meetings," Wendal replied.

"Where were these other meetings?" Lady Arkyn asked.

Wendal shook his head. "Greenwood told Lady Hanzor that Bracken's steward wasn't sure where the meetings were or who they were with, only that it would be some time before he was expected back." Wendal waved an excited finger in the air. "Now here is the kicker." He leaned forward with a toothy grin. "Senator Bracken left on business a couple of days before the magistrate's murder. There was no way he could have been sent from the senate to investigate the murder."

"Because he was not with the senate when it was informed of the magistrate's death," Orres said.

"So what does this mean?" Arkyn asked.

Wendal shook his head. "I don't know," he said with a frown. "That's why I came here, to try to figure it out."

"Perhaps someone got a message to him while he was in the field," Orres said. "Surely another senator must have known where he was. Perhaps they sent him instructions to investigate based on his proximity."

Wendal wrinkled his nose and shrugged. "I guess that makes more sense than what I thought."

"What did you think?" Lady Arkyn asked with a nudge to his ribs.

Wendal shook his head. "No, it's stupid. My imagination just got away from me, that's all."

"Master Wendal," Orres said. "If you have a theory, I want to hear it. Sometimes a pair of fresh eyes are the best cure for a bleak and dreary world."

"I thought that perhaps the senator was on his way to meet Janik," Wendal said. Orres sat back in his chair and folded his arms.

Lady Arkyn leaned in front of Wendal and traced her finger over the map from Kuldiga Academy to Lokton Manor. "Why would he meet with Janik?"

"I..." Wendal paused, glancing to Orres. The sight of the headmaster boring a hole through him almost stopped him from continuing. "Forgive me, but given the revelation about Janik's involvement with the Order of the All Seeing Eye, I thought that Janik had invited the senator for a meeting."

"To what end?" Lady Arkyn asked.

Wendal shrugged. "Maybe to kill him," he offered. "Given the magistrate's murder and the escalating hostilities between the two noble families, it seems to be the perfect time to ambush a senator."

Orres shook his head. "No, that can't be it," he said. "Why kill Bracken? What good does one dead senator do for anyone?"

"Well, if Bracken is one of the senators who handles the high level investigations between noble families, perhaps the warlocks needed him out of their way. They could easily pin the murder on House Lokton and then slip away undetected."

"No," Orres said. "The information I have says that Janik attacked Erik in a secluded part of the forest, away from the battle. Everything indicates that Erik was his target."

"Then maybe Senator Bracken was working with Janik," Lady Arkyn said. The other two stopped and looked at her. She flipped her braid back over her shoulder and returned to her seat. "Think

49

about it. We all know what Lepkin is training Erik for. If it is true, and Erik is the Champion of Truth, then perhaps that threatened Bracken somehow."

"That would help put Tukai's uninvited visit and subsequent attack on Lokton Manor into better context. Tukai belonged to the same warlock order as my brother. Perhaps they formed a relationship with Senator Bracken."

"Why would a senator partner with an order of warlocks?" Wendal asked.

Orres shook his head and thumbed his chin. "I don't know, but I would like to find out." He leaned forward again and dropped his hand on the map so that his thumb rested on Lokton Manor and his index finger touched Drakai Glazei. "Lady Arkyn, do you think you are up for some field work?"

The blonde woman smiled and cocked her head to the side. "Will I get to use my bow?"

Orres let out a belly laugh and held up a hand, waving her off. "Just some reconnaissance work," he told her.

"What about me?" Master Wendal asked.

"Tomorrow I have a meeting with Master B'dargen. During my interview with him I would like you to inspect his office," Orres said.

Wendal's eyes shot wide. "Master B'dargen?"

"He has been receiving some letters from House Finorel. I want to know what they say."

"Is House Finorel a concern for us?" Lady Arkyn asked.

"Yeah," Wendal answered quickly. "Lord Finorel governs the city of Pinkt'hu, which lies on the border with Verishtahng."

Orres nodded grimly. "There have been indications over the years that Lord Finorel is more interested in preserving his own wealth and standing than the integrity of our southern border, or even the lives of his people."

Lady Arkyn raised an eyebrow and pursed her lips. "If that is the case, then perhaps I could travel south and use my bow there?"

"You are bloodthirsty, aren't you?" Wendal chided.

She winked back and him and smiled coyly. "Can't be a hero unless you do something that people remember."

Orres cleared his throat. The other two quieted down and blushed. "It is entirely possible that the letters are harmless. So let's not convict anyone until we prove their guilt, understood?"

"Yes sir," they answered together.

"All right, now let's get to it. I have some students waiting in my office," Orres said.

"Schoolyard fight?" Arkyn asked.

"No, just letters of concern from their parents. Apparently the dueling tournament with Erik has made quite a stir in the kingdom. All the students write home about how a couple of apprentices got injured and all of a sudden I am justifying the entire academy and doing damage control to keep the tuition money flowing in."

"Back to the boring job of headmaster then," Arkyn teased.

*****

Al took a drink from his goblet and studied Erik. Seeing the boy's mannerisms acted out through Lepkin's body was unnerving to say the least, but Al found that if he concentrated on Erik's eyes, it helped him look beyond the physical body to see the young man inside. "Well, at least you're taller," Al said with a grin.

Erik frowned. "A lot of good that will do me," he replied.

Al shrugged and turned toward the others. "Whether the boy is in Lepkin's body or not, I have to take Lepkin to the tribunal. You know the consequences if Lepkin fails to answer the summons."

"So, that is how it must be," Marlin said somberly.

Erik shook his head. "They will see through me," he said. "I may be in Master Lepkin's body, but I am not him."

Al nodded and thunked his empty goblet on the table. "That may be true, lad, but if you fail to answer the summons, then it will be used against us."

Dimwater conjured a shot of absinthe before her with a flaming sugar cube over the glass. She noticed Marlin's disapproving stare as she reached for it. "It helps clear my head," she said with a shrug. She tossed the glass back, swallowing the contents in a single, wide-mouthed gulp.

"My sense of morality aside, such habits would kill a normal person," Marlin commented.

"You and I both know that I am anything but a *normal* person, Marlin," Dimwater replied.

"Still, it can't be good for you," Marlin retorted.

Al shuddered as a puff of thin, gray smoke emerged from Dimwater's nostrils. "Not very lady-like either," the dwarf put in.

Dimwater arched her brow and tossed the glass into the air, where it promptly vanished to another realm. "I never claimed to be a lady," she rebuffed. "Now, shall we debate my habits, or get back to the matter at hand?"

Al leaned forward and ripped a golden brown turkey leg from the platter. Steam snaked up as the skin cracked and the joint snapped apart. He tore a mouthful of the leg off and sucked in a breath around the piping hot bite.

Marlin sighed. "Master Lepkin had been gathering allies to the king."

Dimwater folded her arms across her chest. "To neglect the summons is to further weaken the kingdom," she agreed.

"The Livonian order would likely remain true," Al put in.

"They would remain faithful to the king, but they would ignore Lepkin," Dimwater countered. "As would everyone else. A failure to appear for the summons would be viewed as an insult to the king directly, if not an open act of defiance."

Erik pushed his empty plate away and slumped back in his chair. "Tell me what to do," he said. "I can go, but I don't know what to do when I get there."

The four of them sat for a few moments in silence.

After a while Al tossed a clean leg bone to his plate and unceremoniously wiped his mouth on his sleeve. "I am familiar with the senate," he said. "I accompanied my father many times to senate hearings or other negotiations."

"I thought senators went to Roegudok Hall." Dimwater said.

"That is true now," Al replied with a nod. "Since my brother assumed the throne he has demanded the senate create a liaison to come to Roegudok Hall, but that was not so during my father's time."

"Very well," Marlin said. "I don't see an alternative." He turned to Erik. "This will delay your training, but I can give you some exercises that will help you stay active. When you return, we will resume your training. In the meanwhile, we'll work with Lepkin and find a way to switch you back."

"About that," Al interrupted. "I may know a way." He looked

to Marlin and then to Dimwater before continuing. "Have either of you heard of the Golden Scale?"

Dimwater and Marlin glanced to each other. Dimwater's mouth fell open, and Marlin leaned forward to rest his chin on his knuckles. "The Golden Scale was given to the first dwarf king of Roegudok Hall," Marlin said. "It is rumored to have many magical properties, chief among them is its healing power."

Al nodded and ripped the other turkey leg off and held it up for a moment, offering it to the others. Marlin shook his head and Dimwater dismissed the offer with a wave of her hand. Al grinned and ripped a steaming hunk off the leg and chewed with an open mouth. As he blew some of the heat out, he spoke through a mouthful of half-chewed meat. "On the way back from Drakai Glazei, I'll get the scale and bring it here."

"That could help Lepkin at the very least, if not reverse them both back," Marlin said with a nod.

Al winked and took another bite.

Lady Dimwater tapped a finger on the table a few times. "Will your brother give it to you?" she asked at last.

"He shuns the Ancients," Al said through a hard swallow. "I doubt he would mind."

"Then why not get the Golden Scale first?" Erik asked. "Then Lepkin could answer the summons himself after we are switched back."

"Not enough time," Al said just before taking another bite.

Erik opened his mouth as if to ask something else, but stopped himself and stared at the roasted turkey carcass instead. "And because you know your brother won't give it to you," Erik observed.

Al stopped chewing and set the leg down. He glanced to Erik and reached for his goblet. He raised it to his mouth to wash the rest of his bite down, but the goblet was empty. He set it down and hurriedly chewed the remaining meat. "I guess there is no point in shielding you from it," Al admitted.

"He can see through it," Marlin commented.

"Reaching through with reflexive power," Dimwater added quietly.

"What will your brother do when you ask for the scale?" Erik asked.

Al sighed and folded his thick fingers together. "For now, let's concentrate on the senate. I will deal with getting the scale afterward."

Erik reached for his plate and filled it with bread and turkey meat. The others did the same. The crackling fire and utensils scraping against ceramic plates were the only sounds made for the rest of the dinner. Each person ate in silence, occasionally stealing glances at each other from across the table as they dealt silently with their own demons.

As the candles burned low and the food disappeared from the table, Lady Dimwater was the first to leave. She dabbed her lips with a napkin and conjured another glass of absinthe.

Marlin departed shortly thereafter. He patted Erik's shoulder as he passed.

Al and Erik remained until the candles were nearly completely diminished. The dwarf popped the last hunk of bread into his mouth and looked to Erik. "I can help you learn what Lepkin would do," he said.

Erik sighed and pushed his empty plate across the table. "You expect me to have the presence of mind to act as Lepkin would when I will be attending a tribunal that claims my father is a traitor." Erik finished his water and turned the glass over in his hand, watching the candlelight refract through it. "I don't think I can do that."

Al nodded. "I only expect you to do your best," he assured him. "Besides, Braun is on his way to the tribunal as well. He'll help us if we get into trouble."

Erik smirked. "Or he will cause trouble," he said.

Al licked his forefinger and then began gathering bread crumbs by sticking them to his finger. "You might be right," Al said. He raised his breaded finger up to his mouth and sucked the crumbs off. "Lepkin has a powerful role to play here, Erik. When he is summoned for a tribunal, he gets a vote for the verdict. He also oversees the tribunal itself to ensure there is sufficient evidence against the accused, and that the proper protocol is followed."

Erik jumped to his feet, knocking his chair back to the floor. "How am *I* supposed to do that? I don't know the proper protocol, and I have never even seen a senator. Just standing in front of

Master Orres at Kuldiga Academy makes me nervous, and here I am trapped in Lepkin's body and on my way to a tribunal that is deciding whether my father is a traitor." Erik folded his arms and turned away from the table.

"I will be with you the whole time," Al promised. "I have been there many times. I can coach you on everything that is to be done. Besides, I had not thought you to be one to back down from a challenge when it comes to protecting your family."

Erik turned back and saw Al smiling warmly at him. Erik offered a half smile and picked his chair off the floor and set it right. Then he poured another glass of water and sat back down as he scooped the last few grapes from a silver fruit bowl and popped them into his mouth in a single fistful.

"One other thing I should mention to you," Al said. "On my way here I was attacked by a Blacktongue. He was partnered with another man."

"A Blacktongue?" Erik asked. "Why were they after you?"

Al smiled. "After I put the Blacktongue down I asked the man named Deglain that very question, among others." Al frowned. "Would you like the good news or the bad news?"

"Give me the bad news first," Erik said.

"He was hired by a warlock named Gondok'hr. He said he was part of the warlock's personal retinue, but he didn't know where I could find the warlock or what his plans were."

"So another warlock is after us, and all we know is that he hired the same assassins that Tukai used."

Al nodded and smiled. "And the good news is that he said there are more assassins on their way to make sure we all die."

Erik blanched. "That's the good news?" Erik asked.

Al nodded excitedly. "Sure is. Think about it, this means that we will get some excitement along our journey to the tribunal!" Al said with a winking grin.

Erik sighed and shook his head. "Sounds wonderful." The two of them sat quietly for a few minutes. Quiet enough that Erik was sure Al could hear him chewing the grapes and gulping them down with the water.

"Are you all right?" Al asked.

Erik nodded quietly.

"Let me into that head of yours, beanpole," Al said with a

forced smile. "What are you thinking about?"

"That we are both walking into a trap," Erik replied coolly.

Al's smile stretched wider. "That we are, my boy," he said. "But, we'll beat them," he promised with a wink.

Erik laughed nervously. "You forget I can tell when you're lying," Erik replied.

Al's smile faded. "Well, it was worth a shot," he said with a shrug.

*****

Master Wendal turned the brass knob and pushed the heavy, oaken door inward. B'dargen's office smelled of parchment, formaldehyde, and smoke. Wendal was used to such smells. His own office smelled of them quite often. That was the way with mages. The items they studied often carried pungent odors with them. He stepped inside and closed the door behind him. The large double windows allowed him to see easily in the afternoon sun as the light streamed in, reaching every corner of the room.

He scanned the bookshelves and the small table in the center of the room briefly before proceeding to the desk. A maroon pipe lay in its holder. The cherry flavored tobacco still smoldered, letting its scent waft through the air. Wendal wrinkled his nose and tried to blow the smoke away so he wouldn't have to smell it. Besides the pipe and a couple of books on arcane lore, the top of the desk was clear and clean. He moved on to the drawers.

The first drawer was filled with writing utensils and blank parchment. He also found scissors, an iron stamp and a stick of wax. He picked the red wax up and turned it over. One end had been melted numerous times, indicating that Wendal had been sending several letters. He put the wax stick back and closed the drawer.

In the second he found a couple of journals. He pulled them out and perused through them, but found only general information about how B'dargen believed his pupils were developing. There was absolutely nothing in the journals of a personal nature, so he closed them and put them back. Behind them he found a couple of letters. He pulled them out and started to sort them by sender.

"Three from House Finorel," Wendal counted aloud. He set

the others down, noting the senders' names. He scanned through the three bearing Governor Finorel's signature. The letters spoke of orcs, which was unusual, but there was no mention of working against the king. Wendal put the letters back. He scanned through the other letters, but they hardly appeared sinister. Two were orders for frogs and bats, which Wendal himself had done at least a dozen times for the students to have dissection subjects. Another letter was from a bookstore in Drakai Glazei, responding to an apparent inquiry about text books for the students. A dozen more mundane letters passed before Wendal's eyes before he finally finished. Frowning, he stuck the letters back in the drawer. As he started to close it, a small roll of paper fell out from the side.

"Must have gotten stuck when I opened it," Wendal said as he plucked the paper up and unrolled it. There was no seal, and was signed only with the letter "G" at the bottom. As Wendal read the note his eyes went wide. He rolled it up and tucked it into his pocket. Quickly he closed the drawer and went for the door. Just as he reached out for the knob it turned and the door opened in, barely missing his nose as he recoiled back.

In stepped Master B'dargen. His square jaw was clenched tight under his scowl, and his blue eyes carried the heat of anger inside as he muttered something to himself. Upon seeing Master Wendal, Master B'dargen took a half step back and his brows raised under his blonde head of hair, wrinkling his forehead.

"Master Wendal, what are you doing here?" Master B'dargen asked.

Wendal froze. What should he say? His mind raced, grasping for some reason to be where he was. "I…" he started. "I was coming to ask if you had any bats left over, and see if I could borrow them."

Master B'dargen glanced around Wendal and looked inside his office. Then he motioned for Wendal to step aside and he marched in. "Bats?" he asked. "What do you need bats for? We are already beyond the dissection lesson."

Master Wendal nodded and side-stepped closer to the hall. "True, but I was planning an extra lesson for my students. I was going to reanimate the bats and show them how to throw accurate fireball spells."

The other master shook his head and folded his arms. "Your

students are third-years. They shouldn't be playing with fireballs for another year," he said sternly.

"Yes, Master B'dargen," Wendal said with a bow of his head. "I'm sorry, I meant no harm by it."

"Either way I have no bats left. I only order enough for dissections," B'dargen said.

Wendal nodded and left the room, apologizing as he exited.

Master B'dargen called out after him. "If I was gone, why did you enter my office and close the door?"

"When I came to call there were some students running through the hall and I closed the door behind me. After I saw you weren't inside I was going to leave a note for you, but I had nothing to write with. I was just on my way back to my office to write the note." Wendal shrugged and smiled back at B'dargen, who now stood halfway in the hallway and halfway in the doorway. "Thanks anyway," Wendal said as he turned and briskly walked away.

He could feel B'dargen's hot, angry glare boring into his back as he walked down the hall.

CHAPTER SIX

Leanor pulled her shawl tight around her shoulders and rubbed her arms. She grabbed a leather bag, clamping down on the top. The bag heaved and writhed as the contents inside squirmed.

She saw the basin resting upon a stone. A chill ran down her spine. Her foot hesitated, paused in that slight arch just before the foot leaves the ground to take a step. Her body's reticence reflected that of her shaking will. Many years ago, she had sworn never to return, never to indulge this side of her. She compelled her foot forward, despite the nagging in her gut.

"I hate this," Leanor muttered to herself. She walked toward the basin of ashes and sucked in a deep breath. Scanning the woods around her, she made sure she was alone before pouring the bag out into the basin. A nine-inch long cucumber slug slammed down and slimed its way to the powdery ash, recoiling against the substance. Next came a sheep's eye, a spider's egg sack, a snake head, and a lizard's tail.

She waved her hand over the basin and spoke. "As the day is eaten by the night, the darkness is the truest keeper of the light." She spat into the ashes and they began to glow. "Darkest night, reveal your face and let me partake of your light."

Green flame reached through the ashes, enveloping the slug and the other offerings in the basin. The slug shriveled, but did not char. Instead, the offering simply absorbed into the ash as the flames grew taller. A pale, wrinkled face peered at Leanor from the flames for only a moment before vanishing again.

The oak tree beyond the basin began to swell, doubling, then tripling in size. A knot slid into the center and slowly dilated. The tree groaned and creaked at the effort. Finally a mountainous mass emerged up from the dirt and joined to the back of the mutated oak tree.

Leanor ran her hand through the flaming ashes in the basin. The flames licked and tickled her arm, but she remained unharmed. Her fingers sifted through the ash until she found the round, gelatinous mass. She pulled it from the basin and walked to the tree. She reached forward and deposited the black, smoldering mass into the dilated knothole. The tree closed around her forearm like a mouth, sucking the blackened ooze from her palm and only releasing her arm when all of the slime was cleaned from her skin.

The tree emitted a low, rumbling groan. The knot swelled again until it was large enough for her to pass through.

Ethereal green flames hovered in the air before her face. The inside of the oak smelled like freshly chipped wood, but it resembled stone in its appearance. The magical cave descended steeply into the ground. She steadied herself with her left hand as she exited the tree-like cave entrance and found herself in an earthen tunnel.

The hovering green flame floated before her still, lighting her way enough so she wouldn't trip.

At last, she came to a great chamber. A pair of underground rivers flanked her as she stepped out from the tunnel and into the chamber. The glowing, azure rivers converged in the center of the great hall, forming a living pool of light. In the center of this pool, upon an island of stone, were three women. One was next to a cauldron, periodically glancing to a podium which held a large tome. Another was sitting behind a desk of stone on a chair made of mammoth bones, stirring a solution in a beaker. The third was consulting a looking crystal, though Leanor was too far away to see what she was looking at.

The old, wrinkled lady stood up from the mammoth bone chair and pointed to Leanor. "Ah, Sister Nora has returned!" A smile inched its way across the left side of the old witch's face.

Leanor bristled. "I am called Leanor now, Hairen" she said.

The old witch shrugged. "A panther is always a panther, regardless of what new name it is given."

"Hairen, I am not returning to the coven," Leanor said assertively.

Hairen huffed and pushed the beaker away from her. "Then why have you come?" the old witch asked.

Leanor walked toward the edge of her stone platform,

stopping a couple of paces away from where it gave way to the ever flowing rivers pouring into the pool. "I need your help," Leanor answered.

The youngest witch turned from the looking crystal and placed her hands squarely upon her hips. "Leech," she hissed. "You turn your back on us for years and only come now to demand our service."

Leanor bit her tongue and bowed her head. "I wouldn't come, except I have no one else to turn to," she said.

The middle-aged witch at the cauldron looked up and stepped forward. "What of your shining knight?" She flicked her raven hair over her shoulders. "What was his name again?" She mockingly tapped her chin as if lost in thought.

"My husband is dead," Leanor replied softly.

Hairen nodded her head and the others turned back to their previous activities. "I told you that only sadness would come from marrying a nobleman," Hairen said. Leanor looked, but found no compassion on the old witch's face.

Leanor had forgotten how apathetic and cold Hairen was. "My son is also dead," Leanor said.

"Your son?" Hairen asked. The other two redirected their attention back to Leanor. "How was he killed?"

Leanor started to speak, but the lump that formed in her throat may as well have been stone. She could not force the words to come out.

Hairen took a step forward and waved her hand. A silver mist flew from her and went into Leanor's mouth, nose, and ears. Hairen sucked in a breath and her eyes glazed out of focus. Her spine arched backward and her arms flailed to her sides.

Mist rose from the pool and formed into ghostly images. First, Timon appeared with a swollen hand. "Curse that guttersnipe!" he shouted. "Erik broke my hand!" Timon then walked into a room and picked up a wooden shield. "Eldrik!" he shouted over his shoulder. "I thought I told you not to touch my things!" Timon walked to a shelf near a window and took a wooden sword from the shelf. He then turned back to face the door. He held up the sword and shield. "I found them mom, they were in Eldrik's room," he said with a smile. Suddenly his face twisted grotesquely. He stepped forward with his mouth open and eyes wide. Then he fell to his face. An arrow protruded from his back.

Leanor and Hairen both screamed and fell to their knees, crying out Timon's name and sobbing wildly. The apparition dissolved and was replaced by the figure of Lord Cedreau.

"I will make Lord Lokton pay for his treachery!" he swore.

The younger two witches stole a glance at each other.

Lord Cedreau rode away, only to return as a corpse upon a sled a moment later.

Leanor and Hairen wailed terribly.

The mists dispersed only to reform and unveil a funeral scene.

Leanor trembled. "Enough," she begged. The mists dissolved and the silver smoke retracted from her head. She remained trembling on all fours for quite some time, crying and shaking.

Hairen regained her strength and rose to her feet again. "So, that was your price," she said flatly. Hairen turned to the others. "Get her a bed and make her a bowl of soup."

The other two nodded.

"And Merriam," Hairen said with a stern voice. "No tricks."

*****

Leanor woke suddenly and jerked upright, calling out for Timon.

"We made you some soup," Silvi said.

Leanor drew in a couple of measured breaths and resigned her gaze to her lap and let her hands fall to her sides. "You still have my old bed," she commented. She stroked the black fur blanket, seeking comfort from the familiar softness. "You look as radiant as ever," Leanor forced herself to say.

"Some things don't change," Silvi said with a shrug.

"And others do," Merriam said from the far corner of the room. A book blocked Leanor's view of Merriam's face, but given the years of bitterness between them, Leanor knew better than to look to Merriam for kindness anyway. "I thought you would never return," Merriam added.

Leanor sighed and swung her feet over the side of the bed to the floor. "I have nowhere else to go," she explained.

"What makes you think we would help you?" Merriam asked.

"You helped me before," Leanor replied.

"I owed you a favor," Merriam reminded her.

Leanor sighed again and went to the table. A wooden bowl filled with steaming, yellow broth sat before her. She took the spoon and plunged it to the bottom and gave the contents a stir. Hunks of white chicken meat flittered to the top among a slurry of cubed carrots and potatoes. She took a spoonful into her mouth and slowly chewed the savory bits before swallowing. She then set the spoon down and dropped her face into her upturned hands.

"See, Silvi, your soup is horrendous," Merriam chuckled.

"Hold your tongue," Hairen scolded as she strolled into the bed chamber. "You ought to treat her better, she was our sister."

"*Was*," Merriam emphasized.

"She saved your life," Hairen countered.

"She ruined my life," Merriam quipped. She slammed her book shut and rose from her seat as if to challenge Hairen.

Hairen held her hands out to the sides. "Choose well where you shall stick your dagger, Merriam, for I am not easy to kill."

Merriam fumed and snarled. Her face blushed and veins in her forehead throbbed and pulsed. "It isn't you I hate, it's her!" She spat at the floor.

"Me!?" Leanor shouted. The three witches turned to face her. "You exist only because when Lord Cedreau discovered this place, *I* convinced him to let it alone."

"You stole him," Merriam hissed. "You knew I wanted him."

"He chose me," Leanor shot back.

"But you didn't want him, not as I did," Merriam argued.

Leanor shook her head. "You would have put him under a spell and made him your slave," Leanor shouted. "I loved him as he was."

Lightning erupted through the chamber. A rumbling thunder shook the entire cave so that only Hairen remained on her feet. "What is done, is done. I daresay you had the final victory in the end," Hairen said as she turned a glaring eye on Merriam.

"What do you mean?" Leanor asked.

"Magic comes with a price," Hairen began. "That's why I refused to help you when you returned to me seventeen years ago. Yet, you went behind my back."

Leanor shook her head. "No, you don't understand. After you said no, Silvi offered to help me. I didn't mention anything to

Merriam."

"Seventeen years ago you were barren, unable to conceive. You feared your husband would leave you for another, so I can understand your desperation, but did you really think Silvi could cast such a spell alone?"

Leanor shrugged, mouth agape and tears forming in her eyes. She glanced to Silvi. The raven-haired beauty looked to the floor. Leanor looked back to Merriam. Merriam straightened her neck, puffing her chin up and glaring down at her. Leanor clutched at her chest with her right hand and turned back to Silvi. "Why, Silvi?"

Silvi rose forcefully from the table, knocking her wooden chair over behind her. "You turned your back on us!" she shouted. "We were sisters, bound together forever by a solemn oath, but *you* left us!"

Leanor set her jaw and clenched her fists. "So you cursed my family," she said. "You cowardly hen."

Silvi shrank away from Leanor's glare, but she offered no apology.

Hairen stepped in close to Leanor. "You know the kind of magic you sought comes with a heavy price," she said. "They meant to do you harm, but not this much."

"It matters little what they *wanted* now," Leanor growled.

Hairen nodded. She snapped her fingers. "Both of you should leave. I will speak with Sister Nora," she said.

"That's not my name anymore," Leanor said defiantly. Then she looked to the other two women. "If our paths cross again, I will pay you both back every bit what I owe you. You have my word."

Merriam stopped and started to turn back, but Hairen wheeled around on her angrily. "Get out, you have done quite enough!" she yelled.

Merriam narrowed her eyes on Leanor, but did as Hairen commanded.

After the others were gone, Hairen spoke softly. "I know what you feel."

"No, you don't," Leanor said.

A mist formed in Hairen's hand. "Actually I do," she countered. "Through your memories we were linked. Silvi and Merriam saw images over the pool, but I lived the memories as they played out."

"I hate them," Leanor replied.

Hairen nodded. "You knew there would be a price. That's why I refused to perform what you asked."

"Silvi said she could do it," Leanor sobbed. "She stopped me on my way out after you and I had talked. I told her everything and she said she could perform the spell for me." Leanor paused for a moment and shook her head. "I should have been more careful." She looked up to Hairen's gaze. "When did you know she had performed the spell?"

"I knew the moment it was cast. Magic of that magnitude is not performed in secret."

"Then why didn't you do something?" Leanor asked.

"The spell was already cast. There was nothing for me to do but watch and see how it played out."

Leanor nodded. "I do not have time to dwell on the past," she said. "I am here because of my eldest son. I fear that he will lose his life as well, and then I will be left with nothing. Can you help me protect my son?"

Hairen cackled. "Eldrik is not *your* son," she said.

Leanor held her breath, afraid to ask for the explanation.

"Silvi worked with Merriam to perform the spell you desired. They used magic to switch your dry, barren womb with the fertile womb of another woman. That woman had already conceived with her own husband."

"Who?" Leanor stammered.

"Lady Lokton," Hairen replied.

Leanor stumbled backward and threw her hand out to steady her as she slumped down onto her bed. "Why?" Leanor asked. "That makes no sense."

"Silvi and Merriam thought if you bore a child that resembled another man, then Lord Cedreau would divorce you, and you would be forced to live with the child on the street." Hairen sighed. "They may have tried to curse you, but not in the way things turned out."

"Then why have things ended up as they have?"

Hairen arched a brow and her gaze focused on a distant point. "They were foolish, dabbling in magic they did not understand. That kind of magic demands its own price."

Leanor felt her pulse slow. Her head became heavy and her breathing quickened. Darkness encroached upon her. Oblivion itself threatened to consume her. Then she remembered her eldest son. "No," Leanor said as she willed herself to remain conscious. "Eldrik is *my* son. I have fed him, clothed him, and loved him. He is my son!"

Hairen sighed. "Will he love you after he discovers the truth for himself?"

Leanor narrowed her eyes at Hairen. "After all that I have suffered, I will not let any harm come to Eldrik." Leanor stepped within a hair's breadth of Hairen's face. "If you try to tell him, there is no magic on this plane that will save you from my wrath."

Hairen gently patted the air before her, shaking her head. "I have no intention of telling the boy."

"Then you and Silvi and Merriam should have no issue with me."

"It isn't that simple," Hairen pointed out. "Have you heard of Tukai's prophecy?"

Leanor squinted for a moment and then her mouth fell slack and she gasped. "No, you don't mean the prophecy was about *Eldrik*?"

Hairen nodded soberly. "Who else could it be about?" She paused a moment. "I would wager he has already left for Drakai Glazei to hunt Lord Lokton down and enact his revenge."

"I thought that prophecy was about Erik," Leanor said.

"Erik is not Lord Lokton's son, not by birth anyway. However, Eldrik is a Lokton. You may have raised him, but Eldrik is not yours."

"Curse that warlock!" Leanor shouted.

"The warlock only saw what is to come. He did not make it so." Hairen paused and locked eyes with Leanor. "Your choices have led you to this tragedy," she added coldly.

Leanor rose to her feet, gathering courage and strength from her anger and hatred. "I am leaving now," she said.

"You have decided not to ask for my help?" Hairen inquired sarcastically.

Leanor walked forward and leaned in close to the old witch. "For all of the things you did for me, for taking me off the street and giving me a home, I thank you. Those things are why I am willing to leave peacefully now." Leanor's eyes narrowed hotly on the old woman. "But, if I see any of you again, I will not think twice about ending your existence. From now on the coven exists only because I allow it."

"Do not make idle threats, child," Hairen warned.

"I am Lady Cedreau," Leanor said sternly. "To interfere with my son is to invoke the wrath of House Cedreau on your heads. You will let Eldrik alone, and you will stay far away from me, or else I will bury all of you." Leanor pushed past Hairen and stopped just short of exiting the chamber. "One more thing, Hairen," Leanor said. "It isn't a threat, it's a promise."

CHAPTER SEVEN

The carriage lurched to the side suddenly, throwing Senator Bracken to slam his shoulder into the velvet, padded interior wall of his transport. His eyes bolted open and he quickly steadied himself as the carriage continued to rock side to side for a few moments before finally stabilizing. He reached up with his right hand and shoved the silken curtain up just enough to stick his head out the window. The cool, late afternoon air greeted him with the scent of fresh mud mixed with pine needles.

"Sorry, Senator Bracken," the driver called out from the front of the carriage. "There was a storm here last night, and it created a few ruts and holes in the road."

Bracken curled his lip and barked back "Well see to it that I am not thrown about like a silly doll on the back of a farmer's cart. You are at least that competent, are you not?"

"Yes sir, I will do my best," the driver shouted back dutifully.

"Good," Bracken snapped. "The last thing you want is for me to take the reins from you, I assure you." Bracken caught movement approaching out of the corner of his eye. He turned his face just as Captain Thorgrave pulled up alongside the window atop his stallion.

"Is there anything I may do for you, Senator Bracken?" Captain Thorgrave asked.

Senator Bracken regarded Captain Thorgrave wearily. "No, captain, there isn't," he said quickly. Senator Bracken then arched his right brow and peered down over his nose at the captain. "If I had been in need of your assistance, I would have informed you myself."

Captain Thorgrave nodded dutifully and slowed his horse to allow the carriage to pass without another word.

Senator Bracken flicked the curtain back over the window and slumped into the pillow-backed bench with a sour grimace across his face. He hated to travel this way. He was sick of the pageantry, the sycophantic boot-lickers, and the horribly tortuous snail's pace it forced him to suffer. He would much rather open a portal and be done with it. But, he couldn't afford to expose himself.

As it was, he found it difficult enough to mix his own mercenaries with the standard escorts such as Captain Thorgrave. Needing to additionally make accommodations in his schedule for things like stopping in a village for food as a pretext for getting his prisoner alone in the back of the prison transport was getting to be quite exhausting. But it all played into the role of a pompous senator.

He employed a garish entourage and employed full military protection on occasion when he traveled beyond Drakai Glazei's walls. This visit had been trickier than most, with the need for his military detail to join with him after he had already been travelling, but the soldiers knew better than to ask questions of a senator, and the mercenaries cared little as long as they were paid. Arresting Lord Lokton was the first time he had actually used his military escort for something productive, however. He knew other senators that used their escorts to pick up food from the market, or even to finish yard work that their regular household staff had done improperly.

"Senators," Bracken grumbled while wiggling himself back into a comfortable position in the cushion. "All of them corrupt and too preoccupied with their own petty self-interests to have any real power." They only had the appearance of power, he knew, perhaps with the exception of Senator Mickelson. He was a fairly young senator who seemed genuinely ethical, but his influence was still too small to pose any real threat to Bracken. His family had never been impressive to begin with, and Bracken often wondered why that family had ever been chosen to serve in the senate.

He straightened his left sleeve and shifted in his seat again, finally finding the groove he had been creating during the last couple hours of his nap. As he closed his eyes he thought how pleasing it would be to finally rip off his false identity. He could see the other senators' reactions. They would all stand dumbfounded with their drooling, wrinkled mouths hanging open and not the slightest clue what to do. Many of them were already close enough to him that they would likely remain as supporters, but what of Mickelson and the few that had thus far resisted him? What would they say? What would they do?

Likely nothing, he knew. What could they do in light of his fully revealed power? For now he played the part of a waiting pit viper. He would bait the trap with Lord Lokton. The Keeper of Secrets would have to come. Not only would it discredit Lepkin and his position to ignore the summons, but Erik would demand his father's rescue. Bracken smiled wickedly and cracked his knuckles as a bit of blue fire danced across his fingertips. Master Lepkin would come to rescue Lord Lokton. Then, Bracken would be able to spring his trap. He would kill Lepkin and Lokton in the same day, and destroy any chance Erik might have to grow powerful enough to defeat him.

The warlock senator closed his eyes and savored his anticipated victory. The master would be pleased, and the warlock would be closer to achieving his innermost desires.

"We are approaching the city!" a shout came from outside.

Bracken opened his eyes resentfully. "Perfect timing," he grumbled. He popped his head through the window again and looked up just as the carriage rounded a curve in the road. The late afternoon sun glinted off the copper flecks speckling the black granite walls of the city. The walls stood a foreboding forty feet tall, affording a great vantage point at each of its several towers for the garrisoned forces. Only the king's tower rose above the walls enough to be visible from the road. The great, square spire reached three times as high as the walls, casting its long shadow over the whole valley during sunsets, and creating a sparkling focal point at dawn.

The lower levels of the king's tower housed the main government store houses, living quarters for the garrison, a throne room in which the king could hold court, and a few feasting halls as well. All of these seemed insignificant with the uppermost levels in Bracken's estimation. The twelfth floor housed the king's bedchamber, but it also held the king's library, orrery, and, most importantly, there was a special pedestal atop the tower which had allowed the king to summon the dragons in ancient times. The top of the tower was built specifically for this purpose, Bracken knew. In days of old, the dragons would take turns perching atop the tower and providing counsel to the king, directing the affairs of men and, when necessary, launching offensives from above to maintain order.

Bracken had only seen the top of the tower twice. Once upon the king's ninetieth birthday, and again when the king called a select council to discuss how the kingdom was to continue without a king after their lord's imminent death. The king had advised the senators present to create a list of potential heirs from among the various nobles of the land, but he had not chosen any of them as of yet. Instead he reminded the council that in the event he died without an heir, the kingdom would be ruled jointly by the senate and the Keeper of Secrets.

The warlock snarled as he recalled those words. The time for Lepkin's death could not come soon enough!

Bracken eyed the top of the king's tower. The king hardly ever came down from the top level now. On the rare occasion he did, he had to be carried by several of the king's guard, his bodyguards and special police, in order to descend the great staircase to the lower levels. He usually only went to such efforts for the summer and winter solstice festivals so the people of Drakai Glazei could see their figure head still breathed and walked among mortals. Bracken didn't mind. The old king had ceased interfering with matters of state a couple of years ago. Sometimes his advisors and ministers did so on his behalf, but he was never directly involved anymore.

It made a senator's life extremely easy, and had given Bracken several opportunities to solidify his own power.

It had also given rise to a smattering of smaller factions throughout the kingdom, but Bracken did not concern himself with them unless they could offer him something in return. He found that most nobles were like senators, too selfish and greedy to meaningfully serve any master other than their own base desires. The warlock had found a few nobles he could trust, and the rest he ignored, knowing that their efforts would amount to little more than the sting of a single ant when compared with his power, let alone the might of his master.

Bracken smiled and turned back to beckon for Captain Thorgrave.

"I am at your service," the captain said dutifully as he trotted his horse up alongside the window.

"I do not wish to be disturbed by fanfare and parades today, Captain Thorgrave," Bracken said.

"Very well," the captain replied. "What would you have me do?"

"Make it known that I wish only to deposit our guest into the garrison dungeon. Have him watched by a triple guard and keep him in irons. Then I wish to simply go home, eat, and sleep. I have a long couple of days ahead of me."

"By your command, sir," Captain Thorgrave said. "I shall dispatch my lieutenants ahead of us to make the necessary preparations."

Bracken sneered at the captain. "I don't care to be bothered with the details, just get it done." Senator Bracken pulled his head back inside the carriage and tried to steal a short nap before they made it to the city gates.

*****

Braun hung close to the oak branches supporting his weight high up in the great tree. He had managed to get ahead of Senator Bracken's convoy enough to set up a small camp just inside the forest that flanked the northern road. His perch afforded him a great view of the valley, and he never took his eyes from Lord Lokton's wagon after he had caught sight of it. A pair of sturdy, bearded men stood on platforms on the wagon's side and a driver followed Senator Bracken's gaudy white and purple carriage from the forest road to the paved stone road through the valley that led to the gates of Drakai Glazei.

He was too far away to see Lord Lokton of course, but he still felt as though he could sense his master's sadness as the heavy, iron plated wagon lurched on the road behind eight powerful draft horses. The great wheels were even covered with iron. Even if Al had not offered an alternative plan to rescue Lord Lokton, Braun knew there would be no way for a single man to break a prisoner from that wagon. It would take a small army to hack their way inside, and that was to say nothing of the complementary military escort.

Braun waited not only until the wagon had disappeared

behind the gargantuan iron gates of Drakai Glazei, but also until the sun began to set before he descended the tree and started on his way to the city. The sky was ablaze with purple and pink clouds above the city's black granite walls. His horse trotted along the paved valley road with a perfectly rhythmic *clippity-clop, clippity-clop.*

He passed a couple of local farmers who were driving their carts in the opposite direction, obviously going home for the day. Braun would wave if they waved first, but he didn't slow his pace. Even when one of the farmers called out with cheap bread and vegetables, Braun pushed on.

A trio of guards raised their hands and asked for Braun to bring his horse to them before they allowed him to enter.

Braun pulled back on the reins and swung his leg over the side of the horse as he slid off and greeted the guards.

"Name and business in Drakai Glazei," one of the guards demanded.

"I am Braun Gerble," he said. "Sergeant-at-arms for House Lokton."

The guards looked to each other for a moment. One of them offered a crooked smile. "You aren't planning on busting your employer out of prison are you?" he inquired with a chuckle.

Braun shrugged. "If I was here for that, then I think I am a little ill-prepared, don't you?" He watched the guard's smile straighten and sour for a moment.

"I should warn you that he is heavily guarded, and we will not tolerate troublemakers in Drakai Glazei," one of the other guards said.

Braun scratched the left side of his face and brushed a hair from under his nose. He was unimpressed. "I doubt the city needs to worry about one man armed with only a single sword and a hunting knife," Braun commented. "I am here to uphold House Lokton's honor, nothing more, nothing less."

"They won't let you in the trial," the third guard stated. He stepped closer to Braun and raised a hunk of jerky to his mouth, taking a big, tough bite while he sized Braun up. "Still, if your nobleman demands you follow him all the way to the gallows, who are we to stop you?"

The other two guards looked to the third. "Shall I check his sword?" one of them asked.

"Nah," the third said just before he swallowed the half-chewed bite. "Just let him in. If he is fool enough to raise trouble, then that's his problem."

Braun smirked and offered a hand. "May I have the pleasure of your name?" he asked.

The third guard scoffed. "No, you can't." He took another bite and walked away.

"All right, sign or make your mark here in the log," the first guard said as he produced a thick book with creaky, breaking binding.

Braun took the quill from the middle of the book and placed his name at the bottom of a long list of names. "Do I sign upon departure as well?" Braun asked.

"Yes, you will see a guard house on the inside of the gates. That is where you will stop before departing Drakai Glazei." The first guard took the log book back, closed it, and walked away.

The second guard stayed back and looked at Braun's horse. "Do you need a recommendation for accommodations?" the guard asked.

"That would be appreciated," Braun admitted.

The guard nodded. "What kind of purse has your lord given you for lodging?"

"I have sufficient for a few days board, but I don't require anything fancy," Braun replied.

The guard nodded again and smiled. "Well, the Black Rose is found on the main road about three blocks inside the gates. It is a bit on the pricey side, but the beds are clean and the food is hot. If you are willing to bunk with others, you can get a shared room at the Hungry Man Inn for only a couple of copper a night. Food costs extra, but you have the choice of eating at the inn or elsewhere."

"Where is the Hungry Man Inn?" Braun asked.

"Go straight for two blocks, then turn right and follow the road for about six blocks. It is a bit off the beaten path, but it will save you a bundle."

"I appreciate the advice. Do they have a place for the horse?" Braun asked.

The guard nodded. "Yep, there is a stable out back and it only costs one extra copper to stable your horse there for the duration of your stay."

"Thanks," Braun offered.

"Tell them that Jep sent you, they might give you a free meal for tonight."

Braun nodded and hopped atop his horse. As he directed his steed to the gates he overheard Jep tell the other two guards that he would be staying at the Hungry Man Inn. He stole a glance in their direction and noted that the third guard directed the others to make a note of it in the log book.

As he passed under the gates he was amazed with how busy the streets were for this time of day. Great shadows filled the city as the sun had dipped below the level of the walls, but people filled the streets. Some pulled carts, while others simply loitered about on wooden fences or at street corners.

A barrage of smells mixed in front of his nose. There was the definitive stench of body odor as a group of day laborers passed by, but it was soon carried away by a pleasant evening breeze that funneled through the city. The breeze also brought with it the aroma from a nearby bakery, with its promise of freshly baked rolls and pies.

Braun stopped when he got to the road he was supposed to turn at. He thought about pushing on and finding his own accommodations. Something about the way the guards seemed so interested in where he was going to lodge made the hairs on the back of his neck tingle. However, it was late, and he had never been in Drakai Glazei before. He figured he could spend at least one night at the Hungry Man, and then move to a new location the next day.

He turned his horse and eased it through the throngs of people heading in the opposite direction. By the time he had passed two blocks of shops and taverns, the crowds thinned out considerably. The demographics also shifted noticeably. People in this side of town tended to be middle-aged men, most of them looked native, but many looked as though they had seen more than a few rough years beyond the protection of the great, black walls.

He almost passed the Hungry Man Inn. The sign was faded, and barely legible. The building was nestled between a pair of older taverns so that it blended in as though it were a joining of the two establishments rather than a separate enterprise. An old man, probably in his mid-sixties, sat on the front steps smoking a long, curved wooden pipe.

The man looked up at Braun with one eye. The other was too lazy to follow where he was looking, but he said nothing. He drew a couple of puffs and then blew them out before turning away from Braun and resting his shoulder against the old, cracked wooden railing.

Braun dismounted, hitched his horse to the hitching post and walked up the creaking steps to the front door. The knob had lost its brass finish a long time before. Now it was a dark brown lump of metal that stuck slightly at first. A cloud of smoke assaulted Braun once the rickety door squeaked open. Several men inside had pipes, but some of the smoke was very obviously flowing out from a brick chimney that was no longer drawing away the fire's exhaust properly. The mixture of wood and tobacco was enough to make Braun cough and sneeze a couple of times until he made his way to the back and approached an older, plump lady behind a bar.

She wore a red kerchief in her hair, a pale, dingy gray dress spotted by visible beer and sweat stains with a tan apron over the front. "What can I get fer ya?" she asked as she swept a mug up from behind the bar.

Braun placed a pair of coppers down on the bar and slid them to the lady. "I am looking for a room, and some supper."

The lady scooped the coins into her apron pocket. "We have some chicken soup coming out of the pot now, traveler. It's fresh and hot."

"Jep said you might include the soup with the price of tonight's lodging," Braun said.

The lady eyed him carefully and then shrugged. "If that is what Jep said, then that's what I'll do. Just fer tonight though," she said. "If you have a horse to stable, that will cost you another copper."

Braun nodded and produced another copper coin. "Do you have a key to the room?" he asked.

She shook her head. "No key, just up the stairs and pick a bed that ain't already claimed. None of the rooms have any doors on 'em."

Braun shrugged and dug another copper out of his purse. "Would this be enough to cover an early breakfast in the morning?"

The lady nodded. "Wait here, I'll send the soup out shortly and then you can take your horse around back and put him in stall number four. I'll have some biscuits and gravy ready by the time the cock crows in the morning."

"Thank you," Braun offered. The lady winked half-heartedly and turned away. Braun watched her go, waddling from side to side as her bulbous hips and posterior bounced between the bar and the wall. It was a wonder she could fit through the door that led to the kitchen. She reemerged a couple of minutes later with a crusty wooden bowl full of yellow steaming broth. She set the bowl down hurriedly, sloshing some of the soup over the side and onto the counter. Then she bent over, placing one hand on the counter while she dug around behind the bar with her other.

"Everything all right?" Braun asked.

The woman stuck her tongue out to the left corner of her mouth, revealing a couple of missing bottom teeth, and nodded her head. "Just lookin fer a spoon," she answered. "Aha!" The woman straightened up with a bright smile and tossed a wooden spoon down next to the bowl. "Enjoy, honey," she said. Then she waddled off to serve others.

Braun picked up the wooden spoon and plunged it into his bowl, deciding it was better not to inspect the spoon first. As he brought a mouthful of soup up, a fairly steady stream leaked out through a minor crack in the middle of the spoon's bowl. Braun shrugged and just moved faster as he shoveled the chicken soup to his mouth.

The soup was simple. Just chicken, a bit of salt, and water. But that was all he needed. In the morning he could afford to spend some time looking for more suitable accommodations and food. For now, he was happy to be in Drakai Glazei. He just hoped that Al was faring well in his part of the plan to get Lepkin.

He rushed through the soup, lifting the bowl to drink the rest rather than wasting time with the cracked spoon. This wasn't a place requiring manners anyway, he figured.

After taking his horse to the stable and offering the stable boy an extra copper piece to take special care of his horse, he went upstairs and found an empty bed.

The first room was packed full of people. Many of them were

already snoring upon their beds, while others gambled and drank from open bottles. The second and third rooms were the same. In the fourth room, he saw an open bed near the far corner. He went straight for it and tucked his pack and purse under the flat pillow. He sat down on the straw mattress, testing the bed's strength by pushing on it with his palms before turning and swinging a leg up onto it.

A pair of bearded men eyed him from a nearby card table. They leaned close to each other as if to whisper, but they said nothing. Whatever they were waiting for, Braun didn't care. He knew he could handle himself if needed. He made a point of ignoring them and laid himself back on the bed, placing one arm over his eyes and the other across his stomach, with the palm of his hand resting strategically over the handle of his hunting knife.

He positioned his elbow just so he could peek out from under his arm without drawing attention to himself. He could see the bearded men talking to each other and glancing back at him occasionally. After a couple of minutes, they turned their backs to him and began playing cards.

Braun settled into his surroundings. Listening to the muffled conversations around him to discover what kind of men he was spending the night with. He heard them swap tales of women, adventure, gold, and intrigue, but nothing that seemed out of the ordinary given the kind of inn he had chosen for himself. As the lamps burned low, many of the men turned themselves in and started to sleep. Braun stayed awake. Even after almost everyone was asleep, he couldn't convince himself that he was safe, nor force his body to sleep. Something was amiss.

After a couple more hours, there were only three men left awake in the room besides Braun. The two bearded men that had watched him earlier now played cards with a third man. Braun only caught a couple of fleeting glimpses of the third, but it seemed he was not saying much of anything other than what was required for betting and throwing down his cards.

Then another figure entered through the doorway.

"Long live the king," the man said.

The three at the card table stopped abruptly and pushed back from the table. None of them returned the greeting. The newcomer stalked into the room. He pulled his hood back to reveal a full, red beard underneath a thick head of matted red hair. He pointed to the table.

"Room for a fourth?"

The other three threw down their cards.

"What brings you out here, Desmon?" one of the bearded men asked.

"I heard we might have a newcomer, is this him?" he asked, pointing to Braun.

Braun's breathing caught in his chest for a moment. Newcomer? Newcomer to what?

"Don't know about that; we didn't talk to him. He just came up here and went to sleep."

"I doubt that," the red-head told them. "You probably can't sleep in a place like this, can you?" the man said as he shifted his gaze to look at Braun.

Braun wondered whether he should sit up and confront them, or pretend to be asleep and let things unfold.

The redhead strode over and kicked the bedpost. "You can come out from under your arm, Braun Gerble," the man instructed. "I know you are awake."

Braun slowly pulled his arm away from his eyes and met Desmon's green eyes. "Who are you and what do you want?" Braun asked.

The redhead smiled, clapped his hands and walked back to the table to join the other three. The two bearded men frowned and picked their cards back up. "Braun, won't you join us here at the table?"

Braun rose slowly and stood up. He saw there was a wooden chair near the head of his bed, so he grabbed it with his left hand and plopped it a few feet away from the table. "All right, what is it you want from me?"

"Nothing much," the redhead said. "I just wanted to talk with you and ask you a couple of questions."

Braun eyed the four of them warily, turned his chair around and sat down in the chair backwards so he could rest his hands on the back of it, just in case he needed to improvise a shield "You have the advantage over me," Braun said. "It seems you know my name, but I do not know yours."

"Not to worry, friend," the redhead said. "Mine is Desmon, as

I am sure you overheard while you were pretending to sleep. This here is Craver, and the two bearded brothers are Miles and Sweets."

Braun nodded to each of the men as they were introduced. All but Miles kept their eyes on their cards. "Am I correct to assume that Jep sent you?" Braun asked.

Desmon smiled and touched his finger to his nose. "The bigger question here, my friend, is what your plans are for the near future in terms of employment."

"I am already employed," Braun said. "I am not interested in new employment."

Desmon held a hand in the air. "Hold on a minute there, friend." Desmon reached down and pulled up a small, leather coin purse. "I have a couple reasons you may want to listen." Desmon set the purse on the table. Braun glanced at the purse and clenched his jaw.

"Not interested," Braun said sternly.

"Just consider it a retainer in case you become available for hire," Desmon coaxed. He slid the bag farther onto the table.

Braun shook his head and started to rise from the chair.

"Maybe it's time you open your eyes, mate," Miles said from behind a pair of cards. "Your employer is going to be sleeping with the worms within the week, and you might be out of a job sooner than you think." Braun stepped over and backhanded Miles across the top of his head. Miles' head jerked to the side and he flopped his cards down, but Desmon reached out and held Miles in place.

"My honor is not so cheap as to be bought by a bag of coins in a flea ridden hostel among the company of thieves and mercenaries. You would do well to hold your tongue around me, else you may find it lying on the floor after I sever it from you," Braun growled.

Miles fumed and clenched his jaw. His eyes flicked from Sweets to Craver before he looked at Desmon.

"Easy, friend," Desmon said. "No one is impugning your honor. To the contrary, we are looking for someone exactly like yourself to join us. Let me explain, and then you can do as you please."

"Make it quick," Braun said.

Desmon nodded. "Seeing as you serve a noble, we figure you

have your finger on the kingdom's pulse. You and I both know that our king is not much longer for this world. We are forming a band of brothers to help ensure that power transfers to the right heir after his death."

"His rightful heir?" Braun scoffed. "The king has no heir."

"He has no blood heir, that much is true," Craver put in.

Desmon pointed to Craver and nodded. "But, a special council has named an heir."

"If this council has named an heir, then why form a band of thugs to ensure the kingdom transfers smoothly?" Braun asked.

"Don't play to be dense," Sweets said. "You know how the nobles work. If there is ever a chance that power can be taken, you know as well as we do that they will do anything to seize that power."

"So, we are offering you a spot with us. Help us protect the rightful heir to the throne. You will not be able to save your master from the senate, but you can honor him by ensuring the kingdom does not crumble upon the king's death."

Braun shook his head. "My master serves the king, and the kingdom, that much is true. But I owe my allegiance to House Lokton."

"Lord Sarelle has been named as the rightful successor," Desmon continued. "Several other nobles recognize his right to the throne."

"He has no claim to the throne, unless King Mathias names him as heir. A secret council of nobles holds no authority," Braun answered.

"Still, it makes more sense that the late queen's nephew should rule. He is the closest living relative," Desmon added.

"Unless you would rather have the senate take over the kingdom upon the king's death," Miles put in with an icy stare.

"I will not hear any more of this," Braun said.

"Well," Desmon said with a shrug. "We tried."

"Go and tell Jep to keep his nose out of my business."

"Before you sever it from his face?" Miles put in.

Braun jerked his chair up and slammed it on the floor next to Miles, causing the man to flinch. "Don't press me," he warned. Braun turned back to his bed and gathered his things.

"Oh come now, there is no need to walk out," Desmon said.

"I prefer better company," Braun said.

"Good luck finding any space tonight," Craver said. "Most of the inns are full this time of year."

"I can find better company in a stable," Braun replied.

Desmon chuckled to himself. "I do believe he values his horse higher than us," Desmon jested.

Braun smiled. "I would value the soiled hay mucked out of the stable above the likes of you."

Desmon's smile disappeared. "Well then, go and sleep with your horse. I doubt our next meeting shall be so amicable."

Braun nodded knowingly and then quickly exited the Hungry Man Inn.

CHAPTER EIGHT

Al and Erik checked the straps on their saddles and nodded to each other when they were ready.

"I figure we can make it half way to Buktah tonight," Al said.

"Why are we going there?" Erik asked.

Al shrugged. "Seeing as how you are in a new body, your armor isn't going to fit anymore. So we need to go back to my forge so I can retrieve a new set for you. I usually have a couple of sets in the shop. Besides, it might benefit us all if I send my apprentice here to help with preparations."

"Preparations?" Erik asked curiously.

Al nodded. "The temple is well stocked, but we will need another smith here to make sure we have enough equipment. When you and Lepkin are switched back, you will go back to your training. Given the frequency with which the Blacktongues have followed you, I imagine we will need a smith around here to help us stay ready. I have already discussed the matter with Marlin, and he agrees."

Erik nodded. "Will it delay us much?" Erik asked.

"Nah," Al gruffed. I have some basic pieces in stock. I will have to make some adjustments to them in order to ensure a proper fit, but that won't take very long."

"You know, I never got a chance to use the armor you made for me anyway," Erik said.

Al sniggered to himself. "Don't remind me." Al smiled and clambered up the step ladder that allowed him to mount his horse. "I spent the better part of six months making that set of armor for you. Seems a shame to leave it here." Al bent down and fastened the straps around the top of his left foot.

Erik shook his head. "I imagine if Lepkin wakes up in my body, it may serve him well in case the temple is attacked again."

Al nodded.

Erik watched Al tighten his right stirrup. He wondered how it could be comfortable for Al to straddle the full size horse with his diminutive legs, but he decided not to ask. He almost asked about it, but decided it might be better just to get on with the journey.

Al caught Erik looking at him and smiled wide. "Not all dwarves ride ponies, boy," Al said.

Erik shrugged. "I guess I am not the only one who can see what others are thinking," Erik said. He jumped atop his horse with incredible ease. Being in Lepkin's body definitely had its advantages.

"So, where is Goliath?" Al asked.

Erik frowned. "He doesn't recognize me," Erik said.

"Just as well," Al commented. "It might raise question if people saw 'Lepkin' riding your horse."

"Who would know the difference?" Erik asked.

Al shrugged. "Anyone who works for or with House Cedreau maybe. Come on, let's get to it."

The two spurred their horses on at a gallop, riding away from the stable as quickly as their four legged steeds could go. Erik fell into a rhythm as his horse's hooves gnawed at the stone path leading to the main road in front of Valtuu Temple. The stale, hot air wrapped around him as his speed increased and the valley started to pull away behind him. Lepkin's sword flapped out to the side, slapping into the side of his leg and his horse.

The grasses of the valley stopped just inside the tree line of the forest as bushes and shrubs took over the ground. Great pines and oaks whipped by as Erik and Al galloped along the winding road. Squirrels and birds ceased their chirping to gawk at the two intruders briefly before skittering away. The morning sunlight broke through the leaves, warming the forest and inviting the flowers to open and turn toward the golden rays.

The two of them travelled silently, sacrificing discourse for the sake of speed. The quiet gave Erik plenty of time to ponder the recent events. He found his mind wandering back to the battle near his home and he again saw Janik's face. His grip on the reins tightened and his heart skipped a beat. How could Janik have betrayed him so? Why would he have pretended to be his friend for so long, only to ambush him in the woods outside Lokton

Manor? A dark thought entered into his mind and fear gnawed at Erik's stomach. Erik pulled up short on the reins and brought his horse to a slow trot before halting it. Al caught Erik's movement and pulled his horse back around a few seconds later.

"What is it boy, is something wrong with the horse?" Al asked.

"No," Erik said with a shake of his head. I was just thinking…"

"Think while you ride, Erik, we don't have time to dawdle," Al chided.

"Why did Janik come to Lokton Manor?" Erik asked.

Al shrugged. "I don't know." The dwarf let his horse trot up beside Erik's and tug at a young fern on the ground. "Perhaps he expected you to return from the temple to defend your home."

"But why not just do away with me at Kuldiga Academy? There were plenty of times when I was washing windows with him and no one else was around."

Al sighed. "What's bothering you, Erik?"

"Don't you find it odd that at the same time my father is defending our home, the wizard attacked the temple looking for Nagar's Secret?" Erik looked back down the road and then turned back to Al. "Then, after both attacks are foiled, Senator Bracken arrests my father before you have even had enough time to rest?"

Al stroked his beard and cocked an eyebrow. "It does seem uncanny that all three events happened so quickly," Al agreed.

"And that Janik chose that precise time to attack me in the woods," Erik said.

"Well, we know that Janik was with the Order of the All Seeing Eye," Al put in.

"Was the wizard with the warlocks as well?" Erik asked.

Al shook his head. "No, Marlin told me that Erthor was with the Wyrms of Khaltoun."

"So is it possible that Janik was orchestrating the whole thing?"

"I don't know, but we can talk about it more when we stop for lunch."

Erik nodded and looked past Al. "Will I be able to save him?" he asked. Al didn't answer. "There is still Tukai's prophecy."

Al turned his horse and started off down the road again. Erik begrudgingly followed after him.

*****

Marlin pulled himself upright and pushed down on the side of the granite tub as he climbed out of the crystal clear pool. He reached out and pulled a large towel from a golden bracket and dried himself off. He couldn't see the steam in the room with his natural eyes, but he could feel it enveloping his skin. He took in a deep breath and wrapped the towel around himself. Then he left the bath chamber and walked through a short antechamber to his room. Once there, he grabbed his white, hooded silk robes and dressed himself. He took a green bottle from the top of a desk and generously applied the scented liquid to his hands and neck. Lavender and spice filled his nose.

Next he opened the desk drawer and removed a pair of golden, silk gloves and placed them upon his hands. He slipped his feet into a pair of soft, leather-soled slippers and then exited his room. The cool air from the night permeated the halls of the temple. The halls were quiet and still. He wrung his hands and bit his lower lip. All around him seemed at peace, though he himself was a tempest of doubt, worry, and confusion.

He sensed a presence nearby. He turned to see Dimwater emerging from a nearby hallway.

"You look as though you are going somewhere important," she said.

Marlin nodded. "I have some things I need to tend to. I need to get clarification on these prophecies."

"So you are going to talk to Tatev about the immortal mystic?"

Marlin shook his head. "No, while that would give us clarity, finding the immortal mystic would require a journey far to the east. We don't have that kind of time."

"Assuming Tatev knows for certain where the mystic is and whether the legend is true in the first place, right?" Dimwater finished.

"Precisely," Marlin said.

Dimwater nodded and rubbed the outside of her arms. "So, where are you headed then?"

"I am going downstairs," Marlin replied. He started to turn and walk away, but thought better of it. "I can't offer a full explanation now," he said. "Suffice it to say that there are other sources of knowledge beyond the libraries in this temple."

Lady Dimwater nodded and backed away, turning to return down the hallway from which she came. She took two steps and then paused, turning quickly to face Marlin again. Her lips parted slightly and a hint of a smile tugged at the corner of her mouth. "I wish I could come," she said.

Marlin smiled. "Perhaps some other time," he offered.

Dimwater smiled and walked away, talking softly to herself.

Marlin watched her for a moment, studying her aura. He could see the awe swirling through her. He knew she had guessed what he was about to do. After the light from her aura was long gone, he turned away and walked to a simple, iron crossed door at the end of the hall. Marlin produced a long, slender claw from a pocket and slid it into the opening under the knob. Golden rays snaked out from the brass key plate, reaching and stretching across the iron bands over the door. The metal glowed and vibrated against the wood. Marlin looked back over his shoulder and then turned the knob. The latch clicked open and the door gently fell open.

He removed the claw, stepped through the doorway and pushed the door closed behind him. The steps steeply descended down a tight spiral. Small, goat horn sconces adorned the wall every seven feet to illuminate the tunnel and caused the gold inlay between the red bricks to shimmer and dance.

At the bottom of the stairs the brick opened up into a green marble tunnel. Torches hung halfway down the smooth, hard walls. Marlin's slippers created soft echoes through the tunnel as he made his way to the end of the hall. As he got closer, a golden glow appeared and grew brighter and brighter until he stood in a large antechamber made entirely of gold, with glowing crystals hanging from the ceiling.

A small golden dragon head protruded from the left wall, mouth closed and waiting silently for Marlin. The eyes were open, made of jade, and staring at him. Marlin reached over and slid his index finger over the dragon's head. A small hole opened in the top of the head. Marlin pulled the dragon claw out again and slid it point first into the opening.

The jade eyes began to glow. Marlin held his palm out in front of the dragon head. Green light exuded from the dragon's eyes until they enveloped Marlin entirely. After a few moments, the light died down and then the golden mouth opened, revealing a key on the dragon's tongue.

A door materialized in the wall at the end of the hall. The bricks cracked and crumbled as yellow light ripped through the green marble, revealing the golden door. A large shining eye opened on the door and Marlin slid the key into the pupil and turned it. The tumblers inside clicked and snapped. The door slid back three inches and then sank into the floor below.

Marlin took a deep breath and held it for a moment. The stark darkness beyond the open doorway gave him reason to pause. There seemed to be nothing beyond the doorway. Finally a faint, red glow appeared and Marlin heard the words he was waiting for.

"Enter, Prelate," the deep, thunderous voice said wearily.

Marlin stepped into the darkness and pushed forward, aiming to go to the red, glowing light. A few yards into the next chamber the door behind him rose up from the floor and sealed the way back. Chills ran through Marlin's spine and his feet halted in mid step for a moment. After a couple of seconds he continued going forward. It took him several minutes to reach the red glow in the center of the chamber. A fist-sized garnet sat upon a golden candlestick with smaller jasper stones placed into the base of the stick.

He reached forward and placed his hand over the glowing garnet. The light flowed warmly into Marlin's hand and pulsed through his arm momentarily before withdrawing back into the gemstone. Marlin removed his hand and stepped back from the candlestick. The light intensified from within the garnet and flooded the room. Dark tones of red rippled out through the chamber, bouncing off of nondescript dark forms and bumps. The garnet hummed and vibrated as it started to rise from the holder. It stopped about twenty feet above Marlin's head and began to spin. The faster it spun, the lighter the red tones became throughout the room until streaks of brilliant white light shot through the air, rending the clouds of red and illuminating the room as though it were a small star.

Marlin raised a hand above his eyes and shut them against the searing light.

As his eyes adjusted, he brought his arm down and opened his eyes. A great, golden leg rested before him. He stared at the shield-sized scales briefly before following the leg up to the shoulder. He shuddered at the sight of the long spikes extending from the dragon's spine. He then looked to the great, angular jaws filled with teeth the size of spears protruding over the thin, leathery lips.

The eyes opened slowly, revealing great green orbs flecked with gold and red specks. The long, angled pupil shrank quickly and then widened slightly as the eye shifted to focus on Marlin.

Marlin bowed his head. "I apologize for disturbing you, great one, but I have many troubles on my heart," Marlin said.

The dragon pulled its head back, sliding its leathery neck over its leg briefly until its head was poised to look at Marlin. "Normally I am only awakened to perform the Exalted Test of Arophim," the dragon said. "However, your predecessor woke me for counsel on occasion as well."

"Forgive me, Ancient One," Marlin apologized, using the human title instead of the proper name, Hiasyntar'Kulai

The dragon slowly closed his eyes and emitted a deep, throaty rumble. "My time must be short, lest the power of the book overpower my defenses. Even here, inside this blessed chamber and protected by spells, I can feel its power trying to claw its way in."

"Forgive me, Hiasyntar'Kulai, for disturbing your rest. I have a candidate for the Exalted Test of Arophim," Marlin said. He frowned and knit his brow. "I am worried that this may be the wrong candidate. I have uncovered prophecies that point to a false champion. Before I continue with his training, I wanted to speak with you and seek your guidance."

The dragon opened his eyes. Hiasyntar'Kulai nodded slightly. "The books of prophecy are difficult to decipher, even for those who are well versed in the ways of the mystics." A slim tendril of smoke slithered out from the dragon's nostrils. "I presume you still have faith in the candidate, otherwise you would dismiss him yourself."

"That is correct, Ancient One," Marlin replied.

Hiasyntar'Kulai nodded. "Ultimately, the Exalted Test of

Arophim will decide whether he is the true champion. My advice would be to continue with his training and present him before me as soon as you believe him ready."

Marlin bowed his head.

"Trust your instincts," Hiasyntar'Kulai added. "If you believe in the candidate, then follow your faith." The great dragon slowly dropped his head to rest on his extended foreleg. "I must return to my slumber to keep the power of Nagar's Secret at bay. Allow me to sleep until you are ready to present him before me, so I may be strong enough to perform the test."

"As you wish," Marlin answered.

Hiasyntar'Kulai closed his eyes and emitted a throaty rumble as he sighed.

CHAPTER NINE

Lady Arkyn slithered out the window of the senate building and delicately pressed the stained glass window, spinning it back into place. She inched along the four-inch ledge, keeping her back flat against the exterior wall and using her hands to steady herself. Her green, half-elf eyes amplified the sparse starlight and allowed her to see everything easily.

She paused. Thirty feet below her a guard stepped around the corner. She held her breath and remained perfectly still until he walked past and disappeared around the next corner. Arkyn exhaled and sped along the ledge to the large oak tree near the rear of the senate building, which was positioned adjacent to the king's tower. She pivoted on the ball of her right foot and leapt to the nearest branch. As she gracefully descended, she pulled her bow from her hiding place near an abandoned nest and dropped to the ground as silent as a cat in the night.

By the time the guard made his next round she was already over the fence and stalking the shadows in an alley that would lead her to Senator Bracken's house. Having found nothing in his writing chamber at the senate hall, she hoped there would be more clues at his home.

A pair of men stumbled into the alley ahead of her. Her keen eyes quickly spotted the large, brown bottle the two of them were sharing. She slid up next to a protruding chimney. Rather than risk a confrontation, she decided to wait for the drunk men to pass her by. It took much longer than she would have liked. She rolled her eyes as one of the men tripped and nearly went headlong into the building opposite her. Luckily his friend caught him and the two zig-zagged on without spotting her.

Arkyn peeled away from the wall and went to the end of the alley. She glanced down both sides of the street, gaging the chance of her being seen by the few people still outside. To her left was an old man sitting on the front steps of an upscale tavern. He wore a long, red jacket over a neatly tailored ruffle-shirt. To her right were two senators, still dressed in their white robes, conversing about something. The temptation was too great. Arkyn scrambled up the building to her right and leaned over the front of it just enough to eavesdrop on the senators.

"You heard me," one of them said. "Bracken is offering fifty gold for your vote."

"Preposterous," the other said. "I lose more than that when I play cards. If Bracken wants my vote, he will have to pay me what it's actually worth."

Arkyn peered over the edge of the building. She could only see the tops of their heads, so there was no way for her to identify them unless they used their names. She moved back and continued to listen.

"He isn't trying to buy your vote for the verdict," the first senator said. "He just wants us to hold the tribunal a day earlier."

"Bah," the second man scoffed. "I suppose it doesn't make much difference anyway. From what I hear the case is very simple."

"That's right," the first agreed. "There is more than enough evidence to convict Lokton."

"Seems a shame for House Lokton to fall this way," the second said.

"So, what do you say, will fifty gold persuade you to vote for an earlier tribunal?"

There was silence below. Arkyn restrained herself from leaning over to watch them again. Finally, she heard the second man speak.

"Tell Bracken that fifty gold is too cheap, but I would consider skipping breakfast for one hundred."

The first senator laughed. "Come, let's go back inside. Lord Robair is waiting for us."

Lady Arkyn leaned over the edge, watching them leave. Unfortunately they never turned back so she could only see their backs. At least she had some evidence that Bracken was dealing dirty with Lokton. She looked through the night air toward Bracken's house, glancing between it and the tavern where the two senators had joined up with the old man who had been sitting on the steps. The three of them walked inside, laughing boisterously and entering into a raucous cheer from inside.

She weighed her options. Following them inside could give her more direct information, but she would surely be seen. On the other hand, going to Bracken's house might yield as little as visiting the senator's office in the senate hall, but she would remain a shadow. Arkyn rolled to her right and quickly picked her way down the right side of the building before dashing across the street while it was still empty.

A dog barked as she ran by the back of a large manor. The barking grew louder and closer, becoming angrier with each moment. She turned and saw a medium-sized black dog squeeze under a hole in the bottom of its fence and head straight for her.

Lady Arkyn turned and knelt down as the dog charged. She waved a hand in front of her face and whispered to the dog, "Be quiet, my friend."

The dog stopped instantly, panting heavily, but no longer angry. It cocked its head to the side and studied her carefully.

"Go home," she whispered, pointing to the hole under the fence. The dog turned around and obeyed. Lady Arkyn sighed and brushed the dirt from the front of her pants as she stood back up. Not wanting to waste any more time, she turned and quickly made her way to the back of Senator Bracken's manor.

Crouched at the edge of the back yard, her heart slowed along with her breath. She scanned the area, and she almost smiled as she spied a globe willow tree growing near a second floor window on the south side. Her hands gripped one of the iron rods of the nearby fence and steadied her ascent while her feet propelled her up and over the barrier in a single leap. She tucked her head and rolled into a flip over the fence, landing silently on the balls of her feet inside the yard.

A nearby hedge would provide perfect cover for her bow. She slid the weapon in at the base of the hedge, careful not to scratch herself on the plant's thorns. Then, she was up and off to the willow tree. Running forward, she leapt up and planted her right foot halfway up the trunk and then pushed off forcefully to launch herself up and backward to a thick branch. Her arms caught the limb and easily swung her around to perch atop the branch, hidden from view by the drooping, smaller branches farther out with their veil of leaves.

She jumped straight up and caught onto another branch, this one much smaller than the first. It bent under her weight, but did not crack. She quickly ran to the middle of the branch and leapt out to her left, swinging from another branch and then executing a reverse flip to land on the wall next to the window. Where a thief may have been clumsy and loud, she was effortlessly silent. Her fingers worked like spider's legs gripping the grooves in between the brick and stone.

Arkyn slowly arched her back and leaned to her right, allowing her to see into the room through the window. No lamps burned, but a quick glance with her half-elf eyes allowed her to see the chest of drawers against the north wall, a door in the western wall, and a bed against the southern wall. The bed was empty. She pulled a pin from her braided hair and tapped on one of the four inch square panes of glass in the window, searching for signs of magical enchantments or barriers.

Satisfied that there were none, she used the same pin to dig the wood away from the four inch pane. It took her several minutes, but she preferred silence to speed. Once the pane was loose, she slid it out with her left hand and tucked the glass under her belt for safekeeping. She snaked her right arm through the hole until her elbow passed through, then she bent her arm up so she could disengage the lock. Silently her thumb and forefinger gripped the flat lever and pulled it open. She retracted her arm and then slid the whole window up enough to allow her to slip in. Once inside, she closed the window and replaced the pane of glass she had removed.

Keeping to the balls of her feet, she stalked across the room and put her ear to the door. She didn't hear anything. She then went flat on the floor, peering under the door with her left eye. There was a hallway beyond the door, as she had expected. It was lit, and a red runner covered the middle of the hall, leaving only a few inches on either side exposed so that the wood was visible.

She slowly opened the door and leaned to the side to afford herself a better view. The hallway was clear. She stepped out, looking to her right. As was typical of the few senate houses she had been inside before, she saw several white marble busts of previous family patriarchs. Between these busts were various portraits and tapestries, but nothing seemed out of the ordinary. The hallway ended in grand, double doors of mahogany with two brass rings under lion heads.

"That's the bedchamber," she whispered to herself. Footsteps echoed from the stairway to her left. She glanced over and the light from below increased. Someone was coming, probably carrying a candlestick or a lamp.

"Gildrin," a voice called out. The footsteps stopped and the growing light shifted.

"Yes, master," another man, presumably Gildrin, replied from farther away.

"I am going into the library for the night. I do not wish to be disturbed, do you understand?"

"Yes, master," Gildrin said. "I will ensure you are left in peace."

The light shifted back and the footsteps resumed ascending the stairs. Lady Arkyn shrank back into the room and gently closed the door most of the way. She left only a sliver of a crack so she could watch which way Senator Bracken would go.

As Bracken came up to the top, she saw him holding a small box in one hand. He wore long, black velvet robes, and by the stern look on his face there must have been a lot on his mind. She watched him turn the opposite way and pause before a door. He said a few things to the door that she could not quite make out, but it was obvious he was unlocking magical barriers. Then he disappeared through the doorway and the door clicked shut behind him.

Lady Arkyn wasted no time slipping out toward the bedchamber. She stuck to the wall, just in case she needed to crouch behind one of the many pasty busts. She stopped in front of the double doors and waved her hand in front of her. A pale green shimmer appeared on the doors. They were sealed by magic as well. She inched closer, inspecting the vague pattern of green lines and circles on the doors. She tapped a fingernail to her teeth a few times as she traced the design with her eyes. She shook her head and sighed. There was no way for her to defeat the barrier. She didn't recognize the pattern, or even the style of magic it might have come from.

She looked over her shoulder toward the other end of the

hallway. The corner of her mouth turned up into a sly smile. In a moment she was up and darting down the hallway on her soft, silent feet. She slowed and crouched in front of the door she had seen Bracken go in and pressed her ear to it.

At first all she could make out was a muffled voice. It sounded like chanting of some sort, but she couldn't be sure. Under the door she could see a shifting shadow, then a flash of purple light and the chanting stopped. She backed away from the door momentarily as a bit of thin, gray smoke slid under the door.

A low, throaty voice ripped through the air. "Gondok'hr, what news do you have for me?"

Fear gripped Lady Arkyn's spine. It was as if the voice itself had coursed through her body and uncovered her. She wasn't sure what it was, but the voice did not come from any human. She pressed farther away from the door.

"Master," another voice said from within. "There have been some very exciting developments." This voice was human, and sounded a lot like Senator Bracken, but something was amiss. Lady Arkyn knit her brow and pressed her ear back to the door.

"Then tell me, Gondok'hr, how does Lord Lokton fare? Will he join with us?"

Clanking metal down the hall made Lady Arkyn jump back. She caught sight of a silver tray holding a tea pot emerging from the stairs. Her heart raced and her adrenaline spiked. A man stepped up to the landing, holding the tray. A flanged mace hung from the man's belt, pulling the leather down a bit under his waist. How had she not heard him coming up the stairs? She held her breath. If the man looked down her way, she would be discovered. She didn't bother waiting to test her luck. Instead, she stealthily slipped back out the way she came, and disappeared into the night as easily as a shadow.

*****

Al and Erik entered Buktah from the southern gate and directed their horses through the streets. People looked up from the street and parted when they saw the two on horseback.

"Seems different," Erik commented quietly.

Al nodded. "Things are always different in Buktah, that's one of the reasons I set up shop here. If you are gone for a week, you can miss the whole transformation."

"Still smells like spices and sweat though," Erik said dryly.

Al smirked. "Yeah, that doesn't really change, until winter time," he said. "Even then the spices just increase with the mulled wines they sell along the streets and the cinnamon cakes. The sweat is still there though." Al pulled his horse in close to Erik. "I forgot to mention, but Master Lepkin's sword only bursts into flame for him, so let's try to keep things quiet while we are here."

Erik glanced down to the cold, black Telarian steel. "No, I have used it before without problems," Erik corrected.

Al raised his bushy eyebrow and tugged gently at his beard. "When?" he asked.

"When the wizard attacked Valtuu Temple. I used the flaming sword to slay him."

"Marlin failed to mention that," Al noted with a wide eyed nod and a frown. "Anything else you want to tell me before we get to the senate's tribunal?"

Erik shrugged. "Not really," he replied.

"Well, just don't try to turn into a dragon."

"Why would I do that?" Erik asked.

"Just saying in case you get any crazy ideas since you can apparently use his sword just fine, and you are in Lepkin's body after all." Al shot him a playful wink and then held a finger to his lips as if they were hiding a big secret.

Erik laughed it off and kept his eyes on the road.

They passed by the Rosewood, the Midnight Traveler, and the Spotted Owl Inn. Erik smiled when he saw the old, plain sign with the word "Inn" etched into its side. "This is it," Erik said.

"I know the way to my own shop," Al quipped.

"I..." Erik started to apologize, but something in Al's demeanor stopped him. "What is it?"

Al did a double take over his shoulder before jumping down from his horse. He looked up to Erik and held a finger to his mouth, signaling the boy to remain silent. This time Al was not playing. Erik nodded his understanding and dismounted. He followed Al through the narrow alleyway, turning his body sideways to fit between the buildings. Al slowed his pace as he neared the opening. He held his left hand out, motioning for Erik to halt. All at once there was a heavy scent of burnt wood and something almost metallic in the air.

Al's head dropped down and he let out a long sigh. "Oh laddie, what have you done?"

Erik turned his head to look at the street they had just left. Something gray flashed across his field of vision. He reached out with his right hand to tap Al on the shoulder, but his hand found nothing. He turned back to see that Al was gone. A knot formed in his stomach. A bottle skittered into the alleyway from behind. He turned back, pulling Lepkin's sword from its sheath, but no one was there.

Erik decided that if there was danger, he would be better served in a larger area. The alley was too tight for him to maneuver, and Al was no longer near. He bolted out from the alley to see a smoldering heap of charred lumber around a large, stone kiln. Some of the embers still burned.

Someone had burned Al's shop to the ground.

"Al?!" Erik yelled.

"Keep yer voice down, beanpole!" Al growled. Erik wheeled around to see Al kneeling over his old apprentice.

Erik rushed to Al's side. "Is he?"

Al nodded. "He is alive, but not faring well," the dwarf said soberly.

"We should get him out of here," Erik said in a whisper.

Al shook his head. "It's too late for that."

Erik looked at Al curiously and only upon closer inspection did he notice Al's hammer nestled neatly in his lap with his left hand near for quick access. The apprentice moaned, drawing Erik's attention and showing him that he held one of Al's daggers. Erik realized that something was about to crash down around them.

He slowly rose to his feet, adjusted his grip on Lepkin's sword, and let his anger flow into the weapon. "Well then," Erik said with a nod. "What shall I do?"

"Two on the roof, one behind the burnt shop," Al said softly.

"There were four," the apprentice said.

"I saw him at the other side of the alley," Erik said.

"The Blacktongues will come at us in a matter of moments," Al said. He looked down to his apprentice. "You need to keep yourself out of the way, boy."

"I'm no boy," the apprentice said with a forced grin. He struggled to sit up and locked eyes with Al for a moment. "Give 'em hell," he said.

Erik heard a creak behind him. Instinctively he somersaulted to the left while Al grabbed his apprentice and dashed for an outhouse just a couple of yards away. A pair of throwing knives whistled as they flew harmlessly by. Al's apprentice screamed in agony as his twisted, broken leg dragged raggedly through the dirt and grass until Al plopped him behind the outhouse. The dwarf took only enough time to prop his apprentice's back against the wooden structure before looking back to Erik. He pointed to Erik and signaled that he would go for the roof and Erik should head for the assassin behind the burnt shop.

Erik nodded and jumped to his feet. His eyes scanned the smoldering heap for any sign of movement. A man emerged from behind the kiln. He was already in a dead sprint, coming at Erik hard. Erik saw Al bounding for the alleyway as fast as his stubby legs would carry him. Erik would have to deal with this Blacktongue alone.

Erik raised Lepkin's sword into a high guard. The Blacktongue readied a war axe in his left hand and continued his charge. Erik's heart pounded in his chest. He tried to count how many steps the Blacktongue would need, but the man moved too quickly. Erik was forced to parry and dive to the side as the Blacktongue slashed at his side with the axe. Luck, more than skill, gave Erik just enough clearance to dodge the strike. As good as his training had been with Master Lepkin, Erik was unaccustomed to fighting in an adult body.

He was about to experience the steepest learning curve of his life.

Before he could turn around he heard the apprentice shout a warning. Erik instinctively thrust his sword backward, over his left shoulder. The sword shook violently as the blade scraped against something hard. Erik spun under his thrust, maintaining contact with his foe and stepping out far enough to avoid the dagger strike that followed the Blacktongue's axe.

The Blacktongue struck out with a savage kick to Erik's ribs, knocking him a few inches to the side. Erik was surprised by the small man's strength, but he recovered quickly. He lunged forward with an offensive of his own. He slashed his sword down in a quick chop to drive the Blacktongue back. Then he double-stepped forward for momentum before launching a forward snap kick to the Blacktongue's chest. He connected solidly, sending the wiry man back a couple of feet, but the assassin retained his footing.

When Erik's foot came back to the ground he felt a burning sting in his leg a few inches below his knee. He looked down quickly to see a small rip in his pants over the side of his calf. He looked up and saw a tint of red lining the Blacktongue's dagger.

The Blacktongue drew his thin lips into a crooked, toothy smile and whirled his axe around his left hand. "The legend of Lepkin ends today," he promised. "Tomorrow we will put down his rabid orphan dog too."

Erik felt rage boil up within him. A flash of Timon's purple, broken hand came to his mind, warning him to control his anger. He shook his head. This was not the time to bridle his emotions. The Blacktongue embodied evil and was bent on destroying everything Erik held dear. While he knew he would have to control his anger just enough to maintain control over his thoughts, he welcomed the rage. Anything to give him an edge over this foe.

The Blacktongue charged forward again. Erik resumed his high guard, allowing his anger to flow and course into Lepkin's blade. Flames leapt out from the hilt and ignited the black Telarian steel. Erik let out a yell, summoning his wrath to the surface.

The two clashed as Erik deftly parried the first strike of the axe with Lepkin's flaming sword and kicked away a low stab attempt with a dagger. Erik held the sword in his left hand and caught the Blacktongue in the jaw with a savage right hook. Erik heard something pop and snap. The Blacktongue's chin seemed to dislodge and come forward under the skin while the back of the jaw drooped down.

The assassin reeled back, but he was undaunted. He threw the dagger, but his aim was wild and it only glanced off of Erik's shoulder with the side of the handle. The move might have made Erik stumble back, but in his enraged state it seemed to him barely more than a fly buzzing onto his skin. He pressed forward, not giving the assassin a chance to regroup.

Down came the flaming sword. The assassin blocked it with his axe and the two found themselves struggling against each other.

The Blacktongue reached up with his free hand to keep Erik from bringing the flaming sword down upon him. Erik lashed out with a pair of quick kicks at the assassin's shins. The Blacktongue grimaced and grunted, but he did not stumble.

"Behind you!" the apprentice shouted out.

Erik disentangled himself from his foe and spun out to the right. The fourth Blacktongue had come out of the alley and his sword missed Erik by a hair's breadth as he thrust the blade into the now empty air that Erik had just occupied.

Erik lunged forward, bashing his shoulder into the newcomer and slicing the man's forearm with the flaming sword. The new Blacktongue screamed horribly as his arm fell to the ground, still holding his sword.

The axe-wielding Blacktongue came to his comrade's rescue, but Erik had expected as much. Erik quickly pivoted on his back foot, and with a flick of his wrist positioned his sword tip directly in front of the charging axe-man. The Blacktongue's eyes shot open wide as he ran directly into the flaming point.

Erik withdrew the blade and finished both foes with a strong, sideways chop at neck level. The two bodies fell lifelessly to the ground. Erik looked up just in time to see another body falling from the roof of the inn.

"Three down," Erik muttered to himself. He couldn't see Al, but he could hear his heavy feet pounding and punishing the wooden roof as he battled the last Blacktongue. Erik studied the back of the building for a moment. There was a four-pane window next to the rear door. Above that was a small window with iron bars crossing the glass. It would be difficult, but it was just close enough to the gutter that it might provide Erik a quick ascent.

He quickly moved the sword toward the scabbard. As he did so, the flames extinguished themselves and the metal was miraculously cool. He bolted across the grass, ran up the side of the wall, launching himself upward from the window sill. He reached up with both arms and latched onto the iron bars on the window higher up the wall and pulled himself up to the gutter. He found himself mentally thanking Lepkin for all the pull-ups he was assigned in the past. He had done so many that pulling himself up and over the gutter was almost second nature to him, despite the fact he was in Lepkin's body.

He scrambled to his feet and saw Al somersault between the Blacktongue's legs, punching up into the assassin's groin with his hammer as he went. The assassin stiffened onto his toes and jumped into the air slightly. Erik rushed forward, pulling a knife from his belt and tackling the assassin from behind. The two of them flew over the roof's apex, slamming hard into the old, cracking cedar shingles, knocking many of them loose as they tumbled over each other.

Erik slashed the assassin across the chest and then brought the dagger down into the assassin's left shoulder. The Blacktongue growled and struggled to move his weapon into play, but Erik was stronger. He pinned the man down, holding one wrist to the roof, and disabling the Blacktongue's other arm with a few more quick stabs.

"Who sent you?" Erik asked.

"Don't waste time talking, just finish him!" Al yelled out.

Erik didn't take his eyes off the assassin, but he didn't move to slay him either. He wanted answers. "Who sent you?" he repeated.

A pain ripped through his left thigh. He recoiled reflexively and the Blacktongue wormed out from under him just enough to bring his knife to bear. He slashed out at Erik, but Erik managed to deflect the attack with his thick leather bracer and roll out of the way. The roof shook violently with every move he made. Shingles tore loose from their place and cascaded out over the edge, threatening to trip Erik and send him crashing down to the street below.

The assassin was back on his feet and pulled a long, slender instrument from a peculiar sheath on the side of his leg. He flicked his wrist and sent the steel dart arcing straight at Erik. Erik ducked and shifted his weight to the left. The roof creaked and groaned under his weight and started to crack. Erik could feel his footing giving way, so he jumped farther back to increase the distance between him and the Blacktongue, who was already advancing quickly.

He landed on shingles that held only for a moment before slipping out from under his foot. Erik lost his balance and crashed down to the roof, sliding down and over the gutter. He reached up with his left hand and grabbed hold just in time to avoid falling to the street below. A series of gasps and shouts erupted below him as people in the street spotted the action.

The Blacktongue leapt through the air, knife glinting in the sunlight as the assassin deftly turned it over in his palm, preparing to bring the blade down into Erik's skull. Erik knew he had two choices. He could drop to the street below, likely breaking one of his legs, or he could allow the Blacktongue to end everything.

A hammer spun into view and crashed into the Blacktongue's skull with such force that the assassin's trajectory was altered. The Blacktongue's eyes glazed over and he spun head over heels to the ground below, crashing in a sickening lump on the cobblestone. Erik froze, staring at the dead Blacktongue below.

"I had him all locked up," Al grumbled from above.

Erik looked up to see the dwarf scooting on his rump to the side of the roof. Al planted his sturdy boots in the gutter and reached a hand out for Erik. "Sorry, I thought I could get some information out of him." He jerked up and reached out to grab Al's hand. The dwarf heaved him up and dropped Erik on the roof beside him. Then he patted him on the back.

"Still," Al started. "That was a good hit. Had you not tried to interrogate him you would have won."

Erik reached down and rubbed his thigh. He pulled his hand back when he felt the warm liquid. "What did he hit me with?" Erik asked.

"He had a hidden blade in a sheath next to his knee. It's fairly common among Blacktongues. They can activate them with their feet somehow, and then it helps them get out of tight encounters."

"I should have listened to you," Erik said

Al nodded. "Yes, you should. You should also be more careful. That isn't your body you are flingin' around on rooftops." Erik chuckled a bit at that and went to the back of the roof. Al called out to him. "Seein' as how I saved yer butt, how about you go down and get my hammer before someone takes it? I'll go back and see to my apprentice."

Erik stopped and shrugged. "Sounds fair," Erik said. Going down was definitely more difficult than climbing up had been. Furthermore, a crowd of rough looking men had gathered around the body on the ground below. None of them said anything to him as he walked toward the corpse and retrieved Al's hammer.

Erik nodded to a nearby gawker, and walked back toward the alleyway.

"Hold, there!" someone shouted. Erik felt a chill run down his spine. He turned slowly, maneuvering the hammer in his hand, readying himself for another fight. He saw a pair of men walking toward him. They were each dressed in yellow tunics that covered all but their chainmail sleeves. The closer of the two wore an open-faced steel helmet with a red plume sticking out from the top. He looked at the body on the street and then up to Erik.

"Blacktongue," the man said to the other.

The other guard nodded. "What happened here?" he asked Erik.

"We were attacked by several of them," Erik said, motioning to the dead man at his feet. "We acted in self-defense."

A commotion sprang up through the crowd behind Erik. A couple of men shouted and grumbled as they tripped backward. Erik turned to see Al barreling through the crowd to get to him. "Captain Rufus," Al started. "Don't you know who you are addressing?"

The man with the plumed helmet looked to his partner and then back to Al. "I might have known you were behind this, dwarf," Captain Rufus said.

"Bah," Al huffed with a wave of his meaty hand just a moment before swiping his hammer back from Erik. "Say what you will about me, beanpole, but you watch your tongue while you are in the presence of Master Lepkin," Al thumbed at Erik.

Erik turned his hip slightly so Captain Rufus could see the sword hanging from his belt. Erik saw Captain Rufus' eyes flash wide in surprise for a moment before he quickly regained composure.

"It makes no difference," Captain Rufus said. "We are responding to reports of a burned building and open violence in the streets. We will have to take you in."

Al laughed. "A little late for my shop," he said. "Seems to me you were a little slow in attending to your duties."

"Watch yourself, dwarf," Captain Rufus said.

Erik could see that the other guard was watching everyone carefully. It occurred to him that perhaps the other guard was not as set against them as Captain Rufus was. He decided to play his hand at acting as Lepkin would. Erik folded his arms across his chest, cleared his throat, and glanced from the guard to Captain Rufus. "If you wish to take us in, you may try, but I doubt you will fare any better than the assassins who tried to ambush us while we were peacefully going about our business."

Captain Rufus' face reddened. "Peacefully?" he shot back. "Four men are dead!"

"Interesting," Erik said as he turned a sidelong glance to Al. "There is only one body here, how do you think Captain Rufus is counting up bodies?"

Al nodded and snorted. "Either his math is lousy, or perhaps he threw in with the others."

Captain Rufus bristled. "Arrest them," he ordered his partner.

Erik looked to the other guard, and carefully examined the confused expression on the man's face. "This one is innocent," Erik told Al. "But Rufus here has made a deal with the wrong side."

"I have done no such thing!" Captain Rufus shouted. He looked back to his partner. "I told you to arrest them."

The guard turned and regarded Captain Rufus curiously. "Sir, how did you know there were three others? You only told me that there was a fight and someone had burnt the blacksmith shop."

"I don't need to tell you all the details!" Captain Rufus shouted. "Arrest them, or I will have you court martialed."

The guard stood tall and backed away from Captain Rufus. "I asked you how many were involved, and you had told me you didn't know."

Captain Rufus gripped his sword so tight his knuckles blanched. "This is ludicrous."

Erik turned to the crowd. "Time for everyone to leave. Any man still here after I count to three will be presumed to be with the Blacktongues, and I will not stay my hand from bringing forth justice."

"You have no right to presume such authority," Captain Rufus bellowed. "Fifty gold as a reward to any who help me apprehend these vigilantes."

"I am the Keeper of Secrets, appointed as the dragons' representative to the king. I *do* have the authority to denounce traitors to the crown."

"Well played," Al whispered to Erik.

"I am no traitor!" Captain Rufus shouted.

"I am answering a summons from the senate. I was ambushed by these men. If you have thrown in with them, then you most certainly are a traitor. Stand down, or I shall cut you down." Erik drew his sword and the black blade responded with roaring flames across its surface.

The guard drew his sword as well and turned to the crowd. "Disperse, by order of the guard!"

Captain Rufus sneered. "You have sealed your fate, dragon lover."

Tumult rippled through the crowd. Some tried to scramble away while others struggled to get closer. Remembering his training with Marlin, Erik called upon his powers to identify friends and foes. He side stepped closer to Al. "You deal with Rufus, I will handle the crowd. Not all of them are against us."

"Better I handle the crowd, your flaming sword can do a lot more damage than my hammer," Al replied.

Neither got the chance to move before a loud crack of thunder ripped through the air, sending most of the people to the ground. Al and Erik managed to keep their balance by leaning into each other.

Erik looked around and saw a thin, wiry man with a long, narrow chin underneath a pointy nose step out from the doorway to the inn behind them. His leathery lips stretched into a wicked sneer across his face.

"Master Lepkin, it is an honor," the man said in a nasal voice. Erik noticed the necklace hanging around the man's neck. A golden triangle around an open eye. It matched Tukai's necklace.

"Warlock," Erik said simply.

"Now!" Captain Rufus shouted from behind. Al barreled into Erik, knocking him several yards away as a flurry of arrows glinted off the stone road. Men shouted and screamed as a few were caught with arrows, and others tried to scramble out of the killing zone.

"Rooftop!" Al shouted. Erik looked up and saw numerous men armed with bows.

"Go for the warlock," Erik said. He then turned quickly and sprinted for Captain Rufus. "Traitor!" he shouted. He brought his flaming sword down and it cut through Captain Rufus, chainmail and all, as though the man were a bundle of kindling.

Arrows zinged by him, narrowly missing him while he dealt with a couple of poorly trained mercenaries that advanced on him as the remaining gawkers dispersed. Erik felt a sting as one arrow grazed the back of his right shoulder. He somersaulted away as a pair of arrows sailed right through the space where he had been standing and sank into another mercenary that had been charging at him from behind.

Erik looked up and saw Al throw his hammer at the warlock. The hammer stopped short of the man's face. Caught in a spell, it hung in the air and harmlessly continued to spin. The warlock waved his other hand and Al went flying through the air to crash into a wooden barrel on the other side of the street. The wood splintered and the iron bands snapped as Al's body blasted through the barrel. Water burst out and spread quickly over the road.

Erik took to his feet and rushed the warlock.

"I will enjoy this," the warlock promised. The thin man pointed a finger at Erik. A bolt of purple lightning leapt out through the air. Erik cut through the magic assault with his flaming sword and kept charging.

"You will have to do better than that," Erik growled as he leapt through the air. He swung his sword to the left, aiming for the warlock's chest. The warlock simply raised an eyebrow and disappeared. Erik's sword sliced through the doorway and scorched the inn's wall.

"Over here," the warlock taunted from the end of the alleyway.

Erik was about to charge again when he caught a glimpse of motion out of the corner of his eye. He jumped inside the open doorway and rolled to the left. Arrows twanged into the wall and floor nearby, their shafts still quivering for a few seconds after the heads had bitten into the wood. Erik sighed and jumped up to his feet. He peered out the doorway and ducked back as another pair of arrows flew at his face. One missed, but the other sliced his left cheek. He stumbled back in shock and put his back to the wall. He looked around the room he was in for the first time and saw several people cowering under chairs or behind overturned tables.

"There is a rear exit," a plump lady called out to him from one of the tables. "You can get away through there." She pointed her flabby arm to the back hallway.

Erik nodded, but he couldn't bring himself to run. Al was still out front; he had to find him. He inched closer to the doorway and took in a series of deep breaths.

The warlock appeared in front of him and flashed a dagger at Erik's throat. Erik reflexively dropped to the ground and struck out with his sword. The warlock disappeared again before his blade could connect.

Erik knew he would have to move or he would be killed. He ran forward and grabbed a chair, then he turned and sprinted for the window to the right of the door. He threw the chair through the glass, sending shards of razor sharp glass out to the street. Then he dove through, covering his face with his arms and tucking into a roll when he hit the ground. As he rolled away he searched for the warlock. He spotted him appearing and disappearing around Al, who was frantically trying to lash out with a long knife as the warlock materialized.

The other guard had taken an arrow to the knee, but was still managing to fight off the few mercenaries still in the battle. Erik rose to his feet, quickly analyzing the warlock's pattern, and then let his sword fly through the air at the next spot he figured the warlock would appear. To Erik's dismay, his sword sailed through empty air and crashed into a building a few yards away from Al. Al jumped and looked back to Erik. The dwarf's mouth dropped open and he pointed frantically. Erik turned to see the sneering warlock behind him.

"Now you have no weapon," the thin man said. He raised his arm, but the purple lightning fizzled off his finger and fell to the ground like a worm shriveling in the hot sun. The warlock lurched forward, his jaw slack.

Erik didn't know what was happening, but he didn't wait for an explanation. He lashed out with a savage right hook that whipped the warlock's face to the left and spun the man's whole body to the ground. Only then did Erik see the pair of arrows protruding from the warlock's back. Erik looked up and saw Al's apprentice in the alleyway. He was propped up on his good leg and holding a dual action crossbow.

Erik saluted his thanks and then turned to dash across the

street. He slammed up against the wall where Al was crouched. Al held out Erik's sword.

"You really shouldn't throw this weapon around," Al scolded.

"You're welcome," Erik replied sourly as he took the weapon back. Something thumped into the wall next to them. Erik peered over Al and saw the wounded guard.

"This is not how I thought I would be spending my day," the guard said.

Erik nodded. "How many are still on rooftop?" he asked.

The guard shrugged. "Six or seven, I think."

"How are we going to get to them?" Al asked. "They have us pinned down pretty good, and we are out of allies."

Just then Al's apprentice hobbled into the street and let fly a pair of arrows.

"How did he find that?" Al asked.

A body fell from above and slammed into the stone road in front of them. A bow followed a couple of seconds later and landed on top of the body. Erik rushed out, grabbed it, and ripped the quiver from the dead Blacktongue's body. He furiously strung an arrow and wheeled around to let fly at the first foe he could find. His arrow struck true and slew another enemy.

Al bounded past Erik, somersaulting halfway through the street. As the dwarf spun up he turned around and let his hammer fly. The weapon sailed end over end and slammed into a Blacktongue's skull.

Erik grabbed another arrow and strung it as he back pedaled quickly to avoid the onslaught of arrows coming at him. He fired again, but this time he missed. Another pair of arrows sailed over Erik's head from behind and down went two more Blacktongues.

Three Blacktongues remained. Erik set another arrow to the string and took careful aim as the foes ran across the rooftops.

"Looks like we have them on the run!" Erik shouted. He jogged out to get a better angle just as two of the Blacktongues turned and fired their bows. Erik dove to the side, but the arrows were nowhere close to him. He heard something fall to the ground behind him.

"No, laddie!" Al shouted.

Erik turned to see Al's apprentice lying in the street, wheezing and struggling for breath. Al rushed over and scooped up the crossbow. He worked the contraption furiously, loosing more than eight bolts in a matter of seconds. Erik gave a glance to Al's apprentice before turning back to add his support to Al's shots, but by the time he put another arrow to the string, all of the Blacktongues had several arrows protruding from their bodies.

It was over.

Erik dropped his bow and ran to Al.

"You got anything to stop the bleeding?" Al shouted to the wounded guard.

Erik dropped onto his knees and frantically searched for something to help. Al's apprentice twitched and arched his back as he coughed.

"The arrows have pierced his lungs," the wounded guard said.

"Well, don't just sit there, do something," Al shouted back.

The guard shook his head. "There is nothing to be done," he said soberly.

"Sorry, Al," his apprentice said.

"No, you can't die, boy. I haven't given you permission to do that. There is still work to be done!"

The apprentice forced a chuckle. "The shop is gone, there ain't no work. Not anymore."

"Don't argue with me, laddie, it ain't proper. We have plenty of work rebuilding the shop."

"This is one argument I think I am going to win," his apprentice shot back. He coughed again and jerked to the side. His eyes flinched a few times. "It was a pleasure to work with you, ya old grouch," he jested.

"You were a fine apprentice," Al replied.

"A compliment?" his apprentice coughed. "You feeling all right?"

Al chuckled a bit and wiped a tear from his eye. Then his apprentice jerked up and coughed for the final time before settling back down to rest. Al shook him and gently slapped his face. "No, laddie, don't go."

The guard put a hand on Erik's shoulder and motioned for him to back away.

Al dropped his head. "No."

Erik sighed and bowed his head. "He gave his life saving ours," Erik offered. "He was a good man."

Al remained silent.

Erik rose to his feet and turned back to the guard. "I trust you will see to his burial?"

Al stood up and turned around. Erik watched the dwarf for a minute, as it looked like he was going to say something, but then Al looked off in the distance. Erik turned to glance in the direction Al had been staring, but didn't see anything.

"*I* will see to his burial," Al growled, calling Erik's attention back to him.

"We don't have time for that," Erik said. Al shot him a threatening look, but Erik held his ground. "We were only supposed to stop for a few minutes to pick up some items. We have already lost much time."

"Can you notify his mother?" Al asked the guard, ignoring Erik entirely.

The guard nodded.

"Have you forgotten about the summons?" Erik interjected. The words came out a lot harsher than he had meant them.

Al jumped to his feet and glowered at Erik. "Have you forgotten your humanity?" He pointed down to his apprentice. "He just saved us, and you would cast him off as quickly as the others lying in the dirt here. Where is your heart?"

Al's words stung deep. The shame welled up inside Erik's heart, yet he was unable to shake the feeling of urgency. He knew, and even agreed, that Al's apprentice deserved a proper burial, but that would take time. Time to gather the family. Time to prepare the gravesite. Time to prepare the body and the casket. A proper funeral demanded a lot of time. It was time they simply didn't have,

"We don't have the time, Al," Erik said after a few moments.

Al's face turned sour and the dwarf looked away from Erik. It was subtle, but Erik noticed that Al's eyes went back to the same place he had stared at moments before, and then they looked back to Erik and Al shook his head..

The sound of hoof beats alerted them all to a troop of guards coming toward them.

"I will handle this," the wounded guard said. He stretched a hand out to Erik for some help and struggled to his feet. "They will be able to help us with cleaning the street. They can also see to it that your friend gets a proper burial," he put in.

Al nodded and walked back to the alleyway.

Erik patted the guard's back. "Thank you, for everything."

The guard nodded, but he said nothing and averted his eyes from Erik's.

Erik then followed after Al. He saw the dwarf leaning against the side of the inn with his face buried in the crook of his elbow. Erik wasn't sure what to say, so he went up and put his hand on Al's left shoulder.

Al wheeled around and socked Erik in the gut so hard that Erik doubled over and struggled for breath. Al then reached up and seized Erik's throat with one of his meaty hands and pulled Erik's eyes within a hair's breadth of his own.

"You may be in Lepkin's body, but you are not him!" Al growled. "How dare you order me around? Do you have any idea that other people have lives that don't revolve around you?" Al jerked Erik's head to the side. "Look at Garen's body." Al twisted his wrist enough to ensure Erik was looking directly at the dead apprentice. "He was the closest thing to a son I have ever known."

Erik tried to wrestle free, but Al's grip was like being stuck between two unmovable boulders. "Let me go," Erik said.

"I have known his family for over a century. I have seen them develop into some of the finest people to ever walk this land. He selflessly gave his life for us, and you would be rid of him like a dead rat in the street!" Al tossed Erik back to slam into the wall behind him. "I would walk through hellfire for Lepkin, but you will have to regain my respect."

Erik gasped for air and put his hands on his knees. "I didn't mean…" he started to say between gasps.

Al shut him up with a swift, stinging, backhanded slap. "When you rushed off to save your family, I stood by your side. I stand by you still. I demand the same in return."

Erik nodded. "I will go and help the guards prepare the grave, but then I will go north. The summons will not wait for the funeral."

Al turned his back on him. "Well then get on with it."

CHAPTER TEN

Senator Bracken placed his gold ring onto his left index finger and twisted it until it rested comfortably. "Have the others been assembled?" he asked his servant.

"Yes, sir, the others have assembled in the audience hall and are waiting for you," the servant responded.

"Very well, thank you," Senator Bracken said. His servant bowed deeply and backed out through the open doorway, pulling the door closed after him. Senator Bracken looked into the mirror and straightened his thinning hair over his scalp.

The image in the mirror distorted and faded away, replaced by a darkness that swirled inside the pane of glass.

"Are we alone?" a voice from within the mirror called.

Senator Bracken bowed his head. "We are," he replied. Senator Bracken raised his arm and in response the thick, iron bolt scraped shut across the door, locking out any would-be intruders. "What is your command?"

The darkness parted as if a wind had blown a hole through a hazy, black fog. Deep inside the glass a crimson, scaly face peered back at him. The dragon's fangs hung low, sharp and menacing over his lower jaw. His mouth did not part, but rather his voice was heard inside Senator Bracken's head telepathically. "Did your plan succeed?" the dragon asked.

"Yes, Master Tu'luh, the strategy worked. Lord Cedreau has been killed, and Lord Lokton has been arrested for treason. Lord Lokton has refused to join with me, as I expected, and he will not survive his tribunal."

"Are you certain that Lepkin will come to the trial?"

"Of course," Bracken said slyly. "If he does not, then he will lose his authority and the king will be forced to denounce him. Unfortunately for Lepkin, he will miss the tribunal. I have secured the votes needed to expedite the trial."

"It is vital that Lepkin be separated from the boy," the dragon cautioned.

Senator Bracken nodded. "I know," he said. "I am certain that after the recent battles, they will keep the boy at the temple. Lepkin will feel pressured to continue the boy's training and will come to the trial alone."

"You have foreseen this?" Tu'luh asked.

Senator Bracken nodded. "I have seen it. Lepkin will come to the tribunal without Erik. Sometimes I see him with the dwarf, but I do not see him with the boy."

"Do not fail me," Tu'luh warned. "We will only get one chance at this."

"Have faith," Senator Bracken said. "Everything I have foreseen has come to pass. Two noble houses are ruined and at each other's throats, Lokton's trial will draw Lepkin away from Erik, and then we will spring the trap."

"What of Erthor? He was as confident as you are now, and look what it got him," Tu'luh hissed.

"Erthor was impatient and arrogant. He had neither the ability to foretell the future, nor the patience to work with me when I cautioned him against a premature attack on the temple." Senator Bracken sighed. "He was foolish to attack while Dimwater, Lepkin, and Erik stood united."

"Be careful that you do not fall into a similar trap," Tu'luh warned.

"I have taken additional precautions," Senator Bracken replied. "I have enlisted another warlock, and some assassins to throw at Lepkin along his journey."

"Do not think him so easy to destroy," Tu'luh said. "He is dragon born, chosen for his abilities."

"I understand," Bracken said. "Even if all it does is slow him down, it may be enough. The tribunal will be concluded a day earlier than Lepkin expects it to begin." Bracken ran a hand over his hair, smoothing it back. "I have also spoken with Master Wizard Gilifan. He is aware of my plans and concurs that it should accomplish our goals."

Tu'luh hissed. "I will contact you again shortly," Tu'luh said suddenly. The great dragon turned his head to look somewhere that Bracken could not see.

Bracken nodded. "I will stand by my scrying pool at my home after I am done here. When will you make yourself known?" Bracken asked.

"The time is close, but not yet. I will reveal myself and strike only when the time is right." The mirror went dark again for a moment before clearing to reflect Bracken's image.

Senator Bracken stood silently, contemplating Tu'luh's words. He reconsidered his plans, checking them for weaknesses. He had not told Tu'luh that it had actually been Erik who had killed Erthor. Nor did he tell him that Lepkin had appeared to be unconscious after the battle was over. Senator Bracken had killed the Blacktongue who had returned from the battle. Normally, he tried not to waste the lives of those that had committed to his cause, but on occasion, it was difficult to keep his wrath in check. This particular Blacktongue fell victim to Senator Bracken's anger partly because Erthor had failed to even locate the book, let alone deal with the boy, but also out of frustration that the boy's power had seemed to make a quantum leap beyond what any of the warlocks had foreseen or thought possible.

He was beginning to question whether his order would succeed. Still, he was too close to turn back now. He waved a hand over the mirror and a new image formed from a silvery mist. Rounded, high cheekbones framed by fiery red hair greeted him from behind smiling, full lips. Dark, chocolate eyes twinkled as they connected with his.

"Kyra," Bracken whispered to the mirror. He stepped close and put a hand on the glass. The beautiful face in the mirror continued to smile, but remained silent. Then the image shifted, showing Kyra walking through a flower garden with a baby in her arms and a toddler tugging at the back of her skirt. Bracken called out to them through the mirror, but none of them heard him. They were only mirages, illusions of a long lost memory. A tear slid down Bracken's face and he waved the image away.

"You had better be able to deliver on your promise, Master Wizard Gilifan," Bracken said aloud. The necromancer had promised to restore what was lost, what had been taken from Bracken those decades ago. The additional rewards for the help of his order, the lure of an immortal life with infinite slaves to serve

115

him were enticing as well, but they couldn't hold a candle to the longing he felt to hold his beloved Kyra once more.

He walked to a nearby desk and pulled a folded parchment from a drawer. Upon opening it he examined the writing therein before he exited his writing chamber and walked down the long, broad hallway. He passed by white marble columns and bronze busts of senators past. Their eyes looked down upon him from their granite pedestals. He paid them no mind. He knew that most of them were no better during their lifetimes than he was, they simply lacked the power and the foresight to go after the kind of prize he sought.

The hallway opened into a large ante chamber. Mahogany benches lined the walls, and sat at the base of each gigantic, fluted column that held up the high, vaulted ceilings. Frescoes accented the walls, giving life to the history and myth of the kingdom. A couple of middle aged women mopped the gray floor near the grand entrance that allowed commoners access to this antechamber. In days past, many had come to congregate while the senate convened to discuss matters of state. Now the benches were empty.

Senator Bracken made his way across the chamber to the bronzed doors of the senate chamber. The two sentinel guards nodded respectfully upon his approach and turned to open the great doors. As they did so, a grand light poured into the antechamber with dazzling colors. Bracken looked up to the stained glass window that stood above the pulpit upon the dais. The symbol of Hiasyntar'Kulai, a large golden dragon known to men as the Father of the Ancients, was fixed forever in the window to remind the senate of their heritage, as the Ancients had helped men establish themselves in the Middle Kingdom. Bracken could only view the image as a mockery of men, however. He had called upon the Ancients, and had once been a devout follower of their ways, but they had let him down. They had failed everyone..

He grimaced sourly at the window. The sight of the ancient dragon's image annoyed him. He entered the hall and went to the left to a smaller, maplewood door. He opened the portal and walked into the narrow hallway that allowed him access to his seat, which was fixed inside a balcony raised above the floor of the senate hall.

"Ah, Senator Bracken," someone called out. "I was waiting to see you."

Bracken turned to see Senator Stigs. "Senator, how are you today," Bracken greeted with a warm smile.

"I am well," Stigs replied. "Have you given any consideration to my proposal?"

Bracken nodded. "I have, actually. It looks intriguing. We can discuss it at the banquet next week," Bracken promised.

Stigs smiled, nodded, and raised a goblet in thanks before taking a drink and turning back to a young woman who shared his balcony.

Bracken quickened his pace, paying only as much attention to the others as proper etiquette required. He was adept at hiding his contempt for people and making them like him. Had he not become a warlock, he might have made a good politician in his own right.

He parted the red velvet curtain to his balcony and found another man sitting in his chair. "Senator Mickelson," Bracken guessed. "To what do I owe the pleasure?"

The young, dark haired man turned, holding a charter in his hand. He reached forward and gripped Bracken's outstretched right hand and gave it a solid shake. Bracken could feel the young man's strength through the greeting, which was obviously Mickelson's intent. Mickelson gave a final squeeze to drive the point home before releasing his grip.

"I was just reading the rules regarding tribunals," Mickelson said. "I was wondering why we are being gathered together before the requisite senators have been able to respond to the summons."

"We have a quorum," Bracken replied soberly. "There is nothing in the charter that denies the senate a hearing before the tribunal."

"Interesting," Mickelson said with a huff. He dropped the charter on Bracken's seat and started to walk out, but he stopped just next to Senator Bracken.

Bracken readied his left hand, just in case Mickelson tried to get physical.

Mickelson looked into Bracken's eyes. "I won't let you reach a verdict before the tribunal. Crimes of treason must be handled appropriately. That includes waiting for *everyone* to answer the

117

summons."

Bracken sneered. "You speak of Lepkin," he guessed. "His presence will mean little once I show the senate the evidence against Trenton Lokton. Perhaps you should look to the future. The traditions of the past are fading."

"Not while I am here," Mickelson promised. He leaned in close and dropped his voice to a whisper. "It is the corruption of the past that is fading. There are those among us that wish to see truth and honor triumph over the greed and selfishness that plagues the senators of last generation."

"Be careful, Mickelson," Bracken warned. "Such taunts and insults are not well tolerated. Men have been known to disappear for such words."

"Is that a threat?" Mickelson asked.

"It is a fact," Bracken replied. "Now run along to your seat, we are about to start the pre-tribunal hearing."

Mickelson bristled, staring hard into Bracken's eyes for a few seconds before disgustedly storming out through the red velvet curtain.

"The righteous pride of youth," Bracken said to himself as he swept the charter to the floor and took his seat. He only had to wait for a few minutes until an old senator made his way slowly to the pulpit on the dais. It was Senator Desepp, the most senior senator.

"Welcome, brothers," the old senator said. "We have gathered together today to hear the evidence Senator Bracken will provide in the upcoming tribunal." Senator Desepp leaned on his thin, bony arms and gripped the sides of the pulpit. "As this is not an official gathering, we will dispense with the usual protocol that would normally accompany such an event."

"Objection," someone shouted from one of the balconies on the other side of the senate hall.

"Mickelson," Bracken growled to himself under his breath. How he despised the meddling young fool.

Senator Desepp looked up and strained his eyes. "What is the objection?" he asked.

"There is no basis for holding a pre-trial," Mickelson shouted. "We have only twenty-one of the thirty six senators. We also have not heard anything from Master Lepkin."

Senator Desepp held up his hand and shook his head. "We are not holding a pre-trial, Senator Mickelson," he said. "We are simply allowing Senator Bracken the opportunity to present his evidence now. This, in turn, will allow those of us present extra time to consider all of the evidence in the matter. I am sure you will agree that in matters where treason may be involved, it would be best to handle the situation delicately, and avoid rash, emotional sentences at the tribunal. We have enough of the senate body present to call a quorum. Please remain seated and silent. During the tribunal, you will be allowed to present any evidence or testimony you wish to share."

"This is an outrage!" Mickelson shouted. A couple of senators rapped their knuckles on the bannisters in front of their seats in the balconies.

"Senator Mickelson, I will ask you once more to hold your testimony until the actual tribunal. We are only presenting evidence at this time. As you are a junior senator, I will overlook this outburst. However I will not hesitate to have you escorted out from the hall if you persist to disrupt the assembly."

Mickelson sat back in his chair and held his tongue.

Bracken smiled.

Senator Desepp turned his gaze to Senator Bracken's balcony and he invited him down with a wave. "Senator Bracken, you may present your evidence at this time," Desepp said.

Senator Bracken quickly moved out from the back hallway behind his balcony to walk across the dais. The colorful light from the stained glass window behind him colored the pulpit until his shadow blocked the light's path. How fitting, he thought, for his shadow to blot out the light from the ancient dragon.

He produced the folded parchment from his robes and opened it over the pulpit. "My fellow senators, it is with a heavy heart that I present to you the official account of what has happened over the last several days." He cleared his throat and looked to a few of his allies in the senate. Each of them nodded to him when their eyes met. Then he continued. "You are all aware of Timon Cedreau's murder. He was killed shortly after the local magistrate was found dead in a cabin. I will not bore you with the details of those events, though I ask you to keep them in mind as they do hold meaning for the events I am about to describe.

"I traveled to Lokton manner to uncover the truth of these murders. I had a list of suspects, and a list of official complaints. However, nothing could have prepared me for what I found. Lord Lokton had incited war against House Cedreau, and used his own agents to murder Lord Cedreau during a parlay. These underhanded, dastardly deeds are not the end of Lokton's treachery either. When I confronted him about these crimes, his soldiers were ready and willing to assault me and my retinue. Had I not had my own body guard with me, it is likely that I would be in a shallow grave next to Lord Cedreau."

"This is ridiculous!" Mickelson shouted. "This is not proof of anything! Senator Desepp, you said testimonies must be held back until the tribunal. Are we to take this man's account as fact without allowing the accused to defend himself as the law requires?"

A few senators shouted back and forth. Bracken stepped back from the pulpit and allowed Senator Desepp to retake the position of power. The old senator slammed a stone sphere onto a metal disc on the pulpit. The arguing ceased immediately.

"Senator Mickelson, you were warned. Now, you may either remove yourself from the hall, or I will have you removed by force."

Senator Mickelson placed a hand on the bannister and vaulted over his balcony to land on the floor of the hall. "This is repulsive!" Mickelson roared. "I will leave, but I will not abide this travesty of injustice. I will petition the king to preside over the tribunal."

"Do as you will," Senator Desepp said. "Just do it outside of this hall. You are hereby expelled for a period of one month."

"You can't bar me from the tribunal!" Mickelson said.

"I have the power to expel any junior member of the senate for disobeying procedural norms."

"Procedural norms," Mickelson spat on the floor.

"The expulsion will be enforced by the sentinels," Desepp announced. He slammed the stone sphere three more times and in came a pair of sentinels. Mickelson shook himself free as they went to grab his arms.

"I will not let this stand!" Mickelson swore as he stomped out of the hall.

The sentinels slammed the bronzed doors shut after he left.

The echoes rang through the hall. Senator Desepp stepped back from the pulpit and motioned for Bracken to resume.

Senator Bracken walked back to the pulpit. "Mickelson is correct. My testimony in and of itself may not be enough proof to convince you of Trenton Lokton's guilt. However, as I arrested him and brought him back to stand trial for his crimes, I also brought back the bodies of his agents. Mr. Stilwell, and Sir Duvall were both found in the forest nearby the scene of Lord Cedreau's murder. Also found on their persons was a large coin purse filled with gold, and arrows that matched the arrow which killed Timon Cedreau, and Lord Cedreau himself. The evidence is clear to me. Lord Lokton conspired against House Cedreau, and holds contempt for the order of the kingdom. Therefore, he stands accused of treason. His actions and the wilful disobedience and animosity with which his retinue responded to me and my investigation should serve as the final point of proof. While we may not know exactly what Lord Lokton hoped to gain by removing Lord Cedreau, we all have heard of the tumult in the kingdom. Even the nobles have been jockeying for position, eager to take the throne upon our dear king's death. They circle like vultures in the sky, waiting for the old man to pass before they descend to feed upon the chaos. They presume to do away with the law and overstep their bounds.

"Lord Lokton is even viler than some of the other conspirators. At least they have the decency to wait for the king to pass! Lokton would rather remove rivals now in order to place himself closest to the throne. We cannot allow this would-be tyrant access to the throne, and we certainly must not allow him to escape justice just because he is a noble. We must send a strong, clear message to all traitors everywhere. Betray the king, and it will gain you only the edge of the executioner's blade!"

"Here, here!" Senator Stigs shouted as he rose to his feet and pounded on the bannister. Others joined him.

"We must hold the kingdom together!" another shouted. "Sentence this traitor to death and we may stop others from attempting to take the throne by force!" Others shouted, echoing the sentiment and pounding on their bannisters.

Senator Desepp walked back to the pulpit and dropped the stone sphere on the metal plate. The senators would not respond.

He tried several more times, but still they shouted for Lokton's head and pounded their bannisters.

Bracken smiled. Victory would be sweet.

Senator Desepp tapped the stone sphere on the metal disc again. "Quiet down!" he said. The senators slowly responded and came to order. "Obviously we cannot sentence a man before his trial." Senator Desepp looked back to Bracken for a moment. Their eyes met briefly, and the hint of a smile flashed across Bracken's face. Desepp turned back to the pulpit. "However, in light of the very strong evidence presented here today, perhaps we can move the tribunal up so this matter is settled as quickly as possible. The law allows for me to move the tribunal up a day earlier than the summons originally specified. However, it will require fourteen of you to vote to move it forward."

"I vote aye," Senator Stigs shouted quickly. "The faster we deal with this the better!"

Two others shouted "aye."

Another leaned forward. "I vote nay, and I dare say that Mickelson would agree with me."

"By a show of hands, who votes in favor?" Desepp asked. Seventeen hands went up.

Bracken smiled. Now only one more loose end to tie off.

*****

Senator Bracken stepped forward and raised his finger in the air. Light extended out until a small, golden orb hovered in the air above a great, pillowy silken blanket that covered the sleeping man. The man's eyes twitched slightly as the orb moved to hover directly over his snoring, bearded face.

"Judge McTeabe," Senator Bracken said calmly. "Time to wake up." Bracken snapped his fingers and Judge McTeabe rose sharply in his bed to sit upright. The fat man rubbed his eyes with sausage-like fingers and yawned, groaning against the pain of waking before the sun had brought morning.

"What," he stared through bleary, blinking eyes. "What is the meaning of this?" He shook his head and removed his green, silken night cap from his head to reveal a balding head of gray hair.

"Do you remember the conversation we had about a month

ago?" Bracken asked.

Judge McTeabe's gaze settled upon Bracken and the fat man stiffened. He slightly puffed his chest. "I have nothing to say to you, how dare you intrude upon me at this hour like some spider along the ceiling." Judge McTeabe flung his stubby legs over the side of the bed and rose to his feet, straightening his silken night shirt to cover his hairy, pale thighs.

"The life of a judge appears to suit you well," Bracken noted.

Judge McTeabe sneered back at him. "And a senator leads a pious life?" Judge McTeabe fired back. "Have you really come to discuss my lifestyle?"

Senator Bracken shook his head. "I told you that Baltezer the Brown was a simple priest, protecting his village as best he could. Yet, you went around me and had him executed."

Judge McTeabe folded his flabby arms over the top of his round belly. "Guards!" he called out. "There is an intruder!"

Bracken cackled. "They can't hear you," he said with a shrug. "They have all fallen into a deep sleep."

McTeabe's eyes widened and he glanced to his door.

"There is nowhere to run." Bracken said. "I *told* you not to interfere!"

McTeabe shook his head. "I am a judge, I do not have to listen to your commands. Only King Mathias can command my obedience."

Bracken shook his head and moved closer to the bed. "You ought to have listened to me."

"What will you do now?" McTeabe taunted. "Would you hire assassins to stab me in the back? You wouldn't dare kill me before your tribunal. You know the law. The king has the right to order a review of any senate tribunal, and *I* am the High Judge."

The senator smiled and nodded his head. "All I need to legally convict a nobleman of treason is two thirds of the senate body. I know that more than two thirds will find him guilty."

"But you forget, the king has the right to order a review of *any* tribunal. He will not stand while you take House Lokton to the ground."

Bracken sniggered. "Yes, well I don't suppose I could convince you to align your opinion with mine?"

"No," Judge McTeabe said defiantly. "I will not be bullied by you or anyone else. If the king orders a review, I will do my best to ensure that *all* proper procedures have been followed. Just like I did with Baltezer the Brown."

Bracken waved his hand. A gust of wind threw McTeabe to the ground with a heavy *thump*. The judge's belly rocked back and forth violently and a small amount of blood trickled from McTeabe's nose. "Unlike you, I do not need to *hire* underlings to do my dirty work." Bracken's face melted away to reveal his true visage. "You have not the slightest inkling who you are dealing with."

McTeabe opened his mouth to speak but another wave of wind sent his bulbous body sliding and squeaking across the red hardwood floor until he slammed into the wall.

The warlock produced a paper from thin air and sent it into McTeabe's hand. "That is your confession," he said.

"Confession of what?" McTeabe huffed.

"That letter, written by your own hand, says that you were paid by Master Lepkin to execute an order against Baltezer the Brown."

"I wrote no such letter, this is preposterous!"

"You don't think my magic can copy your handwriting?" the warlock taunted.

McTeabe shook his head. "No one will believe this, why would Lepkin pay me for something like that?"

"Because his lover, Lady Dimwater, is a shadowfiend. She was the one behind the human sacrifices. Baltezer the Brown discovered her secret and so she needed him gone. It's all explained rather nicely in your letter there."

"That is absolutely ridiculous!" McTeabe shouted. He found the strength to stand and started to shake his fist at the warlock. "I will not stand for this madness!"

A length of rope appeared in front of the judge and a noose wrapped itself around his neck. The cord tightened and hoisted the heavy man from the ground, hanging him from one of the great beams that crossed the ceiling of his bed chamber. McTeabe struggled to get his foot to his bed to get away from gravity's deadly grip. His toes just managed to graze the silken blanket a few times before his strength started to flee from his body.

"I should have mentioned that this is a suicide letter," the warlock added. "That should add some credibility to the words you wrote, along with the bribe that your guards will find inside your foot chest." The warlock senator started to turn, but then held a finger in the air, as if he remembered something he had almost forgotten. "Oh, and I daresay that I spoke with your replacement, Judge Nellers, and he is more than happy to provide a review of the senate tribunal that will be almost identical to our finding. So, you see, even if the king does stick his nose in and order a review, I have won."

McTeabe's dying eyes threw daggers at the warlock in the judge's final moment before his inevitable end.

The warlock smiled and congratulated himself. Now, even if Lepkin made it to Drakai Glazei alive, his credibility would be destroyed. Everything was falling into place perfectly.

CHAPTER ELEVEN

Lady Cedreau flattened her skirt across her lap and took in a deep breath. Her chest heaved up slightly as her heart pounded within. She glanced out the carriage window, looking at Lokton Manor and squirming inside. She thought to turn the carriage back toward her home, but before she could utter the command the great entrance to the manor opened and a pair of men came out from the building. They were both wearing simple, yet highly polished platemail that reflected the sunlight back at her painfully. The clinking and clanking grew louder as the armored men approached the carriage.

"Good morrow," one of the men hailed.

Lady Cedreau sighed, resigning herself to finish what she had started. She heard her driver answer the two men, and her own personal bodyguard leaned forward to open the carriage door and step out in front of her. He was a large man, just under seven feet tall, with broad shoulders that had to turn sideways to allow him passage through most doorways. He wore a suit of chainmail under a padded leather hauberk, and a pair of scimitars hung at his sides.

"My mistress wishes an audience with Lady Lokton," he said.

The two Lokton guards shared a glance before frowning back. "I don't see why that is necessary," one of the guards said. "We would prefer that our lady not be disturbed."

Lady Cedreau slid out from the carriage and stepped around her body guard. "Please," she said simply. "My husband has passed from this world, along with one of my sons. I am here to preserve what is left of both houses. I implore you to ask for her patience with me for only ten minutes. What I have to tell her is extremely important."

The guards eyed her suspiciously. "Wait here, milady, I will ask her, but I cannot guarantee a favorable response."

Lady Cedreau offered a slight nod of her head. "I appreciate it."

Off the two went, leaving her there to stew in her thoughts and fears.

"I still don't like this," her bodyguard whispered to her.

"It's all right Derg," she said. "I want this to end."

Derg shrugged his boulder-like shoulders and rested his hands upon his hips, keeping them close to his scimitars. "A truce should not be sought with Lord Cedreau's blood still wet upon the field of battle," he said to no one in particular.

"Hold your tongue," Lady Cedreau said sharply. "I am the master of the house now, and it is not your place to counsel me on strategy."

Derg blushed and nodded his head reluctantly.

Lady Cedreau could understand his sentiment, but he did not know as much as she. As much as she would like to avenge her husband and son, her only hope of salvaging what was left of her family was to make amends with House Lokton.

The doors opened. Lady Cedreau looked up, but she did not see the pair of guards. Instead, Lady Lokton emerged from the doorway in a green dress. A large, gold necklace hung just above her bosom and her hair was pinned up on the back of her head.

She stepped down from the doors and walked slowly, yet confidently toward Lady Cedreau.

"I understand you wish to speak with me," Lady Lokton said as she approached.

Lady Cedreau noted the contempt in Lady Lokton's voice. Still, she kept her senses and nodded her head politely. "I have, milady," she started. "I thought that perhaps we may be able to end the feud between our families and bring peace, and comfort, to our houses once more."

Lady Lokton folded her arms across her chest and stared at the gargantuan guard beside Lady Cedreau for a moment. "It appears as though others here do not agree with your desires."

Lady Cedreau looked to Derg and motioned for him to return to the carriage. She could see the conflict on his face, but a quick flick of her wrist was all it took to dismiss the giant. "Forgive him. Derg is my personal guard, and he was very close to my late husband."

Lady Lokton shifted her weight to her left leg, sticking her hip out a bit. "I don't see what you can offer that will bring peace to us. You have lost your husband, and I have lost mine."

Lady Cedreau knitted her brow. "I had no part in your husband's arrest. Senator Bracken was here to investigate the magistrate's murder."

"That makes little difference now," Lady Lokton said. "As I said, there is nothing you or I can do to salvage anything. My husband will hang for crimes he didn't commit, all because your son murdered the magistrate!"

Lady Cedreau bristled and turned her upper lip into a snarl. "Eldrik did no such thing! If anyone is to blame, it would be Mr. Stilwell, who came and murdered my youngest son, who had nothing to do with any of this madness!"

"Right," Lady Lokton started. "I forgot that Lord Cedreau was completely innocent."

"My husband was betrayed and murdered while in parlay with yours!" Lady Cedreau countered. Her rage welled up in her bosom, lighting a fire in her that had not existed since the time she lived with Hairen and the other witches.

"My husband was not to blame for your husband's death. Trenton is a man of honor; he would never order such an underhanded attack." The two women glared at each other for a moment before Lady Lokton waved her hand to the left. "My home has been under attack several times by liars, thieves, and assassins," she said. "Did you know that Blacktongues came here to kill my little boy?" she asked.

Lady Cedreau shook her head.

"Many of my friends were injured that night, and some were killed. Then, your husband starts a war with our house and brings death to many, many more. Now you come here and beg for peace." Lady Lokton's face grew red and the tears in her eyes were visible. "You don't want peace for the sake of peace, you are asking for mercy now that you realize you have lost. I cannot stomach to look upon you."

Lady Cedreau fought the urge to lash out with her magic. She could cut down Lady Lokton with a blast of fire, or smother her in an earthen grave with a simple incantation. Lady Cedreau pushed the thought from her mind and focused her energy on her son. He was the only thing that mattered now. She could withstand the insults, if it meant that Eldrik could be saved.

"I have come to warn you that I fear Eldrik has taken it upon himself to avenge his father and brother," Lady Cedreau said coolly. "I wished to tell you that his rage has blinded him, and that I have already sent my scouts out to find him. I thought you may wish to inform your guards, and also send out patrols of your own. However, I ask that if you find him, please return him to me unharmed."

Lady Lokton narrowed her eyes on her. "And I am to trust that you will talk sense into him?" Lady Lokton sighed. "I thank you for your concern, but House Lokton will see to itself. If I were you, I would pray that he returns home soon."

"You would order your men to kill a boy?" Lady Cedreau asked.

Lady Lokton froze in place. "No, I would not have them kill a boy, but I would have him hog-tied and delivered to the senate for trial." She then turned her back and walked away. "Good day, Lady Cedreau, may your return home be swift and peaceful."

Lady Cedreau stood there, staring at Lady Lokton's back. Should she confess the truth? Should she tell Lady Lokton that Tukai's prophecy was about Eldrik? Perhaps it would buy some forbearance and mercy from her if they did find Eldrik on Lokton lands. Then again, would Lady Lokton believe her? Lady Cedreau sighed. She barely believed the witches herself, and she had lived with the coven long enough to understand what they were capable of. How, then, could she expect Lady Lokton to believe her? Even if by some miracle the woman would believe her, would her reaction be favorable, or was she still too distraught to have the presence of mind needed in the face of such news?

Lady Cedreau opened her mouth to speak, but only then did she realize that Lady Lokton had disappeared inside her house and the two guards had returned to the front entrance. They were staring at her coldly. She frowned and returned to her carriage, sitting down across from an obviously upset Derg.

"I told you this was a waste of time," he said.

"I had to try," Lady Cedreau said. "Too much blood is on my hands already." Derg looked at her curiously, but she offered no further explanation. "Let's return home," she said. "We need to find Eldrik."

"I would wager ten gold that Eldrik is making his way to Drakai Glazei," Derg announced. "We won't find him coming here."

"Why do you say that?" Lady Cedreau asked. "He could just as easily come here for revenge."

"If my family were killed, I would go to the murderer's trial to ensure justice was served."

"The senate will decide his fate," Lady Cedreau countered.

Derg shrugged. "Still, I would go to make sure that his fate was decided *appropriately*."

She sighed and a worry formed a gnawing hole in the pit of her stomach. She hated to admit it, but Derg was right, and Eldrik had enough of a head start that none of her scouts would catch him in time. She knew there was no chance of foiling Tukai's prophecy.

*****

The words on the page were beginning to blur in front of Lady Dimwater. She blinked hard and forced herself to concentrate. She picked up her mug of mint tea and put it to her lips. The lukewarm liquid did little to satisfy her, and she set the mug down with a *clunk*.

"No absinthe today?" Marlin teased when he walked in the door.

Dimwater looked up from the dusty tome she was examining and glanced to her mug. "Not today," she replied flatly. "Have you had any luck?"

Marlin shook his head. "I have been going through many of the books of prophecy, but I haven't found any additional clues. I am not sure what this false champion prophecy is about."

"I haven't made any great discoveries either," Dimwater admitted with a sigh.

"I brought some flat bread and yogurt." Marlin set the bronze plate of bread down between two matching bowls of pink yogurt peppered with spearmint leaves. "I like to dip the bread into the yogurt."

Dimwater shook her head. "I am not really hungry." She

pushed the book away and rubbed her weary eyes. "I wish Al were here. He might be able to point us in the right direction."

Marlin nodded. "For records kept among men and dwarves that may be true, but I doubt any of them would have any references to what we seek."

Dimwater pulled the paper closer to her where she had scrawled some of her notes. "On the wings of death the champion will ride, laying waste to the seats of white. His anger ushers in the dark tide, and washes the world in the color of night," she read the words aloud.

Marlin sat across from her and tore a piece of flatbread. "Believe not your eyes, for a champion in false skin shall rise," he added as he dipped the bread in yogurt. He placed the bite in his mouth and leaned back.

Dimwater watched Marlin carefully, trying to assess his thoughts before she continued reading. "One touched of the dragon's might, but not born of it, shall save the world from darkest night, and rule from the Stone Pulpit." She shook her head. "Everything I have ever read would point to Drakai Glazei being the Stone Pulpit mentioned by the prophecy. But, I am not sure what to make of the rest of it."

Marlin swallowed and sighed heavily. "As I said before, I believe the first is a warning that there is a false champion, the second warns what the false champion will do, and the third tells us who can stop the false champion."

"Do you really think that Lepkin will have to fight Erik?" Dimwater whispered. "If that was the case, then why would he be so sure that he chose the right apprentice?"

"I don't know," Marlin said with a shrug. "The Keeper of Secrets has many gifts, but he has not the gift of True Sight. As far as I know, he can't even sense or discern auras."

"But you can, did you detect anything inside Erik that would show him as a false champion?"

Marlin shook his head and took another bite of the flatbread. "No, I never sensed any such thing. He has only ever proven to be of incredibly high character."

Dimwater nodded. "That is all I have seen as well, and surely Al would agree if he were here. Erik, despite his stubbornness, is ultimately a selfless person. I can't believe that he would turn the other way."

"The prophecies do not lie," Marlin countered.

"Perhaps we put too much trust in prophecies, and too little in ourselves," Dimwater said.

Marlin frowned and dipped another morsel of bread into his yogurt bowl.

"None of the other books I have come across mention this event. There are others that deal with the Stone Pulpit, and I would agree that they all speak of Drakai Glazei."

A knock came at the door. Marlin stopped and waited for the door to open. A young healer entered. "We have switched shifts with Master Lepkin. We have seen some marginal improvement in his aura, but nothing significant as of yet."

"Thank you," Marlin responded. The young priest nodded and backed out of the room, closing the door.

Dimwater slammed her palm down on the table. "*Of course!*" she exclaimed. Marlin regarded her curiously. She shook her head and pointed to a bookshelf nearby. A small brown book flew from the shelf and landed in front of her. "Look here," she said. "It was so simple, it was right there in front of me the whole time!"

"What is it?" Marlin asked.

"The seats of white," she repeated. "They aren't actually white seats. What color are the senators' robes?"

"They are white," Marlin said.

"Exactly," Dimwater replied. "So not white seats, but seats of white, as mentioned in this history book about the formation of the senate. Listen to this." She pointed down to a paragraph and read aloud from the excerpt. "From that moment on, the power was entrusted to thirty-six families to ensure that only the best men occupied the *seats of white...*" she pushed the book away and looked up to Marlin. "The prophecy foretells that the senate is going to be destroyed."

Marlin slowly leaned forward and pushed his bowl of yogurt away. "On the wings of death the champion will ride, laying waste to the seats of white." Marlin tapped the table with his knuckles. "Of course," he said after a moment. "What is the one thing Erik has always tried to protect?"

"His family," Dimwater answered. "And who is on trial before the senate?"

Marlin nodded grimly. "His father."

"What do we do?" Dimwater asked. "Lepkin isn't awake, so he can't stop this from happening. Shall I teleport there and confront him?"

"No," Marlin said firmly. "To confront him would be to expose him, and it would damage Lepkin's reputation and credibility."

"As it would if Erik, in Lepkin's body, destroys the senate," Dimwater countered.

Marlin stopped tapping his knuckles. "What if the prophecy is not a warning?"

Dimwater folded her arms. "What else could it be?"

Marlin patted the air with a hand and cleared his throat. "You just made me think of something. Erik is inside Lepkin's body, so he is by all physical accounts a *false* Lepkin. Maybe the prophecies were there to help us understand that this was the way the events were meant to unfold."

"You mean Erik was supposed to be inside Lepkin's body while Lepkin lies unconscious inside Erik's body? What purpose would that serve?"

"I'm not sure," Marlin said. "But it makes sense that it could be a possibility. Believe not your eyes for a champion *in false skin* shall rise." Marlin nodded. "It doesn't actually say *false champion will rise*. It says a champion *in false skin*.

Dimwater took a drink of her lukewarm peppermint tea and quickly set the cup back down, turning her nose up. She choked the liquid down. "Peppermint tea turns quite bitter after it has cooled," she said. She shook her head as if it would throw the taste from her mouth and then looked up to Marlin. "Sorry," she offered. "Do you think the prophecies could be that simple?"

Marlin shrugged. "That has to be it. That is the only thing that makes sense. We both have discussed Erik's integrity at length. This is the only logical explanation."

"What of the other part, about the champion riding on the wings of death and destroying the senate, how could that be part of the right plan?" Dimwater asked.

"On the *wings of death*," Marlin repeated with quickened breath. His eyes went wide suddenly. "Oh my," he said. "I think I know what it all means. Come with me, there is something I must show you!" He jumped up from the table, tipping his chair up onto its back legs so that it almost fell over behind him as he turned quickly for the door. "Come quickly!" he urged.

Lady Dimwater rose and clambered around the table in an effort to keep up. She followed him, sprinting through the hallways until the pair stopped in front of a door at the end of the hall which was reinforced by flat iron plates criss-crossing the front. Marlin produced a long, slender claw from his pocket and slid it into the opening under the knob. Golden beams of light slithered out from the brass key plate, reaching and stretching across the iron bands over the door. The metal glowed and vibrated against the wood. Marlin turned the knob and the door gently fell open.

He removed the claw, stepped through the doorway and beckoned for Dimwater to follow him. She pushed the door closed behind them. Dimwater put her right hand out on the wall to keep her balance as she descended the tightly winding steps. She marveled at the gold inlay between the bricks as it shimmered under the light from the sconces on the wall.

At the bottom of the stairs the brick opened up into a green marble tunnel. Torches hung silently halfway down the smooth, hard walls. As they passed through the tunnel a golden glow appeared at the end growing brighter and brighter. Marlin paused, turning and pushing her back against the green marble wall.

"What is this?" she asked.

"You must stay here, and swear that you will never repeat what I am about to tell you," Marlin said.

Dimwater drew her brow together and nodded slowly. "You can trust me," she said. Marlin studied her for a few moments. She knew he was carefully studying her aura, looking for any sign that might tell him not to trust her. Understanding the gravity of the situation, she remained still and let him search for his own verification.

After several minutes he nodded and pointed to his left. "At the end of this hall is a secret, sacred chamber. It is the heart of our temple, and the only real purpose for our existence. It is only shown to people who are about to take the Test of Arophim."

"I'm not taking the test," Dimwater said. "Besides, I know what the room is, I have seen it before, a long time ago."

Marlin held up a hand to silence her and shook his head. "Of

134

course," he said. "I have brought you here to show you something so you can help me understand the prophecies." He paused for a moment. "I could have told you upstairs, but I want to make sure you believe me, and I didn't want to risk being overheard by any of the newer priests who don't already know."

"What is it?" Dimwater said. Her heart started to beat harder and faster. She looked to her right. Torches brilliantly illuminated a large antechamber made entirely of gold with glowing crystals hanging from the ceiling. Her mouth dropped open when she noticed the figurine at the end of the golden room.

A small, golden dragon head with eyes of jade protruded from the left wall.

"Not all of the dragons left after the great war," Marlin said. "One was instructed to remain behind, inside a special sanctuary that the other dragons built for his protection. Inside the chamber he slumbers and conserves his strength so the power of Nagar's Blight cannot overpower him. He is waiting until the Champion is found and given the ability to destroy the dark magic so the dragons may return."

"For what purpose?" Dimwater asked. Though she had indeed been to the temple many years prior, she had never heard of a dragon residing inside.

"To give the Test of Arophim," Marlin replied. "That is why the test is so dangerous, and also why it holds such great rewards for those found worthy. The gift of True Sight has always been granted to humans from dragons. We say that we can pass it along to new members, but the truth is that no human can pass it to another. The gift is only given from dragon to man."

"He stayed behind to find the Champion of Truth," Dimwater gasped.

"Exactly," Marlin said.

"But why would you tell *me*? You know my history, I was expelled from the temple before reaching this point in my own studies here."

"Because of the last part of the prophecies we found." Marlin smiled. "One touched of the dragon's might, but not born of it, shall save the world from darkest night, and rule from the Stone Pulpit."

"All of the prophecies are about Erik," she said breathlessly.

Marlin nodded. "If he is the real champion, then once he passes the Exalted Test of Arophim, he will also be known as *touched of the dragon* because he will receive a dragon's sight, a gift directly from the dragon."

Dimwater shook her head. "By that logic, the prophecy could also be describing Lepkin, as he has an ability given to him from dragons."

Marlin nodded. "I thought of that as well, but what is Lepkin called?"

"Dragonborn," Dimwater replied.

"So he is born of the dragon," Marlin surmised.

Dimwater folded her arms and looked back to the golden dragon's head at the end of the hall. "That seems a bit too easy," she said. "I want to believe Erik is good as much, if not more than anyone else. But I can't see him ruling the kingdom. Besides, there is still the matter of the senate. I can't see how laying waste to the ruling structure would benefit our cause. With the kingdom as weak as it is, it would fall into chaos if the senate were destroyed. Nobles would go to war, fighting for control of Drakai Glazei."

Marlin nodded. "Perhaps I have been too hasty, but I feel like this is right. My soul is screaming to me that Erik is the one we have been waiting for."

"Well, couldn't you just go in there and ask?" Dimwater inquired.

Marlin raised his eyebrows and leaned back. He started to stammer a bit, fumbling for an answer before finally admitting the truth. "I already asked him about Erik."

Dimwater smiled and nodded. "What did he say?"

"Well, he told me to trust my instincts and that ultimately the Exalted Test of Arophim would decide whether Erik was the Champion of Truth."

"So what do we do?" Dimwater asked. "Do I go north and try to see what happens with the senate?"

"If Erik destroys the senate, then we can deal with it afterward," Marlin said. "I still believe in him, and I believe it best not to expose that he is not really Lepkin."

Dimwater nodded. "Shall I go to lend him a hand then?"

Marlin shook his head. "No, with Lepkin convalescing, I would prefer you stay here. There are still other enemies that will be looking to attack the temple if they perceive a weakness."

Dimwater nodded, then she tilted her head to the side. "Do you remember who Al said arrested Lord Lokton?"

"Senator Bracken," Marlin replied.

"Lepkin told me that Senator Bracken was also at Roegudok Hall, talking to the dwarf king." Dimwater bit her lower lip. "Lepkin was attacked on his way here from Roegudok Hall," she said. "That's why he called for me."

"What are you getting at?" Marlin asked.

"Don't you think it strange that Lepkin was attacked just after meeting Senator Bracken, and then the senator arrests Lord Lokton without much of an investigation?"

"Well, Al said that all of the witnesses to the murders were unaccounted for," Marlin countered with a shrug.

"That is an *interesting* coincidence, don't you think?" Dimwater asked.

Marlin nodded. "You think Senator Bracken has thrown in with one of the factions seeking to overthrow the king?" Marlin asked.

"If he has, that would help me understand why Erik would lay waste to the seats of white."

CHAPTER TWELVE

Erik, his backside aching from the long journey and legs begging to be streatched, led his horse to a fir tree near the road. The tall tree towered over a small, babbling brook and had ample grass nearby for his mount. He dismounted and let his horse wander to the water for a drink, nibbling on clumps of grass as it went. After he surveyed the area he also went to the stream and cupped his hand in the cold liquid. Keeping his eyes up to scan his surroundings he brought the water to his mouth and slurped several mouthfuls before going back to stretch out under the fir tree. He removed his sword and set it beside him as he extended and retracted his right leg. The muscles were tight and sore from riding long hours. Suddenly his knee popped, bringing with it a sharp, momentary sting followed by a wash of relief that soothed the whole leg as he let it fall back to the dirt.

He looked back down the road he had been travelling, still half expecting Al to be charging up from behind to catch up. He saw no one. He understood why Al was angry with him, but he still couldn't slow his pace. He knew he had to reach the senate before the tribunal decided his father's fate. What else could he do? Sure Al had known his apprentice, but Erik had never thought the two of them close before Al erupted at him like some miniature furry volcano.

His horse whinnied contentedly and pulled away from the stream to nibble and tug at blades of grass mingled with bits of clover. Erik watched the beast's neck glisten in the afternoon sun as it grazed. For a moment he wished that life could go back to the way it was before Lepkin had made him fight those other apprentices. Life was so much simpler when Erik's worst task of any given day was washing windows with Janik, or helping to clean Kuldiga Academy's stables. Now he was alone and confused. Fate had dealt him an unusually cruel role, he felt. How could he play the part of Lepkin? How could he pretend to measure up to Lepkin's true abilities? He didn't even know the proper protocol for the senate, let alone what Lepkin might say or do in this situation. Yet, his father's life depended on him figuring it out.

"You promised to be with me," Erik muttered as if Al could hear him. He understood why Al had remained in Buktah, but he was still angry with the dwarf for abandoning him. "Well, at least I can count on Braun," Erik assured himself. He knew Braun would never surrender his father to anyone without a fight. The problem was that Erik had never been to Drakai Glazei. How would he be able to find Braun? He thought on it for a moment as he pulled a strip of dried meat from a leather pouch on his belt and chewed on it. At first he was disheartened, but then he realized that he didn't have to find Braun. All he had to do was make his way to the senate's tribunal. Braun was sure to be there. Erik swallowed his bite, coughing a couple of times as a stringy piece of meat got stuck in his back teeth before finally dislodging and going down his throat.

His eyes watered and he coughed a couple more times as he fought to catch his breath. He put the rest of the dried meat away and quickly went to the stream for another drink to help calm his throat.

That's when he saw it.

A flash of black, out of the corner of his right eye. He turned his head, but nothing was there. He searched the clumps of bushes on the other side of the road. Was it an animal? His horse raised its head and its ears went erect, turning this way and that. Something was near.

Erik slid his hand to his sword, but grasped only air. His eyes went back to the bottom of the tree, and saw his sword lying against the trunk. He jumped up and ran to the tree, where he had left his sword, but a sharp pain in his left thigh dropped him to the ground. Dirt flew up around his face and into his open mouth. He spat and wiped his mouth as he rolled onto his right side and looked down. An arrow stuck out the side of his left thigh. The shaft was broken, no doubt from him stumbling onto it. Blood ran down what was left of the arrow, and pain radiated through his entire leg. He frantically looked around for his attacker, but he saw no one.

His horse startled and bucked suddenly before galloping off through the brook and away from Erik, carrying all of his supplies away with him.

Erik forced himself through the pain, trying to stand. His leg would not hold him upright, but somehow he managed to crawl to the tree and lay hold of his sword. He clumsily threw the scabbard free and held the blade out in front of him.

"Face me as a man!" Erik shouted, putting on his best courageous face. His eyes darted about, looking for his hunter. Rustling came from above. Erik looked up just in time to roll away from something as it dropped from the tree branches. A powerful kick slammed into Erik's ribs as he continued to roll away from the tree.

"I am not a man," the attacker said slyly.

Erik looked up to see a beautiful woman. Her raven hair seemed to cascade over her bare shoulders to meld with the dark, long tattoos typical of the Blacktongues that Erik had seen before. Like the others of her order, she wore a simple leather loin cloth. However, while her male counterparts only wore their weapons aside from the loincloth, this Blacktongue also had a bizarre kind of leather shirt that covered and protected her chest while leaving her flat stomach exposed.

Erik struggled to push himself up, but could not force himself through the pain in his thigh. The Blacktongue sniggered wickedly and sneered down at him with a contemptuous shake of her head. "I expected more from you," she teased. She set the tip of her bow in front of her bare feet and slowly drew another arrow from her quiver. "I have been sent to ask you something," she said. "Where is the book?"

Erik glared at her and clenched his jaw. "In my pocket, come and get it," he lied.

The Blacktongue brought her bow up and loosed her arrow before Erik could blink. It seemed to him as though a fire had erupted in his arm as the arrow blew through his left shoulder.

"Agh!" he squealed as he dropped to the dirt on his back. He whimpered and squirmed, noting that the arrowhead had gone through his shoulder. His left hand burned when he closed it, and felt worse when he opened it. All he could do was writhe in protest, crying out in pain.

"I have all day," the Blacktongue said. "I need the book, then your pain will be over."

"Then you will kill me," Erik sputtered through spittle.

"Yes," she said. There was a flash of movement and then Erik froze when he felt her hand on his chest, pushing him flat against the ground. He tried to bring his sword up to bear, but the Blacktongue quickly pinned his right arm down with her left knee. He struggled for a moment, but his injuries only burned all the more as he futilely wrestled against her.

"I won't tell you," he said.

"Well, we will see about that," she replied. She turned her cold, gray eyes to his and smiled. She leaned down, her mouth close enough he could feel her breath on his lips. "I have ways of making people talk," she promised.

Erik twisted his trunk, trying to move her off of him, but to no avail. Her strength was more than he would have guessed from her small frame. That, as well as the two arrows protruding from his left side had him pinned. "You don't understand what the book is," Erik said.

"It is a key to unlock a gate," the Blacktongue answered. Her free hand brought a curved, black dagger up to Erik's face. "Tell me where it is, and I will end your torment."

He used the only weapon he could think of to combat against her. He called his power up, hoping he could use it somehow. Erik looked into her dead eyes and shuddered as he felt her intentions. He found no compassion, no sympathy, no hope. Her soul was as hollow and dead as her charcoal eyes. Erik turned his face away, but she forced him to look at her again by placing the dagger on his cheek and prodding him. He felt anger rise up within him. It was unlike anything he had experienced before. A burning, hot fire seemed to rise in answer to her cold, barren soul.

She pressed the dagger tip into his cheek and opened a small hole. "Tell me where it is," she said

"No," Erik said. The fire burned hotter inside until he could feel it burning in his heart. "NO!" he shouted. At that instant a great light erupted from his mouth, blinding the Blacktongue and causing her to recoil, covering her eyes. Erik seized on the moment and squirmed away from the assassin. He gripped the sword and felt his anger flow out through his arm and into the sword. White flames encircled the blade and reached out from the top to lick at the Blacktongue.

She jumped back and looked at him. Her eyes narrowed and her jaw closed tightly. She replaced her dagger and reached for another arrow. As her arm bent back to the quiver, a hammer slammed into the side of her skull with a resounding *crack*! Her body fell disjointedly to the side, dead.

Erik looked to his left and saw Al riding as fast as he could toward him.

"Are you all right?" Al shouted.

Erik looked back to the dead Blacktongue. His vision started to blur. The flames on his sword dissipated as quickly as they had come and his strength left him. "Al," Erik whispered with a hint of a smile crossing his lips. He slowly fell back to the ground. He just caught sight of a blurry, bearded face standing over him before he closed his eyes.

*****

"There you are," Al said quietly. "You had me a bit worried."

"Where are we?" Erik asked. He tried to blink the darkness away and wipe his face. "I can't see," Erik said.

"Of course not, it's pitch black in here," Al gruffed.

"What do you mean?"

"I brought you to a cave," Al explained. "You had lost a lot of blood, and the Blacktongue had tipped her arrows with a paralyzing agent. So I brought you here to fix you up and make sure we weren't followed."

Erik nodded as though he understood, but he was still pretty foggy in the head. Only when he tried to push himself up did he remember what had happened. He groaned and fell back down as pain ripped through his shoulder followed by warm liquid oozing out across his upper arm.

"Don't move, you idiot!" Al chided. "You'll rip the sutures out."

"I never saw her in the tree," Erik said.

"I know boy," Al said comfortingly. "Blacktongues are like that."

"This one was different," Erik countered. "We saw everyone in Buktah before they attacked. We had time to prepare."

"Not much time," Al interjected.

"But I never even knew she was there," Erik said. "She was like a ghost."

"Truth be told," Al started. "She was in Buktah also."

Erik shook his head. "Then why didn't she attack there?"

"I think she knew her best chance would be to come at us when we thought we had passed through the danger."

"If you saw her in Buktah, why did you let me go on alone?"

Al put a hand on Erik's good shoulder. "Forgive me boy, I had no choice."

Erik snorted.

"I saw her there. So, I thought it would be easier to flush her out if it looked as though we would split up and go separate ways for a while."

"You used me as bait?" Erik stammered.

"Sort of," Al said. "I didn't know which one of us she would go after. But I never left your side."

"Except for the funeral," Erik pointed out.

"No," Al said with a shake of his head. "I walked away from you, but I kept you in my sight. More importantly, I kept *her* in my sight. I left you in order to stalk her. Once I realized she was going after you, I followed." Al came over and thunked Erik with a meaty index finger. "I had thought that you would see through my act," Al teased. "With you being able to tell when others are lying and all."

Erik's scrunched his brow and studied Al's face. "You mean the whole thing was an act?"

Al shrugged. "Not all of it. I was a bit shocked by your behavior, and I was angry that my apprentice had been killed, but I would never abandon you to face the senate alone." Al smiled. "I gave you my word, Erik."

"But, you hit me in the alley."

Al pursed his lips and tugged at his beard. "I'm sorry about that, but I had to make sure to put on a convincing show for the Blacktongue in order for her to believe we were going to go our separate ways."

Erik scanned Al with his power and realized that the dwarf

143

was telling the truth. He had not abandoned him, as he had previously thought. Erik frowned and shook his head. "Then why did you take so long to stop her?" Erik asked.

"She was crafty, perhaps more so than any other foe I have tracked, and I have fought goblins and trolls boy!" Al took his hand back and stood up next to Erik. "She got away from me. It's not something I am proud of, but that is what happened. I was about three hundred yards behind you for most of the way until about twenty minutes before the last hill where the trees started to thin out. Somehow, she slipped away from me then. I searched everywhere for her, but I had to be careful not to alert her to my presence. I didn't want to risk scaring her off and missing our chance to confront her."

"Well, then I guess I should be glad you arrived when you did," Erik said.

"When I heard your horse, I thought the worst. I came as quickly as my steed would carry me, but even then I had to be careful. I wasn't sure where she was, so I stayed under cover as best I could until I saw her descend from the tree."

"Did you see what I did?" Erik asked, shifting the subject.

Al groaned. "That I did boy, that I did." He kicked a pebble out through the mouth of the cave. "Do you know *how* you did that?"

"No," Erik admitted. "I thought I could use my power to turn her, like I did with Master Lepkin, so I tried to look into her soul."

"Bet that was about as pleasant as swallowing a baby porcupine," Al put in.

"Something in me reacted to her. I don't know what it was, but it felt like a fire."

"Well," Al said after a moment of silence. "The important thing is you are still alive. We will rest here tonight and then I will take you in to Drakai Glazei. I have already made contact with Braun, he will meet us outside the tribunal before we go in."

"How did you meet with him already?" Erik asked.

"It is very early in the morning," Al replied. "About three hours ago. I went into the city while you were unconscious, after you were stable of course."

"You left me alone?" Erik said.

"I had no other choice. I had some things to help with your

bandages, but I needed to visit an apothecary in order to counter the poison the Blacktongue had used. If I hadn't, you would be permanently paralyzed from the neck down by morning." Al stopped talking and turned to pat Erik on the chest. "Don't worry, the apothecary is a friend of mine. She'll keep things quiet."

"You seem to have friends everywhere," Erik noted.

"One of the benefits of being a dwarf, you live long enough to meet lots of folks." Al patted Erik's chest one more time and then hopped onto a smooth, flat slab of rock. "Get some sleep," Al said. "Tomorrow you have a big day."

Erik nodded and moved his good hand over to touch the bandage on his left shoulder. "I hope you have a good plan," Erik said. "I don't think I will be in fighting shape for a while."

Al chuckled aloud. "You planning on fighting the senate?"

Erik reached out and placed his palm on his sword. "If I must," he said flatly.

Al stopped chuckling and stroked his beard. Tomorrow was going to be a very big day indeed.

*****

"Sit upright," Al said under his breath.

"I'm fine," Erik replied sharply. "My leg hurts."

"Deal with it," Al gruffed. "These people have a certain expectation of Master Lepkin, and you have to make sure that everyone here sees you as *completely* able-bodied," Al said. "There are people everywhere that gather information. If the senate were to find out you are severely injured..." Al stopped short as a couple of uniformed guards approached.

"Master dwarf," one of them said. "May I have your name for the log book?"

Al scoffed. "You don't recognize us?" he said loudly. "I am Aldehenkaru'hktanah Sit'marihu brother to the King of the Dwarves. I suppose I can forgive your ignorance, but surely you don't need to ask *him* for his name, do you?" Al thumbed to Erik.

Erik straightened his back, fighting the pain in his leg as he pushed down in the stirrups. With his right arm he slid his cloak back to reveal his sword of black, telarian steel. "Go easy on him Al," Erik said in his best impression of Master Lepkin's commanding voice. "Perhaps he is new to the guard."

"Uh, er, I…" the guard stammered as he looked to the sword. The other guard ripped the log book out of his hands and quickly put pen to paper.

"Master Lepkin, excuse us please. We weren't expecting you." The guard scribbled their names down. "How long will you be in Drakai Glazei, and what will you be doing?"

Erik arched his eyebrow in Lepkin's typical fashion. A part of him thoroughly enjoyed watching two grown men squirm in exactly the same way he had himself squirmed under Lepkin's scrutinizing gaze. "I will be here for a few days. I am here in response to a summons from the senate." Erik produced the summons momentarily and let the guards look at it. The guards each nodded and started to respond simultaneously. Erik turned away from them and nodded to Al. "Let's go," Erik said. He made a point of not waiting for the guards to finish their sentences. He was done. Al nodded and turned his horse to the gate. The two of them rode in and Al led them straight for the center of town, where a large, black spire towered over the rest of the city.

""That is it?" Erik asked.

Al nodded grimly. "That's the king's tower. The senate hall is on the other side, adjacent to the tower."

"What do I do?"

"I just told you this morning over breakfast," Al quipped.

Erik nodded. "I'm nervous," he admitted. "Just tell me again to make sure I have it all correct."

"Well," Al started. "The Keeper of Secrets has a unique role in these cases. You will stand on the floor of the senate hall and oversee the tribunal. You will be allowed a vote toward the verdict, but you don't have the right to overrule the senate"

"Unless the senate has broken protocol," Erik put in quickly.

"Aye," Al replied. "Your role is also to ensure that proper protocol is followed."

"How do I do that if I am not given a chance to speak or… what did you call it?"

"Give testimony," Al said. "It is simpler than it sounds, lad," Al began. "I will stand with you on the main floor near the doorway. I will help you observe the proceedings. If I sense something is amiss, I will let you know. Then you can order an

146

injunction, which will stall the tribunal for three days while the king decides whether to order a review of the proceedings."

"And if he does, the high judge will conduct the review, right?"

Al nodded again. "That's right." The dwarf leaned over and clapped Erik on the back. "You have it straight, boy, there is nothing to worry about." Al nodded to a mounted guard as he rode past. "Besides, today we are just going to announce that we have come to answer the summons. The tribunal is set for tomorrow. So we have some time to go over the protocol in depth tonight."

"What happens if the senate finds him guilty, and then the king declines the review? How do I save my father if that happens?" Erik asked.

Al shushed him with a stubby finger and stern look. "Keep your voice down." Al shook his head and moved in close enough to be heard in a whisper. "If that happens…" Al paused for a moment. He thought to make something up, but he knew that Erik would be scanning him to see if he was lying. Finally he relented and told Erik the truth. "I don't know that we can save him, I'm afraid."

Erik turned and shot Al a menacing look. "Then *why* did we come?"

"Because if we didn't come, then the senate could discredit Lepkin, and try to get the king to turn against him. If Lepkin were to ignore an official summons for such a monumental hearing, it would be a grave offense to the kingdom. Some might think it was the start of a declaration of war."

"War? What are you talking about? Lepkin has no army, how could he start a war?"

Al patted Erik's forearm and stopped him to ensure his next words would sink in. "My boy, a war of ideas is far more dangerous than a war of armies ever could be. There are many in the kingdom who follow the older traditions and hold them dear. With all this talk of the kingdom splintering apart, people may look to the last vestige of those traditions to lead them. Lepkin, as the Keeper of Secrets, embodies those traditions."

"So you are saying the senate would claim that Lepkin was making a move on the throne by defying the senate? Why would the people believe that if Lepkin is already set to rule jointly with the senate in the event that the king passes away without a declared heir?"

Al shrugged. "I am not for knowing what you tall folk would do, but I know that that is the scenario the senate would posit to the king if Lepkin fails to attend this tribunal. They would claim Lepkin was associated with Lord Lokton and preparing to advance against the king, or at least against the senate in a move to consolidate power." Al sighed and shook his head. "It would be a self-fulfilling prophecy. As soon as the senate would make the claim, I am sure a sizeable number of people would seek Lepkin out to join him against the senate. There are many who are not happy with the current body of government. Many people believe that after King Mathias passes, the senate is the worst and last body that should be trusted to rule, even if they are only joint rulers with Lepkin. That is to say nothing of the several nobles who have made overtures of their own desires for power."

"So," Erik said with a nod. "We are here to delay the inevitable civil war. Either way, my father will die as the senate will find him guilty."

"I don't like it either," Al said. "I won't tell you how to feel about it, but you must see this through."

"I'll see it through," Erik promised. "And I will find a way to set my father free."

Al gripped Erik's forearm tight. "You can't break protocol. If you do, the senate could still claim that you are siding with rebels. You must remain in character the entire time. No matter what."

Erik said nothing.

"Do you understand?" Al asked.

At last, Erik nodded. "I understand."

"You should know, I spoke with Braun about this as well."

"You told him who I really am?" Erik asked.

Al shook his head. "No, I mean I explained Lepkin's role to him, so he also understands the constraints you will be under."

A slight smirk flashed across Erik's lips. "Are you telling me that Braun is devising a plan?"

Al shrugged and tried to hide his smile. "It is a lot easier to explain the actions of an overzealous bodyguard. A few people might get riled up, but nobody is going to start a civil war over it."

Hope returned as if on a warm summer breeze, washing over

Erik in an instant. "Then let's go."

The two of them continued on their way until they reached the front gate. A trio of black uniformed guards approached them with a logbook. This time, they only needed to look at the pair before the guards scribbled the names in the book.

"Master dwarf," one of the guards said. "You may wait in the antechamber outside the tribunal hall. Master Lepkin, you may assume your usual position inside."

"No," Erik said. "He will accompany me inside as well."

"This is highly irregular," the guard objected. Erik arched his eyebrow in the same, menacing way he had seen Lepkin do many times before. The guard shrank away from Erik's gaze and nodded.

"Thank you," Erik offered as he walked past.

"You may leave your sword with us," one of the other guards said timidly.

Erik glanced to the guard. "My sword stays with me." He walked through the great marble encrusted doors without so much as another word. The guards didn't dare try to stop him.

"That was a little brash," Al whispered after they were far enough inside not to be heard.

Erik shrugged. "After being caught without my sword yesterday, I feel better keeping it near. You never know what kind of trap may be ahead for us."

Al raised his eyebrows and pursed his mouth for a moment before nodding and shrugging his shoulders. "Fair enough," he said.

"Something feels wrong here," Erik commented. "It is similar to the feeling I got before the Blacktongue attacked me by the brook."

Al nodded and checked around. "Let's hurry up then."

The two of them stopped before a grand set of double doors. Erik pushed them open, not arrogantly, but with enough force that both doors creaked and parted before him. His heart leapt into his throat at what he saw inside.

A senator stood behind a pulpit, obviously stopped in mid-sentence as his mouth was agape and his right hand was raised in the air. To his left was a man bent over and chained with his arms behind his back. The iron chains linked to a steel ring in the dais, keeping the man hunched over. It was hard to tell who it was at first. The bruises and lumps discolored Braun's face so that Erik almost didn't recognize him.

"They have Braun," Al whispered in horror.

"And my father," Erik said.

A few feet away from Braun, Lord Lokton was in much the same predicament. His face was swollen and purple around the eyes and cheekbones and he was also chained to the floor with a leash so tight that he had to rest upon his knees with his back hunched over.

"Master Lepkin," the senator bellowed. "I did not think you were coming."

Erik's eyes locked on the man in white robes behind the wooden pulpit. If he could have, he would have melted the man into oblivion with his glare. Erik felt a sharp nudge in his side. He looked down to see Al motioning with his head.

"Say something," Al whispered.

Erik collected his thoughts and put on his best impression of Master Lepkin. He cleared his throat and folded his arms across his chest. "I was unaware that the tribunal would start so soon. The summons I received informed me that the tribunal would commence tomorrow. I came today to announce that I am here in answer to your summons, and I would have assumed you would have either waited for me, or given me ample notice that you would start without me."

"Here, here!" someone shouted from one of the balconies. "For the record, I objected to starting the tribunal without the Keeper of Secrets."

"Senator Mickelson, hold your peace," the senator at the pulpit said. "The senate voted to speed up the tribunal in order to avoid political ramifications, and the vote was in accordance with the law as it currently stands."

"What political ramifications?" Erik asked. Al nudged him.

"Don't speak too much," Al cautioned.

"Senator Bracken thought that holding Lord Lokton might result in revolts in the streets," Senator Mickelson said.

The old senator at the pulpit motioned for Senator Bracken to come up to the pulpit.

"Was I wrong to be careful?" Senator Bracken asked. He pointed to Braun. "This man here threatened city guards, and was found trying to sneak into this very building. What more proof do you need?"

No answer was given.

"I am here now," Erik said.

Senator Bracken turned a steely gaze to him. "So you are." He tapped his knuckles on the pulpit. "Perhaps you can be of assistance then, Keeper," senator Bracken Said. "I was about to call the tribunal's vote."

"The trial is over?" Erik asked.

Senator Bracken looked at him for a moment, studying him carefully. "Perhaps I should remind you that the law allows the senate to accelerate the tribunal if there is sufficient reason to warrant such measures. But, do not worry, the senate understands that you put forth your best efforts to answer the summons we sent, and we find no fault in you for missing the hearing. However, in light of the fact that you did not witness the evidence presented, nor hear any of the testimonies given, it seems you may not wish to vote in this matter."

"Or we could run through the evidence again," Erik said. "For I wish to vote."

Senator bracken sneered down at him. "There is no provision in the law for such a request, Keeper," Bracken said.

"Be quiet," Al whispered harshly.

Erik shook his head. "It is my job to ensure protocol is followed," Erik said. "How is it that these prisoners have come by the bruises on their faces?"

Bracken turned to the other senator and stepped back from the pulpit. The old senator stepped forward and gripped the sides of the pulpit with his leathery, liver-spotted hands. "While normally it is your duty to ensure protocol is followed when summoned to a tribunal, you have no such authority when you miss the hearing."

"You changed the date," Erik growled.

The old senator rapped a stone sphere onto a metal disc. The jarring sound echoed through the chamber. "All that has been done is in accordance with the law and the protocol. We have finished the hearing and now it is time for a vote. If you feel so strongly, you may cast your vote along with us, but I would advise against it as you have not been present for the entire proceeding."

Erik bristled and wiped away Al's relentless elbow. "This isn't right," Erik whispered to Al.

Al nodded. "We can still ask the king for a review, just keep calm."

Senator Bracken made his way back to the pulpit and looked at them both for a moment before turning his attention to the balconies. "All of those who believe Lord Lokton is innocent, please raise the white flag on your balconies."

Senator Mickelson was the first to display a white flag. Three others slowly followed suit. Each flag drew Bracken's ire visibly. The senator's face grew red and he tapped his knuckles on the pulpit before continuing.

"Something is wrong," Erik whispered.

"Quiet!" Al responded in a harsh whisper.

Erik couldn't shake the feeling. Something was terribly wrong. He searched the room and tried to scan for anything that might be out of place. He couldn't find anything. The stone sphere smacked against the metal disc one time, ripping Erik back to the present.

"Those who find Lord Lokton guilty, please present your vote by raising the black flag."

Thirty black flags appeared over the front of each balcony. A wide smile pulled the corners of Bracken's mouth out toward his ears. He nodded, satisfied at the outcome. Then he added his own black flag, displaying it proudly over the front of the pulpit.

"Lord Lokton, you are hereby found guilty of inciting rebellion. You are forthwith deemed a traitor, and sentenced to death."

"No!" Erik shouted.

"Shut it!" Al pleaded, but it was too late. Erik was walking forward to the pulpit.

"Interesting," Bracken said. "So, does this plot go beyond a nobleman and his retinue then?" Bracken swept his arm out to the floor and pointed to Erik. "Fellow members of the senate, what think we about this?"

The room was silent.

"I am no traitor, neither is that man there," Erik said. "Your trial is a sham. You have no proof of anything."

"Oh but we do," Bracken shot back. "You would have seen our evidence had you been more diligent in answering our summons. But I wonder whether you would have accepted the proof? For now it appears that you have thrown in with him."

"This is madness," Senator Mickelson shouted out. "The Keeper has only acted in the interest of the kingdom!"

"And yet, he holds himself above the kingdom," Senator Bracken retorted. "Isn't that right, Master Lepkin?" Senator Bracken walked out from behind the pulpit. "At Roegudok Hall, you recently told me that you were autonomous from the senate, and from the kingdom as a whole. Could it be that you think yourself capable of taking the throne for yourself."

"I do not want the throne," Erik said. He tried to think of something quick to say that would help him out of the predicament and still give him the chance to save his father. "I want only justice. A fair trial, held in accordance with the law. Even your fellow senator said there was a protest against the way this tribunal was conducted."

"You want justice?" Bracken repeated.

"Yes," Erik said.

"You would see justice done in all circumstances?"

"Of course," Erik said.

"As you are aware, a formal protest may be overcome with a senate vote. I had all the requisite votes to proceed with accelerating the tribunal despite senator Mickelson's protest. That means that this tribunal was fair, and in accordance with the law. Now, if you want *justice* I have one proposal that will satisfy both of us."

"What is it?" Erik asked.

"The sentence stands. It is a lawful verdict, reached by majority vote of this senate. If you want justice, then use your sword to take this traitor's head."

Erik's heart fell into his feet. His hands went numb and his throat dried out. He looked to his father's silent, waiting face. He swore he could see Tukai's ghost standing on the dais, laughing with his wicked grin.

Erik shook his head. "I will order a review of this tribunal," he promised.

Senator Bracken pointed and shook his hand. "You refuse to carry out justice? Why would you stall for a review when the verdict was reached by the vast majority of senators present? Are you a traitor, or do you serve the king?"

153

"There is only one way the Keeper can prove himself loyal to the king!" another senator shouted from the right side of the room.

"Enact the sentence or you will stand trial beside the traitor!" another shouted.

"Oh laddie," Al sighed.

Erik glanced around the room. He could see the senators shouting, pumping their fists in the air or spitting on the ground in his direction, but he could no longer hear them. Something pulled at his heart, warning him of an unseen danger. He hadn't identified it yet, but he was searching, scanning each balcony. He called upon his inner power as he tried to discern the truth of the matter.

All became clear as his eyes returned to Senator Bracken. The man's white robes turned dark, the skin on his hands aged and gnarled. His face withered and wrinkled beyond what it had been, and his eyes became black as death.

Erik drew his sword. The heat of his anger coursed through his right arm, down to his hand until the blade itself awoke with a white hot sheath of living fire that swirled over the blade.

"I see the truth," Erik said. "Reveal yourself, warlock!"

"Warlock?" Senator Bracken repeated. "He throws blame from himself by casting spurious accusations! There are no warlocks here, only loyalists and traitors." Senator Bracken motioned to someone that Erik could not see. "Kill them both," he said, pointing to Lord Lokton and Braun.

A large, pot-bellied man strode into view from the side of the dais carrying a large, oversized axe in his hands.

Erik rushed forward. "Stop!" he yelled.

The executioner maintained his gait and moved to put himself in line with Lord Lokton's neck.

Lord Lokton closed his eyes and held his head up slightly. "I am no traitor," he said defiantly.

The executioner was upon him. He raised his axe high above his head.

Erik threw his sword. The flames hissed as the blade whirled through the chamber. Senators gasped as they watched the sword spin end over end until it cleaved through the large axe, dropping the massive blade on the dais. The executioner staggered backward and dropped what was left of the axe's handle.

"You have shown your true colors," Bracken hissed. He

waved his left hand and sent a blast of air into Erik, knocking him backward several yards.

Erik landed hard, almost knocking his shoulder out of socket, but he grit his teeth and forced himself to stand back up. He could feel blood starting to seep from his recent wounds, but he paid it no mind. "And you have shown yours, warlock," Erik said.

"Using magic does not prove I am a warlock," Bracken retorted.

"Reveal your true form," Erik said. He waved his hand, calling upon his power to dispel Bracken's magic.

The shouting ceased and all eyes turned to the pulpit. Senator Bracken's spell dissolved, revealing his true form for everyone to see. The warlock sneered and gave a slight nod of his head. "You are more intuitive than I would have guessed," he said. "I would have thought that only the boy could have..." the warlock's words caught in his throat and he stared hard at Erik. His eyes widened suddenly and his mouth fell agape.

Erik realized that somehow the warlock had looked past Lepkin's body and discovered his identity as well. Erik turned his gaze to the balconies. "The warlock must be brought to justice!" he yelled. As he scanned the balconies he used his power to ascertain which senators he could trust. Many of the men were already scrambling for the exits, obviously wanting no part of what was to come.

The warlock raised his fist high above his head. "All hail Tu'luh the Red, and Nagar the Black, the true prophets of our time!" He turned his attention to Lord Lokton. "Your house shall be no more!" he shouted.

"No!" Erik yelled. Again he started to rush forward, but this time something else awoke in his body. With each step his leg seemed to grow exponentially, his arms too. He felt the fire of his rage burn within his chest as it had with the Blacktongue assassin back by the stream, but this time no light erupted from within. Instead, he felt his body expanding, growing, breaking and transforming. Pain tore through him for an instant, and then it was as if he were towering over the warlock, looking down on the evil man as though he were no larger than a mouse. The warlock looked up with a shriek of horror and turned his spell up to Erik. The blue blast of lightning scorched Erik's face and neck, but he withstood the blow and roared back at the warlock.

Erik's roar shook the entire chamber, and it was then that he felt an immense power running through his chest. He opened his mouth and a stream of fire flowed out to engulf the warlock. Erik could hear shouting and crying as the senators scrambled around him. His hearing seemed more acute than normal, allowing him to hear every leather sole's scrape against the stone floor and every heated, quickened breath from each person in the room. It allowed him to know everyone's position in the chamber without turning his head.

Out of instinct he reached out with his right hand and snatched the executioner up just before the man could bury a sword in Lord Lokton's back. Erik turned to regard the now puny man and crushed him between his sharp talons.

He discarded the executioner and turned back to the warlock, who was still alive, using a magical shell to keep Erik's flames at bay. Erik let his instinct take over. He snapped down with his massive maw and crushed the warlock's defensive shell with his mouth.

Somehow, the warlock escaped out to the side but Erik swung his heavy, spiked tail and caught the warlock through the chest. The man gasped and twitched, then he slid down the wall to the floor in a heap of blood soaked white robes.

Erik could hear Al's approach as the dwarf went to work on the chains that bound Braun and Lord Lokton. The clicks and scrapes of the locks almost echoed they seemed so loud. Erik turned to cover his friends. A few senators had already escaped the chamber, but others seemed frozen in place. While some of the senators who had sided with the warlock appeared to have been manipulated or tricked, many of them held evil intentions within their hearts. Erik's wrath was quick to punish the crooked senators.

As his fire purified the senate chamber, the walls and seats in the room were charred or altogether disintegrated, leaving barely a skeleton of the grand room that had been before Erik unleashed his power.

When he was finished only Al, Braun, Lord Lokton, and Senator Mickelson remained in the blackened hall. Erik looked around and clawed at the stone floor. His talons cut through the granite as though he were slicing through cream. His breathing slowed and puffs of smoke snaked out from his elongated snout. He turned his eyes down to Al and could almost hear the dwarf's thoughts.

"Enough" Al said. Except, the dwarf's mouth didn't move. Erik cocked his massive, scaled head toward Al and scrutinized the dwarf more carefully. "Erik," Al communicated with his mind. "This is enough, you must stop. We have to flee."

Erik wasn't sure whether to respond vocally or if Al could also hear his thoughts, so he just nodded his head. He looked down at his hands, really looking at himself for the first time. During the heat of the moment he had understood what had happened, but now his mind was catching up with his instincts. Only now did it fully dawn on him. Somehow, he had turned into a dragon.

The boy within him became afraid. Would the book snare him now? What had he just done to the senate hall? What would Lepkin and Dimwater say?

Al came up and placed a strong hand on Erik's forepaw. "Calm down," Al communicated. "Close your eyes and think of your human form."

Erik's heart slowed and he did as Al instructed. The fire in his chest dwindled, and as it did he felt himself compress, as though a thick band were wrapping itself around him and squeezing him back to his normal form. Though it seemed to take several minutes, the transformation only last a couple of seconds. When Erik opened his eyes, he was standing shoulder to shoulder with Braun and Lord Lokton.

"That, was…" Lord Lokton started to speak but couldn't finish his sentence.

Braun simply nodded in disbelief and cast his eyes about the room again.

"We must go, quickly," Al said. "Perhaps we should split up."

"Why?" Erik asked.

"Given what just happened, we might have a better chance of all escaping if we go in pairs. Surely the guards will be looking for four men."

"Three men and a dwarf," Braun corrected. "Any way we split up, you are going to draw attention, I'm afraid."

Al nodded. "Let's not waste time discussing it." Al pointed to

Braun and Lokton. "You two make your way to the southern gate. A block away from there you will find a well. You can go down the well to an underground river. That river will take you out to the east, where it will emerge from the ground through a cave. If you are careful, you won't need to go in the water as there is a small path along the bank."

"How do you know that?" Lord Lokton asked.

"A few decades ago I was on the crew that dug that well and plotted the underground river. There is a gate at the cave, but you should be able to pick it easily, just take care as there are usually a pair of guards nearby."

"Sounds better than trying our luck at one of the gates," Braun said.

"We'll go out the same way, but first I think we will need to get to the king.

"To the king?" Braun asked skeptically. "The two of you are just going to walk in and ask him to speak with you after this?"

"We have to tell him what happened here," Al said. "We have to show him that Bracken was really a warlock."

A shapely dark form dropped from a nearby balcony, catching their attention. A long, golden braid bounced over the woman's shoulder as she somersaulted to the floor and began to walk toward them. "I will go with you," she told Al. "I was investigating Senator Bracken, and I have some information that may help you prove your case to the king."

"Who are you?" Al asked. His hand gripped his hammer.

"It's Lady Arkyn," Erik said. He would have recognized her green eyes anywhere.

"It is good to see you again, Master Lepkin," she said.

"Can we trust her?" Al whispered to Erik.

"Yes, you can," Arkyn replied. Al shot her a confused look. "I am half-elf, and my hearing is excellent," she explained with a shrug. "Besides, Lepkin can vouch for me."

Erik used his power to scan her intentions. He found them to be pure. "We can trust her," he said.

"Very well," Al said. He turned back to Braun and Lord Lokton. "The two of you should get moving. Hang around the mouth of the underground cavern until we come out, then we can head down to Hovart."

Braun nodded his head and clapped Al on the shoulder. "Good luck," he offered.

Lord Lokton extended his hand out to Erik. "Master Lepkin, you have my undying gratitude."

Erik took his father's hand and fought the urge to reveal himself. His throat caught, so he simply nodded.

"Come," Al said. "We must go."

Erik could hear shouting from afar off. He nodded and they split up. Erik and Al were joined by Lady Arkyn. The three of them stopped just short of the hallway where Senator Mickelson stood waiting for them.

"What you just did," he started. "That will throw our land into civil war! There will be no way for me to keep the nobles from going at eachother's throats. How can I prepare the king? What do I do?"

Al looked up to Erik. It was obvious that the dwarf wanted an explanation as well.

"Take us up to see the king," Erik said. "What I did, I did because there were those among the senate who would abuse their power to seek the throne. They sought to do away with the law and subdue the kingdom to feed their own greed. Those who were spared, I spared because their intentions were honorable. It will be hard, but it is better to rebuild a kingdom with solid stones, than to use a faulty foundation."

Mickelson nodded and scrunched his brow and nodded. "Very well, Keeper, I trust that you have proof."

"You did see Senator Bracken turn into a warlock, didn't you?" Lady Arkyn chided.

Mickelson stiffened, glancing between the three of them. "All right, let's go see the king."

CHAPTER THIRTEEN

"What in the name of Hammenfein happened here?" Rory gasped.

"I'm not for knowing," Jasper replied. "Come on, let's look around." The two guards quickly scoured the chamber. Rory went along the right side, going from corpse to corpse. Jasper scurried on by the left side trying to hold his breath while examining each charred body for a moment before moving on, hoping to find someone alive. He halted at one of the balconies where he saw a man squirming slightly.

He tested the stone railing before climbing over. It was hot, but he clambered over it anyway, shaking his hands out after vaulting over the side to land next to the severely wounded man. Jasper cupped a hand to his mouth at the sight of the senator's injuries. There was no way for him to identify which senator lay before him.

"Can you hear me?" Jasper asked.

"Help," the man pleaded through labored gasps.

Jasper looked the senator over. There was nothing to be done. Jasper shook his head, fumbling for something to say. It didn't matter though. The senator gasped his last and became still. Jasper sighed and moved on. He walked through the back hall, kicking up soot and dust with his footsteps.

"Jasper, come quick!" Rory called.

Jasper ran through the back hall and stopped on the dais. "Senator Bracken."

"He's been stabbed," Rory said. He rolled Senator Bracken to his side and began checking for vital signs. "It's weak, but he still has a pulse."

"How is that possible? He must have been stabbed at least four times," Jasper noted. Jasper quickly pulled his satchel up over his shoulder and retrieved a roll of bandages out. "Here, let's get these on him as quickly as we can.

Rory took them, shaking his head all the while. "It's hopeless, the injuries are too great."

Senator Bracken slowly raised his left hand and placed it over Rory's arm. "I still have some fight left in me," he said softly.

"Of course, Senator Bracken," Rory said shakily. He removed Bracken's hand and went to work with the bandages.

"What happened?" Jasper asked. "Can you tell us who did this to you?"

"Lepkin," Bracken sputtered. "He and his dwarf friend came in and attacked us to free the traitor."

Rory looked up to Jasper. "Master Lepkin?"

"That doesn't make any sense," Jasper agreed.

Senator Bracken struck out with lightning fast reflexes, pulled Jasper's dagger from his belt and slid it up under Rory's armor and into his abdomen. Rory's eyes went wide. Jasper looked up, but Bracken reached out with his left hand and seized Jasper's arm. He dug his nails into his flesh and before either guard could move, the warlock drained each of them of their life forces. As their faces paled and drained, the warlock's wounds healed and closed. His strength returned to his body and he could feel his magical reserves coming back as well.

When he was done he dropped the two corpses, cast a quick spell over their bodies to vaporize them, and then waved his hand in front of him. An egg of purple mist formed in front of his eyes and twirled, expanding with each second until a cloud of black and purple mist the size of a door hovered in front of him. He reached up and grabbed his amulet. He rubbed the cold, golden image with his thumb and spoke an incantation. Upon his command the mist opened to reveal a bright yellow tunnel. He stepped through and disappeared.

*****

Eldrik stepped up to the apple stand and dug around his pocket and pulled a copper coin out. "How much for two?" he asked the short man behind the stand.

The man looked at Eldrik's clothes and smiled wide, revealing big white teeth. "One copper for three," he said.

Eldrik gave him the coin and picked three apples. He tucked two into his backpack and immediately tore a bite out of the third one. A bit of the juice squirted out onto the front of his chin. He wiped it with the back of his sleeve. He wandered down the road, glancing over the nearby buildings to the black tower reaching high above them.

"First time in the city?" a voice asked from behind. Eldrik turned to see a pair of boys standing a few feet away. He looked them up and down and kept walking.

"Hey, where are you going?" one of the asked.

He could hear their shuffling steps trailing after him. He quickened his pace, taking a sidelong glance over his shoulder at his followers. Eldrik spotted an empty side street and turned down it. He didn't need trouble, but he couldn't have anyone following him either.

"Hey little man," one of the boys called out. "Wait for a minute. We can help you find what you are looking for."

Eldrik stopped and turned in place. "I don't need any help," he said.

"That's where you're wrong," one of them said.

The other nodded his head. "He must be lost, otherwise why would someone like him come to this part of town?"

"Someone like me?" Eldrik asked. "I think you should turn around and leave," he warned.

The two laughed and rolled up their sleeves. It was then that Eldrik noticed the scars over their knuckles. They were roughly the same size as Eldrik. Though they seemed a bit skinnier than him, they looked tough enough to fend for themselves.

"What do you want?" Eldrik asked.

The blonde haired boy stepped forward. "We'll take your backpack."

The brown haired boy pulled a short club from under his belt and slapped it in his other palm. "And I saw you had some copper coins in your pocket, you can give us those as well."

Eldrik shook his head. His father's crossbow was hidden in the backpack. There was no way he was going to let them take it away from him. He pulled the bag off and set it to his side. "I'll give you each a copper piece to turn and walk the other way."

162

The blonde haired boy turned to the other. "If he offers us money to keep his bag, then there must be something good in the bag."

The other nodded and stepped forward, raising his club up in the air.

Eldrik glanced behind them. The side street was empty. There would be no witnesses. His time to strike was now. Eldrik waited for the boy with the club to approach. He put his hands up, as if to wave him off. The boy with the club smiled and slapped his palm again. Eldrik burst into movement, striking out at the boy's right knee with a sweeping kick, followed by a heavy bottom fist strike to the boy's nose. The combination dropped the boy onto his back. Eldrik finished it with a kick to the boy's ribs.

"Bad move!" the other boy growled. He drew a knife out and advanced on Eldrik. Eldrik deftly snaked his right arm up under the boy's wrist, twisting it around and jerking the arm forward. The boy stumbled forward. Eldrik spun around his foe and dropped a savage elbow strike on the boy's spine just between the shoulder blades. The boy flopped forward, tripping over his partner. Eldrik bent down, took the club from the first boy and slammed it into the knife-wielder's tailbone. The boy cried out and rolled off of his partner.

Eldrik dropped the club and quickly made his exit out the other side of the alley. As he did so he found himself staring at a black haired woman sitting inside an azure tent with golden stars painted over the opening. He glanced up and down the street, trying to decide which way to go, but something about the woman in the tent compelled him to go forward.

She reached out, beckoning for him to come to her. He studied the large, round glass ball on her table. He had heard about fortune-tellers from his mother many times while growing up. She had told him that many were no better than common thieves, but that every once in a while it was possible to find an authentic seer and gain the advantage in life. Perhaps this was a sign that his luck was turning for the better. He walked forward and stopped in the tent's opening.

"Eldrik, I have been waiting for you," the woman said.

"How did you know my name?" he asked.

She curled her finger, motioning for him to step inside. He

did so and the tent flaps unfurled, closing the opening behind him. "I know many things," she said slyly. "I also know why you are here."

Eldrik regarded her curiously. "All right then, why is it that I am here?"

"You wish to avenge your father's murder," she said. "I can help you with that."

Eldrik's mouth fell open and his hand trembled as he reached out to take the seat in front of him. "Who are you?" he asked.

She smiled and pulled a curved knife from under the table and placed it in front of her. She then waved her arms and cloudy mists swirled through the glass ball on the table. "The senate tribunal will not end Lord Lokton's life. He will escape. You will be able to find him in an alley near a well. Wait for him there. You may use your father's crossbow, but be sure to also use this knife if you wish to restore your family's honor."

Eldrik looked at the knife, then he glanced to the woman's smiling face. How could she know so much? Could she be telling the truth? He reached forward and took the knife in his hand. "What do you want from me?"

The woman laughed and shook her head. "I want only to make things right." She waved her left hand and Eldrik felt himself falling away, as if the ground swallowed him. A moment later he found himself sitting on a small wooden stool next to a pile of crates. He looked around, trying to get his bearings. A horse and cart moved away from before him and as it disappeared behind a building Eldrik spied a large well made of stone. He slid his hand and went to stand up but stopped when he heard something hit the dirt below. Eldrik looked down and saw the knife the fortune teller had given him.

He bent down to pick it up and then glanced up and down the alley. He tucked the knife into his belt and crouched down by the crates to wait for his target.

*****

"Sir, wait here and I will go check the well," Braun said.

Lord Lokton nodded and stepped back into the alleyway. He watched Braun pull a cowl over his face and walk out into the square. He wiped the sweat from his face and rubbed his wrists. His skin still stung from the iron cuffs he had been trapped in. He ran his fingers over his dented skin and sighed.

"So, she was right after all," a voice said from the shadows.

Lord Lokton looked up and peered into the darkness. The setting sun had begun to cast long shadows in the alleys and behind buildings. He could only make out a pair of legs and most of a torso. Judging by the voice and the person's stature, it was a young man. "Who's there?" Lord Lokton asked. "Erik?"

The voice laughed. "No, I'm not your son," he said. The legs stepped forward to reveal Eldrik Cedreau's face. "You should be hanging from the gallows for what you have done."

"Eldrik," Lord Lokton said. "I haven't done anything."

"Tell that to my brother, and my father," Eldrik retorted.

Lord Lokton held up his hands and patted the air. "Your father and I have had our differences, but I would never have allowed my men to attack your house. You have my word."

"Your word," Eldrik repeated with a curt nod. He sucked in his lower lip and glanced over his shoulder briefly. "Your word won't heal the hole in my mother's heart. It won't replace my father, and it won't bring back my brother."

"Eldrik, listen," Lord Lokton stopped short as a pain ripped through his chest. He coughed and sputtered, staggered sideways and reflexively moved his hand up. He looked down when his fingers bumped into something hard sticking out of his chest. His eyes nearly fell out of his head when he saw the shaft of a crossbow bolt protruding from his body.

"Now, we are even," Eldrik said as he stepped closer. "Don't bother trying to yell for your bodyguard. I dipped the tip in the venom of a tree viper. You are as good as dead."

"I didn't kill your family," Lord Lokton said.

"One more thing," Eldrik said quietly as he leaned in close. "I want you to know that I will find your son, and I will kill him. There is nothing you can do about it." Eldrik drove the dagger up into Lord Lokton's side, just under the ribs. Eldrik pulled the dagger back.

Lord Lokton opened his mouth, but his strength was already fading. His vision blurred and he slid down to his rump. He barely noticed Eldrik walk away as a fever gripped him and burned him from the inside. Beads of sweat fell from his forehead and his stomach knotted and churned. His hands grew numb and his arms and legs tingled. He tried to focus on breathing, which was becoming more difficult with each passing moment. He fell over to the side, nearly splitting his head on the ground as a vice-like pressure gripped his lungs and heart.

*****

"We didn't expect you so soon," a short servant said.

The warlock regarded the short man with his cold eyes. "There has been a change of plans," Gondok'hr said grimly.

"So, no more playing the senator then?" the servant asked.

"No." Gondok'hr rubbed a hand over his chest, checking that his wounds had healed entirely. "Where is Master Gilifan?"

"He is across the water. He is supposed to return next week."

I see," Gondok'hr said. "I need to be left alone for a few moments."

The servant nodded and walked out through the door. "Call for me when you are ready."

Gondok'hr nodded silently and strolled ethereally toward a smooth hexagonal pedestal topped with a great glass basin filled with water. The warlock waved his hand over his scrying table. The surface rippled in response to his hand and turned black. Within a few moments a great, horned dragon appeared.

"You should not make a habit of contacting me so frequently," Tu'luh said.

"The assassins failed," Gondok'hr said flatly.

Tu'luh emitted a low, throaty growl. "I warned you not to underestimate Lepkin."

"There is more," Gondok'hr said. "I think I found the boy."

Tu'luh's scaly lips stretched thin over his long, curved fangs in what could almost pass for a smile. "Then, what are you waiting for? Kill the boy."

"It is complicated," Gondok'hr said. "I believe the boy is inside Lepkin's body."

"Hm," Tu'luh's voice rumbled low, vibrating the surface of the water in the scrying table. "That is interesting. I wonder how that might have happened."

166

"I don't know," Gondok'hr said. "But, the important thing is that Lepkin is not actually with the boy now."

Tu'luh sat quietly for a moment, studying Gondok'hr intently. "Can you complete your task?"

"Of course, master," Gondok'hr promised. "I have a plan, but I wanted your blessing."

"Tell me quickly," Tu'luh commanded.

"I have returned to Kuressar. My men are ready to strike. I will take them and march on Lokton manor."

"Ah." Tu'luh let out a puff of smoke. "So you will force the boy to return to his home and kill him in battle? I do believe we tried that once already."

"True, but this time will be different. The boy is stuck in Lepkin's body, and now he has openly attacked the senate. I will be able to call upon other reinforcements to ensure that Lokton manor is overrun and the boy is destroyed."

"What of the senate?" Tu'luh asked.

"The senate is destroyed," Gondok'hr said. "Most of the senators are dead. Those that remain will surely be scrambling for power in the current chaos." The warlock left out the part that he was also almost killed because Erik was able to access Lepkin's power to transform into a dragon.

"So, the boy of prophecy has started the civil war himself," Tu'luh said with a throaty chuckle. "The irony is delicious."

"So, I have your blessing then?" Gondok'hr asked.

Tu'luh nodded his massive, horned head. "Proceed, but know this, if you fail I will make you suffer."

"If I fail, it will be because I am dead," Gondok'hr said with a nod of his head.

"There are fates worse than death," Tu'luh warned.

"Understood," Gondok'hr replied. "I will mobilize my forces immediately."

"See it through," Tu'luh commanded. Then his image disappeared and the water turned clear again.

*****

Mickelson hardly looked at Al or Erik and he certainly didn't talk to them. A couple guards approached to question them, but

Mickelson waved them off with an abrupt gesture. Had it been any other senator, the guards may have still prevented them from ascending the staircase to the king, but Mickelson's reputation was well known, and there were none among the guards that would question his honor or his intentions.

Only the four guards before the king's door stopped them. "What business have you with King Mathias?"

"Is this a joke?" Mickelson retorted. "There has been a horrible battle in the senate chamber below and you ask me why we want to see the king?"

Al nudged Erik in the side with his elbow.

Erik glanced down and realized he should say something. He mustered his most official sounding voice and tried to stand as if he were Lepkin. "Several senators tried to execute an innocent noble as a traitor as part of an attempt to shift the balance of power in the kingdom."

Al cut in. "We need to speak with King Mathias in order to know how he would like us to handle the fallout."

The guards looked to each other but remained stoic in front of the door.

The door creaked open behind the guards and a thin, scraggly bearded man stood in the doorway wearing a yellow silken robe. "I will speak with them," he said.

The guards instantly bowed and scrambled out of the way. The king looked to Erik with pale blue irises encircled by slightly yellow orbs. His hollowed cheeks sunk into his face and his hands shook when he waved for them to follow him into the room. Despite the agonizingly slow pace with which King Mathias walked, his stringy white hair billowed out with each step.

"Sire," Mickelson began as they crossed through the king's doorway. "Senator Bracken has been killed, as have many others."

"I assumed as much when I heard the mighty roar of the dragon," King Mathias said hoarsely. He shakily leaned over to reach out for the arm of his high-backed chair, guiding himself in as he slowly sat down. "That was your doing, no doubt," Mathias said nodding to Erik.

"It was," Erik admitted. Erik ran several explanations through his mind, but he couldn't find any words.

The king watched him with those pale blue, jaundiced eyes

and then rested his head back in his chair. "I know about Bracken. I know about most of them, actually," he said. "Honestly Mickelson here is the only senator I don't have any negative information about."

Erik glanced at Mickelson and the senator stood silently.

"With respect," Al started. "Why not do something, if you knew they were plotting against you?"

"A wise man once told me that being a king is not about controlling the people with power, it is about controlling the power for the good of the people."

Al grinned and nodded. "My father told me the same thing," he said.

"Then it is a shame you did not ascend to the throne in Roegudok Hall," Mathias said. "I believe that I would have found a friend in you, as I did your father."

Al bowed his head. "It was not my place," he replied.

"Bah, your place is wherever you can best serve your people. You will see the truth of it soon enough," Mathias retorted.

"So you let Bracken play his political games?" Mickelson asked.

Mathias smiled slightly, his thin skin stretching to the point that Erik thought it might split. "Bracken's games," he repeated. "I am the king of the Middle Kingdom. I rule from the northern sea to the Ten Forts that border upon the orcish lands. For generations we have kept the peace as best as we could, but we have always had our enemies. If not Tarthuns from over the mountains to the east, then we had homegrown vipers that laid in wait, trying to poison the throne from within. Whether this Bracken played his games or not it made no difference. Someone always seeks to put a dagger in the back of the king. That is the way of human men." Mathias convulsed with a bout of coughing. Mickelson and Erik stepped forward to help, but the king raised his hand to stop them.

"Bracken was a warlock," Erik put in. "Were you aware of that?" Out of the corner of his eye Erik caught Al's sour, disapproving expression.

King Mathias finished coughing and cleared his throat. He rubbed his bearded chin and shook his head. "No, that I did not know."

"We believe he was conspiring with those who would seek the

book," Al added.

Lady Arkyn stepped forward. "I saw it too, my king. Bracken was deceiving the senate."

King Mathias breathed in deeply and stroked his beard. "So, there are still those who seek the power of Nagar's Secret. That is unnerving, but not entirely surprising."

"My king," Mickelson started. "With what has happened in the senate chamber, we need a plan of action."

"Yes, well with the Keeper of Secrets charring a score of people in the middle of the senate chamber, I imagine there isn't much we can do to prevent riots in the streets. You have triggered a spring that will give rise to a wave of violence as factions vie for power in the absence of their puppet masters. The back stabbing senators were at least useful for keeping each other in check most of the time."

Erik felt as though it were Lepkin, not King Mathias, sitting there in the chair and giving him a lesson in consequences. He didn't know what to say, so he said what was in his heart. "The men who plotted against you would not have waited much longer. At least for now we have stopped those who not only seek the throne, but the dark magic used by Nagar and Tu'luh to enslave men. I cannot apologize for defending that which I have sworn to protect."

King Mathias nodded and pursed his lips. "I have always appreciated the fact that you speak your mind, Lepkin. It is a breath of fresh air to an old king. I trust that as you gathered evidence of treachery, you also martialed additional allies, yes?"

"He has alerted the Lievonian Order, and tried to talk with my brother as well," Al said.

"Well, the Lievonian Order will surely come," Mathias said. "I have already sent the falcon summoning them when I heard the commotion below. The dwarves, on the other hand, I doubt will raise a hammer to help."

"My people are not without honor," Al said gruffly.

"It is not your people I doubt," King Mathias said. "It is only your brother that I have reservations about." King Mathias coughed again briefly before continuing. "Mickelson, I would suggest you stay in the tower until the Lievonian Order arrives." Then he looked back to Erik. "Master Lepkin, you have put me into a very tight predicament. I have not named an heir, but now there is no senate to rule jointly with you."

Erik bowed his head. He had no words to answer the king with.

Mathias cleared a hefty amount of phlegm from his throat. "Is it your desire to rule the kingdom yourself?"

Erik shook his head. "I have no desire to rule at all," he said.

"I will go to Roegudok Hall," Al interjected. Everyone turned to look at him. "It's time to talk some sense into my brother." Al looked up to Erik. "Plus he has something that Master Lepkin needs."

King Mathias grunted. He looked to Erik with heavy eyes. Whatever was on his mind, he did not say. He turned back to face Al. "I wish you the best of luck," he said. "I do not envy your position."

"Perhaps you could grant me a writ of passage, it would make things easier for me considering what happened in the senate chamber," Al said.

King Mathias nodded. "Out of respect for your late father, you may ask for whatever you need. I can send a pair of my personal guard with you as well."

"Is that necessary?" Mickelson asked.

"Mickelson, you come to me to tell me of corrupt senators and fail to imagine that the rank and file guards in the city might also have their own separate agendas?" Mathias said with a grin. "If I send my own guard, no one will interfere."

"I understand," Mickelson said. "Master Lepkin, what will you do?"

Erik thought of his father. "I have some business to attend to."

King Mathias raised a hand. "I trust you are going to Bracken's house?"

Erik had a confused expression on his face, but Al cut in without missing a beat. "Your majesty, he will investigate the possibility of others who were working with Senator Bracken to get their hands on the book. He will start at Senator Bracken's house. From there he will follow the clues he finds."

"I understand," Mathias said. "I am tired," he said suddenly. "I need to rest." Mathias pulled a small brass bell out of his robe

171

pocket and gave it a gentle shake, sending a high pitched ring through the air.

A young man appeared, seemingly out of nowhere. "You rang, sire?" Erik looked at the young man, dressed in a long tailed black jacket and dark trousers.

Mathias nodded amidst a coughing fit. A small amount of blood seeped into Mathias' beard at the left corner of his mouth. "Bring me my paper and writing utensils. I have some proclamations that need to be sent out immediately." The king looked up to Erik and the others. "You are dismissed. Wait in the main lobby below and I will have my servants bring down the documents you will require."

"Thank you, your majesty," Mickelson said. "Come, let's go." The four of them returned to the ground floor, followed by a trio of the king's personal guards to ensure their safety within the city.

Once in the lobby, Senator Mickelson broke off from the group and went to sit on a stone bench, resting his head back against the wall with a heavy hearted sigh.

"We need to talk," Al said as he took Erik's left elbow in a vice-like grip. "Would you excuse us, Lady Arkyn?"

Lady Arkyn nodded. "Before you do that, I wanted to tell you that I was in Senator Bracken's house. I too was looking for evidence that he was corrupt, but I could never have guessed he was a warlock." She glanced to either side and then continued. "If I were you, I would look in his library. I heard him conversing with someone in there. He called him 'master' and talked about Lord Lokton. I wasn't able to catch the whole conversation, but I think if you go there you might find the answers you are looking for."

"Thank you," Erik said. "Where will you go?"

"I must return to Kuldiga Academy. I have some duties of my own to tend to."

"Good luck," Erik said.

"May your journey be swift and safe," Al added. She nodded and disappeared out the door. After she was gone Al pulled Erik to the opposite side of the lobby and pulled him down onto a white marble bench. "What have you done, boy?"

Erik looked to his friend and then glanced around the lobby. He didn't know what to say.

"You know, I once knew a boy who was so overwhelmed

with curiosity that he would stand in awe in a room such as this." Al swept his hand out, indicating the ornately appointed lobby. "This same young boy once stood in the main entrance of Valtuu Temple, utterly dumbstruck by a simple wall mural."

Erik shrugged and shook his head. "I don't know what you want," he said.

"I want that boy back," Al said. "Who appointed you judge and executioner? Who gave you the right to tear down the senate hall? Do you have any idea what you have started?"

"They were evil," Erik said simply.

Al gruffed and folded his massive arms over his chest. "I think you let your emotions get the better of you."

"What should I have done?" Erik said. "My father is innocent."

"He wouldn't have been the first innocent man to be executed by the senate."

"So you would have let him die?" Erik shook his head and looked away from Al. "And you said I had lost *my* humanity."

The words caused Al to recoil. He tugged on his beard and cleared his throat. "I think Lord Lokton would rather have died than thrust the kingdom into civil war," Al stated.

"Bracken was not who he said he was. He was a warlock," Erik retorted. "I know you saw it too when I took away his spell."

Al grunted. "Yeah, I saw it, but that doesn't explain why you tore through the others."

Erik sighed and leaned forward, planting his elbows on his knees and his chin atop his clenched fists. "I don't know what happened. I tried to summon my power, as I had in training. I wanted to discern enemies from friends." Erik stopped talking and shook his head. "I don't know *how* it happened." He fidgeted with his foot, tapping his heel up and down rapidly. "I just remember being so angry with Bracken. He told me to execute my father and all I could think about was Tukai and his prophecy. Then, once I realized that Bracken was really a warlock too, I couldn't contain myself."

"That's an understatement," Al said. Erik turned to regard his friend, and for the first time since the senate chamber he saw compassion in the dwarf's hard face. "How did you transform into a dragon?"

Erik shook his head. "I wish I knew, but like I already said, I have no idea how it happened. I know how to use Lepkin's sword, but I had no idea I could use his dragonborn power to shift into dragon form."

Al grunted again and tugged on his beard some more. He furrowed his bushy eyebrows and started to speak, but instead he closed his mouth and shook his head again.

"Don't you have any ideas?" Erik asked. "You know more than anyone about the dragons, so you should know more about Lepkin's abilities than anyone else too, right?"

"I don't know, boy," Al whispered. "But let's try to keep it under control from here on out. Did you feel the book try to take hold of you whilst you were in dragon form?"

Erik thought for a moment but shook his head. "No."

"Are you sure," Al pressed.

Erik shrugged. "All of my senses were heightened. I could see better, hear better, and even sense movements around me. I could feel everything within my body. I felt my power amplified, but I didn't notice any influence from the evil book."

Al nodded slowly and smoothed out his beard. "Well, that's a good sign I suppose."

"Still, I won't try to do it again," Erik promised. "Not that I would know how even if I wanted too."

Al placed a reassuring hand on Erik's shoulder. "We'll figure it all out, one step at a time." Erik nodded.

The doors at the other end of the lobby burst open and in walked a pair of men dressed as the other servant had been in King Mathias' room.

"We have the papers from the king," one of the servants said once they were within a few yards of them.

"Much appreciated," Al said. "Well, Senator Mickelson, we'll be on our way then."

Senator Mickelson opened his eyes and nodded at them. "May the gods watch over you and keep you safe."

"Same to you," Al offered. The dwarf stood up and took the proffered documents from the servant and motioned for Erik to follow him. Erik did so, and two of the king's guards fell into step behind them on their way out.

Once outside, Erik caught sight of Braun sticking close to a building across the way from them. He didn't say anything, or make any overt gestures, but when Braun locked gazes with Erik he knew they needed to talk.

"Something's wrong," Erik said. He nudged Al's shoulder and pointed with his chin to Braun.

"Aye, I feel it too," Al agreed. "Let's go see what he needs."

The two of them asked the guards to wait for a moment as they walked over to meet Braun. "What is it Braun?" Erik asked. Braun looked up to Erik with red, bloodshot eyes. His shoulders hung weakly and his chin quivered slightly. Erik's heart sank. He sensed the cause of Braun's sadness before the large man opened his mouth.

"Master Lepkin..." Braun's voice caught in his throat. "My master is dead."

CHAPTER FOURTEEN

"I should return home, with Braun," Erik said.

Al looked over at Braun, still waiting next to the king's guards while he and Erik talked privately. "I understand how you feel, Erik, but we have to be careful in how we respond."

"My father has been killed in the streets, like a dog, and you want me to stay here?"

Al backhanded Erik in the gut. "No one knows you are Erik, you have to act as Lepkin would act."

"Lepkin would go to my home and ensure my family was safe," Erik growled through Al's hand.

"No!" Al whispered harshly. "He would stay here to uncover the assassin and help the king. The two objectives are linked. Think about it, if Bracken sent all of those Blacktongues after us to prevent us from getting to the tribunal, doesn't logic suggest that he might have also hired assassins to take care of your father if the tribunal didn't go the way he wanted?"

"I suppose," Erik said. "But if there are assassins here, then what is to stop them from getting to my home?"

Al clenched his jaw tightly and glared into Erik's eyes. "Listen to me," Al instructed. "*If* Lepkin were here, he would stay because whoever killed your father likely did so on orders from Bracken, and the best way to protect your home would be to uncover who Bracken was working with." Al glanced around to ensure no one saw them arguing. "You and Braun should stay here and investigate your father's murder. Call it poetic justice. You can catch and dispose of his killer."

Erik straightened up. "You would approve of me avenging his death like that?" Erik asked.

"It might be the only way to convince you to stay," Al said with a shrug. "Besides, I already said that I am guessing it was a

Blacktongue, and I never lose sleep over a dead Blacktongue."

Erik nodded his head. "All right, I'll stay, but after this is finished I will accompany Braun to my home and ensure my mother is safe."

Al nodded. "Agreed, but remember that you are here at the king's pleasure. You will need to stay close to him if he desires you to do so."

"All right," Erik said. "Before we depart for Lokton manor, we will speak with the king and make sure he grants us leave."

Al nodded appreciatively. "That sounds more reasonable. Remember, you have to try to control yourself. We can't have any more episodes like what happened at the senate chamber."

"Trust me," Erik said. "If I knew how to transform, I already would have."

Al shot Erik a curious look, then shrugged it off. "Just try to maintain control." Al slapped Erik's elbow. "I will be as quick as I can with my brother, and then I will head straight for Valtuu Temple. Don't dawdle."

Erik nodded. The two of them walked back to Braun. The mighty man looked up expectantly.

"What's the plan?" he asked.

"You and I will remain here to search for Lord Lokton's murderer," Erik said.

"Where do we start?" Braun asked skeptically. "I didn't see anyone, and the crossbow bolt is fairly ordinary. I wouldn't even know where to begin. Perhaps it would be better for me to return to Lokton Manor and resume my duties there?"

Erik held up a hand, fighting the urge to tell Braun who he really was. "I think the murder may be linked to Senator Bracken."

Al cut in. "You will start at Senator Bracken's house. See if there are any clues as to who he may have hired. I fear it may be possible that he employed the services of a Blacktongue."

"No Blacktongue would ever make it into our city," one of the king's guards announced curtly. "Our guards are better than that."

"No doubt," Al said. "But, Blacktongue's aren't new to the game. I doubt they would come through the gates."

The guard bristled and turned away.

"Where do you go?" Braun asked Al.

"I have some business with my brother," Al said.

"Come, let's not waste any more time," Erik said. "The longer we wait the colder the trail will become." Erik turned and addressed one of the king's guards. "Do you know the way to Senator Bracken's home?"

"I know the way," the man replied.

"Then let's go."

"Be careful," Al cautioned.

Erik nodded and motioned for Braun to follow him. So many thoughts were running through his head. He kept replaying the events over and over in his mind. Perhaps if his father had stayed with him then he would still be alive. Or maybe if Erik had arrived to Drakai Glazei a day earlier, for the start of the tribunal, then the whole battle could have been avoided. His father's face haunted his mind.

He had shaken his father's hand, but he was unable to tell him who he really was, or tell him that he loved him. Now he was gone, and he would not see him again in this life. The empty, nagging knot returned to his stomach and gave birth to a stone-like lump in his throat. He started to stumble, but a mighty hand caught hold of his arm and steadied him.

"Are you all right, Master Lepkin?" Braun asked.

Erik shook his head. "No, I am not," he said truthfully.

The king's guard paused, watching the two of them curiously. "Do you want to go to Senator Bracken's house or not?" the man asked.

"Of course," Erik said. "It's nothing, just an old wound acting up." Erik lightly touched his shoulder, hoping they would buy the excuse. If they doubted him, they didn't show it. The two pushed on ahead of him. Erik delayed for a moment, trying to regain his resolve. At last he latched upon his anger. He thought of the person who murdered his father. He imagined a leather-clad tattooed Blacktongue stalking his father from the shadows and attacking from behind with a crossbow. Erik seized upon his hatred for that person and used it to push out his sorrow. He knew it was a tactic that Lepkin would not approve of, but for the moment, it would satisfy his purpose. "There will be time for sorrow later," Erik told himself. "Now it is time for the sword."

Braun stopped suddenly and waited for Erik to catch up. "I

haven't known the great Master Lepkin to show pain," he said.

Erik shrugged it off. And just followed after the king's guard. He scanned the streets as they became wider and the rows of shops and guildhalls gave way to large estates and manors. Short, wooden picket fences gave way to tall, wrought iron privacy fences backed by thick green hedges. Erik might have been mesmerized by the white and gray marble pillars supporting the great, sweeping porches if it weren't for the fact that he knew these houses belonged to the senators. The opulence and grandeur served only as a reminder of the evil greed Erik had found within the senate chamber.

"We'll turn here." Erik turned his attention back to the king's guard.

"We might want to consider going in the back," Braun put in quickly, pointing down the road on their left.

Erik looked and saw a mob of people gathering and making their way down the road toward them. He could hear them shouting and yelling. He could see some carrying pitchforks and shovels. A couple of city guards came into view, arriving from a side street just a few yards ahead of the mob. Erik wasn't sure who started it, but in an instant the mob surged forward, swallowing the two men in the crushing, angry wave.

"I have to go for help, if we don't stop this it can spell disaster," the king's guard said.

"Go, we can handle ourselves," Braun replied.

"Two houses down," the king's guard shouted over his shoulder as he started sprinting away.

Erik and Braun ducked away, hopping a large iron fence and crossing the well-manicured grass and flowers surrounding the marble and granite building. An old, lazy yellow dog raised its head off the grass and gave a half-hearted bark as they skirted by him and to the next fence. A medium-sized black dog appeared from around the house, barking wildly and charging them. The two wasted no time getting to the next yard.

Erik vaulted over the cement partition, barely scanning the ground below before landing next to a large rose bush. A thorn snagged the bottom hem of his tunic, but he paid it no mind. Braun landed a foot to Erik's right. The dog jumped onto the fence behind them, scratching and barking at the cement. Erik sighed in relief and Braun offered a half smile. Then the large man pointed to the back door.

"Let's go have a look around," Braun said.

Erik nodded his agreement. The two stalked up to the white marble steps that led up the ornately appointed slate porch. Gargoyles and dragons peered down at the two of them from the stained glass windows. A shadow moved behind on the other side of the colored glass. Braun and Erik each reached for their weapons.

One of the great double doors opened abruptly and a large man with a hawkish snout and fat lips stood in the doorway staring down his nose at them with an eyebrow arched so far that it almost touched his hairline.

"Intruders shall not be tolerated," the man said as his hands went for a flanged mace hanging from his belt.

Braun went to strike but Erik put a hand on the man's shoulder and stopped him. "Your master is dead, and we are here upon King Mathias' orders to investigate possible leads."

The guard peered at Erik for a moment before slowly replacing his mace. "When did he die?" he asked.

"Earlier today," Erik replied.

"And why should I believe you?"

"Surely you recognize me?" Erik added.

The man nodded. "I recognize you," the guard said. "But, if you are here on official business, then why are you skulking about the back door like a thief?"

"Take a look out the front door and you will see an angry mob. We thought it best to avoid that," Erik said.

The guard stood there, shifting his gaze from Erik to Braun. "I don't know you," he said.

"He is assisting me," Erik said. "His name is Braun, he serves House Lokton."

The guard nodded. "And Senator Bracken is truly dead?"

"Yes," Erik replied.

The guard narrowed his eyes on Erik. "Did you see his body with your own eyes?"

Erik sensed something in the man's tone, an eagerness that piqued Erik's curiosity. He scanned the man with his power, discerning the guard's intentions. How he wished he could decipher auras the way that Marlin could. It would be easier for him if he could use a man's energy to learn more about them. However, his own power was not without merit, notwithstanding his elementary understanding of his gift. His scan told him that this man was not a foe, and might even be here against his will. He couldn't be sure, but he decided to take a chance.

"Would that make you happy?" Erik asked.

The guard bristled and cocked his head back. "N-no, why would you ask that?"

Erik sensed the man was lying. He smiled warmly and nodded his head. "You have no need to fear me. I know that your master was involved in the dark arts," Erik said.

The guard's shoulders tensed.

"We also know that he wasn't really Senator Bracken," Braun put in, catching on to Erik's direction.

"You saw his body?" the guard asked again.

Erik leaned in. "I ended his life once I discovered his true identity and his treachery."

The guard looked to Braun, who nodded and affirmed the claim. A smile of relief washed over the guard's face and his shoulders fell slack as he exhaled. He looked to Erik as though a heavy boulder had just rolled off of his back. "That is something I have been waiting to hear for a very long time," the guard said. He stuck out his right hand. "My name is Gildrin, I am Senator Bracken's steward." A frown flashed across his face. "I was away on business when my true master was slain by that wretched warlock. When I returned, I noticed the differences and sensed the man who took his place was only an imposter."

"Then why stay?" Braun asked.

"Have you ever faced a warlock by yourself?" Gildrin asked. "I wanted to leave, but he cursed me. His spell bound me to this house. He cursed me so that if I were to leave the house so long as he lived, my heart would burst from inside."

"So then why not kill him and end the curse?" Braun pressed.

"Believe me, I wanted to do just that," Gildrin said. "The other part of the curse was that I could not raise my hand against him nor design a scheme to have him killed." Gildrin sighed and shook his head. "I tried once, but as soon as I raised my mace and advanced, there was a horrible fire that encircled me. The flames burned my soul, but did not damage my body. After three days of unending fire, he released me from my punishment and warned me that the next time I tried to harm him he would leave me in that agony for a month."

"I'm sorry," Erik offered.

Gildrin nodded. "So, now that he is dead, what can I do for you?"

"We believe the warlock created a plan to assassinate Lord Lokton," Braun said.

Gildrin frowned and wrinkled his nose. "Well, come in. I can take you to his chamber and show you where he would keep his secrets."

Erik and Braun followed Gildrin into the house. The air was cold, and smelled of old leather and smoke. Large vases, sculptures, and trinkets adorned the corners and walls. Great, intricately woven rugs lay over the dark wooden floor, holding the large, plush couches and chairs in place.

"This makes Lokton Manor look like a stable," Braun said.

Erik nodded.

Gildrin grinned. "It was once a lovely place, when my master was alive. The real Senator Bracken was born and raised here, as was his father, and his father before him. The house goes back for many generations of faithful servants to the kingdom." A tear appeared in his right eye, but it did not fall. "If I can help restore this family's honor by helping you, then that would make me the happiest man alive."

"You loved your master then?" Braun asked.

Gildrin nodded. "I looked upon Senator Bracken as a dear uncle. He always treated me fairly, and he dealt honestly with others as far as I was aware." He motioned for them to follow him to a grand staircase. "We are going up," he said.

The stairs creaked and popped the way that old wooden stairs do but the sounds were muffled by a great purple runner held in place by brass bars bracketed into the inside corner of each step. The runner was faded and well worn, but still had years of life left in it. Erik ran his fingers over the smooth, brass bannister, marveling at the opulence.

"How could a senator afford all of this?" Erik asked.

Gildrin shrugged. "Aside from their salary, each senator has access to a wealth of information."

"Not to mention connections forged through their power and authority," Braun added. Erik recognized the disgust in Braun's tone.

Gildrin shrugged it off and kept walking. "My master was not so bad, considering the company he kept. Much of what you see here is the combined efforts of generations, not merely one man's accumulations."

"How did the warlock choose him?" Erik asked, changing the subject.

"I don't know," Gildrin replied. "As I said, I was away at the time."

"You didn't notice anything strange in the time leading up to it?" Braun inquired.

"No, I know it may not speak well of my skills as a guard, but I noticed nothing out of the ordinary." Gildrin paused at the top of the stairs. He turned and held his right arm out, pointing down the hall. "This way is the bed chamber. However," he pointed down the opposite hall. "This way leads to the old library. It is there I would look first, if I were you."

"Actually the library is first on my list as well," Erik said as he recalled Lady Arkyn's words. "Are there any other servants?" Erik asked.

Gildrin frowned. "Not anymore," he said. Braun pushed past them and walked toward the old library. His footsteps muffled by a red runner that spanned most of the hallway's width. The trio stopped in front of the door as Gildrin fumbled through a large iron key ring. "I have a key here somewhere," he said.

Erik scanned the door. It was plain enough, made of redwood and bearing only an engraved "B" in the top panel of the door. The brass knob was tarnished and dirty from years of use. Erik put a hand out to the door and used his power to scan the door. He was concerned that there may be some sort of magical trap.

Gildrin found the key and slid it into place. "Got it," he said.

Erik snatched Gildrin by the wrist and yanked his hand back. "Wait!" He shoved the man aside and motioned for Braun to back away. "There is a magical trap on this door."

"How can you tell?" Gildrin asked. "I have gone through this door many times, and nothing has ever happened before."

"Did you ever enter while the warlock was away from the manor?" Braun asked.

"No, I only..." Gildrin closed his mouth as it dawned on him.

"He must have set it before he left the house," Erik said. "I was scanning the door and everything seemed all right, but when you slid the key into the lock a green symbol appeared over the top panel of the door."

"I don't see anything," Gildrin said.

"Still, I wouldn't argue with Master Lepkin," Braun said. "Can you get around it?"

Erik shook his head. "Without knowing what the spell is, I wouldn't know how." Erik thought hard. Though the others couldn't see the symbol it was obvious that the spell was not any sort of illusion, he would have been able to dispel that. This was a different kind of spell. He had no way of knowing what might happen if they tried to open the door. Perhaps it would explode into flame, or freeze the trespasser's hand to the door. No matter what the spell was, Erik had no way of disarming the trap.

"I bet this has to do with the other night," Gildrin said after a moment.

"What happened the other night?" Erik asked.

"I saw a blonde woman kneeling at the door shortly after the imposter returned home from his travels."

"Did you confront her?" Braun asked.

Gildrin shook his head. "My curse is that *I* cannot scheme against or kill the warlock." He smiled slyly and gave them a wink. "I pretended not to notice and continued on toward the bedchamber. By the time I turned back, she was gone and the window at the end of the hall was slightly ajar."

"Interesting," Braun put in, stealing a glance at Erik. Erik nodded, but neither of them offered to tell Gildrin who had snuck in that night. "Is there another way in?" Braun asked.

Gildrin knit his brow and then snapped his fingers. "There is!" He motioned for the two of them to follow him to the next door in the hall. "This is one of the old guest chambers. Inside there is a dumbwaiter in the wall adjacent to the library. The dumbwaiter has a door in both rooms."

"Wouldn't he seal that too?" Erik asked skeptically.

Gildrin shook his head. "I doubt it," he said. "Senator

Bracken liked books more than he liked the dumbwaiter, so several years ago he painted over the door in the library and put a bookshelf in front of it. I bet the warlock never knew it was there."

Braun turned to Erik. "It's worth a try, I suppose."

Erik nodded in agreement. "Let me scan the area before we bust through, just in case." The others nodded and Gildrin excitedly went through the door into the guest chamber. He walked straight to the wall opposite the large canopy bed and pulled on a brass ring. A wooden panel, just large enough for a man to squeeze through, opened with a puff of dust and a few stray cobwebs.

"This is it," Gildrin said.

Erik rushed up to his side and peered in. "It looks safe," Erik said.

"So do we try it?" Braun asked. The large man stopped short and turned to the canopy bed. "I have an idea." He went to one of the thick wooden supports and hacked through it with a mighty chop of his sword.

"What are you doing?" Gildrin shrieked.

"Your master is dead, so is mine. Let's worry about avenging them, instead of fretting over furniture that no one uses anymore," Braun shot back. Gildrin bristled, but shut his mouth as Braun finished ripping the support free of the bed. The canopy roof cracked and drooped low, but stayed up as Braun walked away. "Just in case there is some sort of trap, I can use this like a lance."

"You sure?" Erik asked.

Braun shrugged. "I'll wait a few moments for the two of you to get back a bit, just in case."

Erik backpedaled to the window and then folded his arms, hoping he was right about the door being safe. Braun turned the support over in his hands, securing his grip and then he levelled it at the hole, aiming for the door to the library. Without a word he charged forward. The knobby end of the support crashed into the door on the other side. Braun ran through with ease, but was jerked to the side when his makeshift battering ram slammed into the bookshelf beyond the door. The wooden support bent and then exploded in the middle, sending wood chips all about the room and tumbling Braun forward at the sudden lack of resistance. Braun managed to catch himself by planting his forearm on the wall just before going into the dumbwaiter.

He backed out with a sly grin on his face. "No explosions," he teased.

Erik nodded and moved quickly into position. He could see light coming in around the massive bookshelf. Only a few bits of the door clung to the hinges. The rest was gone, obliterated by Braun. "Let's grab the three remaining posts and all push together. That should move the bookshelf."

"Already working on it," Braun said. Erik turned to see the man pulling his sword and heading for the bed. "Gildrin, come hold the canopy," he instructed. Erik jogged over to grab the other side of the canopy and Braun used accurate, short chops to remove the other posts. Once the job was done Gildrin and Erik tossed the canopy aside and each grabbed a post from Braun. The three of them then walked to the opening and placed their posts securely against the bookshelf.

"Try to push at the top," Erik said.

"On three," Braun said.

Erik nodded and started to count. "One, two, three!" They all pushed with steady pressure. At first nothing happened, but after a couple of moments the bookshelf started to tip and then it fell, crashing to the floor with a mighty *whoosh*! Books and wood skittered across the floor and dust flew up around the rubbage. Erik smiled. He dropped his post and scrambled through the tight opening.

"Be careful," Gildrin said.

"Nothing to it," Erik replied as he squeezed out the other side. He brushed off the wood splinters and looked around. His mouth dropped open and he stood in utter shock.

Braun was next through the opening. "By the gods," he said as he stepped up beside Erik. They both turned to Gildrin. "Are you coming?" Braun asked.

Gildrin shook his head. "I have seen that room enough to last a lifetime," he replied. "If there is anything to find, it will likely be in the old desk. He brought that with him."

Erik turned. His eyes were first drawn to the tapestries. Each depicting horrendous scenes of carnage. One was a great beast devouring a maiden, another was a dragon drinking the blood of a decapitated minotaur, and others showed various demons delighting in torturing what Erik could only imagine were the souls of the dead.

"What makes a man choose to live like this?" Braun said as he picked up a human skull from a table. "Why would someone encircle themselves with death?"

"Power," Gildrin answered from the other room.

Braun nodded solemnly and put the skull back on the table. "Power," he repeated. He dusted off his hands and pointed to an old desk in the back of the room. "There it is."

Erik pulled his eyes away from the tapestries and saw a great, flat desk with a tall hutch on the back. It wasn't made from any kind of wood he recognized. It was solid black and filled with knots. Thorns and barbs stuck out from the legs and looked menacing enough to slice the unwary to pieces in an instant. Runes were put into the top of the desk, etched in and then inlaid with gold. Erik traced the shapes with his eyes only, afraid to touch them.

"What do they mean?" Braun asked.

Erik shook his head. "I have no idea." He placed his hand under the front, where a drawer should have been, but he found nothing. He bent low and looked under the desk. "There are no drawers here."

"Here," Braun said as he reached for a door on the hutch. The door opened easily, revealing a few jars of powder amidst several multi-colored crystals. Braun fingered through the contents and shook his head. "Nothing here that will help us."

Erik tried the door on the right side of the desktop hutch and found several large, leather bound books. He pulled one out and opened the cover.

"Are you sure you should open it?" Braun asked.

Erik shrugged. "I know the dangers of books better than most, but I doubt anything in this library will harm us without some sort of additional magic."

"If he trapped the door, he might have laid traps on his things as well."

Erik shook his head. "I don't see any. I imagine the warlock was confident enough in his first trap that he saw no reason to add more."

"Or perhaps these aren't the things he was worried about keeping safe." Braun nudged Erik and pointed to a silk blanket

187

covering an object a few yards away. "With all of the hideous things in this room, what could the warlock possibly want to cover?"

From the high, oval shape Erik guessed it was a mirror. He watched Braun go to the object and slowly remove the sheet to discover a life-size portrait of a family. The woman had red hair, and was very fair to look upon. She held a baby in her arms, wrapped in a blue blanket. Behind the two of them stood a man, smiling and happy.

"The brass plate at the bottom is scratched out, I can't read it," Braun said.

"You don't have to read it, Braun," Erik replied. "Look at the man."

Braun turned back to Erik and nodded. "It appears to be a portrait of the warlock," he said. "Though, by the looks of it this was painted decades ago."

Erik paused. "He had a family once," he said. He looked at the picture, studying the man's smiling face. He looked so happy and peaceful. What could have changed? Erik turned back to the shelf with the books and noticed a ray of light glinting off of something in the back. He removed the other books and piled them on the desk. As he pulled the last book from the cubby, he saw that there was a brass lever in the back. He reached in and depressed it. A drawer popped out two inches from the side of the desk.

"What have you got there?" Braun asked.

Erik shrugged and gently pulled the drawer out to its fullest extent. Inside he found a handful of letters, tied into a bundle with old, red ribbon. He picked the letters up and turned them over in his hand. It was then that he realized it wasn't simply a red ribbon, it was part of a necklace. A small, star-shaped pendant hung from the bottom. Erik gently undid the necklace and placed it on the desk.

"Who are the letters from?" Braun asked as he walked up to stand near the desk.

Erik took the top letter and handed a few to Braun. He quickly scanned through the fading ink, careful not to rip the old paper. "Are you sure he brought this desk with him?" Erik shouted over his back to Gildrin.

"As sure as you are standing here today, he brought that desk with him," Gildrin replied.

"I don't think these will help us," Braun said after finishing another letter. He tossed the stack back to the desk. "Old love letters are not going to find the assassin."

"No, perhaps not," Erik agreed. He set his letter down and picked up the bottom letter in the stack. "This one appears to be the most recent, according to the dates on the letters," Erik said.

"I'm going to look around," Braun said as he went for a knotty black bookshelf.

Erik read through the letter. "This one is different," Erik said.

"How can you tell?" Braun asked as he rummaged through a pair of black leather books.

"This is an official letter, from some governor." Erik turned the letter over in his hand and inspected the broken, crumbling wax seal. "It reads; Esteemed Master Pemo, it is with great sadness that I pen this letter. It gives me no pleasure to inform you that your wife, Kyra, and your son, Baldwin, have been slain by a band of Tarthun raiders while you were away in service to me at the border. I blame no one but myself for this tragedy, as I should not have allowed your wife to remain on your homestead while you were away. Please, return from your duties at once and I will help you settle your family's affairs. Sincerely, Governor Randal."

"Governor Randal?" Braun asked. "I don't think I have heard that name before."

"I have," Gildrin said from the other room.

Erik and Braun turned to look through the dumbwaiter, waiting for the explanation.

"It was probably twenty or thirty years ago now," Gildrin said. "But I heard that Governor Randal was killed by a wizard that served in his court. Governor Randal had the duty of overseeing part of the border to the east and protecting the kingdom from Tarthun invaders. Some versions of the story say the wizard returned with an army of Tarthuns and wiped Governor Randal and his city from the map in one night. Another version says the wizard called upon the gods of Hammenfein to help him destroy Governor Randal. Others say the wizard returned at night and buried the city in a cloud of fire and lightning."

"Do the stories say why the wizard did this?" Braun asked.

"That is the strange part," Gildrin said. "All of the stories say that it was because Randal betrayed the wizard and took his wife."

"But the letter says she was killed by an attack," Erik pointed out.

Gildrin shrugged. "I have heard a version where Randal kills the wizard's wife because she will not leave her husband, but never have I heard a version that fits with the letter you just read."

"So, perhaps our warlock was this wizard you heard of," Erik mused.

"To what end?" Braun asked. "If those stories are true, then why would the wizard become a warlock?"

Gildrin snapped his fingers and pointed excitedly to the bookshelf Braun stood next to. "Turn around," he told Braun. "What kind of books do you see?"

Braun turned and pulled a few of them from the shelf. "I can't read most of these," he said. "They are written in strange languages." He pulled a green book from the shelf and opened it. "Wait, this one is in the common tongue."

"It is a book about necromancy, is it not?" Gildrin asked.

Braun turned and nodded slowly. Then he scanned the other books on the shelf. "Of the ones in common tongue, it looks like most of them deal with necromancy," he said.

"That's it," Gildrin said. "That's why he began following the dark arts." The two looked back to Gildrin. "Don't you see? He wants to bring his family back to life."

Erik wheeled on Braun. "That is why he would join with the warlocks of the Order of the All Seeing Eye," he said. "They seek the book."

Braun nodded. "And the book describes how to make an army by bringing the dead back to life."

"He didn't want power," Erik said. "He wanted to use the book to resurrect his family."

"Even so, he was willing to kill a lot of innocent people to get that power."

Erik nodded and sighed. "Not to mention the other powers that the book would unleash."

"What book?" Gildrin asked.

"Nagar's Secret," Erik answered.

The three were silent for a few moments. Erik stood,

rereading the letter from Governor Randal and scanning through the other letters while Braun went back to the bookshelf. After Erik finished reading all of the letters he plopped them onto the desk.

"I do believe that the warlock is the wizard in Gildrin's story," Erik said. He turned back to Gildrin. "How did you hear that story?" he asked.

Gildrin shrugged. "I have been privy to a lot of meetings with senators and other officers of state. You would be surprised by the amount of story swapping they will do after a glass or two of ale."

"Master Lepkin, I have something," Braun said suddenly. "There is a brass ring here behind these books." He reached in and pulled it. The bookshelf swiveled away, scraping over the wooden floor and revealing another covered object. It stood slightly over four feet from the floor. The top was circular, though there were some angles and points seen beneath the covering.

The two of them walked over to it and each took a corner of the purple silk cloth. They glanced to each other for a moment and then simultaneously ripped the covering away to reveal a black basin atop a pedestal of black bone.

"What kind of bone do you think this is?" Braun asked.

Erik inspected the thick, long bones and shrugged. "I couldn't say." Erik ran his fingers around the edge of the basin, studying the curious runes along the outside of the bowl.

"Do you know what this is?" Braun asked.

"I am not sure," Erik said. "Maybe a wash basin?" He leaned over and looked into the liquid in the basin. The black, viscous contents shimmered back at him, mesmerizing him. He stared farther into the liquid, leaning down closer. He reached up with his hands and gripped the sides of the basin. A ball of silver appeared in the center of the black liquid that caught Erik's gaze. Erik watched it grow into a cloud and disperse through the blackness. As the silver spread, an image formed in the center. The basin started to hum and vibrate. Erik wanted to pull back, but something held him fast to the object.

"So, you have come," a voice spoke from within the darkness. Erik's heart quickened. His stomach knotted and flipped. Though he didn't recognize the voice, he could feel its contempt for him as though it were a hand that had reach out and struck him across the gut. The silver cloud was now gone and a great, scaled face peered back at him through the liquid. Massive, downward curled horns pointed to a maw of thick, sharp teeth set inside the long snout under a pair of glowing, red eyes.

"Who are you?" Erik asked, his voice barely sounding louder than the squeak of a mouse.

A throaty, rumbling laugh answered him as the scaled lips parted to reveal the hot fire within the dragon's throat. "You don't know?" the dragon teased. Its eyes bored into Erik's soul, stripping away his courage and leaving him weak in the knees. "The great champion has come, but he is not prepared." Tendrils of smoke snaked out from the dragon's nostrils as it sighed in delight. "You are not ready for what is coming."

"What is coming?" Erik asked.

The dragon's lips curled upward into a wicked smile that petrified Erik more than anything he had ever seen. "Come to Lokton Manor, and I shall give you a taste of things to come." The dragon glared with its red hot eyes. "Come, and face your destiny!" The dragon opened its cavernous mouth and a blast of fire came out through the liquid and burst into a great fireball there in the library.

The scrying pool shattered, spewing shards of bone all about. Erik felt the heat wrap around him, burning his entire being before he flew backward, spinning in the air end over end until he slammed into the wall near the dumbwaiter and slid down into the pile of rubble. The heat continued to sting and rip at him, but he was not aflame. He tried to push himself up, he knew he should be looking for something, but he couldn't remember what it was. He slumped down and let his face fall upon an old book. His vision blurred and he teetered on the edge of consciousness.

Moments later a pair of hands scooped under him and heaved him up. He could hear voices, but couldn't understand what they were saying or who they belonged to. He passed through a small, dark hole and then was placed onto a soft, green bed. He moved his eyes around and slowly recognized where he was.

"Braun?" Erik asked.

"I am here, Master Lepkin," Braun replied.

Erik struggled to raise his head enough to see Braun standing at the foot of the bed. He could see a couple of rips in the man's tunic. Bits of black bone clung to his clothes and some blood seeped out from where some of the shards had landed. After seeing that Braun appeared to be all right, Erik dropped back down and looked up to the other man standing over him.

"Are you all right?" Gildrin asked.

"Can you fetch him some water?" Braun asked. "I will check him for injuries."

Gildrin nodded and disappeared from view.

"Are you hurt?" Braun asked.

Erik tried to speak, but nothing came out. His lips, hands, and feet tingled and stung as though they were waking from a long numbness. A moment later a terrible sharp pain ripped through Erik's shoulder. He reflexively turned his head and saw Braun's bloody hands squeezing his shoulder.

Braun looked up. "Your wound came open," he said. "I can stop the bleeding though, it isn't serious." Braun tugged the sheet out from under Erik and tore it into strips. He quickly set about tying a new bandage onto Erik's shoulder.

"Is he hurt badly?" Gildrin asked when he returned.

"This is an old wound," Braun said. "But I am not sure how conscious he is at the moment."

"I'm fine," Erik whispered hoarsely. "But my head hurts."

Braun finished tying the bandage and grabbed Erik's head, turning it this way and that. "No signs of injury on the outside." He then covered Erik's eyes with his hands and then moved his hands abruptly, letting the daylight wash over him. "Pupils still react normally to light."

"What did you see?" Gildrin asked. "What did you see when you looked into that basin?"

"I'm not sure," Erik said. "It looked like..."

"Like what?" Braun pressed. "What was it?"

"It was a dragon," Erik replied.

The other two stole a glance at each other and then turned back to Erik. "Master Lepkin," Braun started. "Are you sure it was a dragon?"

Erik nodded. "I am positive." He took the water from Gildrin and slowly sat up enough to drink the cool, refreshing liquid.

"What did he say?" Gildrin asked.

Erik closed his eyes and wiped his forehead with the back of his right hand. "I think he is going to attack Lokton Manor," he said at last.

"What?" Braun shouted. "How could a dragon attack Lokton Manor?"

"And why?" Gildrin added.

"I don't know, but I do know that we have to get there first," Erik said. "Help me up."

Gildrin put his arm under Erik's armpit and helped him to his feet. "I have four horses at the stable down the street. We can take them."

"Hold a moment," Braun said grimly. Erik spun his head to look at Braun, who was pointing down to Erik's leg.

Erik looked down and saw a patch of crimson over his thigh. The warm liquid leaked out of him quickly, expanding the red spot over his leg. "It's nothing," Erik said. Gildrin began pushing Erik back to the bed. "No, we have to go," Erik said.

"Go and fetch me some more bandages," Braun ordered. He pulled a knife from his belt and cut a hole in Erik's trousers. Then his massive fingers spread the cloth enough to work his hands inside so he could rip the material away. "This is bad," Braun said.

Erik looked down and saw that his leg had opened. Unlike his shoulder, the blood was pouring out quickly and Braun's hands couldn't apply enough pressure to make it stop.

"Gildrin, hurry up!" Braun shouted.

Erik's lost control of his body. His head felt as though it were detached and floating away. He didn't even notice when he fell back down. He muttered something about going home and then he slipped over the edge of consciousness, giving in to the welcoming darkness around him.

CHAPTER FIFTEEN

Master Orres sat at his desk, nursing a bottle of ale and trying to clear his head. A slew of books were scattered in front of him. Two of them were histories of the southern border, which told of orc attacks and invasions over the last couple of centuries. Another was a chronology of House Finorel. He turned the roll of paper over in his hand, staring at the "G" at the bottom of the page.

"This is pointless," Orres told himself. "There is no mention of anyone in House Finorel with a name starting with 'g' and I can't find anything in the history books to make sense of why B'dargen would be interested in orcs."

The sunlight coming through the window began to fade and turn colors, signaling the last few hours of the day before night would sweep in. He turned to look out the window and catch the sunset, but instead he saw a hawk descending to the perch outside Orres' window. The bird quickly pulled on a red string with its sharp beak and the bell inside Orres' office rang twice.

Master Orres stood and went to the window. By the red and black ribbons tied to the hawk's legs, he knew this bird had come from Drakai Glazei. He pressed the window open and reached out for the small paper rolled in a leather pouch on the hawk's left leg. He unrolled the paper and his mouth fell open. He stumbled back and flopped into his chair, letting the paper drop to the ground. He sat silently, nervously tapping his fingers on his leg and looking back at the bird.

A knock came at the door.

"Come in," Orres said.

Master Wendal walked in and shook his head. "I have finished searching Janik's office, but I didn't find anything about orcs."

"What about any letters with the same signature?" Orres asked.

Wendal shook his head. "No. I tossed the office very thoroughly too, looking in every nook and cranny, but there was nothing."

Orres took the bottle of ale from his desk. "I already figured we wouldn't find anything," Orres replied after a big gulp to finish off the bottle. "The man was clever enough to hide his true intentions for years. It was a long shot that he would have been careless enough to leave evidence in his office. I just wish I knew who he was working with."

"Well, if he was working with Master B'dargen or House Finorel, I couldn't find any proof. What shall we do now?" Wendal asked.

Orres dropped the bottle into a waste basket and shrugged. "I think we should close the academy."

Wendal's mouth dropped open. "To what end?"

Orres took in a breath and turned to the window behind him. He rose from his chair and crossed his arms over his barrel of a chest and sighed. "This hawk has just brought me a message from the king." Orres bent over to pick up the note and read it again.

"What does it say?" Wendal asked.

"That I am to close the academy immediately, send the students back to their families and stand by for further instructions. All of the other masters are to remain here with me until further notice."

Master Wendal crossed the floor and held out his hand for the note. Master Orres gave it to him and waited for Wendal to read it. As the mage finished, his mouth fell open and he looked up to Orres with a blank stare.

"That was my reaction too," Orres said.

Wendal shook his head and handed the note back. "It doesn't say who attacked the senate hall, or even how many senators were killed," Wendal noted. "Maybe we are too late?"

Orres nodded and sighed. "That is possible, but we can't know for sure. I need to send a response immediately. I will ask for more details, but I am not certain how long it will take for the king to respond."

"I can wait outside if you like," Wendal said.

Orres nodded. "You can wait in here if you like. I will need to decide how to proceed closing the academy as well. It would be good to have you here for that." Wendal stepped back to take a seat on an old, yellow couch. Orres went back to his desk and pulled a small piece of paper out. He wrote a short response to the king's message promising to do as the king instructed. He also asked for any additional details the king could offer.

When he finished the note he turned it sideways in his large paws and began tightly crimping the paper over into tight folds that would fit into the leather pouch the hawk wore. Orres held the note in place with a large thumb and reached out for his green wax stick. He stuck the end into a nearby candle, melting then end until a small bit dribbled on the desk. Then he moved it over and pressed the soft end onto the paper, swirling the stick around to ensure a good amount of wax stuck to the paper when he pulled away. Next he took his hand and pressed the ring on his middle finger into the wax. He let it sit in the wax for just a moment before pulling it back and blowing on the wax to cool it.

Satisfied that it was ready he stood and returned to the window. He reached over to a can and pulled a piece of dried rabbit meat out. He slid the note into the hawk's pouch and looped the leather thong around a button to fasten the pouch closed. Then he gave the hawk the piece of meat and the bird flew off, bound for home.

Orres turned back to Wendal and shook his head. We need to call a general council. Go and gather all of the masters into the Bellwood auditorium. I can speak with them there.

Wendal rose from the couch and stopped just short of the door. "Have you heard from Lady Arkyn?"

Orres shook his head. "No word from her yet."

Wendal nodded again and then exited the room, closing the door behind him. Orres went back to his chair and ran a hand through his hair. He leaned back lazily and stretched out, trying to make sense of what was happening. He sat for several minutes, guessing whether it might have been Lady Arkyn or Master Lepkin who had stirred up the senate hall. Or, perhaps it was someone else altogether? He let his eyes close as his mind walked through the various scenarios.

"Napping in the office?" a familiar voice said.

Orres jumped a bit and looked to the door, Lady Arkyn smiled and pushed the door open the rest of the way before slipping in and closing it behind her. "When did you return?" Orres asked.

"Only just a moment or two ago. I saw Master Wendal rushing down the hall, what was that about?"

Orres eyed her warily. "Perhaps you should tell me about the senate hall first," he said.

Her smile vanished. "You heard about that?"

Orres nodded and pointed to the empty perch outside his window. "A little birdie told me all about it."

"Right now I bet you are wondering whether I was too eager to use my bow," she teased. Orres didn't respond. "It wasn't me," she promised. "I didn't even have my bow with me when I went to the senate hall." She came in closer and stood in front of the desk.

"Well then, what happened?"

Lady Arkyn looked at Orres with sad eyes. "Let me start from the beginning. I think that will help you put it all into context."

Orres agreed with a slight nod of his head.

"I went to the senate hall when I first arrived in Drakai Glazei. I thought if Bracken had any secrets, he might hide them at his office there, but I didn't find anything. So, I went to his house and snuck inside."

"You broke into a senator's house?" Orres asked.

Lady Arkyn grinned slyly. "I wasn't able to stay long, I was almost caught by the guard, but I did find something peculiar. I watched Senator Bracken unlock magical barriers on a door in his house, then he went into the room and started talking with someone.

"Someone was locked inside the room?" Orres asked.

Lady Arkyn shook her head. "I am not entirely sure, but I think he was using magic to converse with the other person. He addressed the other man as his 'master' and the two of them discussed whether Lord Lokton had decided to join them."

"Join who?"

Lady Arkyn held up her finger. "I am not sure, but that is not the most interesting part," she said.

"What do you mean?" Orres asked.

"The other man called Senator Bracken by a different name."

Orres leaned forward eagerly, planting both hands on his desk. "What did he call him?"

"It was a strange name," Lady Arkyn commented. "He called him Gondok'hr."

Orres sat back in his seat and stroked his chin. "Gondok'hr," he repeated aloud. He pulled out the note found in B'dargen's office and looked at the signature again.

"Shortly after that, the guard came up the stairs and I had to make my escape or risk being caught," Lady Arkyn continued. "So I thought I would attend the tribunal and see if I could figure out why they had been talking about Lord Lokton."

"Did you?" Orres asked.

She shook her head. "Not really. I did ascertain that the tribunal was completely unfair though."

"How do you know that?" Orres asked.

"I hid near the ceiling, on one of the beams that holds a chandelier. I could see and hear everything. I expected the tribunal to last for several hours while the evidence was presented and the parties involved gave testimony, but it wasn't like that at all. Senator Bracken came out and presented evidence along with his testimony and then tried to call for a verdict."

"Without Lord Lokton being allowed to defend himself?" Orres asked.

Lady Arkyn nodded. "Senator Mickelson put up quite an argument though. Not only did he denounce the evidence, but he tore into Senator Bracken directly in an extremely vicious tirade. He accused him of tampering with the evidence and not following proper procedure during the investigation. He even called for a vote to have the matter reinvestigated by a team of senators he assumed would be impartial."

"What happened then?" Orres asked.

Lady Arkyn sighed. "Senator Desepp brought out another prisoner. He announced the man as Braun, one of Lord Lokton's men at arms. He explained that Braun had been caught trying to sneak into the senate hall during the night and that he was presumed to be trying to help Lord Lokton escape."

Orres nodded. "So, because the senate believed Lord Lokton was trying to escape, he lost his right to defend himself."

"Exactly," Lady Arkyn affirmed. "Desepp ordered Mickelson to refrain from speaking while he presented the evidence against Braun. The senate was just about to call for a verdict when Master

Lepkin walked in with a dwarf."

"Al," Orres corrected.

"Ah, you know him too?" Lady Arkyn asked.

Orres nodded. "I have met him before."

"Well, I don't remember all of the exact words. Everything started to move so quickly after they showed up. Lepkin argued with Senator Bracken over the protocol. Apparently the tribunal had started a day earlier than Lepkin was informed so he missed the proceedings. Lepkin said he would demand a review of the tribunal. Bracken pushed the senate to vote anyway and they reached a guilty verdict. Then Bracken insinuated that Lepkin was there not to fulfill his role in answering the summons, but to help Lord Lokton escape. He said the only way Lepkin could prove his honor was to execute Lord Lokton."

"That is outrageous!" Orres shouted. He jumped to his feet and pounded a fist on his desk. "Had I been there I would have given that senator a piece of..." he stopped and looked to Lady Arkyn. She stood there, looking at the floor and biting her lower lip. "Oh no," Orres said. "Lepkin is the one?"

She nodded. "But it wasn't without cause," Lady Arkyn added quickly. "Senator Bracken was not really the senator. He was an imposter, a warlock deceiving everyone with magic so they thought he was Senator Bracken. When Master Lepkin realized the danger he shifted into a dragon and ripped the senate hall apart. Several senators died, as did the executioner."

"And Bracken?" Orres asked.

Lady Arkyn nodded. "While Lepkin was in dragon form he ran his tail spikes through the imposter."

"So what happened afterwards?"

"Next we went to the king. Master Lepkin and the dwarf told him all that had happened. Senator Mickelson was there with us as well. The king believed Lepkin. He wasn't pleased with the situation, but once he found out that Bracken was really a warlock, he was a lot more understanding. Lepkin then went to investigate Senator Bracken's house. I told them to check the library. They were going to see what other connections the warlock had and who he might have been working with. I came directly here to give you the report in person."

Orres let himself fall back into his chair and he slapped a hand to his forehead. "By the gods, this is a mess."

Someone rapped on the door and poked their head in. "Master Orres, the others are assembling in the auditorium."

Orres flipped his head up to see Wendal. "Thank you," he said.

"Hello Lady Arkyn, I didn't realize you had returned," Wendal said.

Lady Arkyn gave a half smile. "I have only been back for a few moments."

"What news?" Wendal asked.

"You don't want to know," Orres said. He rose to his feet and waved for them to go into the hall. "Let's go. This is going to be a long night," he said.

"Why are we going to the auditorium?" Lady Arkyn asked.

"We have been asked to close Kuldiga Academy," Orres said. She stared at him blankly until he walked around his desk and gently pushed on her shoulder. "Come, I have to inform the staff that they need to get their students ready to leave the school."

The walk to the Bellwood auditorium seemed to take three times longer than usual. Orres' feet felt heavier and harder to move also. Arkyn and Wendal occasionally glanced back to him, but he remained silent. The halls he walked through were colder than normal as he made his way, following the other two. Colder and darker. The sun had all but disappeared behind the horizon now and the incoming night was almost palpable. He stopped at the door of the auditorium and looked in, scanning the forty masters as they mixed and mingled while searching for seats.

A few of the more stoic masters had taken their seats in the front and were sitting dutifully, facing the podium silently. Most of the others were clustering with friends and talking. Some laughed while others leaned in close to each other in whisper. A sour feeling crept into Orres' stomach.

"Standing here won't get the job done," Orres told himself. He stepped through the doorway, returning nods and handshakes as he passed through the others still in the aisle. He tried to put on a smile, but he couldn't. It only took a moment for the others to catch onto the fact that something was terribly wrong. The men and women ceased greeting him and moved out of his way instead, scrambling to take a seat and hear what he had to tell them.

He plodded up the few steps to the stage and marched to the podium. He stuck his jaw out to the right and chewed lightly on his tongue. Speaking at times like this had never been his strongest talent. Of all the tips he learned about overcoming nerves, he found biting on the tongue to be among the best. Nobody could see him do it, and it caused saliva to come into his dry mouth so he could wet his throat and loosen up a bit.

Placing his hands on either side of the podium he scanned the crowd. His eyes stopped on Master B'dargen for a moment. Could the 'G' stand for Gondok'hr? Then again, if Lepkin had killed the warlock, perhaps it was not so important now. Surely there would be much to occupy them once the king called them up. He looked down at the podium, wishing he had prepared remarks.

"I apologize for summoning all of you here at the last minute," he began. "I am afraid I have some disturbing news. However, before I start I must ask for your discretion and temperance." He paused for a moment and looked out over the sea of faces in front of him. "I have received a message from the king that the senate hall has suffered an attack."

Murmurs ripped through the auditorium.

Orres knocked his knuckles on the podium and the people quieted down quickly. "The king has asked me to close down Kuldiga Academy and send the students back to their homes. We are to remain here and stand by for further instructions." A hand shot up from the front row. Master Orres nodded, allowing the question.

"Have any senators been killed?"

Orres nodded. "I do not have all of the details, but there have been some casualties." Pockets of whispers sprang up, and again Orres knocked on the podium to quiet them down. "I have sent a reply to the king. I told him we will have the school closed down tonight. The students are to leave by first light, after a light breakfast. Then, the rest of us will remain here. Remember, as professors at Kuldiga Academy we are here to train students, but our first commitment is to the king and the kingdom. Just as the first masters who opened the academy, we have always known we could be called upon to lend our talents to the king's aid. We represent some of the finest warriors, healers, and mages our land has to offer. If we stand together now, there is no obstacle we cannot overcome."

There was silence in the auditorium for the first time since Orres had arrived. No one moved, whispered, or even sighed. He swore had there been a cricket in the room, its chirping would have been deafening. He surveyed the crowd for additional questions, but when no more came he nodded and slapped the podium.

"Well then, let's get to work. Remember, use discretion when preparing your students. Some of them have long journeys ahead."

"How will they get home?" someone shouted from the back. "We only have five carriages here at the academy."

Orres nodded. "The academy has some preparations in place for just such an event," Orres assured him. "We will send our students south to Fort Drake. There they will be able to receive additional horses and escorts as they make their way from Fort Drake to their homes."

"But, Fort Drake is two days walk from here," someone shouted. "Surely there must be a better way?"

Orres shrugged. "Lady Dimwater is not here at the present time, and she is the only one capable of sending others through magical teleports."

"I can take students with me through a teleport," Master B'dargen called out. "It would take a while, because I can only take one at a time, but it could help."

Master Orres shook his head. "At most you would only be able to transport ten or twenty before the night ended. It would be better to keep them all together and then send them with our carriages. We can also send one or two healers, just to make sure everything goes smoothly." The shouts grew louder and Orres had to rap the podium repeatedly to quiet the crowd. "As I said, sending the students to Fort Drake is our evacuation plan. I will send a message to the fort commander immediately and from then on we can start sending messages to each student's family. That way, if a family would like to make different arrangements, or perhaps meet their child at Fort Drake, they may do so."

The front row stood up all at once. They each bowed slightly to Master Orres and began leading the way out of the auditorium.

"This is going to be a long night," Orres told himself.

CHAPTER SIXTEEN

Master Orres raised his head from the back of his couch as the first rays of sunlight poked in through his window. He lurched forward, bones creaking with effort. He had only just barely closed his eyes a few moments ago. He pushed onto the couch with his hands and propelled himself back to his feet. He was exhausted, but he had to make sure the students got on their way. He went to the window and saw each of the five carriages in the main courtyard. A few men were scurrying back and forth like a trail of ants carrying boxes from a doorway to the carriages. It was the food Orres had ordered sent with the students.

Master Wendal opened the door and announced himself. "Master Orres, I brought you some coffee. I thought you might need it."

Orres waved it off. "I never much liked the stuff," he said.

Wendal set the pitcher and cup on the desk. "I didn't say I thought you might *like it*," he replied.

Orres turned a sour face on Wendal and Wendal shrugged. "Forgive me, I don't mean to be rude. I'm just tired."

The two of them stood and watched as several masters filed out of the academy, leading a line of students behind each of them. The procession only lasted for a few minutes as the students lined up by class and the role was taken.

"I'm impressed," Orres said. "I didn't think it could be done so quickly."

"We managed to catch most of the student body before dinner last night. Once we told them what was happening most of them were quick to pack up. Of course, they are leaving a lot of personal effects behind. We instructed them to take only an extra change of clothes and some biscuits and food for the journey."

"That is good," Orres replied. The two of them watched as

the first carriage lurched forward under the driver's whip. The others followed and led the students out through the southern gates. "I never thought I would see a day like this," Orres commented as he watched them go.

Wendal stood silently, sipping a cup of coffee.

Master Berr appeared in the doorway. "Master Orres, all of the students have been accounted for and are on the road."

Orres nodded. "Very well. Tell the others that they should get some rest, if they can. We need to be ready when the king calls upon us."

Master Berr nodded his bald head and walked away.

"Then, if there is nothing else I can do..." Wendal started. Orres nodded and waved him away.

"Go and rest."

"What about you?" Wendal asked.

"I am already up," Orres said with a shrug. "I'll stay here." He glanced out to the perch outside his window. "I am still waiting for a response from a few families."

Wendal smiled and walked out of the room, calling over his shoulder. "You know where to find me if you need me."

Orres walked over and closed the door behind Wendal. Then he returned to the window and continued to watch the exodus of students. He stood at the window long after the last student had disappeared from his view. He offered a prayer to the gods, asking them to protect the apprentices on their way home, then he went to his couch and slumped down on his side.

He was snoring in less than a minute.

*****

Heavy pounding ripped Orres from his slumber. He sat up on the couch and stretched his sore back. "Come in!" he yelled.

"Master Orres, you need to come outside," Lady Arkyn shouted quickly.

"Calm down, what's the matter?" Orres said as he wiped a hand over his eyes to take the sleep away.

"Senator Bracken has arrived with a company of king's guards," she replied.

"Senator Bracken..." Orres dropped his hand and stood to

look at her. "I thought you said that Lepkin—" Lady Arkyn cut him off.

"I did," she said quickly. "I saw it with my own eyes, but he is here. His carriage just arrived and he is waiting for all of us to assemble in the courtyard."

"No, we can't go out and meet him. You said he was a warlock. If it's really him, then we will be walking into a trap."

She nodded. "I know, but B'dargen and several others have already assembled in the courtyard.

"B'dargen," Orres snarled. He walked closer to the window, peering down across the courtyard where a large carriage stood, flanked by a score of horsemen and several ranks of men on foot.

"Master Wendal told me you were investigating B'dargen," Lady Arkyn said.

Orres nodded. "And now he is leading the others out to meet with a dead senator." He turned back to say something and stopped as Master Wendal came running through the door.

"Did you see?" he asked.

"I see it," Orres replied.

"What do we do?"

Orres looked to Lady Arkyn. "You stay here. Watch through the window. If something happens, we will want to warn the king immediately."

She nodded. "I will see to it."

Orres then looked to Wendal. "You and I will go out to see what we can do." Orres turned abruptly, reaching up to a mount on the wall and pulling his sword down to attach it around his waist. He heard Wendal walk away, but he didn't bother to watch the man. Something was wrong. Orres stole one last glance at Lady Arkyn and pointed to the writing instruments on his desk. He took his ring off and set it on the paper. "Use my seal," he instructed.

He made his way down the spiral staircase, passing Groundskeeper Rick on the way down.

"We have visitors," Rick announced.

Orres nodded at the man and continued down, two steps at a time before jogging out the door and into the courtyard. Orres squinted in the afternoon light until he made out the purple and gold pennants flying above the carriage. One of the riders galloped ahead of the carriage and waved a greeting to Orres.

The horseman wore black platemail with red silk trim lining the edges of his cuirass and pauldrons. A golden dragon was emblazoned into the breastplate. Orres recognized it as the battle dress of the king's guard.

"Hail, Master Orres," the horseman shouted out. He brought his horse to a stop just two yards away.

Orres could see the wet lather on the animal. He knew they had been travelling hard and fast for a long time to reach him. "Well met," Orres replied. "To what do I owe this unexpected visit?"

The horseman pointed to the carriage. "Have you heard the senate has been attacked?"

"Aye," Orres said. "I received a message from the king last night."

The horseman leaned forward. "Did the message contain any details of the attack?"

"Not exactly," Orres said. He glanced to the carriage, wondering who was inside. Had the warlock somehow survived only to retake the form of a man others knew was dead?

The horseman relaxed in the saddle and nodded. "Senator Bracken is here to make a formal address."

"Senator Bracken?" Orres repeated before he could catch himself.

The horseman nodded and pulled his horse off to trot back to the carriage. "Please ensure all of the masters have been assembled," he shouted over his shoulder.

Orres watched the horseman ride up to the carriage. The side door opened a crack and the horseman leaned forward, obviously talking with whoever was inside. Orres turned about and saw the remaining masters filing out of the academy to converge on him in the courtyard. Orres walked up to Wendal and B'dargen. B'dargen stopped talking when he saw Orres approach, but the look on the man's face unnerved Orres.

"I see the others have assembled," Orres said.

B'dargen shrugged. "You created quite a stir last night, Master Orres. Now that the senator has come with instructions, I felt there was little need to wait for your approval to assemble.

Orres nodded and put on a forced smile as he looked around and counted the other masters as they formed up around him.

"Looks like we are all here."

"Save Lepkin and Dimwater," Wendal replied.

Orres frowned and turned back to face the carriage. They waited for several minutes after everyone had assembled. Contrary to last night, none of the masters could be heard chattering or murmuring.

At last the carriage door swung open and Senator Bracken descended the steps to the ground. Orres had to check himself and close his mouth before anyone noticed his surprise. He studied the senator as he walked forward, flanked by two king's guards. A trio of men appeared from the other side of the carriage, scrambling to carry a wooden box out ahead of the senator. They rushed up before them and placed the platform on the ground about fifteen feet away from where Orres stood. They took care to ensure it was level and stable before hurrying back to disappear behind the carriage once more.

Senator Bracken stepped up onto the platform and surveyed the crowd. The bottom of his white robes waved in the gentle evening breeze. The flanking guards halted their horses just behind the platform and watched the crowd. Senator Bracken held his arms out to the gathered masters. "My fellow brothers, and sisters" he greeted. "I come to you with terrible news." He paused for effect. "The senate has been attacked, and many of my fellow senators have been murdered."

Murmurs rippled through the gathered crowd, but Orres stood, stoic and still, watching the senator carefully.

"It gives me no pleasure to say this, but one of our greatest heroes has betrayed the crown!" Senator Bracken's shoulders drooped and he shook his head. "The senate tribunal met to decide the fate of a traitor, Lord Lokton, for inciting war with House Cedreau."

The murmuring grew into a cacophony of shouts, gasps, and protests. Master Orres would normally have silenced them, but he kept his eyes fixed on the senator, looking for any hole in the illusion so he might uncover who really stood before him. The knot in his stomach grew and he felt the hairs on his forearms and neck rise to stand on end as chills coursed through him.

Senator Bracken patted the air and called for silence. "I know you all know those two houses well. These are troubling times indeed when the nobles forget their place and squabble over petty differences and greed." He waited a few moments for the last of the whispers to die down before continuing. "The greatest treachery, however, came from one of your masters."

Orres' heart skipped a beat and he felt a rage start to build up within him. He didn't like where this was going.

Senator Bracken looked to Orres and arched one of his gray brows at him. "Master Lepkin forced his way into the tribunal and desecrated the senate. Instead of enacting the just and righteous sentence, he attacked the senate and killed many of my colleagues. I, myself, barely escaped with my life."

Orres held his tongue, but others did not. Master Wendal stepped forward amidst shouts and protests. "Why would Master Lepkin do such a thing? He is one of the most honorable men within the kingdom!"

Bracken turned a glaring eye on Wendal. "Hold your tongue," Senator Bracken warned. His voice carried the weight of thunder, silencing all within the courtyard. "My mission here is twofold. I am to ascertain who here is loyal to the crown, and who else may have been involved with Master Lepkin."

Master Wendal shrank back to stand beside Orres. "Lepkin is an honorable man," he whispered to Orres. Orres gave Wendal a slight nod to show his agreement and then raised a finger to his mouth.

"We are all loyal to the king!" one of the masters shouted from the crowd.

"We knew that cast-away was trouble!" another shouted in reference to Erik.

"Yeah, the cast-away and Master Lepkin were always causing trouble!" another yelled out.

Orres turned to discover who among his colleagues was speaking, but could not see through the sea of faces. He boomed over the din and commanded silence.

"Let them speak, Master Orres," Senator Bracken said.

Orres felt the senator's glaring eyes on his back. He turned to face the senator again, but offered no apology.

Senator Bracken pointed to Master Orres. "We must hurry if we are to stop the chaos that Lepkin has unleashed on us. Even now there are riots and mobs in the streets in Drakai Glazei. Those riots will spread if we fail to stop them. Every able-bodied person is called upon to aid the king in bringing the traitors to justice. The task of apprehending Erik Lokton has fallen to me. I call upon all who are loyal to the crown to stand on Master Orres' right hand. Those remaining on his left will be considered friends of the enemy and put in jail to stand trial after peace has been restored."

"Let's go!" Master B'dargen yelled. "Let's stop the traitors!"

The two king's guards trotted around to the front of the platform.

Orres stepped forward, trying to salvage the situation before it spun out of control. "Forgive me senator, but you did not mention Erik was party to the attack in Drakai Glazei. How is he connected?"

"He's with Lepkin, that's enough for me!" Master B'dargen shouted. "The two of them were as thick as thieves and they were always scheming together. If Lepkin attacked the senate, then you can bet Erik was involved!"

Orres kept his eyes on Bracken. "That is not enough for me. If someone is pronounced a traitor, I need to know exactly what they have done."

Senator Bracken sneered wickedly. "My dear Master Orres," he began. "You really don't see it do you? Erik Lokton and Master Lepkin are the catalysts, just as your fellow master has declared. Tell me, how was Timon's hand injured here at the academy?"

Master Orres bristled, but managed to maintain his wits about him. "I filed the report," he answered. "It is a matter of public record."

Senator Bracken chuckled. "Then everyone here knows that it was Erik who wounded him, and Master Lepkin who orchestrated the duels. Does that not make you stop and question their true motives behind the duels?"

"Master Lepkin was teaching Erik a lesson in honoring his word," Master Orres replied.

Senator Bracken shook his head. "Master Lepkin was setting his plans in motion by inciting House Cedreau to violence!"

Orres could hear whispers growing behind him. He was losing the argument. "I was present when Lord Cedreau came to House Lokton during Erik's Konn Deta ceremony and attempted to dishonor the boy."

"But were you there for the subsequent murders?" Bracken shouted back. "I was charged with investigating them. I found evidence that pointed to Lord Lokton's treachery. That is why he was arrested after he had started a war with House Cedreau and surreptitiously murdered Lord Cedreau under the pretense of negotiations. Then, when the tribunal assembled for Lord Lokton's trial, Master Lepkin arrived and tore us apart to save the traitor from his fate."

The wave of angry protests and shouts all but deafened Master Orres and drowned his response in a sea of vengeful rage. Orres turned to Master Wendal. "What do we do now?" he asked as most of the masters made their way to stand far to Master Orres' right.

Master Wendal shrugged. "Perhaps we side with the devil for now in order to live another day," he said.

Orres shook his head. "That isn't in my nature." He turned to Senator Bracken. "What would you have us do to prove our loyalty?"

The senator's sneer widened into a toothy grin. "We march to Lokton manor. There we will apprehend the traitors and bring them to justice."

Master Orres walked back several paces, pushing through the crowd and jumping up to stand on the edge of a fountain. He drew his sword and slapped the side against the bronze statue of a cherub spouting water. "I am loyal to the king!" he shouted. His voice boomed out over the din and echoed off the academy walls. "I am also headmaster here at Kuldiga Academy. I know Erik better than you. I know that most students never befriended him on account he was adopted and not born a noble. But, I tell you as sure as I am breathing here and now, that boy has a noble and true heart. He is no traitor."

"Watch yourself Master Orres," Senator Bracken warned. "I have no qualms adding you to my list of traitors."

"And that is the problem," Orres fired back. "You are quick to judge as long as it suits your purposes. If Master Lepkin attacked the senate, then he must have had his reasons! I have known him for decades and he has always been true!"

"And what of Janik?" Senator Bracken retorted. "Didn't you consider him to be honorable as well? It appears that you are no more than a simple fool, easily blinded by others."

Master Wendal walked over to stand in front of Orres. "I'm with you," he said loud enough for many to hear.

Master Orres glared back at Senator Bracken. "You are right," he said. "My brother deceived me. He was a member of a warlock order that sought after dark arts."

"You only prove my point that you are not a reliable judge of character," Bracken snarled.

"Janik was not the only warlock to don a disguise and fool others was he, Senator Bracken?" Orres questioned. He wasn't about to let the other masters be fooled if he could help it.

"Whatever do you mean?" Bracken cackled.

"You know exactly what I mean, Gondok'hr," Orres shot back. "The reports I received said Senator Bracken was slain in the attack!"

The crowd froze. A few masters made their way through the throng to stand with Orres.

"Are you insinuating that I am a warlock?" Bracken asked. "You think a warlock could go unnoticed in the senate? Why do you fabricate such fantasies? Is it to save your friends, or is it because you are with them?"

Several masters broke out of the crowd and joined behind B'dargen, who stood prominently where the senator had instructed those loyal to the crown to stand. Only a handful of masters remained undecided in the middle. After the groups were divided Master B'dargen stepped forward and addressed the Senator.

"Senator Bracken, we stand with the king, and with you. We are ready to prove our loyalty however we can."

Senator Bracken looked to Master B'dargen and smiled wickedly. "Very well," Senator Bracken said. He raised his hand and a group of seven horsemen came up to his side. He leaned down and whispered to one of them, who saluted in response and led the others to the group standing with Master B'dargen.

"Something is very wrong," Master Wendal said.

Senator Bracken turned to the group of loyalists. "If you wish to prove your loyalty then join in with these seven king's guards and take the others into custody. Don't let any of them escape."

"Master Orres, he is turning them on us," Wendal said.

"I cannot allow them to get to Lokton manor," Orres said. "If any of you wish to surrender, you would be wise to move away from me now."

"No, we stand with you." Wendal said. "There shall be no deals with the devil today."

Orres smiled "Glad to see you come around," he said. "On my mark, everyone will run into the main hall, we'll make our way toward my office. There is an armory near there so those of us without magic can better defend ourselves."

"And those of us with magic?" Wendal asked.

"Fall back with us, we'll be stronger together."

Senator Bracken shouted over them. "Did you hear me, Master Orres?"

Master Orres looked up to see the seven horsemen ready to charge beside the horde of angry masters. "I heard you," Orres replied.

"Surrender peacefully," Master B'dargen ordered. "We will use whatever force is necessary to arrest you."

"Shame on you, Master B'dargen," Orres replied. "All this time here at the academy and you throw your lot in with House Finorel in the hopes that he would help you. What did Gondok'hr promise you?"

Master B'dargen blushed and bristled. "You all heard Senator Bracken. If they don't stand with us, then they stand against us! You know what is at stake, you heard the message from the king. We were to await further orders, and now Senator Bracken has come and issued those orders. Will we idly sit by while others denounce the king?"

"If I were you, I would surrender," Senator Bracken said. "You are outnumbered and the king's guards will not hesitate to slay traitors to the crown." He raised his hand and seven more horsemen rode to join with the others.

"We are not traitors," Orres said. "But I would gladly take your head, coward. Stop this act and show us who you really are!"

"He defies the king and tries to shift the blame onto me with this ridiculous accusation!" Bracken yelled. "Everyone here has heard what the king expects of them." He then turned his glowering eyes back to Orres. "Take the traitors into custody if you can, kill them if you must," he said.

"It will be done," Master B'dargen swore.

Bracken quickly made his way back to his carriage. The rest of his cohort closed in around it, forming a defensive wall.

"There are only seven of us," Wendal said.

Orres nodded and looked to the small group of undecided masters still standing between the two groups. "Wait for my signal," Orres reminded Wendal.

"Surrender!" Master B'dargen ordered.

Orres turned and pointed his sword at B'dargen. "Come at us and I swear I will take your head myself you leach!"

Master B'dargen blanched momentarily, only to have rage replace his fear. "You will not live through this day!" he swore.

"Wendal, take the key to the armory." Master Orres gave him an iron key and stepped forward. "It's time for you to run, now!"

"But what about you?" Wendal asked.

Orres spun on the man, eyes ablaze and breath hot with battle fury. "Get them inside to the armory. Make your stand there, I will make sure you have the time to get inside."

"Let's go," Wendal said. He turned and started pushing the others toward the closest door.

"They are trying to escape!" one of the king's guards shouted.

Orres shouted at the group standing in the middle. "Get inside to safety, now!" Some of them instantly burst into a sprint for the nearest door, while others stood there looking back and forth between the two groups. Orres tapped the side of his sword to his brow. "I hope you knew what you started, Lepkin." He walked forward, swinging his sword and loosening his muscles. "Let Master B'dargen come first, unless he prefers to stand at the rear while others do battle for him!"

The horsemen charged forward. Orres breathed in rhythmically, adjusted his grip on his sword, and widened his stance. Ravenous hooves tore at the ground as the soldiers sped toward him. To Orres' horror, the king's guards took down several of the masters that still stood in the middle. Many of the masters shouted and cursed the callous killings and started to flee or fight amongst themselves, but most standing with B'dargen still stood firm, shouting their loyalty to the king and denouncing Orres as a traitor. The shouts seemed to fade as Orres concentrated on the task at hand. He knew he was not the same as the great and mighty Lepkin, but these men were soon to find out that he was no meager, old has-been.

The first rider lunged forward with a spear. Orres slashed down and to the side, sweeping the spear away as he spun to the side and brought his blade up to slice the horse's neck. The beast shrieked and went down hard, flinging the rider into the air to land in a heap of clanking metal several yards away. Orres maneuvered his sword to his left just in time to deflect a powerful chop aimed at the nape of his neck. He then deftly reached out with his left hand, grabbed the reins and yanked the horse around, stumbling the animal and giving him an open shot to the rider's side with his sword. As he ripped his sword free he leapt atop the horse with the grace of a man thirty years his younger and turned to meet the other riders.

He managed to dodge a series of quick stabs from the third challenger and lashed out with deadly accuracy, slipping his blade up under the small opening above the cuirass' neck hole and below the jawline of the rider's helmet. The man's head fell limply to the side and the horse charged away.

He turned to face the next rider, but failed to get his horse around in time. The rider slammed his mount straight in, pinning Orres' leg and knocking his horse to the side. Somehow the animal managed to keep its footing, but Orres was at a disadvantage, struggling to turn enough to face his foe. Fortunately, he was able to avoid a savage stab to the chest, but his enemy cut back as he retracted, opening a gash on Orres' shoulder.

Orres roared out and pummeled the rider with the jeweled pommel of his sword. The pointed stub bore down through the helmet, bending the metal until the force of the blow knocked the rider back and out of the saddle. The man tumbled over the horse's rump to land on his head on the ground.

Master Orres turned to face the next rider, but instead he caught a blue ball of fire to the chest. He flew off his saddle and landed in the fountain. As he slammed into the ceramic tile bottom and the water crashed back over him the air left his lungs in a series of pearl-like bubbles. His spine popped and creaked, but he managed to sit himself up and emerge from the water.

Horses galloped past as the rest of the king's guard tried to run down the others. Orres turned and took heart when he saw that they had already made it inside. He turned back and saw

Master B'dargen preparing another spell. Several masters lay at his feet, while others had formed a protective wall around B'dargen. "Second rate caster," Orres mumbled under his breath. He knew that if Lady Dimwater had been the one to throw the spell, he would have been killed. Lucky for him, Master B'dargen was only her replacement. Orres jumped up and sprinted for the entrance, zigging and zagging as B'dargen threw more spells at him.

One of the blue balls blasted into a horseman, knocking the man and horse down to the ground before they could reach Orres. "Thanks!" Orres shouted back over his shoulder.

"Face me!" B'dargen growled.

Orres glanced back to see the tumultuous mob charging forward. He redoubled his efforts, going as fast as his thick legs would carry him. The mounted riders were all filing into the academy now, squeezing in two at a time. He replaced his sword and checked the pair of long knives he kept at his belt, ensuring they were loose and ready to be retrieved. None of the soldiers noticed his approach until it was too late.

He slammed into the last two guards, knocking their heads together in his massive hands and then tossing them aside as he barreled forward. He ripped a helmet off of another and used it to beat in the soldier's face before he turned on the next and pummeled him to the ground.

"At our rear!" one of the soldiers shouted after he caught sight of Orres.

Orres drew his long knives and went to work. The entrance they had used turned sharply upward into a spiral staircase. The close quarters prevented the soldiers from flanking him and only gave enough space for two soldiers to advance at a time. With their large weapons and clunky armor their motility was severely hampered, whereas Orres was able to work fast with his knives. He dodged a clumsy sword swing and answered his foe with a series of quick stabs into the elbow hinges between the plates of metal. The soldier roared in pain and dropped his weapon. Orres finished him with a massive kick to the chest that flattened him against the stone wall.

The next two soldiers leapt down at him, but Orres was quick. He worked one blade into the visor's gap in the left soldier's helmet and drove his knife through the other man's chest plate.

Both men died instantly, but Orres was unable to retrieve either knife as the helmet snagged one out of his grip and his other blade snapped after piercing the chest plate of the other soldier.

Orres moved forward, undaunted. He picked up the next guard, whipped him over his back and dropped him head first onto the ground. A sword came down at him, just narrowly missing his chest as the point sailed through his armpit, slicing into the inside of his left arm. Orres recoiled reflexively and tried to regroup as the soldier came on, shouldering Orres into the wall.

Orres' head knocked into the brick wall. A few spots of yellow light appeared before him and his head rang as if it were a bell, but he didn't let it slow him down. He reached up with his left hand, grabbed the guard's sword arm and then hooked the man's head with his right. In one deft move Orres spun out to the right and drove the man head first into the wall. As soon as the guard connected with the solid surface, Orres reversed his direction and slammed the man into the opposite wall. The guard slid down slowly, and then teetered over to tumble down the steps.

Master Orres turned up to face the next guard, but instead he saw the last one fall backward, tumbling down the stairs with a gaping, smoldering hole in his chest plate. Orres looked up to see Master Wendal.

"We found the armory, and the other masters have taken refuge."

"Thanks," Orres said. Then the large man bounded up the stairs and followed Wendal down the hall on the third floor. The two of them stopped next to a suit of armor displayed proudly next to a glass case with an ivory handled scimitar.

"Give me a second," Wendal said as he weaved his hands in front of the suit of armor. The armor groaned. The legs moved forward as it stepped off its pedestal, metal plates scraping against each other. The helmet angled down to face Master Wendal. The mage smiled back to it and pointed to the pedestal. "Go back to your place. Stay still and wait until you see soldiers wearing black armor with red trim. When you see them, spring to action and let none of them pass. The golem nodded and stepped back to the pedestal, remaining still as it had been before Wendal's spell animated him. Wendal turned a pleased smile to Orres. "The next person who passes by is in for a treat."

Orres nodded appreciatively and slammed his fist through the glass. He retrieved the scimitar and gave it a practice swing. "This should work well in the halls," he said noting its balance.

"Never thought I would see the day when Kuldiga's Headmaster would vandalize our sacred relics," Wendal put in with a wink.

"Stormfang is a great weapon, and as it aided the founding battle for the land on which the academy sits, I think it suitable that it should come out of retirement now to defend it."

Wendal nodded. "We should get back to the armory."

The two of them sprinted as fast as they could. They heard the clambering footsteps coming up the stairs, followed quickly by shrieks and shouts as the suit of armor came alive and started bashing the trespassers.

Orres and Wendal stopped abruptly at the armory and Wendal waved his hand over the door. It opened in response to his command and the two slipped inside. The door closed behind them and Wendal once more waved his hand over the wooden portal. It began to hum rhythmically as a soft green hue descended over its surface.

"We should get to the rear of the room," Wendal instructed. Orres nodded and they joined with the others. Two of the other masters had donned full battle gear, appropriate for the room. Shirts and leggings of chainmail under padded leather hauberks. Each carried a sword and shield as well. Lady Arkyn and another master were perched upon the wooden beams near the vaulted ceiling with bows resting across their laps.

As Orres looked to the people around him he wondered whether his decision was really made from the point of honor, or whether his pride had landed them all in this predicament. Wendal, apparently reading Orres' face came up and placed a hand on the headmaster's shoulder.

"You were right to resist," Wendal said.

"How can you be sure?" Orres asked.

"Aside from the fact that the senator is actually a warlock imposter, the riders are not king's guards. As I fought my way to you I removed the helmet of one of the riders. He was not human."

"What do you mean?" Orres thought back to the men he had

unmasked, and he had surely seen only humans.

"The first I found was an orc," Wendal replied. "However that was not the interesting part. I removed two more helmets, expecting to find more orcs, but I found one human and one dark elf. I believe that they were all resurrected soldiers," Wendal explained. "Reanimated corpses that…"

"I know what the term means," Orres said. "So who brought them back to life?"

"My guess would be that either the fake Senator Bracken did, or he is working with someone very powerful, a necromancer perhaps."

"If that is true, it would give me an understanding of why Lepkin would attack the senate."

"You know of Erik's purpose," Wendal said. "I would put my faith in Lepkin long after every senator denounced him."

"Me too," Orres replied. "I might have questioned his motives attacking the senate to get to one warlock, but if the warlock works with necromancers, then that would explain everything. Necromancy has been banned since the dragons left."

"And any time the realm has seen necromancers, they have always sought after Nagar's Secret," Lady Arkyn put in.

The footsteps and clanging armor came closer.

"It sounds as though my golem is about to be defeated," Wendal said. "What do we do now? We are about to fight against our friends, all because a warlock is spinning lies to gain power."

Orres nodded. "We are to spare everyone's life if we can. Use only the force you must use."

"They will not be so kind to us" Lady Arkyn pointed out from the rafters.

Orres looked up. "Spare them if you can, but put them down if you must. We cannot let the masters join with Senator Bracken. I will go out to meet them."

Just then the door to the armory exploded into a cloud of noxious green gas. People started coughing and sputtering as they flopped to the floor. Master B'dargen stepped through the gas, protected by a white sphere of magic.

"Surrender, traitor!" B'dargen shouted.

Orres stepped forward, motioning for Wendal to move back. "You have been deceived," he shouted to B'dargen and the group.

"Those were not king's guards! They were reanimated corpses, sent here by a necromancer who is working with Senator Bracken."

"Lies!" B'dargen cried out.

"Go look for yourself!" Orres shouted. "We'll wait right here for you."

"I am not falling for your tricks. We all know that Master Wendal could create such illusions to make us think you were telling the truth."

Orres drew a line on the floor. Blue lightning arced from the tip of the blade to singe the redwood floor. Wisps of smoke rose from the ashen line, creating a thin veil of gray between them as the blade scraped its way through the wood. Orres grinned determinedly, flashes of blue lightning reflecting off his blade as he held it up at the ready. "I propose a duel then," Orres said. "I win and everyone goes back to check the corpses. They will find among the others an orc and a dark elf. We all know that neither of those races have ever been in the king's guard, especially not an orc."

"Again, illusions that Wendal could easily conjure up to deceive us," B'dargen refuted.

"So then you would have us fight each other because you are too proud to investigate the truth for yourself?"

"He's telling the truth!" someone shouted from the hallway. "There is an orc here at my feet, disguised in king's guard armor."

"Didn't you hear that Master B'dargen?" Orres asked.

"I already said Master Wendal would use magic to trick us!" Master B'dargen replied.

"I want no academy blood spilt," Orres said.

"I won't fall for your tricks," B'dargen hissed.

"If I lose the duel, then everyone else will surrender peacefully," Orres offered.

"No, it's too late for that!" B'dargen shouted. He raised his hand and charged a spell. Orres flipped the sword over in his hands and readied his stance.

"Or is it that you are so set on killing me to cover up your own secrets?" Orres shouted. "You already know that I am telling the truth. You know everything I said is true."

B'dargen smiled and arched an eyebrow, but he never got the chance to send his spell.

A sharp whistle pierced the air and an arrow shaft appeared in the center of B'dargen's chest. B'dargen's eyes went wide and his spell fizzled and fell over his hand like a cup of spilt water. He fell to his knees and then over onto his face. A few of the masters backed away from the dissipating green cloud, but a horde of footmen stepped through the doorway. They looked down to B'dargen's body and then up to Orres.

"Open your eyes," Orres shouted at the masters behind the footmen. "That isn't Senator Bracken down there. He is a warlock! Go back and look at the other soldiers and you will see what I say is true. Why else would Lepkin have attacked the senate?"

"It's true, I saw it with my own eyes," Lady Arkyn yelled from above.

A tall, black haired master stepped through the throng of footmen and laughed wickedly. "You expect us to believe you when you so readily kill one of our own?" Master Gri asked, pointing to B'dargen's body. "Why should we?" Master Gri looked to the masters behind him and then back to Orres. "I cannot disobey a direct order from a senator."

"You stubborn fool," Orres said.

Master Gri chuckled. "Interesting words to come out of your mouth."

"I won't surrender, Master Gri." Orres raised his sword.

"You dare wield Stormfang?" Master Gri chided as he drew a scimitar of his own. "You are a disgrace."

"For the king!" a footman shouted as he raced forward.

"Spare as many of our comrades as you can!" Orres commanded.

The room broke into a flurry of movement. Arrows rained down from above, catching several masters in the knee or shoulder while dealing death to the footmen that invaded the room. Spells zinged through the air to knock others against the walls or push them back into the hall and block the entrance. Orres charged forward, lightning leaping from his blade to strike down Master Gri just before the man could come close.

Master Lin, a renowned swordsman, replaced Gri in an instant, appearing out of the throng and swinging his scimitar at Orres, catching him in the side. Orres jolted away and brought his blade back just in time to deflect a stab that surely would have gone through his chest. Master Lin spun and wove his sword in and around Orres' defense to score a gash on Orres' right shoulder. Master Orres pushed through the pain and lashed out with a savage left hook, but it caught only air. Master Lin had already spun back three paces and was poised to launch another offensive.

A footman came charging in on Orres' left side, screaming and yelling something completely incomprehensible. Orres threw a massive, left backhand strike that knocked the man on his rump, and then finished him with a quick stab to the chest. Unfortunately, Orres' strike opened a window that Master Lin exploited perfectly. His scimitar went in and pierced Orres' exposed right hip. The blade went in through the layer of fat over Orres' thick trunk and stopped only when it struck bone. Orres fell to the floor and Stormfang tumbled out of his hands.

Master Lin pulled back and swirled away from a pair of arrows just before ducking and somersaulting under one of Wendal's spells. Then he came back in to finish Orres. Master Orres summoned all of the strength he had left into a primal rage. He rose to his feet, grabbed Master Lin's scimitar with his left hand, ignoring the sting in his arm and brought his massive right fist down to shatter Master Lin's jaw. The man reeled back, grabbing at his face and finally fell when a trio of arrows pierced his heart.

Orres turned on the oncoming wave of footmen. There was no time to pick up his weapon. He formed a bloody fist with his left hand and staggered forward to meet them. Stings and cuts appeared on his body as he fought through the throng, knocking enemies together or throwing them into a wall to put them out of commission. With each new slice or gash he could feel his strength slipping away. He caught a couple mild fireballs to the chest as a pair of strange mages emerged through the doorway. He stumbled backward and fell to one knee.

A trio of footmen rushed forward, one of them scooping Master Lin's scimitar up and aiming for Orres' neck. Just before the blade connected, another sword appeared over Orres and stopped it from completing its deadly arc.

"We're here," a wheezy voice yelled. Orres looked up and saw Master Wendal wielding a sword in his left hand while throwing fire balls with his right.

"I'm out," Lady Arkyn shouted as she dropped from the rafters above to the floor. Orres saw her pick up Stormfang and rush to stand beside Wendal. The other masters were working their way forward too, cutting through footmen and dodging blades and spears.

Orres tried to push himself up, but he had no more strength left. He fell to his face with a *thud*. The wood floor vibrated under his face as heavy footsteps danced all around him. As his blood leaked out of his body, he felt hope going along with it. There were far too many footmen. He knew that the cause was lost.

"Wendal, get them out," he said. "Get them out." It was hard to breathe now. "Escape," he whispered.

*****

Eldrik sat in the stable, still shaking and breathing hard. Vengeance had come quickly, but it had not ended his pain. He struggled to understand why instead of satisfaction he felt remorse. He scooted his back against the corner of a stall and kicked a horse apple out of the way. "Mother will be proud," he told himself. "Mother will be proud."

"That's right," a voice said from the darkness beyond the stall.

Eldrik looked up, peering into the darkness. He rubbed his cold shoulders. "Who's there?"

"No need to be afraid, boy. I am a friend."

Eldrik could tell the voice was female, but he didn't recognize it. "Who are you?" A woman stepped just out of the shadows enough for him to make out her shapely figure. She was not as tall as he, but she was definitely older. He could tell that from the width of her hips and the tone she used speaking to him. If she would only take one more step forward, then the moonlight would illuminate her face.

"I am the one who helped you find Lord Lokton," the woman said.

"What?" Eldrik reached up to the side of the stall and pulled himself up to his feet. The woman stepped forward. As the moon revealed her face, he did recognize her. "You are the fortuneteller," Eldrik said.

"And I helped you find the alleyway Lord Lokton would come through and where you could hide to catch him."

Eldrik swallowed hard, though his throat was dry. What did

she want?

"Don't worry, I am here to help you again," she said.

"I don't need more help," Eldrik said.

"Don't you want to know *how* I knew where Lord Lokton would be?" she asked.

"What do you want from me?" Eldrik pressed, finding a sprout of courage from within.

"You have great potential, Eldrik Cedreau," she said. "I am a friend of your family, and I am here to help you develop your talents."

"I don't recognize you," Eldrik said.

"That doesn't matter," she assured him. "I spoke with your mother, and she wants you to come with me. We can help you rebuild House Cedreau and make it great again."

Eldrik stepped forward. "What do you mean you can make my house great again?"

"You think the only thing Lord Lokton took from you is your father?" she asked. "He took more than that. Many years ago your family owned all of the lands now under House Lokton's control. Your great grandfather was conned out of the land by Lord Lokton's grandfather. You see, they have always been scheming against your family."

Eldrik felt the fire return in his chest. "How do you know this?"

"Come with me, I will show you the truth about the treacherous Loktons. You will be a hero!"

"A hero?" Eldrik asked.

"The senate had sentenced Lord Lokton to death. He escaped and ran down the alley you found him in. So you see, you are a hero for catching a convicted traitor and giving him the justice he so deeply deserved. Now, I can help you regain your family's true stature and you will be known for generations as the noblest among the Cedreau clan. The king will likely reward you himself."

Eldrik smiled at the thought. It was tempting, very tempting. "What is in it for you?"

The woman smiled wide. "Oh, well you see I owe your mother a great deal. This will be my way of repaying her the kindnesses she has shown me over the years."

Eldrik smiled. "Then I accept." He stepped forward and

looked in the woman's eyes.

The woman smiled wide and said, "Come with me, we have a lot to discuss, and the others are anxious to meet you."

"The others?" Eldrik asked curiously.

"Yes, there are many who would see House Cedreau return to its former glory." Eldrik nodded as though he understood. The woman put a hand on his shoulder. "Of course, they will be looking to have their loyalty rewarded, but we can see to that once your family has been restored to its former glory."

"What shall I call you?" Eldrik asked.

She smiled wider and squeezed his shoulder. "I am Merriam."

CHAPTER SEVENTEEN

Eldrik walked into the chamber wide-eyed and mouth open slightly. His pulse raced within him. His mind soaked in the sights before his eyes and his skin tingled at the cavern's coolness. It was as if he had finally returned home, only he hadn't the slightest idea where he was or who this Merriam woman really was. Still, a part of him coveted the power he sensed within her. Instead of being repulsed by the magic mixture that opened the door to the underground cave, he had been elated. He thirsted after the power.

"This is your new home," Merriam said as she gestured out with a sweep of her arm. "We can train you here, and you can raise your army from here as well."

"My army," he repeated. He liked the sound of that. "We have men at Cedreau manor," he put in quickly.

Merriam nodded. "Yes, but for the task at hand you will need men who are more, shall we say, experienced.

"You said there were others here waiting for me, where are they?" Eldrik asked.

Merriam nodded and motioned for him to follow her. Eldrik did so, following her and gazing into the mysterious pools of glowing water. Occasionally he saw a frog, or a long tailed colorful fish that he didn't recognize, but otherwise the cavern was empty, save for a large cauldron, a few desks and some bookshelves.

They left the main cavern and walked through a short tunnel to a secondary hall, filled with benches and pews. A dais with four chairs was positioned at the front of the room. Two women were sitting already. An older woman sat at the far left and a younger woman sat at the far right, leaving the two middle chairs open.

"Come, we should be seated," Merriam instructed.

As Eldrik crossed the brown stone floor a few people started to filter in from side tunnels and sit at the pews. Some of them wore regular clothes, others wore leather armor or long robes. Eldrik didn't recognize any of them.

"These are friends of my family?" Eldrik asked as they took their seats on the dais.

The old woman leaned over and placed a hand on Merriam's leg. Eldrik couldn't make out what she whispered, but he could tell by the look on her face and the way that Merriam averted her eyes that something didn't sit well with the old woman.

The young woman leaned in and brushed Eldrik's hair off his brow. "We are happy to have you here," she said. "I'm Silvi."

Eldrik turned and found himself falling deep into her blue eyes as though he were diving into two cool pools without a bottom. He wanted to say something to her, but he managed only to offer a goofy smile. Silvi giggled and patted his back before sitting back in her seat.

He soon forgot everything else in the room except for Silvi. He inched to the edge of his seat, trying to be a little closer to her, stealing sidelong glances at her as the chamber continued to fill. He didn't notice the disapproving frown Merriam shot Silvi, nor did he catch Silvi's nonchalant shrug.

After a while the old woman stood up and walked to the front of the dais.

"Welcome, brothers," she said. "May the night grant its blessing to all of you."

The seated audience responded in unison. "May the shadow encircle us all in its wisdom."

The old woman turned back and pointed to Eldrik. "This young man is destined for greatness," she said. "I have seen the signs, and read the portents. House Cedreau shall be great again."

The audience cheered and clapped, stomping their feet against the stone floor. "The woman produced a knife from the folds of her robes. Eldrik watched with heightened interest as the blood-stained blade was held out in the woman's left hand. It was the knife he had used to kill Lord Lokton.

"How did she get that?" Eldrik asked.

Merriam leaned in from his right. "You dropped it outside the stable, so I picked it up before coming in to speak with you." She looked into his eyes, but he did not find comfort there. Silvi put her hand on his leg and he turned back to her. Instantly he felt at peace as he looked into her beautiful eyes.

"It is a necessary step in regaining your power," she said. "Do not be afraid. No one here means you any harm."

Eldrik nodded dumbly and went back to watching the old woman. She chanted a phrase that he did not understand, and then the knife began to hover in the air, pointing down at the ground and spinning slowly. The blood began to glow. Eldrik watched the blade intently.

"What is happening?" he asked.

"Come with me," Silvi coaxed. She slipped her hand around his and gently pulled him up to stand before the knife. Merriam rose and stood opposite him, obscuring the audience from his view. Silvi pushed him closer to the knife and then stood so that the three women formed a triangle around Eldrik and the spinning blade.

Merriam added her voice to the chanting and the blood began to grow brighter. Eldrik found himself mesmerized by the blade. He watched as the blood once again became liquid and started to drip from the blade until the knife was clean and bright. The droplets never touch the ground, though. They hung in the air just below the knife.

He wasn't sure why, but he reached out with his right hand to touch the blood. As his finger pushed into the red orb it rippled and jiggled. He could feel the heat inside it. What's more, he felt a strange surge of power as he pushed his finger inside the orb. As he marveled at the spectacle, the blood coursed up his hand, tickling the hairs on his forearm, and disappeared under his shirt as it travelled quick as a snake to rest on his chest.

The three women clasped hands and their chanting grew louder. The men in the audience rose to their feet, adding their low, rumbling voices to the chant. A dark purple light appeared around the dagger, forming a column from the ground to the ceiling. Eldrik felt the blood on his chest start to heat up and bubble on his skin. The heat scorched and stung his skin for only a moment before a tentacle of purple light reached out from the knife and shot through his shirt to the spot on his chest where the blood boiled. Searing pain ripped through his body and the dagger began to spin faster and faster. The chanting grew louder and louder. Some of the men were shouting while others were wailing in an orchestra of shouts and mumbles that assaulted Eldrik's ears.

The dagger vibrated and hummed as it rotated up so that the point aimed at Eldrik's chest. His eyes went wide as the knife slowly traveled down the purple arm toward his chest. To his relief the dagger stopped as the tip rested on his skin. It twirled quickly, opening a small hole in his skin and then all of the blood from the knife vanished into his own body and the purple light coursed into him. Instead of pain, he felt only heat and power. His body tingled from his head to his toe as the light continued into his body. The light pulled back then, taking the knife with it until the blade hovered in the exact middle of the triangle.

Merriam and the others had ceased chanting now and only wailed and screamed. Eldrik's body grew numb and then became very heavy at the same time. His heart rate slowed until he was sure he had no pulse at all. He fell to his knees momentarily and then he felt a rush of strength and power fill him from within. Eldrik rose back to his feet and instinctively took the knife from the air.

The handle was cold as winter's first snow, but he took it anyway. It vibrated in his hand. He could feel his skin sticking to the handle, forming a bond with the weapon. His hand began to glow and the same purple light that had coursed through him went out from his hand and into the knife. The blade turned dark and then the bond with his hand dissolved and the ritual was complete. The three women let go and broke the triangle. The audience ceased their chanting. It was as if they had all been connected somehow, and knew exactly when the ritual had finished.

Eldrik turned the knife over in his hand. It was still extremely cold, but now there was no humming. No vibration. It was as inanimate as it had been before. "What just happened?" Eldrik asked.

"You have been initiated into the fold," Merriam said warmly.

"You, are the newest warlock in our coven," Silvi added.

Eldrik tucked the knife into his belt. "A warlock?" he said.

The old woman turned to him. "To restore House Cedreau, we must return to the old traditions. Your great-great grandfather was once a warlock in our coven. That is why our cavern is located on your lands. However, when your great grandfather lost half of House Cedreau's lands, your grandfather denounced him and turned his back on us. These men here tonight are here to see the coven restored, and House Cedreau will flourish with their aid."

Eldrik nodded. He could still feel the new power and strength running through his veins. "I thought warlocks were evil?" he stammered.

Silvi turned him to look into her eyes. "Warlocks are only what they are," she said. "Are *you* evil?" she asked.

Eldrik melted into her eyes again and shook his head. "No, I want only justice."

"Then let us help you find that justice," Silvi coaxed.

Eldrik nodded. "What must I do?"

"For tonight, you have accomplished enough. Now it is time for you to sleep. In the morning we will continue with your next task."

Merriam stepped forward and took Eldrik by the elbow. "Come with me, I will show you to your room." The two of them quickly walked out of the chamber.

The old woman approached Silvi. "You ought not to have hypnotized him, Silvi," she said.

"We are too close to let him slip through our grasp, Hairen," Silvi replied.

Hairen chuckled and shook her head. "Perhaps you are right, but I think he would have joined us of his own free will without magical coercion."

Silvi shrugged. "It matters little now," she said. "Have you chosen a sacrifice?"

Hairen surveyed the crowd. "I will ask John Popper to stay behind." She flattened her skirt and looked back to Silvi. "He has reached the pinnacle of his talents, and his power would be better utilized by the boy."

Silvi nodded. "That is a suitable choice. Shall I bid the others leave?"

Hairen shook her head. "No, give them a proper feast. Some have made an extremely long journey." She started to walk away and stopped suddenly. "And *all* of us have waited for this night a very long time."

Silvi smiled. "Does this mean you are no longer angry with Merriam and me?"

Hairen scowled. "No, I am still unhappy with the way Nora has been treated."

"But you approve of the results?"

Hairen nodded. "I believe the boy will do splendidly."

CHAPTER EIGHTEEN

Al slowed his horse down to a trot and pulled up on the reins just before exiting the forest. He slid over the side and down off the animal. He crept up to the tree line and looked onward at the giant, rocky mountain. It had been well over a decade since the last time he had laid eyes on his former home, and even then he was only passing by.

He let his right hand fall to brush the top of his hammer. His fingers traced the etching and his thoughts went back to the arguments he had had with his father. Part of him wondered how things might be different had he taken the throne. The resources of Roegudok Hall could be at his fingertips even now, ready to augment the warrior monks at Valtuu Temple. His mind went back to Erik. He clenched his jaw and started walking forward. He saw the pair of dwarves standing guard at the entrance to Roegudok Hall.

Even from a distance, they recognized him. "The king has decreed that you are not welcome here," one of the dwarves said.

Al peered at the dwarf with a steely, calm gaze. "I am Aldehenkaru'hktanah Sit'marihu. I am the *elder* brother of Threntonsirai Sit'marihu. I have come to take my rightful place as firstborn heir to the throne."

The two guards glanced uneasily to each other. Then one of them puffed up his chest and stepped forward. "The *king* has decreed that you shall not be allowed inside. You have been disowned after you abandoned your people. You are not welcome here."

"I am the rightful heir to the throne, and I have come for my birthright. To deny me my right is to turn *your* back upon our people, and our traditions."

The second guard ran back and disappeared behind the doors

to the cavern for a moment. He reemerged with a score of dwarven guards, fully armed and donning battle gear.

"You will not pass," the first guard said decisively.

"Stand down!" someone shouted from the side.

Al turned to see another dwarf running toward them from the side of the mountain.

"What are you doing here?" the first guard bellowed.

"Easy now, I am not trying to sneak back in. Perhaps I can persuade Master Sit'marihu to come away peacefully with me."

"Alferug Henezard," Al said. "It has been a long time. What are you doing away from court?"

"The king no longer requires his services," the first guard said. "Now move along or we will be forced to apprehend you."

"Come," Alferug said. "Let us leave these feeble minded sheep to their duties."

Al looked to the guards and let his fingers drift back to his hammer.

"Master Sit'marihu, come with me, please," Alferug pleaded.

"Go with your girlfriend," the first guard taunted.

"When I am king, you will lick the bottom of my boot," Al spat. He turned and walked away with Alferug. "I need to get the scale," Al said as soon as they were far enough away that the guards couldn't hear.

Alferug nodded. "That is an interesting thing to come back for," he said. "You do realize that the scale is fastened to the king's belt. It covers the buckle."

"I know *where* the scale is," Al replied.

"You know there is no way your brother will give it to you."

"I am aware."

Alferug waved his hand and continued. "The only way you will get it is if you are king, and the only way that will happen is over Threnton's dead body."

"Yes," Al said. "I know."

Alferug stopped midsentence and turned to face Al. "As much as I would like to see our people return to their proper traditions, I must advise against this."

Al nodded and kept walking, putting as much distance between them and the guards as he could until they rounded the side of the mountain. "You know that I am the first to admit I am not the one who should be king. It is not in my blood."

Alferug raised a finger to point out Al's error, but thought better of it and kept his mouth closed.

"This is for something much more important," Al continued. "It is needed to aid the Keeper of Secrets."

"Master Lepkin needs the scale?" Alferug inquired as he scratched his wrinkled forehead. "What could he need it for?"

Al smiled politely. "That is not for everyone to know," he said. "Just trust that it is required in order for him to fulfill his mission."

"So, he has found the champion then?" Alferug asked.

Al nodded. "I believe he has."

"Has the champion passed the exalted test of Arophim?"

Al shook his head. "He has not yet taken the test." Al veered off and cut up the base of the mountain.

"Then how do you know?" Alferug pressed as he scrambled up behind Al.

"He has the gifts, I have seen it," Al said. "Now come, let's go. We don't have much time."

"Where are we going?"

Al clambered over a boulder and scanned the ground for a moment. Then he smiled and pointed down at the ground. "Here it is." He marched onward, beckoning for Alferug to follow him. "We are going to the rear door."

"The rear door?" Alferug asked. "What are you talking about?"

Al laughed aloud. "It is known only to me." He walked onward, quickening his pace. "My father passed the secret to me, in case I ever wanted to come back and my brother wouldn't let me in the front door."

"Does your brother know of this rear door?" Alferug asked.

"No, it was passed only from king to king."

"But you aren't king," Alferug pointed out.

"No, but when my father finally relented to let me walk my own path, he told me of the rear door and begged me to keep watch over Roegudok Hall. He said the time may come when I might have to come back and knock some sense into my brother."

"It would appear that that time has come," Alferug said with a smirk.

Al pushed on, ascending the mountain side as the loose dirt gave way to patches of gray shale and round pebbles. His thick fingers easily found the niches in the stone wall as he started up a sheer cliff, scurrying up the face like a squirrel climbs a tree. Alferug was only a few feet behind him until they reached the top and stood on the first shelf.

Al turned and surveyed the area below. "Let's move a little farther east before we climb up. I don't want to risk being seen by any guards."

"Bah," Alferug said with a wave. "They won't be paying attention to the mountainside. They barely stand watch at the gate as it is."

Al shrugged. "Still, better to be cautious." He made his way along the shelf. At times the flat shelf gave way to steep drops where rockslides had occurred over the years. A man might have easily fallen down any one of the dangerous slopes, but Al was a dwarf. His feet were in tune with the mountain and the rock. He often joked that when it came to climbing mountains, dwarves were more akin to goats than to their taller human cousins.

They walked for the space of an hour before Al judged they had gone far enough to avoid any possible detection. He scanned the ascending slopes, looking for the best route up the mountain. It didn't take him long. He pointed a sausage-like finger at a jagged crevice and went straight to it. His hands found purchase quickly and his feet propelled him up. He had all but forgotten how much he enjoyed the feel of rock in his hands. A part of him began to come alive that had long lain dormant. A great smile stretched across his face and he increased his pace, scrambling up the mountain as though he were a strong summer wind, bending up to crest over the peak.

Once they arrived at the second shelf, Al led them on a winding trail to a place near the back of the mountain. They were about two thirds of the way up the great peak, but Al knew there was no cause to go any higher. The door was somewhere nearby. The trick was to find it.

"We'll make camp over there," Al said, pointing to a flat area recessed in a small nook where the mountain curved into itself and hidden by a patch of scrub oak. "I have some biscuits we can share until nightfall."

"Why wait?" Alferug asked. "I thought you said that time was of the essence."

Al nodded. "We can only see the door when the moon shines upon the mountain."

"Ah," Alferug said. "A moonstone?" he asked.

"Aye, a moonstone is set above the doorway. It glows blue in the moonlight. It should be somewhere nearby."

The two of them rolled a couple of sizeable rocks out onto the flat area so they could sit comfortably while they waited. Al reached into his backpack and pulled out three whole biscuits and the remnants of one that had obviously been smashed during the climb.

"I'm sorry I have nothing to contribute," Alferug offered.

"I'll take the broken bits and one more," Al said. He gave the other two whole biscuits to Alferug. "Tell me what caused my brother to expel you from the court."

Alferug frowned and tugged on his long, gray beard. "There isn't much to tell, I'm afraid. It happened when Master Lepkin and Senator Bracken visited the king."

"Master Lepkin came with Senator Bracken?" Al asked.

"No, they came separately, but were seen at the same time by your brother," Alferug clarified. "Anyway, they spoke to him and Master Lepkin asked whether King Threnton would come to King Mathias' aid in battle if the need arose. Your brother told him exactly what he thought of the tall folk and then expelled Lepkin from Roegudok Hall."

"To imagine that the dwarf king should dishonor the Keeper of Secrets so," Al murmured.

"It gets worse," Alferug said. "Master Lepkin insulted your brother pretty harshly."

"What did he say?"

"Well, your brother had just finished renouncing the Ancients, so Lepkin told him that for the sake of the dwarves he hoped that Threnton would not live to be king for much longer."

Al choked on a bit of biscuit and coughed violently. After successfully dislodging the dry bite from his throat he shook his head in disbelief. "I can't imagine that set well with my brother at all."

"No," Alferug confirmed. "And that is why I was sent

packing along with him. Expelled and forbidden to return."

"Well, no more forbidden," Al said. "Whether I choose it or not, I do believe the time has come to put the sense back in my brother's head."

"I said it before, but he won't sit idly and let you in." Alferug took a big bite of biscuit.

"I know," Al said. "But I don't have much choice in the matter. He has what I need and the fool is too blind to see what is happening around him." He took a bite and swallowed without chewing. "Senator Bracken was actually a warlock imposter," he put in. He watched Alferug's disbelieving eyes and took another bite. "It's true," Al said through a mouthful. "I saw it with my own eyes. I don't know exactly what he was planning, but he was an evil, evil man. Threnton should have paid more attention to the affairs of men, then perhaps he would know what perils lie in wait for our people should we fail to act." Al slid down to the ground, kicked his feet out in front and crossed his legs at the ankles as he leaned back against the rock and closed his eyes. He was long overdue for some rest, and there would be a few hours yet to wait before the moon would be high enough to reveal the door.

Alferug sat silently, allowing Al to rest. He finished his dry biscuits and then walked to the edge of the slope they were on to look out. To the east he could just make out the great, jagged snowcapped mountains that separated the Middle Kingdom from the lands of the Tarthun barbarians and raiders. Slowly he brought his gaze down and swept it out across to the west. Everything looked so still and peaceful. To some it would have been an amazing, beautiful scene to behold. Alferug wrinkled his nose and walked back to his seat. He preferred the cool, damp air of his underground home.

He sat still, like a gargoyle perched upon the rock, until the sun dropped behind the western horizon and ushered in the dark night. Stars began to appear as the last colors of the day faded away. Twinkling blue and green dots littered the sky, fighting the night's shadow as best they could, but no moon shone. Alferug searched the sky. His eyes were used to discerning shapes and objects in the dark, so for him it was easy to spot the massive, thick clouds that hung in the air, blocking the moon.

"Well, that is some luck to have tonight," Alferug mumbled to himself. He glanced back to Al and rubbed his hands over his knees. "Never would have dreamed that the rightful king would return, and certainly not like this," Alferug said to himself. He rose to his feet and scanned the side of the mountain, searching the crags and nooks for any sign of a glowing moonstone. After failing to locate anything he moved in close to the rock wall and ran his fingers over the hard, unyielding stone. He moved his hands over every reachable inch in the next hour and a half before he finally gave up and cursed the clouds.

"What is the matter?"

Alferug shook his head. "I can't find the doorway, and the clouds have blotted out the moon. We will not be able to gain entrance this night."

"And why should that trouble you so, my old friend?"

Alferug looked up, expecting to see Al, but instead he saw a familiar face from years long past. The dwarf looked much like Al, strong and sturdily built, with eyes that held much wisdom. Only this dwarf had died a long time ago. It was Al's father, the former dwarf king. His body seemed to glow faintly, as though he were made of the same essence as the blue stars above. "My king," Alferug greeted humbly as he dropped to one knee.

"Alferug, my friend and loyal servant, you have no need to bow to me now." He moved forward, floating more than walking.

Alferug looked up, but remained on his knee. "I have failed our people, your highness. They have turned their backs on the Ancients, and forsaken our pact with the humans."

The king smiled warmly. "Our people have been misled, but they have not altogether forgotten their way. They only need someone to show them the correct path." The ghost turned and gazed upon his sleeping son. "Long have I waited to see him return."

"Shall I wake him?" Alferug asked.

The king turned back and smiled. "My time grows short. Listen carefully. I will move the clouds and show you the door. You and my son will enter and travel along the corridor which will bring you into a private chamber used by kings past to read and meditate. You will be discovered shortly after that and imprisoned. Tell my son to remember the fishing hole we used to frequent when he was a small child. That will help him escape. Then he should challenge Threnton in front of the court. It is of the utmost importance that the entire court be assembled when he issues the challenge. Only then will there be enough support." As soon as the king stopped speaking, he faded away into the night.

"My king, don't leave," Alferug pleaded. No response came. The delight he had been filled with upon seeing his dear friend now flittered away, leaving him alone and void. He sighed and wiped a single tear from his right eye. He rose to his feet and glanced back to Al, still sleeping as peacefully as he had been before. Suddenly the area around Al became illuminated with pale, silvery light. Alferug looked up to the sky as a fierce wind pulled his long beard to the side. He smiled as the massive, thick clouds sailed away, uncovering the full moon. "Time to wake Al," he told himself.

Alferug bounded over to Al and poked him on the shoulder. "It's time!"

Al's eyes snapped open and he jumped up to his feet in one fluid motion. He looked up to the moon and nodded. "My father's spirit is with us this night, I can feel it," he said. Al clapped his companion on the shoulder and moved around him to scan the rocks. It barely took more than a minute to locate the glowing stone. "There," Al said.

"Incredible," Alferug commented. "I was searching for the door with my hands, and I am certain I ran them over that very spot at least twice."

Al chuckled. "The door is not simply invisible, it is sealed in the rock until the moonstone glows. Even had you known its exact location, you would not be able to open it so long as the moonstone is dark." Al rushed over and placed his hand below the moonstone. "I Aldehenkaru'hktanah Sit'marihu, command the door of kings to open and allow entrance to Roegudok Hall."

The mountain groaned. Shale and pebbles bounced and vibrated away from the landing they stood upon as the rock itself came alive, sliding and scraping as it writhed before them. A massive, arched slab of slate and granite removed itself to the side and revealed a shallow cavern that covered a glowing blue doorway, covered in runes and designs of stars and moons.

Al walked inside without hesitating. He reached up to the side of the cavern, grasping a brass tube.

"What is that?" Alferug asked.

"It is the secondary key." As Al twisted the brass tube a stream of light emerged from the end and shone upon a small spot on the door. Satisfied that he had adjusted the light correctly, Al walked forward to the door.

"It appears a jewel is missing," Alferug pointed out.

"Indeed," Al said. He traced his finger in the empty space where a jewel should be and let the light from the brass tube dance upon his skin for a moment. "Our ancestors were quite clever." Al reached up and pulled a thin leather thong from around his neck up and over his head. "My father passed this to me when he told me of the rear door." Al lifted the thong to reveal a small, wooden sphere. He place his hands on either side and twisted once, separating the two halves. Then he slid a covering away to reveal a pink gemstone. He placed the stone into the empty mount on the door and took a step back.

The silver light from the tube refracted in the pink gem, splitting its light and sending rays to the several other blue stones in the door. The runes sang in answer to the light and the door glowed brighter as each of the jewels soaked in the light.

"Why does it not open?" Alferug asked.

"Patience," Al said. "There is yet a third key."

Al stood waiting as the door grew brighter and brighter. As the brilliance grew, the two dwarves shielded their faces until their eyes adjusted to the intense light. As the entire cave danced with the dazzling colors emitted from the stones, a pattern became visible in the center of the door. A golden dragon's face glowed in the stone itself.

"It is a reminder of the Ancients, who gave us life and built our home," Al stated simply. "It is also the third key." He stepped forward and put his forehead to the image of the dragon's head, locking eyes with the glowing eyes in the stone. A yellow light emerged and created a conduit between Al and the image in the door. The light was warm, and inviting as it entered his eyes gently. The whole ordeal lasted only a few seconds before the light pulled back and the golden dragon turned white. Then the door simply vanished, allowing entrance into the great dwarven kingdom.

"Incredible," Alferug said.

Al turned back and smiled. "Like I said, they were clever."

Alferug dropped to a knee, "My king," he said.

Al shot him a confused look and told him to rise. "I am not king yet," he said. "Let's get moving."

The counselor did as he was told and the two walked through the corridor until it came to an end. The wall was smooth and flat.

"A fourth key?" Alferug asked.

Al shook his head. "No, the keys are only used at the entrance. My father said there would be a secret button to push in the left side wall near the end. Al ran his hands over the surface and grinned when he wiped away a patch of old, dry clay to reveal a small hole. He wiggled his pinky finger in and depressed the button inside. A series of clicks and snaps were heard. Then the sound of a heavy chain winding around a windlass echoed through the cave above the din of the stone slab sliding up into its sheath.

Al stepped through, into a round chamber filled with shelves stocked with books and tomes. The domed ceiling gleamed with magic stones that emitted a vibrant light. The desk in the center was covered with a thick layer of dust, as were the two books resting atop the desk's surface. Al walked over to the desk and gently opened the nearest book.

"My father must have been the last person to use this library," Al said.

Alferug nodded thoughtfully and scanned the room, twirling about in place as he took it all in. "Even I never knew such a hall existed here. Surely this must be the wealth of kings that your father always referred to."

Al chuckled. "Threnton always thought the wealth of kings was some lost mine in the lower depths. He used to bait me into following him down there when we were younger." The smile on Al's face disappeared then as he realized the gravity of his purpose. "Come, there will be time for reflection later." Al walked to the other side of the room where a large window was fitted into the wall with a hefty golden frame around it. "Do you recognize this?"

Alferug approached and nodded. "It appears to be the hall in front of the king's bedchamber."

"That is curious," Al commented. "I must have passed by this mirror hundreds, maybe thousands of times before I left Roegudok Hall. I never would have guessed it concealed this room." Al reached out and pulled the jeweled handle on the glass door.

The heavy door moved silently on perfectly hung hinges. The

two of them stepped through and the door closed behind them. Al turned and inspected the mirror. There were no indications how the portal would open from this side. He heard a faint click and knew that the door had sealed from the inside. He gently pressed on the glass, but it held firm, as though it did indeed hang upon a wall of stone.

"Very clever," Al said.

"Halt!" a voice shouted from farther down the hall.

Al turned to see a trio of guards coming around the bend in the hall. His hand curled into a fist and he shook his head. "I am Aldehenkaru'hktanah Sit'marihu, and I have come to see my brother."

"Stonebubbles," one of the guards cursed. "Apprehend them both!"

Another guard retrieved a small whistle made of bone and blew forcefully. The door at the other end of the hall opened and another trio of guards came rushing into the hall from the other side.

"Al, listen to me," Alferug pleaded. "Do you remember the fishing hole you used to frequent with your father?"

Al turned a bewildered eye on Alferug. "What are you talking about?" A sudden blow knocked the air out of Al's lungs and the dwarf fell to the ground. Out of his peripheral vision he saw numerous boots swarming around him. He felt a series of kicks and jabs and then hands moved quickly upon him, stripping him of his gear. He faintly heard Alferug cry out as others descended upon him. Then everything became dark.

CHAPTER NINETEEN

Erik blinked his eyes a few times, clearing the blurry scene around him. A heap of bloody rags sat in a large ceramic bowl upon a small round nightstand next to him. His body ached, but he could move again. He slowly reached up with his right hand and pulled the blanket away to inspect his wounds. His shoulder was bandaged, and only a small round spot of blood was visible. Shifting his gaze down to his left leg he saw that almost his entire thigh was wrapped in bandages. He bent his right arm back to prop himself up and then he wiggled the toes on his left foot.

"You lost a lot of blood, but fortune was on our side yesterday," Braun said. "The king's guard who brought us here returned shortly after I managed to stop the blood and he was able to send for a healer." Braun smiled. "The healer worked into the late evening making sure the wounds were closed properly and casting spells to ward off infections."

Erik nodded and looked to his left. "Thank you Braun," Erik said.

Braun nodded and rose from his chair. He wiped a hand over his face and then approached the bedside. "How is Erik?" Braun asked.

Erik smiled and looked back down to his leg. "He is all right," he said.

"No one else is here," Braun said. "Gildrin is downstairs preparing new clothes for you, and the healer has gone out to get some things from the apothecary."

Erik shot Braun a confused look.

"Tell me the truth," Braun pressed. "I heard you cry out for your father last night." Braun put a hand on Erik's left arm. "I wouldn't believe it, had I not heard you myself."

Fear gripped Erik's heart for a brief moment, but then he felt a wash of relief. If there was anyone he could trust with his secret besides Al, it was Braun. "Yes Braun, it's me," Erik said.

Braun chewed on his bottom lip and squinted one eye down at Erik. "How?" he asked.

Erik sighed. "I am not sure. It happened after I went back to Valtuu Temple. Master Lepkin had turned into his dragon form to fight a nightwing."

"A nightwing?" Braun asked.

"A dragon that has been turned evil by Nagar's Secret," Erik responded. He looked off into the distance. "Lepkin managed to slay the beast, but he had been in his dragon form for too long. Nagar's Secret had warped his soul. I used my power to try to save him." Erik stopped and his eyes watered.

"Did you succeed?" Braun asked.

Erik shrugged. "I'm not sure. From what Lady Dimwater and Marlin say, Lepkin and I went into comas and when I woke I was in Lepkin's body."

"And Lepkin is in yours?"

Erik nodded slowly. "We think so."

"You don't know?"

"He hasn't woken up yet," Erik replied.

A knock came at the door and then Gildrin walked in, holding a silver tray with a plate of eggs and bacon. "Braun I thought you might like some..." he stopped in his tracks upon seeing Erik awake. "Master Lepkin, how do you feel?"

Erik shot a glance back up to Braun and then answered Gildrin. "I am much better, thank you. I appreciate your hospitality."

"Nonsense," Gildrin replied. "It is the least I can do for the man who slew my captor." Gildrin moved in and set the tray next to Erik. "Braun, would you mind if I let Lepkin eat this? I can make a new plate for you."

"That is fine," Braun said quickly. "He needs it more than I do."

Gildrin nodded and left the room quickly. "I'll be back in a few minutes," he said as he left.

After the two of them were alone again Braun looked back to Erik. "Well, as always, Master Erik, I stand at your service."

Erik smiled. "I know, Braun. Thank you." A tear fell from

Erik's eye and he fought the lump in his throat. "Thank you for standing with my father."

Braun squeezed Erik's arm but said nothing. He directed Erik's attention to the food and went to sit back down in the chair. As he watched Erik eat the food he cleaned his fingernails with a short knife. "Tell me something," he said. "How did you turn into a dragon?"

"I have no idea," Erik said. "I guess somehow I was able to tap into Lepkin's ability since I am in his body."

"Hm," was the only response Braun gave as he went back to cleaning his fingernails.

Gildrin returned with another tray and brought it to Braun. "When would you like to be off?"

Braun looked back to Erik. "I will leave that to Master Lepkin," he said.

Erik let his fork clank down onto the plate after his last bite of egg and wiped the corners of his mouth with his forefinger and thumb. "I would like to check the bedroom before we leave."

Gildrin frowned. "I don't think there is anything in there. He never even locked that room when he went on trips outside the city."

Erik shrugged. "Even so, we are here now so it would only take a little bit of extra time. I would rather make sure we don't overlook something."

Braun piped up through a mouthful of bacon. "I can go now and search the room," he offered.

Erik started to move and then stopped suddenly. "Did the healer say I had to take it easy with my leg or anything?"

Braun shook his head. "No, he said the wound itself wasn't so bad, it's just that it had nicked an artery."

"But he said he was able to completely repair it with his magic," Gildrin added quickly. "He said you might ache for a day or two, and there may be some seepage from the wounds, but otherwise you should be all right after that."

Erik nodded and slowly swung his feet down to the ground. He gingerly pushed himself up and tested putting his weight on his legs before standing up fully. It stung slightly as he shifted his weight, but it was not overly bothersome. Next he carefully shrugged his left shoulder up and rotated it around. "I think it's all

245

right," he told Braun.

"All right then, let's go check out the other room."

"I'll gather the trays and be right behind you," Gildrin said. He took two steps forward and then stopped. He looked at the tray next to Erik and frowned. "I suppose I don't need to do that anymore." Gildrin stared at the tray for a moment with longing eyes and then motioned for Erik and Braun to follow him. "Come, I'll show you to his bedroom."

Erik limped at first, mostly because he wasn't sure how his leg would respond. It felt a bit tight as he took the first few steps, but it loosened quickly and he was almost walking normally by the time he exited the room.

He followed Gildrin through the hall, noticing that the man was slowing his pace just enough to look at each bust in the hallway. Erik looked down at the first one and realized that the figures were an homage to ancestors past. Each held a brass plate in its base with the name of the individual the bust represented as well as his birthdate, date of death, and how many years he served in the senate.

Braun seemed unimpressed by the busts and started to pass Erik and Gildrin on his way to the large double doors at the end of the hall. "You said he never locked it?" Braun asked.

Gildrin nodded. "That's right."

"Still, perhaps I should check it first?" Erik said. Braun reluctantly stopped and waited for Erik to catch up. Erik called upon his power to search for any spells or barriers. He found none. He nodded to Gildrin and Gildrin pushed the doors open with hardly a care as he strolled into the room.

The curtains were drawn over the windows, nearly blocking the sunlight out entirely. Gildrin was quick to open them and tie the fabric back in place with gold silk tassels. "I am not sure where you would want to look," he said. "There are a couple of bookshelves there, a desk there, and..."

"How about the locked chest?" Braun asked.

Gildrin frowned. "What chest?" he asked.

Braun walked over to the side of the bed. A metal corner poked out just enough to be visible under the black coverlet. "This one." He bent down and pulled a long, rectangular box out from under the bed. Erik inspected the cold, dull gray metal as Braun set the box on the bed. There were three bands of black iron, each with hinges and heavy locks upon them. Braun tapped on one of the locks. "It might take me a few minutes, but I can probably get these open."

Erik nodded and went to the desk. This one was not like the desk in the library. It was made of cherry wood and was extremely simple in design. A short hutch held two cubbies and a small drawer. In one cubby was a gold plated hourglass. In the other was a small figurine of a mammoth carved out of ivory. Erik opened the drawer and found some writing instruments, but nothing of interest. Next he turned his eyes to the books on top of the desk. One was a treatise on senate protocol, and another was a history of the senate.

"Did he spend much time reading these?" Erik asked.

Gildrin shrugged. "I would find him perusing them on occasion, but most of what I would call his study time was spent in the library."

Erik nodded and fanned through the books to see if any notes had been left inside. Other than an old, pressed yellow rose he found nothing. He turned the preserved flower in his hand and then gently set it back inside the book. He then reached down to pull the side drawer out. Inside he found a tray for rings and other jewelry. They looked nice, but none of them were particularly special from what Erik could tell. Most of them were simple silver rings with various patterns etched into them.

"My former master enjoyed those," Gildrin said from the other side of the room. "He often purchased a silver ring while he was traveling on business.

Erik closed the drawer.

"I got it," Braun said. Erik turned and the last of the locks popped open. Erik turned and walked over to Braun.

"What's inside?" Erik asked.

Braun frowned and gently pushed the lid back. "It looks like he might have been the wizard from that tale after all," he said.

Erik peered inside and scooped up a short, wooden sword. It was very light, obviously made as a toy for a small child. Under that was an old, threadbare doll with one of its button eyes missing. Erik pulled it out and set it next to the sword. Next he saw a long yellow silk dress. As he unfolded it, a large gold ring with a ruby cut into the shape of a heart fell out and clanked inside the chest.

"Am I correct in assuming these are the warlock's?" Braun asked Gildrin.

Gildrin nodded. "They do not belong to my real master. Senator Bracken never had a family of his own."

"What is this?" Erik asked. He reached down and pulled a small leather bound book out of the chest. The binding had come apart and been stitched together with new thread. The pages loosely hung in place and were well worn. "It looks like he read this many times." Erik said.

"What is it?" Braun asked.

Erik turned the book over in his hands, searching for a title. "It looks like the title has been worn off of the cover." Erik opened the book and gingerly turned to the title page inside. Part of the page had torn away and was missing. "It is hard to make out the title," Erik said. "All I can see is 'Aikur's Wa' the rest is missing."

Gildrin walked around the bed and took the book from Erik. "Of course," he said with a nod as he thumbed through the pages. "Aikur's War," he said. "Have either of you heard of it?"

"I have," Braun said. "Isn't that the legend about the man who travels into Hammenfein to rescue his family's souls?"

Gildrin nodded. "The story says that the gods themselves helped him do it after his family was murdered."

"Look at this," Erik said as he pulled out several journals. He opened them to find hand-drawn maps, notes about ancient relics and spells. "It looks like he spent a lot of time studying this book to figure out how to bring his own family back to life."

"But the legend isn't true, it's just a story," Gildrin retorted.

"Story or not, it looks as though he took it as fact," Braun said.

"There are a lot of notes in these journals," Erik said. "We should take these with us."

"With us?" Braun asked.

Erik nodded. "It would take too long to read all of them thoroughly. There are six journals here, each with hundreds of pages. We can start working on them as we travel to Lokton Manor. Maybe something in here will help us."

Braun shrugged. "I could pack them into saddle bags." Braun turned to Gildrin. "Can you help me prepare those four horses you mentioned?"

"The horses are in a stable nearby, but we can pack the bags here and then take them along with us."

Erik nodded. "Let's go."

The three of them left the room and descended the stairs to the main room on the first floor. Erik stopped at the bottom as his left leg began to ache and spasm.

"Are you all right?" Braun asked.

Erik nodded. "Perhaps I should sit for a moment before we depart for Lokton manor," he stated.

Braun and Gildrin nodded. Erik rested on a couch near a fireplace by the rear entrance while Braun and Gildrin went around the house preparing provisions for the journey. Once they were ready they returned to Erik.

Erik stood and nodded to them. "I am doing a lot better than I was," he said.

"Good, let's go," Braun said decisively. "I am not going to let Lokton Manor fall."

The three of them walked out the back door and started down the steps. Gildrin cried out and dropped the backpack he was carrying. Erik and Braun turned to see him grabbing his left arm as he fell to his knees and tumbled down the last two steps to land face-first in the flowerbed.

Braun left Erik's side and rushed to Gildrin. "What is it?" he asked. He turned Gildrin over and saw the man's eyes frozen open in pain. Braun put a finger to the man's neck, searching for a pulse he would not find. "He's gone," Braun said.

"The curse," Erik said as he realized what happened.

"No," Braun retorted. "He said the curse was only active while the warlock was alive."

"I know,' Erik said.

Braun turned a confused look to Erik. "You killed him yourself, he's gone."

Erik looked down to Gildrin's body and shook his head. "Somehow, the warlock is alive."

Other Books by Sam Ferguson

The Sorceress of Aspenwood Series

The Dragon's Champion Series

The Wealth of Kings

The Netherworld Gate Series

The Dragons of Kendualdern series

The Fur Trader by Sam Ferguson

Other Books by Dragon Scale Publishing

The Protector of Esparia by Lisa M. Wilson

Kingdom of Denall Series by Eric Buffington:

The Troven
Secrets at the Keep
The Changing

Tales of the NoWhere and NeverWhen by Jason Hauser

Wisp the Wayfinder
Puck the Pathwinder
Nobb the Nightbinder

The Lost City of Alfarin by Keaton James

Gryl the Enchanter by Tamlin Moore

Also available exclusively on the Dragon Scale website:

Tharzule's Tome of Wishes by Malinda Smiley

Orcs and Elves by Bethan Owen

ABOUT THE AUTHOR

I like to call myself a well-traveled story teller of Irish and Cherokee heritage. I count seven U.S. states as home. I have spent many years abroad, first as a missionary in the Baltic States and later as a Diplomat in the U.S. Foreign Service. When I'm not wrestling with my sons or hefting iron in the gym I can be found at home relaxing with my wife or setting pen to paper, bringing stories to life.